PRAISE FOR *THE HOUSE GUEST*

"This riveting novel twists and turns through the page-turning story. . . . Events turn shocking, with revelation after revelation in a thriller that never forgets to touch the heart."
—Lisa Scottoline

"*The House Guest* is great! Ryan creates memorable characters—then pulls off the nearly impossible: she orchestrates half a dozen twists, turns, and backflips—and then sticks the landing. What a pleasure to read this!"
—James Patterson

"Hank Phillippi Ryan weaves a twisted tale of love, revenge, and betrayal. *The House Guest* kept me on the edge of my seat from start to finish."
—Tamron Hall, author of *As the Wicked Watch* and Emmy Award–winning host of *The Tamron Hall Show*

"*The House Guest* is a thriller lover's treat! Propulsive, smart, twisty, and impossible to predict."
—Gilly Macmillan, international bestselling author of *The Long Weekend*

"Compulsive and absorbing, this is a fast-paced, highly intriguing, and binge-worthy read."
—Hannah Mary McKinnon, international bestselling author of *Never Coming Home*

"Ryan is at the top of her game in this fiendishly clever, rocket-paced thrill ride. Another stellar outing for powerhouse Ryan."

—Lisa Unger, *New York Times* bestselling author

"Ryan does it again with this clever cat-and-mouse chase of a mystery that will keep you flipping the pages until the deliciously twisty end."

—Wanda M. Morris, award-winning author of *All Her Little Secrets*

"Suspense, intrigue, and glamour galore—plus a twist you won't see coming! What more could you want?"

—B. A. Paris, international bestselling author of *Behind Closed Doors*

"A tantalizing, beguiling thriller . . . Ryan has done it again!"

—Samantha Downing, international bestselling author of *My Lovely Wife*

"Binge-worthy . . . This cat-and-mouse story will have readers wondering who is the cat and who is the mouse."

—*Library Journal* (starred review)

Books by Hank Phillippi Ryan

Trust Me
The Murder List
The First to Lie
Her Perfect Life
The House Guest

THE JANE RYLAND SERIES

The Other Woman
The Wrong Girl
Truth Be Told
What You See
Say No More

THE CHARLOTTE McNALLY SERIES

Prime Time
Face Time
Air Time
Drive Time

THE HOUSE GUEST

HANK PHILLIPPI RYAN

Tor Publishing Group
New York

THE HOUSE GUEST

A Forge Book
Published by Tom Doherty Associates/Tor Publishing Group
120 Broadway
New York, NY 10271

www.tor-forge.com

Forge® is a registered trademark of Macmillan Publishing Group, LLC.

ISBN 978-1-250-84958-8

Our books may be purchased in bulk for promotional, educational, or business use. Please contact your local bookseller or the Macmillan Corporate and Premium Sales Department at 1-800-221-7945, extension 5442, or by email at MacmillanSpecialMarkets@macmillan.com.

First Edition: February 2023
First Trade Paperback Edition: August 2023
First Mass Market Edition: January 2024

Printed in the United States of America

10 9 8 7 6 5 4 3 2 1

"You may not control all the events that happen to you, but you can decide not to be reduced by them."

—**Maya Angelou**

For all of you, readers. Yes, you. And you, and you and you. You are tough and brave and smart and perfect.

And for Jonathan, but he knows that.

FRIDAY

ONE

Alyssa swirled the icy olives in her martini, thinking about division. She stared through her chilled glass to the mirrored shelves of multicolored bottles in front of her at the hotel bar. Division, as in divorce.

Not only the physical division, hers from Bill, but what would happen after the lawyers finished. They'd already created a ledger of their lives together, then started the Macallens' financial division. Which would be followed by the devastating subtraction.

Bill had subtracted her from his life, that was easy math. With a lift of his chin and a slam of the front door and a squeal of Mercedes tires. She'd asked him why he was leaving her, *begged* to know, yearned to understand. But Bill Macallen always got what he wanted, no explanation offered or obligatory. She had done nothing wrong. Zero. That's what baffled her. Terrified her.

She jiggled the fragments of disappearing ice. *Division.* The Weston house. The Osterville cottage. The jewelry. *Her* jewelry. The first editions. The important paintings. Club membership. The silver. Money. The lawyers, human calculators who cared nothing about her, would discuss and divide, and then Bill would win. Bill always won.

All *she'd* done for the past eight years was addition. She'd added to their lives, added to their social sphere, organizing and planning as "Bill's wife," fulfilling her job to make him comfortable and enviable and the image of benevolent success. She'd more than accepted it, she'd embraced it, and all that came with it. And then, this.

I need a break, he'd told her that day. She pictured that moment now, a month ago, could almost smell him, a seductive mixture of leathery orange-green aftershave and his personal power. Bill talking down to her, literally and figuratively, wearing one of his pale blue shirts, expensive yellow tie loose and careless, khaki pants and loafers. A *break*! As if his life with her was a video he could casually put on pause while he did more important things. What things?

The music from the speakers in each corner of the Vermilion Hotel's earnestly chic dark-paneled bar floated down over her, some unrecognizable tune, all piano and promises, muffling conversations and filling the silences. A couple sat at one end of the bar, knee to knee. On vacation, on business, clandestine. Impossible to tell.

At the other end, a sport-coated man, tie askew, used one finger to fish the maraschino cherry out of his brown drink, popped it into his mouth, and licked his fingers before he went back to scrolling the phone in front of him. Alyssa was in the middle. Alone. She drew in a deep breath, all peaty scotch and lemons and strangers and elusive perfume. Alone.

Alyssa felt her shoulders sag, assessing the other parts of her life grouped on Bill's side of the ledger. She understood, she did, it was difficult when a couple split. Social allegiances were tested. Loyalties strained. She jabbed at the closest green olive with the little plastic stick. But Bill had taken the friends. Every single one of them.

And now—at the Club, at the gym, at the mall—Alyssa got only pitying glances. Fingertip-hidden whispers. As if they, in their hothouse world of affluence and connection, understood something she didn't.

When she and Bill first met, that night at the charity event, they both had big plans. Now only *he* had them. When she wasn't Bill's wife anymore, who was she? And did she have the power to change that?

Her phone lay on the zinc bar, its glowing screen taunting her with the proof. No matter how many times she looked at it, her calendar messaged her new reality.

You have no events. No. Events. Only blank days, one after the other, calendared out in front of her. She scrolled back through her past, the listings grayed out now, ghosts of occasions. Charity balls, gala dinners, speeches by successful entrepreneurs, and a fundraiser where they'd auctioned off A Day with Bill Macallen. That went for thousands. Everybody loved Bill, and somehow, calculating again, Alyssa was the plus-one. Now, in the excruciating math of marriage—addition, division—she was the minus.

Nothing had changed for *him*. Bill was always jetting off, to New York, or Chicago, or someplace exotic. She reached into the shoulder bag hanging from the curved back of her barstool, slid her hand into a side pocket, and pulled out a postcard showing palm trees, like they used to see in St. Barts. Bill, she knew it was Bill, had sent the unsigned postcards, pictures of tropical flowers and cobalt skies, simply to provide his own manipulative entertainment. *Here's where you aren't.* He was taunting her, distant and nasty and gloating. *Here's where you will never be again.*

Here in Weston, where she *was,* she had slush. Spring in Massachusetts. Her husband, fifteen years older, was off having fun. That didn't seem fair.

She imagined Bill walking in and seeing her, alone on a Saturday night, on this well-worn stool at a suburban hotel bar. Her brown roots showing. Manicure failing. And courtesy of the doomed-to-divorce diet, gone almost scrawny at five pounds thinner. If Bill had caught her here—which he wouldn't, she'd picked this place because it was out of their orbit—he'd have sneered that dismissive sneer at her vodka with three, now two, olives. Alyssa Westland Macallen, almost-divorced at thirty-five.

"May I get you another?" The bartender, high cheekbones and multi-pierced ear, paused in front of her, wiping out a champagne flute with a blue striped towel.

She looked at her watch, pretending. "Oh no," she said. "How did it get to be so late? Everyone will be expecting me."

"Ah." The bartender held up the flute to the row of tiny lights twinkling above them. "Of course. If you're sure?" Alyssa watched as he checked the glass for spots, then, turning away from her, slid it into place on a thin wooden rack.

Bill. William Drew Macallen. *Where are you? And with who?* There could be no other reason but that he was prowling for wife number two.

She stared at the pale place on her finger where, for eight years, three months, and twenty-seven days, her wedding ring had been. A piece of jewelry the universe prescribes to indicate one is married, and happy, and off-limits. There was no piece of jewelry denoting sorrow, or confusion, or disequilibrium. Or fear. Now her once-welcoming home was empty; and when the nights got dark and long, it terrified her. She knew Bill was lurking. Watching. Waiting. Bill was present in every shadow. Every noise. She hated being alone in that house. Hated it.

She'd rather be in a random bar alone than be by herself in that house. Maybe she'd simply drive around. Forever.

"Just the check," she said to the bartender.

"But it's early."

The voice beside her—inquiring, hesitant—startled her. She hadn't noticed anyone walking up behind her, and Alyssa was not here to find companionship or conversation. In fact, the last thing she wanted was to talk to anyone. What would she even say? Even the simplest of questions—*How are you?*—could send her to tears.

The newcomer's fingernails were bitten and nubby, and her pilling sweater just the wrong shade of blue and uneven across the shoulders. She slung a raveled canvas tote bag over the back of her stool. Her curly-wild hairstyle had been an unfortunate decision, as was her hair's artificially not-quite-auburn color.

But that was . . . unfairly judgmental. And the world wasn't all about Alyssa Westland Macallen. It felt like it right now, but this woman was proof it wasn't. To this newcomer, the world was about *her.* That was just as valid. Alyssa should at least be civil.

"Early? Oh, well, maybe, but I have to get home," Alyssa said. No reason to take out her personal bitterness on a complete stranger. "Tough day," she added, explaining.

"Tell me about it." The woman shot her one sarcastic glance, then looked back down at the polished metal bar.

Not a chance, Alyssa thought. She poked at her last olive. The well of her loss could not be filled with chitchat. But a weight seemed almost visible on this woman's thin shoulders. She'd made herself as small as she could, elbows close to her body, bare legs twisted around each other, one chunky heel of her scuffed black shoe hooked in the rung of her barstool.

Alyssa fingered her right-hand diamond, embarrassed at its extravagance. Her birthstone, a gift from Bill during the first April they'd known each other, and not even her seething annoyance with him would convince her to take that off. She turned her hand palm up, hiding the ring.

"I'm sorry," Alyssa said. "Better days will come."

"Huh," the woman replied, more a huff than a word. She shrugged, one pilled blue shoulder briefly raised. "Have a nice night."

She'd hardly looked up, which gave Alyssa a chance to look at the newcomer in the expanse of mirror across from them. Dancers, the skilled ones, can express themselves with simply a gesture, or a posture, becoming a dying swan or an ill-fated fairy. *Poor thing*, the words came to Alyssa's mind at this woman's body language. She swiveled her stool toward the stranger. Not an invitation, simply an acknowledgment of shared humanity. The music from the dining room behind them drifted in, silkier now, an encircling shimmer.

"You okay?" Alyssa had to ask.

"Sure," she said. "Thanks."

Alyssa recognized the sorrow in her voice. Maybe—defeat.

"Get you something, miss?" Even the bartender's voice had softened.

"My treat," Alyssa said, surprising herself. She hadn't meant to say anything.

"Oh, I—" The woman had turned on her stool, and now looked almost grateful. "Couldn't possibly."

"I insist." Alyssa felt her shoulders square, and a glimmer of empathy. Even the background music had shifted to a major key, optimistic. This was good. This was positive. This was progress. Maybe if she heard someone else's troubles, it would diminish her own. It couldn't make them worse.

TWO

Alyssa smiled for the first time in she didn't know how long. "Everything I start to say comes out wrong," she confessed. "Like a bad movie."

The bartender had placed a square gold-bordered white napkin on the bar in front of the newcomer, and a dark globe of burgundy on top of it. He slid a tiny bowl filled with salted brown and orange bits, nuts and crispy things, next to it. "Enjoy," he said.

"How about—what's your sign?" The woman took a sip of wine, signaled her approval to the bartender, and angled her body toward Alyssa's. "Or your major in college?"

"That was a long time ago." Alyssa risked a quick assessment. "Longer ago than for you, I guess. How about—new in town? What brings you here? We can try all the classics."

"I'm thirty-two. New in town, that's an easy one. Yes. What brings me? That's more complicated."

And then silence. The couple down the bar had ordered onion rings, and the salty, pungent fragrance wafted close to them. Black leather booths along the back wall were filling, Alyssa saw in the bar mirror. The gathering layers of conversation wove a murmuring soundtrack.

"Complicated?" Alyssa had only meant to share a quick drink, and leave the woman to her own life and concerns. But now it seemed only polite to chat with her. For a few minutes, at least. This woman's hair reminded her of her high school friend Kiereen, who'd walked out of sophomore French class one day and never returned. Madame Lemaire had explained to them, in French, some story about a sudden illness. We were *friends,* Alyssa remembered sobbing to her mother. She didn't tell me *anything*.

"Friends," her mother had sneered, stabbing out the charred end of a cigarette. "There are true friends, and false friends. Kiereen's family is rich, and they are not like us." Alyssa, who'd confided in Kiereen, and trusted her, hadn't understood that back then. Now she did. She also understood feigned sincerity, and the adjustable life span of friendship. Friendship based on expediency, necessity, opportunity. Money. The friends Bill brought to the marriage had left it along with him. Or he had taken them.

This woman's eyes seemed unhappy, like Kiereen's once had, and she now stared into her burgundy as if she were seeing something Alyssa couldn't.

"I didn't mean to guilt you into talking to me." The woman's voice held no accent, no history. "When you said you were leaving, and I said it's early—it was simply an observation." She lifted her full wineglass. "I'm fine. And you're very generous. But I'm fine."

"You keep saying that," Alyssa said. "My mother used to say that. *I'm fine*. It meant—leave me alone."

"Oh, and now I've offended you." The woman's eyes welled, and she faced Alyssa full on. "I didn't mean it that way, I was just—letting you off the hook. I'm Bree."

"I'm not *on* the hook—Bree?"

"Embry," she said. "Bree. Lorrance."

"Alyssa—" She paused, martini glass raised, wondering if this was the opportunity to go back to her birth name. She could be Westland, starting now. It wasn't like this encounter was going to be any longer than the length of a martini. It was after ten, pushing ten thirty, and Alyssa was eager to be done with this day. "Westland. Alyssa Westland."

"Nice to meet you." Bree clinked the edge of her glass, the red liquid sloshing, then finding its balance.

Three tones chimed from inside Bree's canvas tote bag. Bree startled, flinched, and a splash of burgundy spattered the white napkin.

"Oh, I am so—did any get on you? That beautiful white shirt?"

Three more chimes. Bree pulled a black cell phone from her bag, peered at the screen.

"No, not at all. Look. Not a drop." Alyssa waved off her concern. "You need to answer that?"

The woman's face darkened. She closed her eyes a fraction of a beat, then opened them.

"I should turn it off, I know that," Bree said. "I just worry it's—it doesn't matter. But it's never anything, it's always—" She grimaced as the phone rang again, and scratched her forehead with what was left of her fingernails. A red welt appeared above her left eye.

The phone went silent. The silence seemed louder than the rings.

"Finally." Bree jammed the phone back into her bag.

The onion ring couple, arms draped across each other's shoulders, walked behind them, laughing. Alyssa watched their progress in the mirror, saw the woman wobble in her heels, saw the man catch her, steady her, and pull her closer. Saw the woman kiss his cheek.

"Why don't you refuse the call?" Alyssa asked. "When you see it's a person you don't want to talk to? Sorry, and I'm being pushy, but I mean, hit the button that says *not now,* or whatever it says?"

"Because then he knows I know he's called," Bree said. "And I've responded. And that means he knows I have my phone, and I'm looking at it, and he's *making* me react. I refuse to engage. I refuse to—"

Looking at Bree's face hardening, and seeing Bree's hands curl into fists, Alyssa wondered if anyone in the world was happy. Besides Bill, of course. Any *women,* maybe, a better question. Which she knew was her own bitterness, not reality. Alyssa had once been happy, and needed to remember everything in life was ephemeral. Even the bad things.

"Men." Alyssa offered a one-word indictment.

"So true."

The bartender approached, his towel now tucked into the strings of a striped apron. Pointed to Bree, then Alyssa, inquiring.

Alyssa put her hand on top of her empty glass. "Driving."

"Sure," Bree said. "I'll put it on my room."

"Oh," Alyssa regrouped as the bartender turned away. Edited her speculative biography of this woman. "You're staying here?"

"'Til the money runs out. Which might be soon." Bree puffed out a breath. "Or until . . ."

Alyssa waited. The woman was not finishing most of her sentences, as if she'd run out of steam or intent, or words of explanation.

"Until?" Alyssa finally prodded her, curious. She couldn't figure this woman out, a thirtysomething from out of town. Staying in a hotel. Unhappy, it seemed, and wanting to talk but not wanting to. Alyssa's one year at New England Law—which she'd loved until she loved Bill more—had taught her that every story had a secret, and every storyteller had a motive. Maybe this woman had left her—husband? Boyfriend? She'd seemed to agree with Alyssa's indictment of men.

"Or until what?" Alyssa asked again.

Bree picked up her glass, swirled the last of the deep red wine.

"Or until he finds me," she said.

THREE

Alyssa fished her house keys out of her jacket pocket as she climbed the three brick steps to her red-lacquered front door. The forsythia flanking the flagstone front walk had gone from bare branches to flowering yellow almost overnight, and blooming crocuses made a ribbon of white along each edge, some blossoming brighter in the sudden glow of the motion-activated security lighting. The front steps, cleanly swept caramel-colored brick, were as pristine as when she had left them. One forsythia flower, the one she had carefully positioned on the center of the second step, was still there, as perfectly formed as when she had placed it. No one had stepped on it.

Sometimes, when the lights came on, she imagined that Bill had actually flipped the switch, welcoming her home. She imagined his eyes lighting up, too, when he saw her. Sometimes the loving memories of Bill emerged unbidden, the good Bill, and they threatened to engulf her. She would tamp them down, stomp them, destroy them. She could not allow that. Those days were gone.

She thought about the woman in the bar. *Bree.* Whatever else Alyssa had to complain about, it was nothing compared to what Bree Lorrance had described. Hounding bill collectors, a harassing boss at some bank, and an abusive boyfriend who used the phone as a weapon.

Her key turned in the front door, and she clicked it open, the lights now on and the alarm clamoring. She tapped in the code. She'd changed it, in case Bill tried to sneak in. It had been his idea, the separation, so now he had to live with it.

He'd signed a legal agreement promising he'd only come to the house if he called in advance. *Promises.* As if Bill knew the meaning of that word. As if he cared about a piece of paper. As if he cared about an alarm. And in reality, it was still, technically, his house.

She felt the silence surround her. Sixty-five hundred square feet, Bill had proudly told her. And anyone else who would listen. Which was everyone, of course, he was Bill Macallen. They even laughed when he said *size matters,* as if that stupid joke was funny to anyone but a fourteen-year-old.

Those little things, things she had forgiven him when they were happy, seemed teeth-grittingly annoying now, pompous and even embarrassing. She'd never corrected him, though. She'd seen what happened when someone crossed her husband, a thing that once impressed her and now repulsed her. That was power. Only impressive when it was on your side.

Sixty-five hundred square feet. The living room, the movie room, the extra party room, and what Bill called the reception room, where long tables covered in white damask often served as bars or dinner buffets or arrays of fountains gushing dark chocolate with chefs creating dessert crêpes to order, stuffed with fresh raspberry or lemon curd or brandied peaches.

Bill's office-study, all muted rainbows of immaculately shelved books, with mahogany-paneled walls and elaborate furniture. Bill thought it showed strength. Alyssa thought it showed arrogance. Her glorious kitchen, restaurant-worthy and shiny with stainless steel, then the screened-in porch and redwood deck and, upstairs, an array of bedrooms and bathrooms. The pool in the back, shaped like a shimmering turquoise island. Gardens, a changing cabana, and then the guest house. All that, and now it was just her, alone, in this expanse of terrifying excess.

She set her bag on the slim hall table, an act of defiance. Bill never liked her to put it there. Said it ruined the ambience of the entryway.

It was always Bill's house, though he told her he'd bought it for her. For *them*. But, she thought now, more accurately, it was for Bill and his possessions. As it had turned out, she was one of those possessions.

The *ambience of the entryway*. Bill words. So many things in the house were described by Bill words, including herself. She'd been Alice until the night they'd met—but he'd whispered she was "more like an Alyssa," and persisted, even teasingly, intimately, introducing her as Alyssa, and soon she'd felt like Alyssa, too; glamorous, beloved, to the manner born Alyssa. And eventually she'd embraced her Bill words: her names, first and last. No longer Alice Westland. But Bill's possession, Alyssa Macallen.

She'd loved it, once, as she'd loved him. Until the division. Or again more accurately, the subtraction. Her mother had warned her, back in the days before she died. They'd been leaving her mother's sad little real estate office, where Alyssa had secretaried until she escaped to law school. "Be careful," Mama had said as she'd clutched her daughter's arm. Alyssa could hear it now, an evil queen's menacing admonition. "If he leaves you, you'll be back to having nothing."

Now, the crystal chandelier glittered twinkles of light across the pale yellow walls, deckling the curved cut-glass vase of white tulips, the jewel tones of the patterned fringed rug on the black-and-white tiled floor. Alyssa remembered the first time she'd seen this place, when Bill brought her here. Eight years, three months, and twenty-seven days ago. Twenty-eight now.

The 1894 Victorian had been spotless. Empty. *Do what you want, Lissie,* he had told her. *Sky's the limit.*

But then he'd told her what *he* wanted, and she'd done that. Antique rugs, elaborate bookshelves, heirloom mirror over the Florentine side table. She'd loved it because Bill loved it. And now she was here. Alone. And love had nothing to do with it anymore.

She felt as if there were a line being drawn through everything in the house. Half a chandelier, half a leather couch, half a Travertine marble fireplace. She imagined the lawyers going into the wine cellar, dividing the reds, and then opening the wine fridge, dividing the whites. She felt herself being cut in half, too, into before and after. She'd gotten used to the ease of this life, the access and the privilege. A month ago, the day he'd walked out, she'd decided to embrace it for as long as she had it, then make do. The way she always had.

The entryway alarm pad, hidden by the vase of tulips, now glowed green, signaling all was safe. But there was never a moment when Alyssa believed it. Nothing was safe. Nothing was safe from Bill.

She counted the flowers. Still twelve. She squinted

at the marble table, flecked with gold and black and brown. Two of the flecks were dots of black eyebrow pencil she had carefully placed to mark the position of the vase. If someone deactivated the alarm, and was not careful, they would move the vase.

Tonight, the vase had been moved. No question. The curved right edge of the crystal now covered one dot, and that was not how she had left it. Had she moved it herself, forgetting, when she silenced the alarm?

Possibly. *Possibly.* Maybe she'd been distracted, thinking about that woman in the bar. And spaced on—had she?—the second thing she always checked when she came home. First, the flower on the steps. Then the vase. Then the third thing.

It was silly marking the vase, she knew it, but two weeks ago, when she came home from shopping—one of the few activities she could do alone without anyone noticing, or remarking on her situation—she knew someone had been sitting in Bill's chair in his office.

She'd stared at the worn leather cushions, certain that the impressions in the seat had not been there when she left. And there were smudges, two of them, on the glass protecting the wooden desktop. As if someone had put their hands on it.

It wasn't Thursday, so Tammy would not have been there cleaning. No one should have been there.

She'd put a hand on the seat back, wondering if it was warm. But felt only the smoothness of the leather. Only Bill would have sat here. She opened the top desk drawer, remembering Bill had left it unlocked after he cleaned it out. Now there were two black pencils and a twisted metal paper clip. Had he left them? At the time, she'd been crying too hard to notice. She closed the drawer, and it was so quiet she could hear the pencils roll to the back. Had Bill been here?

Would that be a bad thing? She'd tapped her fingers against her lips, staring at the leather chair. Almost envisioning him in it, hair mussed, shirtsleeves rolled up, that elaborate watch on his tanned arm. Owning it.

That's when she'd set up her secret Bill-alarm system. To test him. To see if he'd broken their legal agreement.

The third test was the secret compartment.

About a week after they'd moved in, on her birthday, they'd still been organizing the house, arranging Bill's collection of first editions—his precious books, which he would not let anyone else touch—and hanging paintings, with Bill directing the museum-trained installer. After the man packed up his collection of special hammers and measuring tapes and driven down the driveway, Bill had said he had a surprise for her. Back when surprises were good things.

She remembered her heart had fluttered at his touch.

He'd held one of her hands, pressed his other against the small of her back, and guided her up the staircase. Their photos hadn't been arranged on the walls yet, so the deep cranberry high-gloss stairway paint was pristine, untouched, so shiny it almost reflected their movements, a couple illuminated by their own electricity.

He'd opened the door to the bedroom, the door creasing a half-moon in the thick pile of the new-smelling dove-gray carpeting, and she'd pulled back, teasing. "That kind of surprise?" She fluttered her lashes at him. "At least let me take a shower after all that heavy lifting."

"You only lifted your iced tea," he'd teased back.

She pouted, then flirted again; her heart had been so full then, so buoyant. "What if you come into the shower with me? Will that make it all better?"

"I'll show you what will make it better," he'd said. "Come with me."

"*Bill!*" She'd pretend-protested.

But instead of the bed, he'd led her to the closet. He'd pulled open one white louvered door, and pushed aside some zippered black canvas clothing bags they had not yet opened.

"In the closet?" she asked. There had been stranger places, she remembered. A private room in the Boston Public Library during the Literary Lights gala, in the ladies' room of the Isabella Stewart Gardner Museum, and once in the back of a black catering truck parked outside the governor's house in Swampscott. Her hair had smelled like soy sauce afterward. The salty brown fragrance and the taut possibility of discovery had been washed away by a late-night swim in their own backyard pool, naked in the moonlight.

"This is just for you," Bill had said. "Count two panels from the left side, then see this knot in the wood?"

She clamped her hands on her hips, skeptical. "What's behind it? The secret room with the crazy relative?"

Bill, busy tapping the back wall of the closet, hadn't responded.

"Ah!" he finally said. "Ready?"

And he'd rapped the back wall with his knuckles, *tap-tap,* then pushed, and a slat in the wall had opened, revealing a black-lined compartment. Empty.

"How perfect is this?" he'd asked.

"*So* perfect," she'd said, humoring him. A place to conceal cash. Jewelry. Passports. Legal papers.

"You'd never see it, right? We can put things here. And oh, what's this?" He'd reached an arm into the compartment, farther in than Alyssa had calculated it would go. Pulled out a tiny robin's-egg-blue box.

"Happy new home, Mrs. Macallen," he said, handing it to her.

She'd opened it, misty-eyed with delight, and had worn the necklace whenever she could. He'd chosen a tiny house of gold with a square-cut emerald as the front door, the jeweled charm dangling from a braided gold chain.

Bill had looked so proud of himself, although he always did. He had a lot to be proud of, she had to admit, one of the reasons she had loved him. Raising money for charities, magnanimous and benevolent, when with his family income, he hadn't needed to do anything but play golf and spend the interest accumulating in his trust funds, inheritances, and bank accounts that seemed as mysteriously deep as that closet's secret compartment.

He enjoyed the public approval, Alyssa's armchair psychology had decided. The glowing news coverage, the fawning attention. Maybe his parents hadn't praised him enough. But, she'd decided, if Bill helped others to help himself, if "doing good" made people admire him, so what? That math worked. Win-win, and that meant she won as well, finally feeling secure, and even generous, if mainly by association.

She'd tried to help people, too, starting in law school, but Bill had persuaded her to leave. Not really persuaded, she corrected herself, she'd swooned with wanting him. Being Bill's wife, she'd soon learned, was a job in itself. No bar exam, but in this privileged world there were other tests, constant and sometimes intimidatingly puzzling tests. Tests of manners and money, of actions and clothing and hierarchy. Still, she hadn't missed law school, or her friends from back then, not for a second. Not for eight years, at least.

Then, a few months ago, Bill had grown—complicated. Moody. Seemed to become more high-strung, wielding his power. Criticizing her, snappish and belittling. Accusing her of being forgetful, pouncing on her mistakes. Closing his study door. She'd written it off as business, part of Bill-money-world. She'd tried to be patient.

But she couldn't resist. She'd looked them up, the symptoms. *How to know if your husband is cheating.* Embarrassed but obsessed, she'd taken the quizzes in *Marie Claire* and *Psychology Today.* Moody, yes. Dismissive, yes. Changed, yes. Demeaning, vague, volatile. Yes, yes, yes. On a scale of one to ten, does he seem to be trying to bait you? Does he go out of his way to taunt you? Scare you? Ten, she checked the box. *Ten.*

At least Bill never hit her. Never physically harmed her. It seemed like Bree had a different experience.

Bree. She trudged upstairs, thinking of the woman in the bar.

Alyssa knew unhappiness when she saw it. After tonight's conversation, tentative steps on emotional thin ice, Bree had let Alyssa pay for her second wine, thanked her politely, then said goodbye.

Alyssa had written her own phone number on a napkin, and slid it across the zinc bar to Bree.

"Call me if you need anything. Really." Alyssa had hesitated, fearing it might seem too forward. Too aggressive. Too intrusive. But men did that without a second thought. Bree had accepted the napkin, tucking it into a pocket, but had not offered her own number in return. And with a wave, she'd walked away, leaving Alyssa alone.

Now Alyssa washed her face, drew on a big soft T-shirt. Sliding under the covers, she put her phone on the white bedside table, and plugged it in to charge. Its green aura lighted the otherwise darkened room.

Forsythia intact on the front steps. Questionable tulips. The third test was usually the secret compartment in the closet. Should she get up to look? But no. There was nothing inside, she knew that. She promised herself she'd stop being paranoid, stop wishing for secret messages, start facing reality. She closed her eyes, resolute.

She thought of Bree, in that not-quite-seedy hotel, equally apprehensive and ambivalent. Why were women always the ones who were harmed?

The sounds of the night surrounded her, the sounds of her solitude, and her anxiety. Had someone moved the tulips? No one had stepped on the front-steps flower, so how could they—*Bill*—have gotten in? *A million ways,* her mind rebuked her. Instead of sheep, she counted fears, individual nameless fears. She was afraid to go to sleep. What if she'd missed something? What if someone was inside? What was Bill trying to do?

But if she stayed awake, there was danger in every sound. Sixty-five hundred square feet, and a guest house. And every square foot was paved with uncertainty.

SATURDAY

FOUR

She leaped out of bed, convinced. The clock showed 3:00 a.m. Sleepless and duvet up to her chin, she couldn't stop thinking about that hiding place in the closet.

Maybe Bill had left her a message there. An apology, or regret, a recapitulation, a plea. He'd know she was smart enough to look for it. To find it. And she would do whatever it said, call him or go to him or answer him or be with him. He had been in their house. And he *had* moved the tulips, on purpose. To send her a message. To test her.

She yanked open the slatted double doors. Pushed aside the clothes. Sometimes, when he tormented her, not physical, and never physical, but emotional enough to hurt, he'd teased her afterward, telling her she could not take a joke. Which was true, she couldn't, not jokes like he made. And when she'd finally laugh, agreeing that he was silly and teasing, he would say, *See? I was right. I'm always right.* Bill loved proving he was right. Bill loved testing her.

Counting two sections from the left side, she tapped, *tap-tap,* and pushed. The secret door opened.

She held her breath and slipped her hand inside.

And there was nothing there, of course there wasn't. There was no test. She was an idiot. A failure. And this was her life, looking for treasures that didn't exist.

That black hole in the closet was like her heart.

Dark and empty. In collapse and defeat, she lowered herself to the plush carpet, its pile just as deep as it had been the first day they saw it.

She must have slept, because when she awoke, the carpet had left lines and bumps on her face, and the morning had vanished. As she burrowed back under her rumpled duvet, she wished she could simply sleep for the rest of her life. At least for as long as it took the lawyers to decide what her life would be.

When she could hide no longer, she'd stared at herself in the bathroom mirror, a rectangle of silvered glass surrounded by professional makeup lights. She stood, shocked for a moment, and touched her fingers to the carpet creases in her cheek.

"*This is not me,*" she'd whispered to the mirror, "this is *not* me. This is what Bill is trying to make me." She'd watched her expression change. Toughen. "And I do not accept it." Her voice had changed, too.

She was thirty-whatever years old. With sixty-whatever years to live. Not a chance she would waste them. Not anymore. Not a chance she would spend them in sorrow and regret and wishful thinking. What did she have to worry about, in reality? Alyssa could reach out her hand and get fluffy towels, and diamond jewelry, and anything she wanted in a refrigerator as big as the Ritz. She was being whiny and annoying, and if she were her best friend, she'd tell her that. She washed her face, threw on clothes, stomped downstairs, left the alarm armed, punched on the coffee, and flipped open the kitchen laptop.

Bree Lorrance, she typed into Google, sitting on a wicker stool at the kitchen island. Through the french doors, she saw the sun shining, that tentative May sun, with its promise of warmth and renewal, and it layered a slash of bright across the speckled black countertop.

"Let's just see," Alyssa said out loud. Bree Lorrance, whoever the internet revealed her to be, *she* was the one with a problem.

Last night, at Vermilion, Alyssa had coaxed out more details. With decreasing reluctance, Bree had described a hideous emotionally manipulative boyfriend—why some women called those men *boyfriends* Alyssa could never understand—and her debts, and the terrible low-paying bank job with the predatory boss, and someone calling and calling and calling her cell phone. Bree had felt so pressured and hunted and terrified, she'd explained, that she'd left town. "I don't want to burden you with it," Bree had apologized. "It sounds worse than it is. Let's let it go. Okay? Other people have problems, too. I'll be fine."

Alyssa puffed out a breath now, annoyed with herself. And here she was complaining because her house was too big. "Get a life," she muttered. She simply had no one to talk to, no one, and how did anyone survive that? "Shut *up,* Alyssa," she said, and that only made it worse.

She focused on her computer search. The results were skimpy, but there they were.

First, the Stateside Bank website, with a photo of Bree Lorrance. Set in a grid of tiny rectangles on the page labeled "Our Staff," curly hair and all. From the site of a public school in Amherst, Massachusetts, an even tinier high school black-and-white graduation photo, a Bree with too-short bangs and a heart-shaped necklace. One from a state university yearbook, too, showing her in Math Club, Drama Club, and Mensa.

So Bree Lorrance existed as presented, raised in Amherst, and worked in a bank. And Mensa meant smart.

Alyssa grabbed her coffee, added milk. *Smart.* What if Bree had looked *her* up?

Clicking the laptop keys, she watched the screen fill with bits of her life, as if Google were eager to remind her what she'd lost.

First, of course, a picture of her with Bill. She might as well have googled *Bill Macallen's wife* as search for her own name, since that's how even Google characterized her.

She scrolled, mesmerized—a before-times Alyssa, coiffed and polished, gazing adoringly at Bill, posed arm in arm with big shots in front of banners emblazoned with bank logos and charity themes and medical emblems and once, even the seal of the president of the United States. Were there any photos of Bill looking at *her*?

Her eyes had welled, blurring the taunting computer screen. It was difficult to give up when you'd thought your dreams had come true. Difficult to admit you were wrong. Easier to keep dreaming, to imagine you were mistaken, or had misinterpreted. Easier to dream a new dream; to imagine a surprise, or an explanation. Alyssa was fully awake now. Her dream had ended.

But Bree had bigger problems. Maybe Alyssa could help her with those. Money changed everything, that's what friends were for.

• • •

"This is a surprise."

Alyssa saw the bartender's eyebrows go up as she approached. He wore a black T-shirt tonight, the same striped apron tied around his waist. She pulled out her barstool, the same one as the night before. She'd looked for Bree as she entered the Vermilion bar. Quickly, casually, as any Saturday night newcomer would. She'd worried about Bree. More than she would have predicted.

"I hadn't pegged you for a return visitor." The bartender wiped the polished bar with his towel, then centered a square napkin where Alyssa's drink would go. "Same as last night?"

"You can't possibly remember that," Alyssa teasingly challenged him. "Dozens of people come here every night. Especially Fridays. And we all must look the same."

"You're right about the dozens." The bartender fussed with a container of salted Chex Mix and peanuts. "But you don't all look the same. That's part of the fun." He filled a white china saucer with the salty mixture, put it in front of her. Might have glanced at her diamond ring.

She used her thumb to hide it, but he might have seen that, too. And now he probably thought she didn't trust him.

"Martini, right? Vodka. Top shelf."

"You got me," she said. Then winced at how lame that sounded. But he wasn't why she was here.

"I'm Emmett," he said.

"Alyssa."

"Are you meeting your friend?" The music in the background tonight was different, not jazz but some baroque classical arrangement, mathematical and repetitive.

"Friend?" *I have no friends,* she did not say, and knew this was how some bartenders passed the time, chatting with single women. Single drinking women. Of which she was definitely not one, no matter how it looked. It had been a long time since anyone paid attention to her that way. Once she was Bill's possession, the level of off-limits was incalculable.

She was reassured, she had to admit. Being discarded was not good for one's ego. Alyssa had dressed with a deliberate casualness, in black slacks and a black silk shirt. *Saturday night,* her outfit telegraphed, *and I'm confident and happily alone.* Her clothing was lying, but one step at a time.

"The woman with the reddish hair, the one you were with last night," Emmett went on.

"Hmm?"

"She's a guest here," Emmett told her. "She came back after you left, put another glass of wine on her room tab. She told me they're having problems with the heating system, and it's stuck on high. Maybe it was more comfortable down here."

"Hmm," Alyssa said again. She'd never thought about hotel bartenders, how much they knew about their guests, when they arrived and who they left with. *Bill,* she thought for the millionth time. *Where are you? And with who?* She had to wonder if some bartender somewhere knew more about her husband's whereabouts than she did.

She shifted on her leather barstool. If Bree was gone, there was no reason for Alyssa to be here. But Emmett had said she *is* a guest here, not *was* a guest here. Alyssa winced at her amateur-sleuth deduction about verb tense. She wasn't *that* needy, and she wasn't *that* interested. She was simply a little concerned. And it was a relief to think about someone other than herself.

The undercurrent of classical music seemed louder now, the rondo unbroken, repeating, strings separating and coming back together, weaving the melody. She heard a rumble of masculine laughter from the end of the bar. Two men were clinking glasses, their shoulders angled toward each other. Seemed like their tawny drinks had done their job.

"Alyssa?" The bartender—Emmett—interrupted her thoughts.

She looked at him, reorienting herself.

"I'm fine," she said. "Just thinking."

Emmett cocked his head toward the entrance behind her. "Look," he said.

FIVE

Tonight's flower-on-the-step, a purple crocus blossom, was exactly as Alyssa left it.

She turned, seeing Bree's questioning face spotlighted in the glow from the motion-activated porch lights.

"Nope, I mean it," Alyssa said, beckoning her. "Bring your suitcase on up here. And this is the last you'll mention it, right? I wouldn't have offered the guest house if I hadn't meant it."

She put her key into the front door latch. This was such a good idea. Alyssa was weary of being alone, and Bree needed a better place than that soul-crushing hotel where the shower water was arctic and the heat relentless. And Alyssa's persistent paranoia-sorrow-imagination-fear did not translate to reality. Plus, no one had disturbed the crocus.

"There's Wi-Fi, there's a fridge. We'll go through and out the back way. If you want to leave tomorrow, all good. Your call. It's just me."

Bree pulled her bag up the front walk, closer to the door. "You and the dog," she said, smiling, as the barking continued.

"The—?" Alyssa held up her key fob. Clicked a button with her thumb. The barking stopped. "Electronic dog," she said. "Motion-detector thing. It's easier, and pretty efficient. I'd dearly wanted a real dog—a rescue—but Bill's allergic." She swung open the front door, and tapped the code on the keypad. Even Bree's presence made her feel safer. She checked the tulip vase, though, this time for sure. It had not been moved.

Bree stood in the entryway, hand still clenched on the handle of her fraying suitcase.

Alyssa watched her guest take in the crystal chandelier, which had automatically clicked on as the dog silenced, glittering lights across pale yellow walls. The fresh tulips, the fireplace, the stairway, the living room, the long hallway. Alyssa saw it all through Bree's eyes, and couldn't decide whether to be proud or embarrassed. What must Bree be thinking? She'd just left a bare-minimum hotel; she herself had described the thin gray towels and the smell of must and silent impermanence. And now she was trading that for opulence. For one night, at least.

"Beautiful," Bree said.

"Thanks." Alyssa decided to own it, and go on.

Bree still had a death grip on her suitcase handle. "I promise I'm not the crazed husband stealer," Bree said. "I mean—"

"Well, that dubious title has probably been retired," Alyssa said. "As I told you in Vermilion. Which is why we're here alone. And you can't be the crazed killer nanny, because we—I—don't have any kids."

"So that makes *you* the bad guy," Bree said. "Picking up vulnerable women in hotel bars. Ha ha."

"I'm too wiped out to be the bad guy," Alyssa replied. "And too old. So, coffee? Wine? Brandy?" Might as well hit the good stuff before her entire life fell apart.

And might as well share it while she could. Karma, all that. Sisterhood. And she wouldn't be alone.

"Leave your bag here for a minute. We'll raid the kitchen. There's cheese, I know. Did you have dinner?" She paused, realized how much she'd assumed. "Is this weird?"

Bree tilted her head, the light emphasizing her pale blue eyes and the dark roots of her hair. It wasn't that Bree was unattractive, Alyssa thought, annoyed with herself for judging. Though she'd obviously once colored her hair, she hadn't kept up with it. Something had interrupted her life.

"Men do it all the time, don't they?" Bree was saying. "I mean, not inviting women to stay in their guest houses, and we'll cross that bridge at some point, but picking up women in bars and taking them home? Isn't that called *dating*? I mean, we're standing here like it's bizarre, when *men* make an entire life out of it."

The chandelier's twinkling lights were electric stars, framed in gilded stucco. "We're *standing* here," Bree went on, "all awkward, in your gorgeous entry hall, with that elegant stairway, and secretly wondering whether we've had too much to drink. Making jokes about being serial killers and psychopaths. If you were a man, you'd have already tried to get me upstairs. And I wouldn't have come home with you, guy-you, if I hadn't expected that. True?"

Alyssa frowned, hoping Bree hadn't misunderstood. "True. But—I'm not—"

"Me, either. Don't get me wrong, you're very attractive, but . . . I'm not into women that way," Bree said. "So—"

"Well, we've just spent two evenings complaining about husbands and boyfriends, right? So we were pretty clear on preferences. You just looked like you needed a friend. Not to mention a place where the heat worked."

"Same could be said for you, Alyssa. The friend part, at least."

"Follow me to the kitchen, friend." Alyssa tossed her handbag on the bottom stair. "It's down the hall. Leave your stuff."

"The dog will guard it, I suppose."

They both laughed, and Alyssa felt the atmosphere change, some decision being made. An alliance.

As they walked down the carpeted hallway, Alyssa imagined Bree wondering about the empty rectangles between the photos on the galleried wall. Alyssa had taken down some of the black-framed photographs, the ones of their honeymoon in Bali, and vacations in their St. Barts beach place, in Bill's office at the grand opening, and the silly one where they'd dressed up as Bonnie and Clyde for a fundraising event. Bill's idea, to be Bonnie and Clyde, two doomed thieves. *Maybe we should pick a couple who lived*, Alyssa teased at the time.

Bill had patted the fake gun in the plastic holster strapped under his double-breasted pin-striped suit jacket. *They did what they wanted, right?* he'd argued. *And died on their own terms?*

"Lovely," Alyssa muttered, opening the fridge door. A blast of cold air hit her. Her stainless steel refrigerator was always stocked, and Tammy was wonderful about keeping things organized. And mopped, and ironed, and dusted, and vacuumed. Another part of her life that the lawyers were probably gleefully about to eliminate. As if *she* had done something wrong.

"Huh? You said 'lovely'?" Bree had come into the room behind her, and Alyssa heard her pull out one of the wicker stools by the center island.

"Nothing. Thinking out loud." Alyssa selected a wedge of brie—smiling as she did so—and held it up as she turned. "How about—?"

"Damn it," Bree said.

"Okay, not funny, I guess. And probably not the first time for the cheese joke." Alyssa grimaced, and started to put it back into the cheese drawer.

"No, no," Bree said. "My phone's buzzing again. I put it on vibrate, but it's just so inescapable."

"Him?" Alyssa organized cheese, knife, crackers. Fig jam. Uncorked a sauterne. Placed them on the island's marble counter.

Bree rested her face in her fists. She stared past Alyssa, past the french doors and into the backyard and garden, azure forget-me-nots aglow in the security lighting.

"It's been a long time since I felt safe," she finally said.

"Me, too." Alyssa fetched two wineglasses, filled them halfway. Gave one to Bree. "I'm trying so hard not to pry, but . . . you want to tell me about it?" It hit her that she hadn't had any food recently, hadn't even nibbled on the crispy things at the bar. She rotated the makeshift cheese tray toward Bree. "Kinda hard to ignore. The calls. And your reaction. Might as well talk. We're living together now."

Bree's eyes flared, and her back stiffened.

"Joking," Alyssa said. Maybe this hadn't been such a good idea. It had seemed expansive, generous, even compassionate. But what was she supposed to say now? *Never mind, this is too strange, better go back to the hotel*? Not a bad idea, come to think of it.

"Bill never thought I was funny, either," Alyssa went on. "Not recently, at least. Listen, maybe we're both tired. And you know, martini, wine, after midnight. I can call you an Uber, anytime. Or drive you back. Your hotel room is still paid for, remember? As you said, so he'd think you were still there. If he ever knew you were there in the first place. Whoever he is."

Silence from Bree.

"Okay." Alyssa put up two palms. "I'll stop asking." It had been an impulse to invite her to stay in the guest house. The same impulse Alyssa'd have felt if she'd found a stray kitten, and brought it home to keep her company. Not that she could have, with Bill's allergies.

But the intensifying loneliness had been nibbling at her edges, nagging her. She'd kept thinking things were moved, or missing. Her jewelry rearranged. A favorite dress dangling from a hanger. A bread knife on the kitchen floor. It might have been the housekeeper, Alyssa had decided. Or maybe Alyssa herself.

Or Bill. It might have been Bill. Mocking her, proving she was defenseless. That he was unstoppable.

So the idea of someone to talk to had seemed tempting. But tomorrow, Bree would leave, and it'd be an episode in Alyssa's rearview. She took a sip of the sweet wine. Having Bree here, though, was almost like having a friend. And it was a treat to have someone to talk to, someone who liked her for herself, not because of Bill.

"I hope you won't be mad," Bree finally said. She curled her fingers around the stem of her wineglass. "I have a confession to make."

SIX

"Confession?" Alyssa stepped back from the center island, caught herself looking at the shiny knives stabbed into the wooden rack on the drainboard, then, embarrassed, actively *didn't* look at the knives. Trapped in a kitchen with a stranger was not the best prescription for good outcomes. She imagined the explanation she'd have to give to the police after whatever horrific thing that was about to happen actually happened. If she were alive to tell it. She could imagine the headlines. *Idiotic suburban housewife invites* . . .

Bree didn't look sinister, though, or threatening, just a thin-shouldered thirtysomething in a cheap sweater and a too-long skirt, but what did bad people look like?

"That's a funny thing to say," was all Alyssa could come up with. The freezer kicked on, the metallic clank making her heart flutter. She wished her imaginary dog were real.

Bree sighed, and twisted her glass. The caramel-colored wine rippled and swayed, and Bree held it up to the light.

"I was going to keep it from you," she said. "Because you were being so nice."

"Bree?" Alyssa eyed her own wine, deciding she didn't need any more alcohol, now or ever.

"Oh, it's nothing bad." Bree winced, apologizing. "I

put that all wrong. But remember when you went to the bathroom? At the hotel? I googled you."

"You—"

"Yeah. You'd told me your name, Alyssa Westland, and we'd already talked about me coming to your guest house, which was either awfully nice, or awfully—" She paused. "Unusual. So I real fast looked you up. I mean, you seemed lovely, but getting into a car with a stranger, lock, stock, and suitcase, and without checking out of the hotel, has got to be high on the list of dumb decision-making. Wouldn't you agree?"

"Okay, wow." Should she admit she'd looked Bree up, too? No, too intrusive-creepy. "Did I pass your test?"

"Yes, eventually. But I didn't find an Alyssa Westland. Which kinda scared me. Because—why would you make up a name? But I did find Alyssa Westland *Macallen*. With a photo of you. And your husband? And there was nothing about him being mysteriously murdered, so that was a good sign. So now I know he's a big-deal charity fundraiser, and you're—"

"Not." Alyssa finished the sentence.

"Separated," Bree said, "was what I was planning to say. When I saw you coming back, I was so embarrassed that I closed the search, and I wasn't going to mention it, but then I felt guilty because I definitely would have said something to let you know I knew things, and then—that wouldn't be good. So yeah. That's my confession."

"That was prudent, of course. Looking me up." Alyssa thought about that. "What would I find if I googled *you*?"

"Do it." Bree pulled her phone out of her skirt

pocket. "Here. Use *my* phone. It's open." She tapped it, and offered it across the island. "Seriously. Do it."

Alyssa reached for it, knowing if she didn't, she'd have to admit she'd already searched, and that moment had passed. Bree's home screen was black, just showing the time, 2:15, in green numerals. Alyssa's own home screen had a photo of Bill in the sunlit archway of their house in St. Barts. She should delete that.

"I don't need to," she said. "Come on."

"No, no, do it, Alyssa," Bree encouraged her. "I'll feel less guilty. We'll be even."

"Fine. But only because it's the middle of the night, and the middle of the bottle, and you're insisting." Alyssa touched Bree's screen, figuring the search would protect her in case she mentioned Mensa or something. The phone vibrated.

"I didn't—" she said, surprised. "Push anything."

Caller unknown appeared on the screen.

She held the phone, gingerly, like a live thing, showing Bree. "Is this—?"

A wash of dismay shadowed Bree's face, her forehead furrowing. "I can't take it anymore."

The phone buzzed again.

"He's just never going to st—"

"Hello?" Alyssa said into the phone.

Bree's eyes widened. "No," she whispered.

Alyssa held up a finger, listened, then shrugged. "Hel-lo?" Mouthed the word *nobody.* She stood, and put on a secretarial voice, the non-inflection of an answering service. "Who are you calling for, please?" Just like inviting Bree home, she'd answered the phone after a snap decision.

She paused. Silence.

"This number is no longer in service," Alyssa said. And she hung up.

"What are you *doing*?"

"I don't know." Alyssa paced to the windows, looked out into the empty night, turned back to Bree. "But this is nuts. If some guy is hounding you, then someone needs to tell him to go away. If you don't want to talk to him, you shouldn't have to talk to him."

Bree nodded. "I know."

Alyssa pulled up a stool opposite her. "If you're frightened, have you gone to the police?"

"No, because what would I tell them? Nothing's happened."

"Okay." Alyssa thought about that. "Proves my point. So why not just ask him? He's on the phone, not in the room. How do you even know it's a man?"

"I did ask, once. And he said my name, and I said, 'Who is this?' And he hung up. It's a man. But, Alyssa? Sometimes I see a shadow. A reflection in a window. Headlights following my car. All these calls. You heard it for yourself. I got a new phone, it's one of those whatever they call 'ems."

"Burners?"

"Right. That you can't trace. But somehow he has the number. That's why I left my car back home. I took the train here, an Uber to the hotel. I'll, I don't know, take the T to work for the new job."

"When do you start?"

"Two weeks. And yes, okay, it might be idiot Frankie. *Might* be Frankie. My kind-of ex. But maybe not. I want to be by myself for a while. Be happy."

"How's that working for you?" Alyssa set the phone on the counter. It was as if a third person were in the room. *Frankie*. "Got to say, 'happy' was not the first word that came to mind when I saw you."

Bree drained her wine, then broke off a cracker, popping sesame seeds across the counter. "Alyssa? I know you're trying to help, and it's very sweet. I was lucky to meet you." She smiled. "This was the first bar pickup in my life that didn't end in a misunderstanding or a disappointment."

"Ha," Alyssa said. "But don't try to change the subject. You should answer the phone if he calls again. Ask who it is and what he wants. If you won't, I will."

"Really, no. Better to leave it alone."

"Why? We've known each other for . . ." Alyssa paused, counting. "Five hours in total. This Frankie person has been a major topic of conversation. So."

Alyssa was tired, and maybe a little fuzzy-headed from the wine, but this was like—a challenge. She pursed her lips. "The caller ID is the same every time?"

"Yes. Caller unknown."

"Bill collector, crazy boss, stalker UPS guy, unrequited suitor from high school. Spam? The bank, or wherever you worked? A *customer* in the bank?"

"You're funny," Bree said. "And you can list all the possibilities, but don't you think I have, too?"

"I suppose," Alyssa said. "Trying to help."

"No, it's a relief, having someone to talk to," Bree said. "But some problems cannot be solved."

Alyssa sighed, considering that. Elbows on the counter, she rested her face in her hands; exhausted, and over-wined, and a little embarrassed at elbowing her way into Bree's life.

"They can," Alyssa finally said. "Be solved. We just don't know how to do it. Yet."

"You think?" Bree's eyes widened. But in hope or sarcasm, Alyssa couldn't decide.

"I do." Alyssa pointed to the last of the brie and crackers. "You want? Or should we call it a night?"

"Good idea." Bree gestured toward the back. "So, should I—?"

Alyssa tapped on the kitchen's alarm system pad, and two short beeps followed. "That opens the blue door of the guest house, see?" Alyssa pointed. "I can show you where everything is. Towels, soap, bed."

"I can go myself, if you're okay with that," Bree said. "Anything I should know?"

"There's a coffee maker. Coffee's in the little fridge. And yogurt, I think. I'll be up at seven-ish, so meet me here whenever. I need to set the alarm system, but you'll see the kitchen lights come on. And oh." Alyssa winced, remembering. "Don't come before that, because the dog will bark."

"That's almost irresistible," Bree said. "But I'll try. And I'll call if I don't see you. I have your number, remember."

"Good. We'll have coffee, then you can decide what to do."

"Sounds nice. Civilized." Bree's expression quieted. "I'm grateful, Alyssa."

Alyssa didn't know how to respond, to the solemnity of Bree's voice or the appreciation on her face. She still felt surprised at the impulsive offer she'd made, and also at the comforting peace she felt in having someone to talk to.

"Not a problem. It's one night."

"Agreed." Bree trundled her suitcase to the door, put her hand on the knob. "Night," she said.

"Night."

The door opened, then clicked closed, and Alyssa watched her guest wheel her bag along the flagstone walk. Bree stopped as she arrived at the blue door, and looked back toward the kitchen, raising her hand in a silent salute.

Alyssa raised her hand, too, acknowledging, and wondered if Bree could see her. She saw the interior lights of the guest house go on, and then the door closed.

The refrigerator motor kicked in, its hum seeming louder than usual, and the red light from the alarm system blinked reassuringly from the panel on the wall. Alyssa stared out into the night, and watched a wide-winged moth flutter into one of the outside security lights, frantic and needy and throwing itself into the irresistible and lethal brightness.

SUNDAY

SEVEN

Poor Bree, Alyssa thought. She pulled on her big white T-shirt, dimmed the bathroom to night-light. But maybe, in this case, at least, comparison was healing. Bree had taught Alyssa to count her blessings, and share them. Alyssa had offered Bree safety and support. This had been a good day. For both of them. The nightstand alarm pad showed a red shield, the overnight mode. If anyone tried to come in, the dog would bark.

As she put her phone next to the alarm pad and climbed into bed, she remembered she hadn't checked the closet hiding place. *No,* she told herself. *Leave it this time.*

She clicked off the nightstand light, determined. She had to conquer her suspicions. Bill had made her miserable. On purpose. Made her feel dismissed and then disoriented. It had taken more than eight years to pour and set the concrete of her married existence. Then Bill became the jackhammer that broke it apart. She needed to sweep up the pieces and throw them in the trash.

The light on her cell phone screen flashed, as it sometimes did; she swore it had a life of its own. What did that remind her of?

She laughed out loud in the darkness. The movie room, in their own house. Bill had gotten on a Hitchcock kick and streamed *The Birds,* and *Strangers on a Train,* and *Rear Window.* Alyssa had swooned over Grace Kelly, and Bill had bought her a little square Hermès bag, just like in the movie. When she was a teenager, movies only meant what was on their unreliable TV. Her mother had told her—daily, sometimes—that they couldn't afford movie rentals or cable, let alone going to the theater. Bill had provided unimagined luxury, to watch whatever they wanted, whenever they wanted. With a popcorn machine. Bill teased her about it; what felt mundane to him was captivating to her.

One night, sharing popcorn and champagne, she and Bill had watched *Gaslight,* where the creepy husband tried to convince his wife she was crazy when she insisted the lights were flickering. Alyssa had felt sorry for the deceived heroine, even though the story seemed far-fetched.

"No one would fall for that." She'd dismissed it, curled up into the curve of Bill's shoulder. "That woman should stand up for herself."

Now the glow of her phone had reminded her that *he'd* seen the movie, too. Understood the power of manipulation, the vulnerability of love and fear and need. She wondered if Bill was doing that to her. Wondered about the crocus and the tulips and the hiding place. Wondered about her own fears, and whether someone—Bill—was truly trying to harm her. Trying to leave her behind. Leave her broken. Leave her with nothing.

She'd fallen asleep, thinking of unreliable lights, and awakened as the real sunlight came through her bedroom window. She checked her phone. No messages. Not from Bill, not from Bree, not from anyone, but no matter. She'd take control of her own life.

Exactly as she'd suggested to Bree, she'd become her own best friend. She rolled her eyes at the mawkish pseudo-philosophy. But it was true. That woman in the movie hadn't stood up for herself—not at the beginning, at least. Alyssa wouldn't wait as long. And Bree, her new friend, shouldn't wait either.

• • •

Bree arrived at the kitchen door fifteen minutes after Alyssa had flipped on the lights and started the coffee maker.

"Have you seen *Gaslight*?" she asked Bree as they organized their Sunday-morning coffee. Alyssa had warmed the cinnamon rolls that Tammy had stocked, and she and Bree ate them the same way, unwinding the fragrant dough to expose the sticky cinnamon sugar inside. "The movie?"

"A classic," Bree said, adding milk to her coffee mug. "Sure. The woman was an idiot, though. What made you think of it?"

"Just—life." Alyssa poured her own coffee. "Bill."

"He's gaslighting you?"

Alyssa pushed the thought away with both hands. "No, of course not, just stream of consciousness. You know what? Let's have a day for ourselves. I say—manicure."

"Manicure?"

"And hair."

"Hair?"

"Yup. My salon is open, Sunday's not crowded at Aubergine. I bet I can get us appointments. And I won't take no for an answer." Alyssa held out her hands, fluttering her fingers. "Look at this. Embarrassing, right?"

Bree seemed skeptical. "Not really."

"Well, I need a manicure. And a haircut. And I'd love you to come with me. We'll have a spa day. We deserve it."

"Deserve?"

"Whatever." Alyssa pulled out her phone. "It's something we can control. Right? I mean, I'm not—special. As my mother reminded me every day. I'm not especially smart, or beautiful, or brave. But some people, ordinary, like me, are just—looking for happiness. We have one life, right?"

Bree dabbed up the remnants of cinnamon sugar from her plate with the last of her pastry. "If you say so," she finally said. "I do need a haircut. But I'll pay you back."

• • •

Four hours later, coiffed and manicured, Alyssa felt like a different person. And Bree looked like one.

Heads turned as they approached the mahogany hostess desk of the country club dining room. Alyssa surveyed the expanse of the Club's white tables, each draped in floaty white linen and topped by three tiny bubble vases holding mini-bouquets of white lilies of the valley. This time of afternoon, verging on too late for regular lunch, held the last of today's customers, maybe waiting for a tee time or a tardy spouse. Alyssa saw a few members stop, coffee cups midway to their lips, as they noticed her. And Bree. She might have been imagining it, but the hum of conversation she'd heard walking up the hallway toward the Club's exclusive Sunday Room seemed to have decreased in volume when she entered with the newly gorgeous Bree by her side.

Bree had emerged from the back room of Salon Aubergine, almost blushing, her now strawberry-blond hair sleek and shiny, cut longer on one side than the other. The stylist had also done some makeup magic; brought out the blue in Bree's eyes, puffed peachy blush high on her cheekbones, added an almost invisible sheen of warm-toned lip gloss. Bree had one of those faces, Alyssa saw, that came to life with a touch of color. Even Bree's posture had changed, her shoulders relaxed; her expression was one only women could understand. Bree had clearly looked into a mirror and seen something surprising.

Alyssa knew she would never have a daughter of her own, and the emotion she felt, familial pride or connection—she'd missed that. She'd wanted a family, and vowed she'd do better than her own embittered mother, but Bill had taken that potential joy from her, too. Today, seeing Bree blossom, it almost felt like she'd gained a younger sister.

And maybe this could be the beginning of not only the new Bree, but the new Alyssa. Lunch. At the Club. And damn them all.

Alyssa—even the new Alyssa—felt as apprehensive as the first time she'd set foot in here, a grand nineteenth-century mansion once owned by a shoemaker magnate who'd bet on the certainty of spats, lost his fortune, and then lucked into oil and moved his family to a showier mansion on the Hudson River, leaving his fifteen-bedroom, three–dining room, and five-fireplaced estate behind. The Club was still surrounded by now-lofty weeping willows and a stand of the shoemaker's original elms, framed by a fragrant shaded garden of sweetly ephemeral lilies of the valley.

The heavy solid oak front door had opened into a vast entryway, glowing with polished mahogany, round marble tables holding crystal fishbowls dripping with stargazer lilies, their scent so pungent it transformed the foyer into a fairyland.

Now Alyssa felt as nervous as Bree looked. She had not called in advance for reservations, reluctant to negotiate with the hostess, a misleadingly prim-looking woman who wielded enormous power. Camden Hollis knew the Club hierarchy, knew who had won today's tennis or who was delinquent on their bill, knew whose iced tea should be laced with bourbon and who deserved the corner table by the lily garden windows.

Camden Hollis could make you or break you with reservations, and with access. With one turn of her back and lift of her nose, she could make you feel invisible. Alyssa had not wanted to risk a frosty "We are fully booked today, Mrs. Macallen" response. She was Alyssa Macallen, no matter what her impending marital status, and the Macallens could always get a table.

Bill could, at least.

With an enigmatic smile, Camden had told them she needed to "go check." That sounded ominous, but Alyssa had held her ground. Looked at her watch. With a matching smile of her own, she'd politely responded, "Do you?" and now here they were. Alyssa and Bree, and all eyes on them.

The Club had long ago dumped its once legendary and then embarrassing admissions policies, and welcomed all through its venerable doors. All who were affluent enough. Now, suspended in no-reservations limbo, Alyssa struggled to keep her confidence. At least she had a companion, albeit a companion who was not hiding her curiosity about the antique furnishings and the embossed wallpaper and the carefully random Persian carpeting and the opulent flowers. The room smelled of vanilla and coffee and cinnamon and peaches, warm and redolent and welcoming.

Alyssa, however, did not feel welcome.

Camden returned, heels silent on the thick carpeting, dark bob sleekly in place, holding a Montblanc pen. "We haven't seen you for a bit, Mrs. Macallen," she said. "But of course we have room for you."

"Marvelous, Camden," Alyssa said, all bright graciousness, mustering every bit of her acting abilities, including the position-announcing first-name choice. "Thank you."

"Follow me, ladies." Camden pointed with her bulky pen. "Such a beautiful day, isn't it?"

Quite the welcoming hostess now, Alyssa thought, as if someone had given her permission to allow them into the room. Who had she called?

"It's amazing," Bree whispered as the three of them, single file, walked from the hostess stand to a table as far across the dining room as it could be. Alyssa held her chin high, her diligently confident expression unwavering. The tables on either side of theirs were empty, too, and Alyssa understood that Camden had placed them in a deserted part of the room. Whether that was out of pity, or concern, or, in derision, as some sort of schadenfreude entertainment, to parade them by the other women—for they were all women—who did not even attempt to hide their scrutiny of her.

Alyssa had lost the husband game, they'd be thinking, as if they'd always predicted she would, as if the *she was never one of us* label was Alyssa's inevitable destiny. A dark expletive, not appropriate for this sunlit room, crossed Alyssa's mind, though she managed to keep her expression serene.

At least she looked Club-worthy, and Bree did, too. Alyssa had stopped at home and grabbed low-key blazers and pearls for both of them. Like dress-up, Alyssa had said, without actually being dressed up.

Now, though Bree didn't know it, they were walking through a minefield. Lylah Rhodes was there, with pre-teen daughter Windsor, far enough away to pretend not to have noticed her. But Alyssa saw how intently, now, they weren't noticing. Eleanor Mbowe and Cecile Grant shared a corner table, and neither acknowledged her, either, deep in conversation and focused on each other as they seemingly were. Lylah and Eleanor and Cecile. She'd considered them friends. Now she saw their furtive glances, their up-and-down assessments, the raising of eyebrows as they returned to their curried chicken salad with white grapes and golden raisins, and sipped their minted teas.

That was the Sunday casual brunch, de rigueur here. A whippet-thin waiter, whose name tag said Imrie, now poured their own iced tea, and set a silver salver of lemon slices and two sets of tiny silver tongs on the white tablecloth. "Good afternoon," Imrie said. "The chicken?"

Alyssa saw Bree's confused expression.

"The chicken salad is . . . fabulous." Alyssa heard her own voice falling into the artificial cadence of her other life. "Everyone has it."

"Of course." Bree unfolded her white damask napkin, and spread it over her lap. "*Fab*ulous."

Now Bree not only didn't look like Bree, she didn't sound like Bree, either. Alyssa remembered seeing Drama Club in Bree's yearbook. Talk about drama.

This mannered lunch, with the two of them center stage, seemed like a milestone. The next act in her journey to a new life.

"I'm a little on overload," Bree was saying as Imrie walked away. "I don't feel like myself, or look like myself, and I . . . don't want you to think I'm, I don't know, taking advantage of you in some way. Honestly, you've done too much, so I will happily devour that delicious-sounding chicken salad, and then just as happily pack my bag and go."

"We'll talk about that when the time comes, and not until after lunch." Alyssa fussed with her silverware. She was torn, she had to admit, between the reassurance and companionship of having someone around, and the unsettling almost-weirdness of having a stranger as a house guest. But Bree wasn't angling to stay, and this was just lunch. She'd take her own advice, and talk about it when the time came. "Agreed?"

"If you say so," Bree acquiesced. She'd been seated with her back to the restaurant entrance, but Alyssa could watch who came in. And they could see her, directly in the line of sight from the hostess station. Had Camden called Bill? Would he arrive, in golf shirt and tousled hair, and what would he do then?

Alyssa selected a lemon wedge with the silver tongs, promising herself to remember to forget, and settled the lemon into her tea, the translucent yellow bits rising then falling in the russet liquid. Then she clasped her hands together, rested her chin on them.

"That was *him*, right? Who called you when we were at the salon?"

Bree chose two sugar cubes from a white porcelain container. Her long-handled spoon rattled the ice and clattered against the sides of the tall glass as she stirred.

"Yes. How'd you know? Did I have a funny look on my face when I came out of the bathroom?" Bree took a careful sip, then another. "What kind of tea is this?"

"Bree? Yes. You looked upset. What did he say? Did he threaten you?" Alyssa leaned toward her friend, needing her to understand. "Honey, you have to face this. You can't keep running. Facing your problems is the only way to handle them."

"I know, " Bree said. "I almost told him. I almost said—I know who you are, Frankie, and—"

"You do? You did?" Alyssa leaned closer, fingertips on temples. As if focusing her words. "So *was* it Frankie?"

EIGHT

"But I hung up." Bree's eyes darted to the still-empty tables flanking them. "I couldn't do it."

"I knew it," Alyssa said. "Your ex. It was—forgive me, Bree—impossible that you had no idea about this. Unlikely, at least."

Imrie had glided up beside them, one gold-edged white plate in each hand, the mound of chicken salad, arranged on a tender bed of baby lettuce and topped with a chiffonade of fresh parsley, glistening in the center.

"For you, Ms. Macallen," Imrie said, settling one in front of Alyssa. "And for your guest. May I get you anything else?" She paused, inquiring. "No? Then do enjoy."

And she was gone.

"Gorgeous," Bree said. "I'm starving."

"I am, too," Alyssa lied. It was all she could do not to keep watching the hostess stand, not to scan the room, not to let her nerves show. "So about the phone call—"

"Listen." Bree had picked up her fork. "Let's have lunch, and then you can ask me whatever you want."

"Deal." Alyssa selected a grape, tasted the sweet-tart burst of flavor. Funny how one taste of one grape conjured another life.

The murmur of voices in the room had clicked up a notch or two in volume. Alyssa, ridiculously, realized she was listening for the sibilance of her own name, trying to pick out which of the conversations was gossiping about her. She had to laugh at herself. Did nothing ever change? So many years ago, she'd whined to her mother, fretting that classmates were whispering about her in the middle school cafeteria. *They're making fun of me,* she'd tearfully confided. *I know they are.*

Her mother had dismissed it, outright, with a wave of her perpetual cigarette. "Don't be silly, Alice. And stop crying." Her mother had rolled her eyes. "You're not one bit special. Why would they waste their time on you?"

But even if no one cared about her, not Bill, and not these harpies in the dining room, the Club was equally her place as anyone's. And at least *she* could authentically care about someone else. That's why she felt connected to Bree. She could guide Bree, or reassure her, or even solve her problems. It would prove Alyssa was a good person.

It was just . . . *was* she?

She hardly thought of herself as Alice anymore, that person from another life. Maybe she'd take her name back. Forget "Alyssa," forget Bill, and forget the houses and the tulips and the imaginary dog. Forget the fear. After all, now she had money, but she was still afraid. So many things, she was learning, were not solved by money.

But some were.

"So delicious," Bree was saying. "I owe you for this, too, Alyssa, and someday when my life changes, I'll pay you back, for everything. I will. And tonight, back at the hotel—my vending-machine tuna will—"

"No pre-fab tuna," Alyssa said. "And you can stay

at our house—*my* house—the guest house—as long as you like."

"Absolutely no."

"Absolutely yes. And after you tell me about the call, you're going to report it to the police. Because—" She stopped, mid-sentence.

"What?" Bree must have seen Alyssa's face change.

Alyssa watched Lylah Everly Rhodes approach. Lylah, as always, announced her virtue in off-white, today a cashmere sweater and wool trousers, cinched by a gold belt. Her hair was a curtain of chestnut, signature bangs flawless. Her immaculate lipstick was unmarred by the assault of chicken salad, her lip color a bespoke deep red Alyssa knew she'd had manufactured specially for her.

In the old days, in the before-times, Lylah and Alyssa had talked constantly, planning charity balls and fundraisers and banquets with the determination of five-star generals. Lylah was an Everly of the Philadelphia Everlys, her husband, Simon, a college classmate of Bill's. Alyssa knew a lot more than that, too.

After the "unfortunate events," as Lylah had deemed them, she'd called, once, almost commiserating, then made a lunch date. Which Lylah had postponed, and postponed again, and then, apparently, forgotten.

"Hello, Lylah." Alyssa felt her fists clench, and tried to keep her voice even. "This is . . ." She paused. "My friend Bree Lorrance. Bree, this is Lylah Rhodes."

"How nice," Lylah said. "Lovely to meet you." She touched the pearls at her throat. Her pale manicure matched the pearls' elegant luster. "How do you know Alyssa?"

"We've known each other forever," Bree said. "Alyssa is fabulous."

Alyssa blinked.

"I've been on assignment in Paris," Bree went on. "The Faubourg Group? You're aware? No? Ah. No matter. It's rather—exclusive. And Alyssa and I, honestly, we simply could not *wait* to catch up."

Alyssa put her fingers to her lips, trying to suppress a laugh. Bree had somehow changed her intonation to gushing society-edged enthusiasm, almost the same as Lylah's, and with that had also managed to put the newcomer off balance, as if Lylah wasn't quite certain if she was being mimicked, or lampooned. Or outclassed. It was the best Alyssa had felt in months.

Lylah blinked, her eyelashes grazing the edge of her bangs.

"A shame you'll miss this year's gala." She eyed Bree, assessing, then focused on Alyssa. "You always had the most *interesting* ideas. Perhaps you can tell your friend all about them."

"Why is she missing the gala?" Bree had widened her eyes, the ingenue. "Is that conflicted with our Amalfi Coast trip, Alyssa? Oh . . . Lylah, is it? How very sweet of you, but I'm sure your event will be just lovely."

Alyssa saw a shadow darken Lylah's carefully proper bearing. Lylah shifted her attention, a fraction, almost put her back to Bree. She leaned toward Alyssa, as if trying to speak to her alone.

"We're all hoping you'll feel better, dear. And we're devastated about your troubles." Her voice had dropped to almost a whisper. "I'm sure you're being quite the trouper. With your little iced tea and all. If that's what it is."

"I—" Alyssa began. "Better?"

But with a swish of her hair and a twist of her tennis-taut hips, Lylah was gone.

Bree straightened in her chair, settled her iced tea on its filigreed coaster. "What was *that* about?" she whispered. "'Little iced tea'? I can't turn around to see what that woman's doing now. But—bizarre. Wasn't it?"

"You're hilarious." Alyssa widened her eyes in surprise, whispering back, trying not to giggle. "Where did that Paris thing come from? And that . . . accent?"

Bree waggled her head side to side, proud of herself. "Well, that woman looked at me like I was—whatever. I couldn't resist. I have my moments." She pursed her lips. "When someone hurts a friend."

Alyssa felt her eyes mist, here in this place where kindness was rarely shown. That's what she'd missed. Kind words, some acknowledgment of herself as a person on her own, not "Bill's wife" or "Mrs. Macallen" or "also seen in the photo." Alyssa had actively chosen this life, but now she could choose a different one. In two days—was that all it had been?—Bree, this needy stranger, had changed her.

"Does she dislike you?" Bree was saying. "Why?"

"No idea. Bill must have said something to her. To all of them. Poisoned them to me. It's how he works. He recruits people. Tests them. Uses them. Discards them. He plays with them, like a cat with an injured mouse. This time, I'm the mouse."

"But why . . ." Bree bit her lower lip. "Forgive me. You can tell me about Bill, if you want to. Or not. Either way."

"Bill is—charming. As long as you do what he says. If not, that's different." Alyssa leaned forward, searching Bree's face. "And in a divorce, the friends choose sides. Lylah Rhodes chose Bill. She came over here to sniff out who you were."

"Rhodes like the Rhodes Corporation?" Bree asked.

"Hmm." Alyssa watched Lylah, now back at her table, leaning toward her daughter, talking behind a cupped hand. "I love how people think they can dismiss you. That woman was my friend, whatever the word means around here." She closed her eyes, a brief pause, remembering. "She has no idea how much I know about her. About her husband. About her daughter."

"Really?"

Alyssa put up a palm. "Don't get me started."

"Come on. *We're* friends now, right? And I may be headed back to Paris any moment."

"Should we get wine? Instead of dessert?" Alyssa couldn't believe she was suggesting that. "Seems very . . . Parisian."

"Why not? Everything else today is so 'Alice.' Curiouser and—"

"So 'Alice'?" Alyssa interrupted.

"In Wonderland. When she said—"

"Oh, right." As if she hadn't instantly recognized the reference. "Sure."

She held up a hand, signaling, and Imrie appeared. Before Imrie returned with the wine, Lylah and her daughter left, without a backward glance. Cecile and Eleanor departed soon after; Alyssa, apparently, remaining invisible to them. Alice again, Alyssa had to admit. *People come and go so quickly around here.*

Bill had not materialized at the hostess desk, so maybe Alyssa had been wrong about who Camden Hollis had called. Maybe she hadn't called anyone. But if she had, then Bill would know she was here. And not only here, but not at home. Today she'd left a tiny fern frond on the front step. Re-penciled the tulip eyeliner, positioned the padded hangers just so in front of the closet compartment. And she had definitely set the alarm.

"So, that woman," Bree was saying. "Lylah Rhodes? You were going to tell me—what?"

NINE

Oh," Alyssa said. "Lylah." She sniffed her wine, a fragrance of buttered honey coming from the chilled liquid. "Nothing important."

"Sure, no pressure." Bree looked at Alyssa through her wineglass. Then took it down. "You're . . . good, Alyssa. A good person. Those people, those women, make your life *miserable,* so no reason to talk about them, right?" She nodded, then fluttered her eyelashes, provocative. "Even though they're gone, and they'll never know, because who's going to tell them?"

"True. I suppose. They talk about *me,* that's for sure. No question Lylah has already reported on our conversation. And on you. Probably tried to google the Faubourg Group." Alyssa shook her head, remembering. "That was classic."

"Let her try looking it up," Bree said. "She probably can't spell it, anyway."

"Sometimes it makes me so annoyed, you know?" Alyssa took a chance, confessing. "They project this vision to the world, this slick society image of ease and privilege, and yet inside, in their real lives, they're—a mess. Pretending to themselves, half the time, rationalizing and covering up and erasing."

"They totally sound super charming. When I was little, I used to think about what it would be like to be rich." Bree seemed to turn wistful. "I always longed for it. I loved numbers, and math, and it seemed like money changes everything."

"Oh, it does. It does indeed. Just not always the way you might think." Alyssa paused. Remembering how her mother's entire focus had been money, the wanting it, or the lack of it. She'd screamed at Alice, once, for throwing away a deposit bottle. But those days were gone. "So, okay. You saw Lylah's daughter? Windsor. She's nine."

"Looked older than that. I would have said fourteen."

"I agree, but they rush them. It's depressing. With makeup, and hair straightening, and clothes meant for someone older. They all want to be what they're not."

Bree nodded, seeming to agree with her criticism.

"So. Speaking of what they're not. Once, Lylah and I were having lunch here, and I mentioned her husband's name, in connection with a project Bill was doing, I suppose, and this look crossed her face. I thought she was about to cry."

"About what?"

"Well, I asked, because she seemed so unhappy. So, she'd had a few wines, as always, and finally she told me that her husband had demanded she prove Windsor was his biological daughter."

"Whoa."

"I know. But apparently—"

Imrie appeared, wheeling a white wicker cart carrying silver platters piled with rainbows of tiny macarons. "May I tempt you?" she asked, pointing at the cookies with a pair of silver tongs.

"I couldn't," Alyssa said. "Bree?"

Bree chose a pink and white and pale green. Imrie

slid them, and a few extra, onto a tiny glass plate. Then left them alone again.

"So biological daughter, you were saying," Bree prompted her as she examined a jewel-toned cookie. "The husband. Did he make the daughter take a paternity test? Like a DNA test? Or however that would work? Whoa, that's a big ask. Imagine *that* conversation."

"I know," Alyssa said. "How are the cookies?"

"Delicious. Sure you don't want one? Did they work together much? Simon Rhodes and your husband?"

"He worked with all of them." Silly, but Alyssa felt guilty divulging more about Windsor. There was still honor, even if it was one-sided. Easier now—and less risky—to focus on Bree's questions about Bill, who was at least old enough to be responsible for his own decisions.

"Bill would get them to make huge charitable donations," she went on. "That was his thing. Then they could take big tax deductions. He told them how to do it, and it was win-win-win as Bill used to say all the time. *All* the time." She rolled her eyes, remembering Bill's puffed-up bragging, as if moving money from one place to another showed some unique skill or aptitude. "But all for the best. You can be a good guy without being sincere about it. The recipients of the charity don't care if you're sincere."

Bree stacked one cookie on top of another. "Your husband—Bill—was he like, um, was that his professional job?"

"Oh, he's a registered fundraiser, if that's what you mean. And he always said the charities and whatever got more donations than they would have otherwise."

"Otherwise than what?"

"Well, you know how it works."

"Not really," Bree said. "These are so yummy."

"Aren't they like the ones you had in Paris, ha ha?" Alyssa asked.

"Oh, exactly." Bree drew out the word, making it a parody of her own parody. She brushed some cookie crumbs into her hand, and tapped them back onto her plate. "I'm making a mess," she said. "No, I don't know how it works."

Alyssa puffed out a breath. "The easy version is that Bill convinces people to donate money, the charities get the money, the donors get deductions, Bill gets paid."

"Like a percentage? Paid by the charities, or by the donors?"

"Hmmm," Alyssa began. Bree worked in a bank, and said she loved numbers, maybe that's why she seemed interested in this. "It was different for each organization, I suppose. A percentage, or some sort of payment. It must all be in Bill's files. Wherever they may be."

"Sure," Bree said. "So you were saying about the daughter? Windsor, you said her name was?"

"I know, right?" Alyssa said. "Anyway, apparently Simon Rhodes had done some sort of 23andMe thing, some sort of genealogy test, and found—what?"

Bree had put down her cookie. "Nothing. I just need to run to the bathroom. Too much tea." She waved her hand toward the hallway. "Out there?"

"To the right," Alyssa said. "I'll sit here and try to stop myself from swiping that pink macaron."

"It has your name on it," Bree said as she stood. "I'll be right back."

Camden Hollis had reappeared at the hostess desk, carrying her rubber-band-wrapped red leather reservations book, and glanced in Alyssa's direction as she laid the open book on her lectern. Alyssa's instinct was to look away, as if she hadn't noticed, but damn it, she *had* noticed, and she was a member of this country club, and Camden was the hostess, and Alyssa had every right to be there. She held up her wineglass, toasting. Then instantly regretted it. *I saw your wife at the Club,* she imagined Camden reporting to Bill. *She was with a woman. At four thirty in the afternoon. On Sunday. Drinking.*

Camden acknowledged her, the very picture of courtesy. Went back to her reservations book.

Alyssa imagined Bill's disdainful laughter, imagined his reaction to Camden's report, derisive, and critical, like *so what else is new?* She could almost hear his voice, his allegiance more to Camden than to her. And what had he said to Lylah that soured her attitude? And when?

She thought about that movie *Gaslight* again, how what's-his-name the husband had deliberately tarnished his wife's mental condition in public, creating a damaged persona for her, impossible to battle because everyone believed the *man.* Was that true now? Alyssa could walk in here and get a table, order chicken salad and wine with the rest of them—but Bill had contaminated her new reality. Not satisfied with making her miserable, but greedily needing to make sure everyone else did, too.

"I'm back." Bree's voice and the sound of her chair pulling across the carpet brought Alyssa back to the present.

"Find it okay?" It was a relief to deal with someone new, someone without the complicated baggage of Bill-and-Alyssa. Someone who could judge her—if that's what people did—for her true self.

"Sure." Bree looked distracted. Fidgety. Her white napkin fell to the floor, and as she bent to pick it up, her new hair brushed across the pink macaron.

"You okay, Bree? You were gone for a long minute there. Do *not* tell me Frankie called when you went to the bathroom. Come on."

"Come on what?" Bree settled herself back into the chair. Blew across the cookie, considered it, ate it.

"Kidding me? Frankie only calls when I'm not around. At the salon, and here. You go to the bathroom, you get a phone call."

"Well, no." Bree swallowed. "Not really."

"Okay, then. Whatever you say." Bree had a life apart from her, she needed to respect that. Shadows were lengthening through the lofty dining room windows. Alyssa deeply dreaded the prospect of being alone, rattling through her home's empty rooms and twisting shadows and lingering memories. The constant threat.

Alyssa knew Bill sneaked in. He moved things. Changed things. Making sure she always felt vulnerable. Reminding her that he was ignoring their agreement. Bill was his own gaslight, flickering constantly at the edges of her worry.

She'd watched the manipulative tactics Bill used on his business adversaries. These days, her divorce lawyer used that very word to describe how Bill and his lawyer thugs characterized *her.* "Adversary." And the divorce was a "battle," with "tactics" and "strategy." Not about love, or sorrow, or remorse. Or guilt.

"Lyss?"

"Hmm?"

"Don't worry about the phone calls. It's not your problem. At all."

Alyssa fingered her teaspoon, frowning. "I still think, if Frankie is harassing you—"

"Okay." Bree cut off Alyssa's criticism. "I'll call the police. I will. I should trust you."

"Good. And I trust you to call. And as soon as you do, I'll stop hounding you." She pointed the spoon, emphasizing. "I'll even change the subject."

"Deal."

"Okay. So—why did you look upset when I mentioned Simon Rhodes? And Windsor?"

"That's got to be the dumbest name ever."

"Don't *you* change the subject. Do you know Simon Rhodes?"

"No."

"What, then?"

Silence. Alyssa heard sounds of laughter from outside, saw silhouetted shapes glide past the wide gauze-curtained windows. People having lives; tennis, and slim tanned legs, and catered dinners with too many appetizers and massive linen napkins and wrapped in their carefree assumption of luxury.

Money itself wasn't a bad thing. Not until bad people used it.

"Bree?" She mentally played back her own words. "The only other thing I said was *23andMe*. Genealogy. Was *that* why you looked upset?"

Bree attempted to take a sip of wine, but her glass was empty.

"A*ha*." Alyssa jabbed a finger at her. "Did you put in your samples? Into one of those genealogy things?"

"It wasn't my idea."

"I'm not getting up until you tell me."

"My mother gave it to me. Made me send it."

"A genealogy test."

"Mom was kind of a . . . flake. A good flake, but a flake."

"Did you get results?"

"I never checked," Bree said. "Life is hard enough with the relatives I have. Had."

Alyssa nodded, thinking about her own relatives.

"Did you ask her why she did it?" Alyssa was prying, but she could tell Bree was upset.

"Never got a chance to," Bree whispered. "She died. A while ago."

"I'm so sorry."

"Life," Bree said. "No way around it. It's okay. I'm fine about it."

Alyssa paused, wondering how raw Bree's grief would be. She began again, tentative.

"Maybe there was something she wanted you to understand, but couldn't think of how to tell you. Was it kind of . . . her last wish?"

Bree's face changed. "Oh. I never thought about it that way."

"What if it was wonderful?" Alyssa yearned to finally make a good choice. Help someone. She could do that now. "Seriously, Bree, I understand your hesitation. But as you yourself said, 'Life, no way around it.' If you ignore it, it still exists. Might as well face it. Whatever she wanted you to know."

"An imaginary brother, maybe." Bree half-smiled. "Like your imaginary dog."

"Until he's real." Alyssa latched on to the smile. "Or maybe a sister. A cousin. Uncle. Doesn't have to be a brother."

Bree blinked at her.

"*My* mother would never have . . ." Alyssa took a deep breath. "Let me put it this way. Yours loved you so much, she gave you a gift. As a kid, I wished every day to have a mom who cared about me like that. Seems like your mother wanted to share her life, and from what you say, it must have been done out of love."

"You think?"

Bree looked like she was about to cry. Alyssa had touched a nerve, she was sure of it.

"So?" *Sometimes things happen for a reason.* She hated when Bill used to tell her that; it always sounded like a phony-commiserative brush-off of her concerns. But maybe he was right. In this case, at least.

"Well . . ." Bree seemed to be considering it.

And then the thought hit her, how it all *might* make sense. Why Bree might not have known the identity of the person who seemed to be pursuing her. Alyssa could easily imagine an abusive relationship, a lover or boss or adversary, but she might have assigned Bree her own painful reality. Maybe Bree's reality was something else. Something good.

"Bree? What if he—or she—is the one who's calling you?"

MONDAY

TEN

"So?" Alyssa had barely poured the first cup of coffee when Bree appeared at the back door. She'd knocked, then opened it, letting in the clammy humidity of the murky Monday morning. Alyssa's mind had been racing over how astonishing and rewarding it could be if Bree really had a brother, or uncle, or cousin, because hadn't she said the voice was a man's? Of course, that wouldn't mean the guy was a good guy—or woman—or reveal how the rest of the story would unfold, but one step at a time. Bree had promised to think about it, and Alyssa hadn't pushed.

"That smells great," Bree said now, wiping her woven sandals on the raffia doormat. "Wow, your backyard is beautiful. It's starting to rain, I think, but I love all the flowers. And the pool. The guest house. My room at the Vermilion smelled like bleach, but yours is all lavender and pink grapefruit. And has much better towels. It must be fun to live here."

"Help yourself to coffee," Alyssa said. "And thanks. Yeah, it is. Fun." *For however long it lasts,* she didn't add. She'd done without things in the past; faced a thrumming teenage uncertainty about the outcome of every day, embarrassed at picking quarters up off the street. Her mother, suffused with resentment, making do. It had been easy, with Bill in her life, for Alyssa to get used to comfort, but soon, so very soon, she'd be losing it. She couldn't decide whether to be enraged or depressed. Sometimes she was both.

"But I totally see what you're doing, Bree," she went on, back to the present. "Stalling. Fine. Mug on the counter. Milk in the fridge. Muffins." She pointed to a straw basket. "But you know I'm—"

"Freaking out." Bree opened the refrigerator.

"Eager to hear what you found."

"Right. Well, nothing."

"Really?" Alyssa hadn't expected the stab of disappointment.

"Yet. Nothing *yet.*" Bree stirred milk into her coffee. "I'd waited this long, and it was your idea, so I figured I'd let you be there when it happened. For better or for worse."

"Really?" Alyssa almost had tears in her eyes. Bree, this newcomer, was more thoughtful than any of the women who had purported to be Alyssa's friends. She'd always speculated about precisely what kind of friends they'd been to *Bill,* but that way lay madness. She had better things to do now.

"Plus, if it was nothing"—Bree parted the corners of the flowered napkin lining the muffin basket—"oh, blueberry. If I'd told you it was nothing, you'd never have believed me. Until you saw it yourself. In real time. Isn't that right?"

Alyssa sat on a wicker stool, picking up muffin crumbs on the white plate in front of her. "Teasing me aside," she said, "it's a life moment for you, potentially. I'm honored you're allowing me to share it. I mean, we barely know each other."

Bree took a sip of coffee, then coughed, holding a hand to her chest.

"You okay?" Alyssa stood, halfway.

"Oh, sure, just went down wrong." Bree cleared her throat, and wiped under one eye with a finger, recovering. "I was going to say, you sure you don't write Lifetime movies? It's quite a tale you've spun here."

"Tell me after it's nothing," Alyssa said. "Then we'll see. Did he call again?"

"Last night? No. I turned off my phone. And it was so peaceful in the guest house," Bree said, "and I felt so safe. Shows you how one person can change your life."

Alyssa looked at her, now sitting at the kitchen island with her coffee and muffin, the sound of the quickening rain clattering the roof, splattering against the multi-paned french doors to the patio, blurring the garden to impressionist greens and blues. Even Bree's sweater was a muted blue, a crewneck, T-shirt underneath.

"Sometimes," Alyssa agreed. She'd thought the same thing about Bill, assuming the change he'd offered in her life would be for the good. Which it was, until it wasn't. And then everything wasn't. But today was about Bree.

"You ready to do this?"

"Before my muffin?" Bree was smiling. "Okay, here goes."

She picked up her phone, started tapping buttons. It was all Alyssa could do not to look over Bree's shoulder.

Bree showed Alyssa the phone screen, displaying a green circle with a yellow question mark in the center. It wasn't Ancestry, or 23andMe. But there were so many of them.

"Do it?" Bree turned the phone back to herself.

"Don't want to pressure you . . . ," Alyssa began.

Bree laughed, her head thrown back for a second. "Pressure. Right. Okay, doing it."

She tapped the screen again.

They waited, the pattering rain filling in the silence. *Families.* Alyssa's own parents were both dead, like Bree's. Bill had been enthusiastic about her lack of relatives. *No greedy in-laws or predatory cousins to deal with,* he'd told her. *Just us.*

Alyssa had hoped for children, hoped from moment one, but Bill urged her to keep taking her pills. *Let's wait,* he'd said, and soon the pill-taking became a nightly ritual; the pill, and then a kiss, and then more. But finally, one night, entwined after wine-fueled passion, he'd confessed he had no interest in children, and didn't she agree?

No grabby descendants waiting to pounce on all the money he'd made. He'd drawn her closer, persuading her. Not to mention the trust fund his parents had provided, and its seemingly ever-burgeoning investments. *We'll spend it all on ourselves,* Bill had held her as he whispered, *and we'll have an amazing life.* She'd agreed, because what else could she do, because it was back when everything Bill did or said was right. He'd traced a finger down the side of her face, and touched her chin, clinching the deal. *And who needs children if we have each other?*

She did, but it didn't matter what she'd thought.

And now Bill was off to another life. And she was alone.

Bree was still staring at her phone screen.

And she had to focus on Bree now. "Is it—?"

"Oh," Bree whispered.

Alyssa wiped her palms down the thighs of her

black jeans. She had no stake in this, so it was silly to care. But she did.

"There's only one listing," Bree said. "Possible . . ."

Alyssa yearned to see for herself. "Oh?" She tried to keep her voice steady.

"Possible . . . possible brother."

Alyssa blinked, afraid to say any more. This was Bree's moment, no matter how it had come about, and Bree had to do this on her own. She watched Bree's chest rise and fall, saw the woman's eyes focused on that little screen. A simple-looking black rectangle of computer chips and connections and magic, where you could push a button and find out something you never knew before.

"It wants to know if I want to know more."

"Mmm," Alyssa said.

"All I have to do is tap 'Yes,' it says. Should I?"

"Your decision," Alyssa said.

"Do you know the ancestry of *your* family? Or your husband's? Any surprise relatives ever pop up?"

Alyssa scratched her neck, deciding how to answer. Maybe Bree was nervous, making conversation, stalling. But Bree's family *was what it was*—another of Bill's platitudes—whether she embraced it or not.

"Nope, my parents never talked about it," she said, giving Bree some space. After all, her life wouldn't be the same after she tapped that button. "Bill's family was from Scotland, they think. And no, no surprises. That I know of."

Bree shrugged. "I suppose Mom figured she'd be alive to explain it to me. Because of course I would ask questions. And why get me the test if she didn't *want* me to ask them?" She nodded, as if agreeing with herself.

"Mmm." Alyssa tried to stay noncommittal.

"Or I could ignore it."

"Sure."

Bree took a deep breath.

Alyssa's eyes widened as she watched her.

Bree tapped the screen. Waited. Then burst out laughing.

"It's asking: 'Are you sure?'"

Alyssa had to laugh, too. "I suppose they're trying to be careful. Once you know it, you can't unknow it."

"What if I wait?" Bree said. "And the next time he calls, *if* he calls, I answer, and see if this is why."

"Your decision. Look, I admit I pushed you," Alyssa said. "Because you were unhappy about the calls, and whatever else. If it's not Frankie, and if *this* is the answer, your 'possible brother' did not handle it in a very logical way. Maybe he's as nervous as you are." She offered the coffeepot, inquiring. "But remember, since he's used this site, he already knows about *you*. You're simply evening the score."

Bree held out her mug. "Huh. So instead of worrying, I could—"

"Take control." Alyssa poured for them both, the fragrance of dark roast blooming. "That's always best."

In the silence, Alyssa played it out. "If he's even the one calling," she felt she had to remind Bree. There was a lot of assuming going on. "This might be a goose chase."

"True," Bree said. "But let's do it."

ELEVEN

The windshield wipers worked hard to slosh away the rain, but Alyssa still had to lean close to the Volvo's steering wheel to feel in control. The Mass Turnpike was insanity on wheels in any weather, but the morning's steady drizzle was relentless, turning up the volume on itself. May had been a rainy mess, Boston's one dependably splendid month a soggy failure this year.

"We could have waited until this ends," Bree said. "My gorgeous hair is gonna be ruined." The two had dashed from the kitchen into the garage, yanking hoodies close around their faces, leaped into Alyssa's Volvo, slammed the doors shut, and pulled out of the driveway, Bree tapping the address into the car's dashboard GPS.

"Nope, nope. Today's the day." The headlights of the oncoming cars barely pierced the gray, and Alyssa needed to concentrate on the white lane lines. At least people were driving near the speed limit, half-respecting the intimidating weather. "It's Monday just past noon, and it's pouring, but we can check his house and see if anything looks familiar. Like a car, maybe—you said you'd seen one following you?"

"Yes, but that was in Amherst, not here," Bree said.

"Look. Google only lists one Collin Riley Whishaw in Massachusetts," Alyssa reminded her. "And he lives in Marbury, about halfway between Amherst and here.

He's thirty-five, and single, and there's no reason not to go see. What else should we do this morning, sit and discuss it forever?"

"Probably get just as far," Bree said. "I keep thinking of how we got here. One drink in a bar, one exchange of niceties, and now we're all Thelma and Louise."

"I hope not." Alyssa risked a glance at her, then back to the highway.

"You know what I mean," Bree said.

"They killed a guy." Alyssa remembered the movie scene.

"He deserved it, right?"

"We're not going to kill anyone." Alyssa took one hand off the steering wheel to wave away this whole conversation. "Maybe Bill, though, if I ever got the chance."

"Or *I* could," Bree said. "Kill him for you. And then you kill my stalker-brother. Or whatever he is."

"Oh, right, *Strangers on a Train*. In Weston, Massachusetts. Brilliant."

"You ever consider it?" Bree asked. "Like, uh . . ."

"Daily. Hourly. Minute-ly, if there's such a word. Bill is such a bastard. But in real life, no one gets away with killing anyone, especially husbands. In real life, every hired killer is an FBI agent. And hey, *Strangers on a Train* is a movie. Even in the movie, they didn't get away with it. Spoiler alert." Alyssa clicked her turn signal, shifted lanes. "Tantalizing to think about, though."

The wipers clacked, then again.

"We might," Bree said. "Get away with it. The old crisscross, as the movie says."

"And then we'll both go to prison forever, and

that'll be that. No more blueberry muffins. No more wine. You're apprehensive, I get it." Alyssa could tell Bree was kidding. Covering up her nerves. "But, hurray, we're not going to prison. We're simply going to see who this person is."

Another mile marker flashed by.

Bree puffed out a breath. "He's not necessarily the person who's calling me, don't forget."

In her peripheral vision, Alyssa saw Bree digging into her bag, pulling out her phone. Seemed to be checking for messages. "I have to admit I'm kind of embarrassed," Bree said. "I was upset the night we met, and feeling pursued, and might have been making too much out of it. Maybe it was just spam calls, everyone gets those. Sometimes I feel so alone, I forget what the real world is like."

"I know what you mean," Alyssa said. "But your sorrow seemed so close to the surface. I guess that's why I talked to you, not my usual playbook. But hey. As a result, I don't mean to be sappy, but this could be important. Life-changing."

"Life is strange," Bree said.

"And I have to tell you," Alyssa went on. "I've barely thought about Bill since you and I met. Not as much as usual, at least. So you've helped me, too. I was feeling pretty sorry for myself. Alone. And yes, one moment in a bar, and—"

"Everything changes."

"In one mile, take the next exit to Marbury," the GPS voice said.

"Ready for this?" Alyssa imagined them walking up to the guy's front door. And then they'd say—well, right now she had no good ideas. They'd scope it out, first. No phone number had been listed anywhere.

"So, your husband," Bree said. "Does he still live around here? Boston?"

"My soon-to-be ex-husband? Listen, Bree, I have no idea where he is. He moved out, two suitcases and a computer, and left for parts unknown. Lucky for him. If I knew, it'd be hard not to . . . I don't know."

"So you two aren't friends? Don't talk at all? Is he still in his regular office, like, working?"

"Turn right," the GPS voice said.

Alyssa aimed the Volvo onto the highway exit. *Slow for curves,* she'd made out the warning sign on the raised side of the road. The rain slushed out from under the tires, and the cant of the exit briefly tilted them sideways.

"Talk? Bill and me? About what? Who he's sleeping with, and how much money he has? Maybe about how he's going to take me for all I'm worth, since that's zero, and he has all the power and the . . . the everything."

"Yikes," Bree said. "That's harsh."

"Oh, Bill and his money." Alyssa stopped at the red light before the road split in two. Marbury to the left, she saw. Ashwood to the right.

"Are soon parted?" Bree finished the old saying. "Is it a lot? Of money? *Oh.*" She clapped a hand over her mouth, sheepish. "That was incredibly rude. Forgive me. But I work in a bank. Money's kind of interesting to me. And numbers. So much potential."

"There's no rude in divorce," Alyssa said. "It's knives out, and wallets, too. Bill will do everything he can to cut me out. The law in Massachusetts gives judges a lot of leeway. Where that'll leave me is anyone's guess."

"You have a lawyer, though, I'm sure," Bree said. "Light's green. Go left. I'm turning off the GPS voice, she's annoying. I'll watch the map."

"I do," Alyssa said. "And my lawyer keeps calling me, as if he's trying to prepare me for disappointment. Bill is a big rich pit bull. Even when he's doing what seems good and generous, he's doing it for himself. Money begets money. Money begets influence. Money begets whatever woman you want, and makes the wife a used car. Just ask my almost-ex."

"I wish I could," Bree said.

Alyssa steered onto the suburban street, inching past the stop sign, wary of oncoming headlights. Driveways were empty, garages closed, sheets of rain sluicing off rooftops and gushing onto manicured shrubs and hedges.

"Not likely this Collin Riley Whishaw's going for a walk," Bree said. "Maybe he's at the office, like normal people are on Mondays. Let's just leave."

"Leave? One step at a time, Thelma," Alyssa said. "What would you've been doing this morning back at the hotel, otherwise? Something more interesting than this?"

Bree reached over the console, touched Alyssa's arm for a fraction of a second. "That would have been pretty bleak, Alyssa, seriously."

"And now we're on an adventure. But not like Thelma and Louise, okay?" Alyssa slowed for another stop sign. No kids in yards, with school still in session, and with the rain pouring, no dog walkers or even delivery trucks. "Where do I turn?"

"Two more streets," Bree said. "Then, according to the GPS map, it's halfway up Partridge, on the right.

Number 2357. Oh, cool, prime numbers that add up to a prime. I'm still not sure what you're hoping to find."

"Your brother, of course."

"*Possible* brother."

"Hey, that's what the site said. Don't kill the messenger. And—wait. There. That one." Alyssa pointed, then eased off the accelerator. "Remember, your mother wanted you to know."

They headed closer to the split-level ranch, the bottom red brick and the top white siding, and well-kept lawn. Boxy shrubs lined each side of a three-stepped porch, and a white front door was covered by a white-framed screen. A closed black metal mailbox was attached beside the door.

"I'll pull up in front of the house next to it." Alyssa eased the car to the curb, shifted into park. "So he won't think we're arriving for him."

"Very spy-ish." Bree rolled her eyes. "We don't look suspicious at all. Too bad we didn't bring binoculars."

"Brilliant idea." Alyssa leaned across the seat, popped open the glove compartment, took out a black leather case.

"Kidding me?"

"Listen, if your husband was a jerk, you'd have binoculars, too. Don't judge." She unclicked the silver clasp on the case, opened the flap. Pulled out the binocs.

"Alyssa," Bree whispered. "Put those down. A car's coming. Behind us. *Damn* it. Start the engine again, as if we're leaving."

"We're fine." Alyssa heard it now, too. "It's a street, there are cars. That's what streets are for."

The car slowed behind them. Alyssa turned on the

engine. "Okay, whatever," she muttered. "I'll pretend we're looking for directions."

She shifted her rearview mirror, and watched a white Camry slow as it approached.

Bree ducked down in her seat. "What're you seeing?"

"Why are you down there? It's just a guy—wait."

"What?"

"He's turning. Into the driveway. Into. *The*. Driveway. You're the numbers person. Remember this: KVC 442. That's the license plate, KVC 442."

"Okay, that's a helpful thing," Bree said. "Not. You might be a little too into this, Lyss."

"He's getting out. He's tall. Thin, white guy. Thirties, maybe. He's going to the front door. Okay, buddy. Let's see if you have a key."

Bree sat up again.

"This might be your *brother*, Bree. Collin Riley Whishaw. And you can ask him face-to-face why he keeps calling you."

"You've put two and two together to make forty-seven," Bree said. "The brother thing is one piece. The calls are another. The connection is all conjecture."

"It's got to be connected. I'll bet my life on it," Alyssa said. "Or at least . . . I'll bet all of Bill's money."

TWELVE

Alyssa didn't take her eyes off the man walking to the front door, and figured Bree was similarly engrossed. She'd buzzed down the window a fraction to keep the interior from fogging, so sprinkles of rain were misting the left shoulder of her hoodie and the left side of her face.

"Here's my thought." Alyssa kept looking straight ahead. "We go up to the door, and ask."

"And then say what? 'Guess what, so fun, you've got a sister'?"

"But that's the key. He's waiting for that. He wouldn't have signed up for the ancestry report if he hadn't wanted to know."

"*I* signed up, remember? And I didn't care about knowing," Bree argued. "My mother made me."

"Like I said. Maybe she made *him* do it, too." The man was almost at the end of the flagstone front walk. If he rang the doorbell, it would be all about who answered. "Because it could be, you know, the same mother."

Bree made a choking sound. "That'd sure give us a topic of conversation. I should have gone to a different hotel the other day."

"Things happen for a reason," Alyssa said. "Okay, look, he's patting his pockets. And bringing out a—key? No. A phone. Maybe someone called him. Or he's calling someone."

"This is *so* fun," Bree held up her phone, pretended to listen. "He's not calling *me,* that's for sure."

"Shush. Okay, he's stashed the phone. Now he's getting—"

"Lunch."

"A key. He's got a key and is opening the door. He's in." She turned to Bree. Eyes wide. "Should we do it?"

"Leave? Yes."

"No."

Bree puffed out a breath, stared at her phone screen.

"Honey?" Alyssa put the binoculars back in the glove compartment. "I understand that you're nervous."

Bree dragged both palms down her face, then rested her chin in her fingers. "Okay, yeah. Who wouldn't be?"

"Right."

"And now here we are, and there's my maybe-brother, and you, a virtual stranger, are suggesting I go knock on the door and say guess who's coming to dinner."

Alyssa nodded, acknowledging. "Yeah, I understand. I do. As much as I can. But when life offers you doors, you can't be an ostrich about it."

"You think?"

"Oh, he's turned on the lights." Alyssa narrowed her eyes, leaned forward, watching through the rain. "In what must be the living room. Look, do you have a better idea? Google gave us nothing, and this was our only choice. Do or not do."

"The guy has the social media profile of the invisible man."

"Right. But we're smart women, and we found him. What can it hurt?"

Bree laughed, then covered her mouth quickly, stopping the sound. "What can it hurt. Good one." She took a deep breath. "Okay. Let's do it."

"Truly?"

"Oh my gosh, I just said yes, let's do it before I lose my nerve."

"And the rain is even stopping."

"You wish. No, it isn't. And this'll ruin my new hair." Bree pulled her hoodie up over her hair and down to her eyebrows. "If you wear your hoodie like this, too, we'll look like home-invading housewives."

"There's a roof over the porch, so it won't be super miserable. And we can fix your hair."

"This had better be good," Bree said.

They dashed to the front porch, then paused, catching their breath at the door. The rain splatted on the white awning above them, so the wooden slats of the wide porch were dry underfoot. To one side of the front door, three cherry-red Adirondack chairs sat in front of a window box full of cascading green ivy. Fake ivy, Alyssa noticed.

"Ready?"

But Bree had already jabbed the black doorbell button with one forefinger. The *bing-bong* echoed inside, then again.

"I hear footsteps," Alyssa whispered. "You talk, Bree. Just be natural."

"Natural? Hell no. *You* talk. This was your idea. You can say—"

The inner door swung open. The screen stayed closed. The tall man, with a long face and a shock of sandy hair, Alyssa saw, wore a long-sleeved button-down shirt and jeans.

"Yes?" he said.

"I'm—" Alyssa began.

"Excuse us," Bree said over her. "We don't mean to bother you. And we're not selling anything, and we're not bill collectors. Or the police. And nothing is wrong. Forgive me, I know this is strange, but are you . . . Collin Riley Whishaw?"

Alyssa felt like the world was on pause. She could almost watch this guy's brain at work. He didn't look dangerous, but more traditional and conservative, preppy, even, like somebody's favorite college professor. Or an accountant. Someone unthreatening like that. Collin Whishaw was a perfect name for him, Alyssa decided.

"Why do you ask?" The man seemed to stand a little taller, adjusting his shoulders as he posed his question.

Bree put her palms to her lips, as if in prayer. Then pointed her fingertips at him. "Okay, I know it's odd, and I'm so sorry to arrive out of nowhere, but a Collin Riley Whishaw is my—" Bree stopped.

"Her—" Alyssa began.

"Brother. *Might* be my brother. I did an ancestry test." Bree's words came faster and faster. "Although it wasn't my idea. The results showed I had a brother. And his name is—"

"Collin Riley Whishaw," the man said.

Alyssa listened for sounds coming from within the house, conversation, or footsteps. But all was silent behind him, and he'd kept the front door close to his back, blocking Alyssa's view of whatever, or whoever, was inside.

"Yes," Bree went on. "Possibly. As I said, my *mother*

made me do the test, I probably wouldn't have on my own. Then she recently, unfortunately, died before I could check the results. Or ask her why."

"I'm sorry to hear that." The sound of the rain muffled everyone's words, diffusing them. A car hissed by on the street.

"It's okay." Bree nodded.

"You were the only Collin Whishaw in Google in Massachusetts." Alyssa had tried to stay quiet, let the two of them have their potentially momentous conversation, but she couldn't stand it anymore. She pointed to Bree, explaining. "I'm her friend."

The screen checkered the man's face into little mesh squares, and the amber light behind him made it difficult for Alyssa to read his expression. He didn't look like a stalker or a harasser, or a person who would do anything but balance your ledgers or grade your essays. Alyssa felt as if she were witnessing family history, and remembered to stay respectful. If this all went bad, it would be her fault.

"And I apologize." Alyssa was concerned by the man's silence. "If you're not Collin Whishaw, we won't take up any more of your time. This was the address listed for him, though, so if you aren't Collin, do you know him? Or *are* you Collin?"

The man shook his head, slowly, and seemed to be studying the beige carpeting under his polished cordovan loafers.

Alyssa silently checked with Bree, making a questioning face. He either is or isn't, Alyssa thought. But if he wasn't Collin, this guy was at his house, so he should be able to point them in the right direction.

Bree gave a tiny shrug in response, and lifted her eyebrows. *What now?*

The man looked at Bree, then Alyssa, then Bree.

"You're Embry Lorrance." It wasn't a question.

"What?" That was the last thing Alyssa expected to hear.

Bree had taken a step backward, away from him, almost falling off the porch. Alyssa grabbed her arm, catching her. If this guy knew her name, he must be her brother. Which meant Alyssa had been right. Crazy unlikely, yes. But right.

She'd succeeded. She'd done a smart thing, a good thing, and she'd done it on her own, calling on her wits and her instincts. She felt protective. Responsible. As if Bree were now her charge.

Alyssa came closer, felt the space between them shrinking. The rain rattled the slats of the awning above, and she raised her voice to make sure he'd hear her.

"So you *are* Collin," she said. "Otherwise, how would you know her name?"

"He's dead," the man said. "Collin Whishaw is dead."

THIRTEEN

"Help me with her," Alyssa demanded. Bree had crumpled. One moment, she had been staring at the man behind the screen, the next, her knees had hit the porch floor. Alyssa crouched, meeting her eye to eye. "Honey? You okay?"

Bree stared at Alyssa as if she might have once recognized her. Then focused over Alyssa's shoulder into the distance. "Sure," she whispered. "I'm fine."

"Get her some water," Alyssa demanded, still on her knees. She wasted a second, glancing at the man as he turned away from the door. What kind of an idiot tells someone their brother is dead like *that*?

"Bree?" Putting one hand on each of Bree's shoulders, Alyssa felt the woman trembling. "Can you stand up? Water is coming, if that nitwit has any sense."

She puffed out a breath, helped Bree to her feet. Embracing her like a heartbroken child, she guided Bree to the closest red chair, then eased her into place.

"I'm fine," Bree said again. She pushed back her hoodie, tried to wipe the dust from the knees of her jeans.

"I am so sorry," Alyssa whispered, dropping to eye level in front of her. Alyssa felt her heart break, her high hopes drowning in the relentless rain. Would no one in her life, no one, ever be happy? Alyssa had browbeaten a stranger, maybe even out of a selfish longing to be a hero, and now Bree's life was worse than before. "I never imagined it would turn out this way."

The front door opened, then the screen door closed with a bang.

"Here's water," the man said. "I didn't mean to upset her."

Alyssa took the half-full glass, and offered it to Bree.

"Here, sweetheart," Alyssa said. She glanced at the guy. "Thanks."

Bree was staring at the porch floor.

"Bree? Drink a little, slowly. You sure you're okay? I know you had a shock."

Alyssa took the opportunity to glare at the man. "So, ah . . . ," she began, trying to keep her voice pleasant. "Not quite sure you made the best choice on how to handle that situation, if I may say so."

"I was surprised," he said.

"Clearly." Alyssa still wondered about Bree's stalker. If this was him, she might need to be careful. But if he *was* a stalker, he was the most inept one imaginable. She settled her palm on Bree's back, protective. "Forgive me, but who are you? Why do you know Bree? And what happened to her brother?"

"Listen," the man said. "I'm Desmond. Desmond Russo. Dez. With a Z. And I'm . . ." He took a deep breath. "The administrator of the Whishaw estate. That's why I'm here. To collect his documents, and arrange for the sale of the home. And that's why I've been trying to contact her. Embry Lorrance, correct?"

Alyssa nodded, wary. Bree was still staring at the floor.

"So I was startled when you two rang the doorbell," he said.

"You'd been trying to contact her? Why?"

He cleared his throat, and didn't seem to know where to look. "This isn't how it was supposed to go. But your friend Embry, here, is now the sole heir. To the Whishaw estate. The only Whishaw relative in existence."

"The—" Bree sat up straight.

"Nothing," Alyssa said. "Let me deal with this." Desmond. With a *Z*, for god's sake. "Give me a break, Dez," she said. "That's the lamest story I've ever heard. We're supposed to believe that? I know what I'm doing when it comes to . . ." She paused, choosing her words. "If you are indeed the representative of a law firm or some other legal entity that handles the fiduciary administration of estates, or a probate heir finder, why didn't you contact Ms. Lorrance using the proper channels? I'm baffled by your process. Or lack of it."

She paused again, wondering if that was really the main point now. "One step at a time. What happened to Collin Whishaw?"

"Mr. Whishaw—that's under investigation," he said. "Have the police contacted Ms. Lorrance at all?"

"About what?" Alyssa asked.

Bree had come to her feet.

"You know what?" Alyssa tucked her arm around Bree's elbow. "If you're with some law firm? Or whatever? Give me your card." She narrowed her eyes. "We'll meet you at your office. During office hours. In a proper setting. With all the principals involved. Then we'll discuss this."

Alyssa tried to stay calm. She was the one who'd pressured—yes, pressured—Bree into checking her results. And now that there didn't seem to be a happy family reunion in the works, she understood she may have caused a personal avalanche for Bree. Except for being the "sole heir to the Whishaw estate," whatever that meant.

"So? A card?" She held out her hand, moving Bree behind her. "And shall we make an appointment?"

"Tomorrow? Anytime." Russo patted the pockets of his khaki trousers, then grimaced. "The office is always closed on Mondays. In Boston, One Beacon Place. But my wallet's inside. Stay here. Two seconds. I'll get a card."

The screen door slammed again. The rain had slackened, diminished to a lackluster drizzle. The sun was trying to make its way from behind the dense clouds, but fighting a losing battle.

"I am so—," Alyssa began.

"It's okay," Bree whispered.

"We'll get his card," Alyssa went on. "We'll make some calls. Are you sure you've never heard the name *Whishaw*?"

"My head is hurting, Lyss," Bree said.

"I know, I don't blame you." She glanced at the front door. This Russo had a key, and wasn't hiding his presence. And he hadn't been expecting them. They were the intruders. Without Alyssa and Bree, this morning would have been business as usual for him. Whatever that was. "We'll go back to my house, and you can lie down, and we'll get this sorted."

"Did he say *inheritance*?"

"Kind of. He said 'heir to the Whishaw estate.' So that could mean some kind of inheritance. I guess." Alyssa nodded, speculating. She took a deep breath, and the green fragrance of new grass and emerging flowers, unmistakable springtime, seemed intensified by the vanishing rain. "But who knows whether anything is real at this point. He did know you, though. Knew your name. Which cannot be random."

"Inheritance. I could sure use—"

"Shhh. Here he comes." The doors opened again, closed.

Watching him emerge, Alyssa realized she'd make a terrible detective. But at least she'd figured out what she needed to ask before they left.

"Mr. Russo? You said you'd been trying to call Bree? Embry, I mean. On her cell?"

"Yes, but she never answers. And this was too important to leave in a voice mail. She'd think it was a robocall."

"Did you go to her home?" Alyssa went on. "Her work?"

"Ah, yes, once. Twice, maybe. But then I was told—it doesn't matter now." He held out a white business card.

Alyssa didn't reach for it. This simpleton and his lamebrained clumsy methods had scared Bree within an inch of her sanity, made her fear for her life, and stampeded her into leaving her own home. She lifted her palms, appalled.

"Just a thought, but how about sending her a letter? From your firm, whatever it is? Wouldn't that have made more sense?"

"Look, ma'am, there's been a proliferation of—what's called *heir-finder scams*. Bad guys send letters to people, saying they've got a relative who's passed, and that they have an inheritance." He gestured with the business card. "Then they say, for a fee, they'll provide the relevant information. But it's a scam."

"Oh. Yes. I know about those from work." Bree came closer to Alyssa, touched her arm as she spoke. "They ask for your bank data, saying they need to make a direct deposit, and then get access to your accounts. So instead of *getting* money, you lose it. We've had it happen at Stateside. It's awful. Devastating."

"Right." Russo nodded. "And so many people are suspicious of it now, they ignore the letters. Our firm has decided phone calls are the most effective."

Alyssa rolled her eyes at him. "Right. I always answer phone calls from strangers. Don't you, Bree?"

"It's okay, Alyssa," Bree said.

"Usually, we have contact information for an attorney, Ms.—ah, I didn't get your name. Ms. Lorrance, shall we say Tuesday morning at ten?" Russo offered the business card to Bree. "My firm and I are prepared to present the full story, and the accompanying documentation. Answer all your questions. Equally happy to do that here, now, if you wish. Though your friend doesn't seem comfortable with that."

"Tomorrow. Sure." Bree took the card, glanced at the white rectangle, tucked it into the back pocket of her jeans.

Alyssa frowned, uncertain. Bree handling other people's money at the bank was one thing, but Alyssa knew handling her own would be another. One Beacon Place was as exclusive as an office address could get, and open to the public, so Bree wouldn't be in any danger. Physical, at least. But Bree should not go to this meeting on her own.

"Thanks." Bree started down the front steps, gesturing for Alyssa to follow as she headed toward the car. "C'mon, Alyssa."

"And, Ms. Lorrance?" Russo had come to the edge of the porch, and stood with one hand on the wooden railing.

"Yes?" Bree stopped, looked up at him. Alyssa did, too.

"I'm sorry about your brother." He shoved his hands into his jeans pockets. Looked up at the white awning, then directly at Bree. "But, ma'am?"

"Yes?" Bree said again.

"If you have financial advisers, you might want to contact them."

FOURTEEN

"How much do you think it is?" Bree finally asked. She'd stared out her car window, silent, for the first ten minutes of their drive home. "When I was little, I always used to think, *If I had a million dollars . . .*"

"Didn't we all." Alyssa'd wished for *five* dollars some days, when she was a kid. Wished not to fear being hungry, or cold. Over the past years, she'd almost managed to forget that life, dulled with constant and hollow wanting. Now she feared all that might be creeping back, closing in on her. Bill's fault. She could not let that happen.

The rain had slowed, and traffic zigzagged and froggered as Mass Pike drivers, apparently unleashed from the constraints of the weather, flew along the still-glistening pavement as if each of them were pursued or in pursuit. "What did you decide to buy with your million dollars back then?"

"A pony," Bree said. "And a barn, which would have been difficult in the suburbs, right? And a saddle. And a friend to ride with. And a Barbie doll, and clothes for her, and a trunk for her. I mean, I was, hmm. Eight? How old were you when you learned about money?"

Alyssa flinched as a monster truck barreled by them.

"When I wanted something my mother said we couldn't afford," Alyssa remembered. "Which was always. I would ask why she didn't just write a check. I had no concept of a check, you know? I thought it was the same as printing money. I remember being so disappointed by the reality. It defines you, doesn't it? Money? You're immediately a have or a have-not. And everyone can tell which you are. We're all so—assessive, is that a word?"

"It is now," Bree said. "Oh, I had a piggy bank, a white china pig, and I'd put in the pennies I'd find under our couch cushions. I never opened Money Pig, though, because I'd have to break it. And that seemed too sad."

Alyssa heard her sigh.

"I wonder where that is now? I never looked when I came home from college, and I haven't thought of Money Pig for, I don't know, however long. And now, I meet you, and boom."

"*I'm* Money Pig?" Alyssa glanced at her.

"Come on, Lyss. You know what I mean."

Eyes back on the road, Alyssa had to admit she was relieved that Bree was talking. Allowing herself to reminisce. As they'd pulled away from the Whishaw house, she hadn't engaged with any of Alyssa's initial questions, and given only cursory answers. Of course she was unsettled after an encounter like that, who wouldn't be? She remembered the moment at Vermilion she'd first seen Bree, waiflike and untethered, seemingly at loose ends. All this might not have happened, Alyssa thought, but for the predictable unpredictability of the world.

Since that night, Bree had learned she had a brother, and then that he was dead. And that she had an inheritance.

"So, Lyss? Do you think it's a lot? Like a million

dollars? Hey," Bree said. "I could repay you for my hair." She pulled down her sun visor. Flapped it back up. "Okay, I'm losing it. How am I supposed to wait until tomorrow? We should have gone inside and gotten the scoop."

"This'll give you time to think straight," Alyssa said. "And . . . hang on, this is our exit." Of course Bree was coming back to Weston; her belongings were in the guest house, and there were decisions in the works. "It'll all be fine," she said. Then wondered if she was telling the truth. Someone had died, after all, and there were so many still-unanswered questions.

Contact your financial adviser, Dez Russo had suggested. He wouldn't have said that if the inheritance, if it were real, was a drop in the bucket. Bree Lorrance might be on the verge of a life-changing windfall, and impossible to predict what would happen after that. Getting a million dollars—an imaginary million dollars, at this point—seemed destined to be a good thing.

But life with Bill had also shown Alyssa the destructive side of affluence. That it bred only the relentless desire for more, more of everything. And the constant terror of loss.

"I just realized," Bree interrupted her thoughts. "Dez never told us much about my—brother." She fussed with her seat belt, letting it snap back into place across her chest. "Should I be sad or happy? I'm confused about how to feel."

"Of course you are," Alyssa said. *Poor thing* meant something completely different now. But she still felt like that about Bree.

"We can try looking up what happened to him when we get home," Bree was saying. "I mean, *your* home. If I can stay one more night? I'm kind of at loose ends, Lyss. My mind won't turn off. But if it's trouble, tell me. I'll be fine."

"Bree. Don't be silly."

"Thanks. I need—I'd feel better if—oh, I'm always taking from you, Alyssa. But wait. There's one good thing."

Alyssa heard Bree's voice brighten.

"I won't need to take from you anymore. We'll be equals. Sort of. I'll be able to pay you back for lunch, too. All those macarons."

"You're funny, Bree. That's ridiculous. Lunch was just lunch." Now that she thought of it, Bill would be paying for that lunch. Since all the invoices were sent to him. She enjoyed the thought of that, making him pay.

Bree pulled her cell from her purse. "I'm going to look up Collin Whishaw again now. See if there's anything we missed."

As Bree tapped her screen, Alyssa replayed their lunch. The dismissive Lylah Rhodes, and her troubled daughter. The rebuffs of Eleanor and Cecile, with their opportunistically shifting loyalties. The manipulative Camden Hollis. She did not know one of those Club people, not one, who was truly happy. Sometimes those people destroyed each other. Just as Bill was trying to destroy her.

Money changes everything, Bree had said. But no one talked about *how.* Money was the ultimate magician—it could hypnotize you into forgetting reality.

"Lyss?" Bree was still tapping her phone. "He must have died pretty recently, or Dez wouldn't have been at his house. I've been getting the calls for maybe, ten days? Two weeks?"

Alyssa nodded. "That's what you said."

"There's so much I should have asked," Bree went on, "but my mind wasn't functioning. Thanks for stepping in. Saving me."

"It was such a surprise," Alyssa agreed. "I wasn't on my A game, either."

"I'll make a list." Bree was still tapping on her phone. "To ask tomorrow. Okay, there's still nothing on Google. So, looks like you were right. I had an older brother. Who I didn't know, and who now I'll never know. Because he's dead."

"I'm so sorry, Bree."

They rode in silence, past carefully constructed moss-covered stone fences, and pristine white pickets, hedges of cheerful bluebells and dense ferns. The rain had saturated the earth, and now that the fickle sun had returned, it transformed the remnants of this morning's downpours into nature's diamonds, the landscape refreshed, renewed, and ready to face the world. It left Alyssa and Bree damp and waterlogged, but changed, too.

"Which is worse, do you think?" Bree asked. "To have something and lose it, or never to have had it at all?"

"That's a tough one." Alyssa slowed to navigate a five-pointed rotary intersection. A bronze statue of a minuteman stood sentry in the center, forever pointing his musket at invisible enemies. "What're you thinking?"

"I'm thinking it's a good thing we didn't *Strangers on a Train* him. I might have lost a million dollars. And you'd be paying for everything again."

Alyssa laughed, such an unexpected reaction, such an unfamiliar sound, that she almost didn't recognize her own voice.

"True," she said, turning onto Loralee Drive. "And if I'd killed him, the way you suggested, not only would I be on my way to prison, but you'd be out your inheritance. Why'd you say a million dollars? When did he tell you that?"

"Please, I'm making this all up," Bree said. "And we shouldn't make fun of death, or a dead person, or killing people. It seems like bad luck." She sighed again, and Alyssa saw her expression change. "This is all very difficult."

"Emotions are unpredictable, honey," Alyssa said. Now, enmeshed in someone else's dilemma, she recognized how long it had been since she'd felt so confident. "It will all turn out fine."

TUESDAY

FIFTEEN

Alyssa tented her fingers over her mouth to hide her smile. It wouldn't have mattered what she did, she realized, as she shifted position on one of the black leather chairs in Dez Russo's picture-windowed conference room. Poor Russo had no eyes for her, or for the spectacular Boston skyline outside, or for the last of the fluffy cappuccino deflating in a monogrammed china cup on the glass-and-metal table. He seemed transfixed by Bree. *Nothing says "baffled" like a man seeing a beautiful woman.* Alyssa took a sip of her coffee to help conceal her amusement.

The already-awkward Russo, in such perfect navy pinstripes that his suit seemed almost a costume, had entirely lost his words on seeing the new—and dry—Bree Lorrance. After stuttering through a compliment that twisted into an apology and then back again, and assured by Bree's good-natured reaction, he'd regained his equilibrium, and guided them to this hard-edged room, rigid with glass and sharp corners. Given them the black leather chairs with the vista views. Coffees had arrived on a glass tray, served by a white-coated assistant who vanished as quickly and silently as the steam from the saucered circle of cups.

Any woman, seeing "the new Bree" as Alyssa had dubbed her, would have cataloged the changes in quick bullet points: strawberry-gold hair still perfect in a knife-edged bob. Pale lipstick, courtesy of Alyssa's drawer of samples, and a touch of blush. Alyssa had offered a peachy silk blouse, and a strand of pearls, but Bree had balked.

"My bank clothes are fine," she'd said, appearing in a simple white blouse and black skirt. "You've done enough, Lyss. I love the new me, but I'm still the same old me underneath this, okay?"

Alyssa knew enough not to argue. But if Dez Russo was telling the truth, Bree's "old me" was about to enter a different world.

"And if I *am* getting however much money, I'm paying you back," she'd insisted. "Every cent."

"Sure." Alyssa had agreed, just to end the conversation. The One Beacon Place elevator had carried them to the twenty-first floor, and Alyssa wondered, as the green buttons glowed one after the other, how she'd wound up so far from where she'd started a few days ago. Bree, too.

"We'll wait for my colleague." Russo was patting a stack of papers, separated with sturdy black metal clamps, on the table beside him. "If you don't mind."

"Mr. Russo?" Bree's voice was softer than Alyssa had heard it, and from the look on Russo's face, he'd caught something in her tone as well.

"Dez," he said.

"Dez." Bree shifted in her chair, and her sleek hair fell across one cheek. "Can you tell me how my—how Collin Whishaw died?"

Dez took a deep breath, his maroon-striped tie and white shirt shifting with the movement. "I wish I could," he said.

Alyssa felt like an intruder. An eavesdropper. To balance the loss of a brother you never knew you had with the gain of his financial bequest seemed like an impossible task. Bree's emotional equation was unsolvable; how to mourn someone she'd never met, but celebrate, because the death of a stranger meant her reward. Death changed everything, Alyssa thought, then chuckled at her own obvious conclusion.

"But police haven't released that." Dez twisted off the cap of a black fountain pen, then twisted it back on.

"Did he die at that house?"

Alyssa kept silent. Bree was asking the right questions.

"I'm not keeping anything from you," Dez told her. "I was assigned by my firm to find and contact you. Now that I have—"

Alyssa almost laughed, couldn't help it. He was taking credit for finding Bree? She and Bree had found *him*. But every story depends on who's telling it.

"Now that I have," Dez went on, "I'll tell the estate's lawyers, and they'll discuss those elements with you. Our company is simply the—"

"Liaison," came a voice from behind them.

The newcomer paused in the doorway. Alyssa heard the creak of a chair as Dez got to his feet, then Bree, and then she did, too. As if the woman, at fortysomething, understood how to control and command simply with her silence and self-possession. She'd positioned herself precisely under a ceiling pinspot, Alyssa noticed, so she was brighter than anyone else in the room. Though maybe that was simply coincidence. Once all eyes were on her—an immaculate figure in black pantsuit, white silk blouse, and tautly chignoned dark hair—she took yet another beat.

"Thank you for your patience," she said. "Dez, is

this . . . ?" She paused, watching them, as if deciding which of the women should have the focus.

"Sorry, Ms. Jain." Spell broken, Dez hurried from behind the table, and moved toward Bree. "This is Embry Lorrance, Ms. Jain. Embry Lorrance, meet Roshandra Jain, our senior partner. She's—oh, and this is Alyssa Macallen, Ms. Lorrance's . . ."

"Friend," Alyssa provided the word that seemed to be eluding him.

"Bree is fine," Bree said at the same time.

"Roshandra," she said. Her careful pronunciation of her own name might have been designed to subtly correct her colleague's Americanization. "Shall we? Everyone?"

She took the center seat at the table, behind the stack of black-clamped papers, and with an almost imperious nod, indicated they should be seated. Dez flipped open his silver laptop, and Bree sat, straight-backed, with her newly manicured hands folded in her lap.

Curtain up, Alyssa thought. If some usher had handed out playbills, this could not have felt more like a drama unfolding in front of her. She'd taken a spectator seat, where she belonged, but she knew she was part of the story. Whether she'd have lines in this scene was yet to be determined. It crossed her mind to take notes—Bree had admitted she felt overwhelmed. Alyssa pulled out her phone, checked that no one was watching her, and surreptitiously tapped Record. She could always delete it.

"Let me begin by giving you my condolences," Roshandra was saying. "Not only for your loss, and we are concerned to know what happened to your brother. But let me apologize personally for the manner in which we apparently failed to properly seek you out. Dez, as I am sure he told you, is new to our organization, and I hope his methods did not unduly—"

"It's fine," Bree interrupted. "I'm here now."

He scared the hell out of her, Alyssa wanted to say. She thought of how haunted Bree had looked just two days ago. Dez Russo had been given this one job, and he'd pretty much blown it. Alyssa glanced at him to see whether he'd reacted, but he was typing into his laptop.

"As you say." Roshandra chose one stack of papers, and handed them across the table to Bree, the metal clip clanking as it hit the glass surface. "Here are some of the documents relating to the Whishaw estate. Dez, perhaps you could point out the relevant pages."

It was driving Alyssa crazy not to be involved with this. She carefully tucked her recording phone under her purse on the chair next to hers. She yearned to look at the papers herself, draw up beside Bree and make sure she knew what she was looking at. She'd left law school before graduation—Bill again—but she hadn't forgotten her classes on contracts and translating legalese. Turned out, Alyssa was the perfect friend right now.

"You are, as Dez explained, the only living relative identified in the Whishaw family. Mr. Whishaw's father is—was . . ." Roshandra touched her hand to her chest. "This is delicate, and I am happy to speak with you privately if you prefer."

"It's fine," Bree interrupted her. "This whole thing is, I have to say, incomprehensible. And frankly, I'd rather not hear it alone. I might not believe it later."

"As you wish. Mr. Whishaw's father was actually your father. And I apologize if that is painful to you. It was a short-lived marriage with your mother, and was legally performed and then legally dissolved. Collin—you were too young to have remembered him—stayed with his father. You will see that from the records I've included in your file."

Bree kept silent, shaking her head. Alyssa tried to imagine how she felt—but remembered, again, how little she knew about Bree. Bree's mother had allowed her own son to stay with his father—or been forced to in the divorce—and for some reason, had actively decided not to tell her. Bree's stepfather must have known, too, and kept the secret until he died. Alyssa was concocting this story out of her imagination and probably too many old movies, but it made sense as Roshandra Jain went on. It was after Bree's stepfather died that her mother had given her the genealogy gift. Merry Christmas.

Your father kept secrets from you, Alyssa imagined her saying. *And I helped him. Until he died.*

What a wife will do for her husband, Alyssa thought. Even ex-husband. Bree's mother, for some reason, had protected him until the end. And only then had she told the truth.

In this version of the story, at least.

"To eliminate your suspense—and to prevent you from what might feel like unseemly questions, let's begin at the end. Then rewind to the beginning." Roshandra used the eraser of a pencil to turn the pages of her file. "If you will examine the penultimate page in your documents? It shows the estate's assets, including estimated deductions for fees, taxes, and other charges that ordinarily incur. Dez and I will answer whatever questions we can. We are at your service."

Bree had licked a forefinger, and flipped pages from the bottom corner as if she were in a teller's cage, counting actual currency. Alyssa tried to assess the demeanor of the two executives, but they'd both gone still and impassive, two sets of eyes now focused on Bree. The only sound in the sunlit room was the swish of paper; and in Alyssa's personal soundtrack, the ticking of an imaginary clock.

And then a gasp from Bree. Alyssa saw her only in profile, watched her silently look at Roshandra, then Dez. Then, as Bree turned toward her, Alyssa saw the full intensity of her reaction.

"Alyssa," Bree whispered, holding out the sheaf of papers. "You need to see this."

SIXTEEN

"Yes, it's real, but it's not an important Cézanne," Alyssa explained. "According to Bill's appraisers. I love it, though." She and Bree stood in Bill's office—now hers, until the lawyers got hold of everything—examining a framed watercolor, all mossy brown trees and turquoise sky. A mysterious shape hovered in the background, but Alyssa could never quite figure out what.

"It gets more complicated the longer you look at it." Bree tucked her new hair behind one ear. "So simple, at first glance, and then the depth begins to emerge. Like life. We never know what's behind anything, really, do we? And with a shift of the light, the entire world is different."

Alyssa toasted her with a bright red mug of tea. "If you want to talk about art, happy to. I know you've got a lot on your mind. Take your time."

"You're an angel, Alyssa. But not so angel that I didn't see you put that slug of Jameson in our teas." She clinked with her own mug. "Yeah, I need to calm down a bit. This whiskey is perfect."

When they'd returned to Alyssa's after their meeting with Dez and Roshandra Jain, Alyssa had half expected Bree to head back to the guest house. But she'd accepted the cup of tea, and Alyssa figured she was still processing her newfound fortune. And family.

She was honestly glad Bree would stay one more night. Nothing unsettling had occurred since she'd been here, nothing strategically moved or tauntingly missing or disturbingly out of place. That was either because it was all in Alyssa's head, like the ghosts of a missing limb, or, because unlike the fake dog, Bree was real protection.

Alyssa had parked in front of the door. They'd walked up the flagstone pathway side by side, the yellow flowers of the forsythia bushes catching and releasing them as they went, the shadows of the spiky branches lengthening with the afternoon. Earlier, after their meeting ended, Dez and his boss had escorted them to the elevator.

Roshandra Jain had held out a hand to Bree, and as Bree accepted it, Jain placed her other hand over Bree's. "I know you're confused now, Ms. Lorrance. Possibly overwhelmed. That's to be expected. Think everything over. Contact an attorney. Contact a financial adviser. Show them the documents—we'll courier you copies."

"Thank you," Bree said. "I'm not quite sure what to say, or how to handle this."

The elevator door opened, and Dez caught it with one hand, holding open the rubber edge. "I understand."

Not a very comforting response, Alyssa thought.

"We'll be in touch, Ms. Lorrance." Jain showed them into the boxy elevator. "And, Ms. Macallen, thank you. You deserve the credit for changing your friend's life."

Bree touched Alyssa's arm. "I owe her everything," Bree said. "I'll never forget that."

"You owe me nothing." Alyssa felt the emotion in Bree's voice, and her eyes had welled a bit.

"Let us know whatever you need," Jain said. "And when you are prepared to continue."

"I will," Bree said.

"I'd be happy to escort you downstairs," Dez offered. "You both."

Who was he kidding? This was only about Bree. But Bree declined, and the elevator doors closed him away. Dez was as obvious as a besotted schoolboy. And Bree's seeming windfall was enough to light anyone's fire.

Seven million dollars. Alyssa had contemplated the inheritance as they drove toward home. They'd been warned it could take months to settle the estate, but also that it was a sure thing.

"You okay, Bree?" Alyssa had asked. "You want to—get lunch, or go for a drink? At Vermilion, for old times' sake? Leave that cute bartender a big tip?"

"Well, maybe. But maybe I don't want to be out in the world right now. I'm not sure how to think about anything."

And that had brought them back to Alyssa's. Funny, if Bill's lawyers tried to sell the house from under her, maybe Bree could afford to buy it, and Alyssa could stay in the guest house. Stranger things had happened. Bree was proof of that. One night in a bar.

"So this is where your husband worked, huh?" Bree now looked at the study ceiling, corner to corner, then back again. Ran a hand over the top of the brown leather chair pulled up close to the desk, then pointed at a row of fountain pens slotted into a mahogany holder. "He didn't take his pens."

"He's more of a computer guy," Alyssa said. "The

pens were gifts from charity clients, not that he cared. He had a real office, in Boston."

"He was in finance, so funny. Too bad I can't talk to him about—" Bree stopped. "Okay. Not the best idea."

Alyssa scoffed, out loud, at the possibility. Then tried to calculate how serious Bree might be. "He wouldn't be a good choice, anyway. Unless you want to give your money away."

Bree drained her mug. "Oh, never mind, forget it. My brain is fried, don't even listen to me." She paused. "What was that? Doorbell?"

The three chimes faded. "Yup. Probably some political thing, or FedEx. Annoying."

The chimes sounded again. "Be right back," Alyssa said.

"'Kay."

"Don't steal the Cézanne." Alyssa made a conspiratorial face. "Or, you know, do. Bill won't miss it."

Alyssa reached the door, peered through the peephole, then took a step backward. Maybe it was the Jameson, but this day was getting stranger and stranger. And it had started out pretty damn strange.

"Dez," she said as she opened the door. She pursed her lips, thinking. "How did you know where I live?"

"Bree told me," he said. "Remember?" He held a manila envelope in one hand, and carried a handled coated-canvas grocery bag in the other. He still wore his conference room clothes, though he'd loosened his tie, as if stepping into casual territory. "I brought those copies Ms. Jain knew Bree would need. Is she around?"

Alyssa waved him inside. The second visitor to be in her house in the last few days. All because she'd had a drink at the Vermilion bar. "I'll get her," Alyssa began. Then decided. "She's in the study. Come on in."

"Dez?" Bree stood as Alyssa heralded their guest's arrival. "What brings you here?"

An excuse to see you, Alyssa didn't say.

He handed her the manila envelope. "Your document copies. From this morning. Roshandra decided it was faster than a messenger."

"She did, huh?" Alyssa teased. But Dez wasn't noticing her.

"Safer, too," he went on. "Happy to do it."

Bree took the proffered envelope, set it on the seat of the other club chair. "Thanks."

The three of them stood in silence, each hesitating, a triangle of uncertainty.

"Would you like a—" Alyssa began.

"What's in the—" Bree said at the same time.

"And this is—" Dez said.

They all laughed at the tumble of words, and Alyssa took the lead. "Okay, then, one at a time. I was going to ask if you'd like something to drink," she said. "Bree and I have tea. With Jameson." She lifted her cup. "You could have yours without the tea, it being after five and all."

"That makes it my turn." Dez reached into the shopping bag, and drew out a silver foil wine bag, tied with a curly white ribbon bow. "Champagne."

He seemed to gulp, searching for words. "It's not in celebration, because I know there's a sorrow that goes with wills and bequests. And I am sorry for your loss. But it might be a new beginning for you."

Bree nodded, acquiescing. "Thank you. But . . ." She accepted the champagne. "You didn't need to."

"I wanted to apologize," Dez said.

Dez seemed even more awkward, Alyssa thought, as if that were even possible. She was used to watching Bill deal with strangers, used to his ease and confidence. Bill would never have shifted from foot to foot, never have bitten his lip trying to figure out what to say. Bill would have known what to do in a situation like this—where the transfer of money was involved, and the jockeying for position. But Bill had many years more experience than Dez. It was definitely showing now.

"Apologize?" Bree said.

Dez set the shopping bag on the floor. Something else was inside, Alyssa judged from how it stayed upright on the rug.

Bree still held the champagne, didn't seem to know what to do with it.

"I'll take that," Alyssa said. "Put it in the fridge." She paused, now holding the beribboned bottle. But Bree and Dez were looking only at each other.

"O-*kay,*" Alyssa muttered as she headed toward the kitchen. "You two don't care about me, that's obvious."

"Apologize for the methods I used to contact you," Dez was saying. "Roshandra was pissed."

"It's fine," Bree said.

Alyssa stopped in the study doorway. This was getting interesting. Maybe Roshandra Jain had forced him to come apologize. Men sucked at apologizing.

"I had to tell her how *you* found me, which was . . ." He looked at the ceiling, as if searching for an emotion. "Thanks for not throwing me under the bus."

"Sure," Bree said.

Dez leaned down to the bag beside him, reached inside.

Alyssa felt her eyes widen, had a heartbeat of wondering what he might be doing. She didn't know this guy, this stranger. And now he was in her home.

Like a party magician, he pulled out a nosegay of yellow and white daisies, wrapped in flimsy green tissue paper. "Peace offering."

Bree didn't move. "Flowers?" she finally said. She perched on the arm of the club chair, the manila envelope still on the seat beside her. She reached out for the daisies, held them gingerly. "Um, thanks. These are so pretty."

"I'll put those in water." Alyssa felt like someone's mom, taking the flowers, too. On prom night. On a prom night that happened because someone had died. A chill went up her back, but then—her disquiet was her own fault. She'd lost a lot of herself, mourning Bill, and now, like a skittish kitten, she worried that the rug would be pulled out from under her again.

"No need to apologize," Bree was saying. "I'm sure you followed all the rules, or whatever you do. It's just so confusing now, with that." She pointed to the manila envelope.

By "that" she meant seven million dollars, Alyssa thought.

"Like I'd explained to Alyssa—bad job, hideous boss, nutty boyfriend, no family, nowhere to turn." Bree looked at Dez, then Alyssa, sheepish. "That's why I was so relieved when Alyssa offered the guest house. I wasn't sure whether I could make it, financially, at that hotel. I was really on the edge. I didn't mean to interrupt your weekend, Lyss." She picked up the envelope. "But I have to say, I'm glad I did."

"Yeah, well," Alyssa said. "Money changes everything."

"That's for sure," Dez said.

SEVENTEEN

They'd opened the french doors of the kitchen and moved out onto the screened-in back deck, where Alyssa's all-weather chintz furniture created an open-air living room. One after the other, Alyssa clicked the switches on the array of ivory battery-powered candles arranged on the wrought iron coffee table, then placed the bouquet of daisies among them. Bree and Dez, champagne flutes in hand, sat next to each other in flowered armchairs, a white wicker table between them. A bright mandarin-orange pot overflowed with waterproof silk ivy that trailed to the wooden deck, and the chirp of the season's first crickets, tentative, sounded through the growing twilight.

"It's so peaceful here." Bree leaned back in her chair, propped her black flats on the coffee table, then quickly whisked them down. "Oh, " she said. "How rude—I didn't mean to be so—"

"We're outside, Bree, anything goes. And I'm happy you're comfortable. Put those feet right back up where they belong. You, too, Dez. Workday is over. It's about time you both relaxed." Alyssa lifted the green champagne bottle from the silver ice bucket, the cubes clattering as they resettled. The container's curved sides, embossed with clusters of grapes, dripped with condensation. "Oops. Almost empty. Who wants the last of this? It was perfect, Dez. I'll go get another bottle. And maybe some chips. And cheese. Yes? I promise no more brie jokes."

"I couldn't intrude—" Dez began. He'd left his suit jacket in the study, draping his striped tie on top of it, a slash of maroon on the navy pinstripes. He'd rolled up the cuffs of his starched white shirt, and somehow seemed more sure of himself. More powerful, with that chunky silver watch on his wrist. And with some new attitude. Engaged. Almost flirtatious.

"Oh, please," Alyssa interrupted, lifting her half-full flute. "You're hardly 'intruding.'" She was three glasses in now, and her rough edges, as well as her suspicions, were fading. Life was unpredictable, and she was having an experience that had nothing to do with Bill. Her own life, her separate life.

Maybe it was time to enjoy it. It had been long enough since she'd enjoyed anything. She'd reset the alarm system, and felt safe and protected.

"Champagne on a Tuesday night," she went on, taking it all in. "Basically no one else has been in this house for weeks. And, Dez, all's well that ends well. Next time, you won't be so—"

She paused.

The doorbell chimed again. And the "dog" started barking.

Alyssa stood, deciding. Whoever had arrived would see her car parked in the front. Dez's car, too. She took another sip of champagne. Might it be . . . Bill? He'd shown up unannounced before, flouting the "call in advance" agreement he'd deigned to sign. He was oblivious to anything but his own desires. He'd rung the bell this time, maybe to enjoy the shock on her face when she opened the door. Alyssa, entertainment on demand.

"I'll be right back." What if it *was* Bill? Alyssa put down her glass, wiped her hands on the back of her jeans. "I'll bring the snacks then."

"Sounds good," Dez said. "We'll be fine."

"You okay?" Bree asked. "Want me to come with?"

The doorbell again. The dog was programmed to pause, then bark, then pause. "Two seconds," Alyssa said.

She picked up her glass again and headed to the door, thinking about Bill. Preparing. He'd be surprised, she thought, to see she had people over. People drinking champagne, and enjoying themselves. People with money of their own—Bree at least—and not hangers-on whose poorly hidden motives were to snag invitations to fancy parties or to be assigned to sit by Bill at a gala. These people wanted *her,* Alyssa. For herself. She'd invite Bree and Dez to stay for dinner. She'd cook.

She did a little shoulder wag as she walked. Toasted herself. She would make this work. She was tough. Self-sufficient. Young, enough, and attractive, enough, and smart. Time to take back her power. And she still had her whole life before her.

She squinted through the peephole, and made out someone standing on the porch wearing a dark suit, maybe, with a white shirt. Raising money for some cause? At first when Bill left, she'd sometimes spent wildly, as if she'd never have money again, which, indeed, she might not. She figured he examined all her credit card bills, knew precisely where she was going, what she was doing or buying.

She easily imagined herself—constantly imagined herself—financially precarious, divorced, alone. Early on, before their city hall wedding, she'd offered to sign a prenup. But Bill had refused. *You're the best, Lissie,* he'd purred, *but there's no need for that.* She could almost hear his voice, honey and promises; he'd actually been feeding her chocolate-covered strawberries at the time. *We don't need a bunch of accountants and lawyers pawing through our assets, babe. I promise to take care of you forever.*

Now, approaching the end of forever, she was at the mercy of Bill and his relentless legal team. And of some mercenary probate judge, certainly in Bill's pocket. And even of her own lawyer. Burke Slattery was supposedly the best in town, but she knew he was cringingly intimidated by Bill's influence. There was nothing more she could do. Bill would concoct some tactic to leave her with nothing.

A woman, short-cropped bleached-yellow hair, big round glasses, and gold earrings against dark skin now rapped on the door, the sound sharp and confident.

"Mrs. Macallen?" A square black shape appeared in the peephole, covering Alyssa's view.

"May I help you?" Alyssa asked through the door. The dog barked again. Why was this woman blocking the peephole? Was she trying to hide? Or maybe she was trying to show Alyssa something. The security cameras were motion activated, so she'd have pictures if she grabbed the screenshots. They deleted themselves after twenty-four hours, so hard drives weren't overloaded with captured images of letter carriers and Girl Scouts.

"Can you see what I'm holding up?"

"No." A guessing game?

"Open the door, please, Mrs. Macallen."

The woman's voice had hardened, all business. Not a fundraiser.

"Tell me who you are, please." Alyssa matched her attitude. Challenging. She'd left her phone—somewhere? Probably out on the back porch with her guests—and now stood here with only a glass of champagne for protection. But then, she didn't have to open the door.

"I'm holding up my identification, Mrs. Macallen," the woman said. "I'm Special Agent Hattie Parker. FBI, ma'am. Will you make sure your dog is secure?"

Now Alyssa couldn't move fast enough. She clicked off the alarm, opened the door. The woman wore a gold badge around her neck, like a necklace. Her suit seemed carefully tailored, and she'd popped her stiff white collar to frame her face. Alyssa closed the door behind her.

"What's wrong?" This had to be about Bill. Didn't it?

"Ma'am?" The woman held up the identification, an American-flag-logoed card in a black wallet flap. "The dog?"

"There's no dog. Did something happen to my husband?" The possibilities raced through her head. A federal agent on her doorstep. Bree and Dez drinking champagne on the porch.

"Is he here? Your husband?" Agent Hattie Parker, she'd said her name was.

"What's wrong?" Alyssa asked again, not answering. The woman was blocking her way out. Not that Alyssa had anything to run from. "Is my husband okay?"

"He's okay. I don't want to frighten you." Agent Parker scanned the entryway, corner to corner to corner. "But sometimes we need to move as fast as we can. This is one of those times."

Alyssa heard footsteps.

"Alyssa?" Bree's voice.

"All good. One minute!" Alyssa called out. "I'll be right back."

She wondered how close Bree was, and how to get her to go away. She had to find out about Bill. The agent asked if he was here, so he couldn't be dead.

Bree's footsteps stopped in the hallway. "You sure? You need anything? Your phone?"

Her voice sounded airy and carefree. And why not? *Bree's* world was about to take on the buoyancy of ease and security. The opposite of Alyssa's. Alyssa, now facing an FBI agent in her foyer.

The woman stood, motionless, probably taking it all in. She settled her shoulders, smoothed a perfect eyebrow.

"Nope, all set," Alyssa copied Bree's casual tone. "Get the cheese and crackers. Make yourself at home. I'll be right there."

"No prob." Bree's voice was softer, farther away. "On it. Take your time."

"Is your husband here? In the back?" Agent Parker touched her on the arm, kept her voice low. "I need to know that, ma'am. Don't call out to him, please, if he is on the premises. Just tell me." Her badge rose and fell on her starched shirt, and she edged closer, a stealthy invasion of Alyssa's space. "We're hoping you'll help us, Mrs. Macallen. You can call the main office if you want to check my credentials."

Alyssa heard Bree's footsteps diminish and disappear.

"What do you mean, help you? My husband is not here. We're separated." Alyssa put down her champagne glass, wishing she hadn't brought it with her. She probably looked like a pitiful day-drinking soon-to-be divorcée.

Agent Parker smiled, an expression Alyssa couldn't decode.

"I need to talk to you in private," the agent said.

Fear mixed with curiosity, fueling her imagination. Maybe this was why Bill had turned ugly. Why he'd begun showing a maliciously critical side of his personality that had first baffled her, then left her crying, alone, in their often-empty bedroom. She'd seen him play hardball with business competitors, but he'd only been gentle and loving with her. Mostly. Until recently. Now, if Bill wasn't dead, and the FBI was here, that meant Bill was in trouble. Maybe that was why Bill had left her.

"Is he okay?" Alyssa persisted. "Just tell me that."

She'd be better off if Bill were dead, the thought came into her head. No more pre-divorce mathematics, no more division, no more subtraction. Bill had definitely thought the same about *her.* Even threatened her about it, one particularly nasty evening when she'd questioned his increasingly volatile moods. *My problems would be solved if you were dead,* he'd said. She remembered his menacing face, the venom in his voice. *Goes two ways,* she'd retorted; devastated, but ready for battle. Now Bill was gone. And an FBI agent was here.

"You would have heard if there was something wrong with him, ma'am," Parker said. "I'm sure. But if you have ten minutes? I'd be grateful to talk with you about his activities. If you could point me in the right direction."

"His activities? Right direction? I have no idea

about 'directions.'" Alyssa saw their reflections in the gilded mirror and almost didn't recognize herself, tense and wary. Should she call Burke Slattery? Would her divorce lawyer be the right person?

Alyssa retreated a step, regrouping. The FBI doesn't randomly show up on your doorstep. "Wait. No. You need to tell me, right now, why you're here."

"Happy to. In there?" Parker pointed to the living room, her earrings catching the chandelier's lights. "Or, maybe . . ." She pointed the other direction. "That looks like a study?"

"I'll go tell my guests." Alyssa started for the patio.

"Stop."

"Stop?" Alyssa kept her voice even, didn't want Bree and Dez to think she was arguing. Could she not have *one* good day? "You're telling me to stop? In my own house?"

"Again, I do apologize, ma'am," she said. "And you might want to be sitting down. This is delicate, I'm afraid, and this is always difficult. But we're doing this for your sake."

"Sitting *down*? Delicate? Are you sure Bill is okay? I need a lawyer." Somehow this had escalated. Her cell phone was still out on the deck. She'd call Burke. But maybe—no. She'd call—"I'll get my phone."

"Let's not do that right now, Mrs. Macallen," Parker said. "What I mean is that I'm on *your* side. The agency is on your side."

"My *side*?" She frowned. "Why are there sides?"

"I have some things to share with you," Parker went on. "To ask about."

"Let me tell my friends," Alyssa said again. "If I don't return soon, they'll worry."

Or they won't, Alyssa thought. They had champagne

and they had each other. And even though Alyssa had wished Bill were dead, she'd never meant dead-dead. Now maybe, he was. Or hurt. Or in deep trouble. She had to find out.

"I'll come with you," Parker said, adjusting the strap of her shoulder bag. "We'll tell your friends I'm from your divorce lawyer's office. I need some paperwork, and we'll be ten minutes. And then we can talk more, you and I, privately."

Alyssa understood Parker's tactics. She didn't want Alyssa talking to anyone—or calling anyone—if she couldn't hear what she said. Which meant Parker didn't trust her. Which meant she might be in trouble, too. Bill. *Damn it.*

"Agent Parker?" She tried not to let her precarious emotions show. "More about what?"

"More about your husband's financial activities." Agent Parker's face seemed almost apologetic. "And, possibly? About yours."

EIGHTEEN

"You want to search? Here?" Alyssa stood in the doorway of Bill's study, taking in its entirety with one broad gesture. When they'd returned from the kitchen, Agent Parker, a hovering shadow, had asked to be shown Bill's office. And to search it. "Why?"

"Mrs. Macallen? I know your husband often works here."

"My husband—soon-to-be *ex*-husband," Alyssa emphasized, "no longer lives here or works here. This was once his study. Now it's mine."

"Then could you show me? If you want to get back to your . . . friends."

She and Parker had found Bree and Dez in the kitchen, Dez unwrapping a chunk of cheddar, Bree arranging crackers on a flowered plate. Someone had turned on the sound system, and sinuously smooth jazz surrounded them. Alyssa felt like someone's mom again, a chaperone. But those two were the least of her worries.

"You okay?" Bree had asked. Alyssa saw her eyeing Agent Parker, who had not introduced herself.

"From my lawyer's office." Alyssa had practiced the cover story in the thirty seconds it took to get to the kitchen. She tried to make it seem inconsequential, commonplace. "She needed to pick up a few papers. We're getting some water."

"Sorry to interrupt the party," Parker said.

"No worries, we're fine." Bree acknowledged Parker, the welcome given an insignificant stranger, then went back to the crackers. Dez seemed to barely notice the interruption.

Alyssa took down a chunky drinking glass and filled it from the filtered-water pitcher, trying to decide how to handle this. Wondering if she'd tell Bree and Dez the truth after Parker left. Wondering why she couldn't ever be—free. There always had to be some obstacle. And it always had to do with Bill. Recently she'd longed for her law school days, before she met Bill, when her future was still a shining possibility, where she made decisions on her own, and things might even turn out the way she planned. Where surprises were good surprises. She'd hoped Bree was a good surprise, but now the FBI of all people, bringing the nagging specter of Bill, had interfered with that, too.

Parker had accepted her decoy water, and even drank some, playing her part.

Now the glass sat, ignored, on a side table in the study.

"You want to search," Alyssa said again, not even trying to keep the apprehension out of her voice. She was furious at Bill. Enraged. This was his fault, his mess, and now she was tangled in it, too. Had he left something behind? Intentionally? By mistake? Either might be a problem. Alyssa drew on her one year of law school. "If that's what you're asking, I think you need a warrant."

Even though she knew it wasn't true, Alyssa conjured a wall swiveling to show a secret room, or a hidden safe that appeared when the agent pushed the right book, like in the classic movies she and Bill used to watch.

And how about that compartment in their upstairs closet? An FBI search could never discover that place. Could it? Even if it did, there was nothing inside. Last time she'd looked. But she hadn't checked it recently. Because of Bree. She felt a prickle at the back of her neck, tried to ignore it.

"I only need a warrant if you insist." Parker unzipped the side of her shoulder bag, pulled out a cell phone. "I can call a judge, and get one very quickly. It'll take—oh, half an hour. And I'd wait here. I warned her I might be in touch."

Alyssa'd assumed Bill took everything he thought mattered, but what if he'd left something? If she let this woman search, she'd at least know. This was *Bill's* world. *Bill's* life. But he still controlled hers, no matter where he was.

Alyssa sat in the armchair. Bree's manila envelope of documents was still tucked into the cushion beside her. She pushed it down farther. Alyssa crossed her legs, tapping one toe on the rug. Wondered what this visit was really about.

"Are you investigating *me*?" Alyssa asked. "If you are, you have to tell me. And I'm calling a lawyer." She smiled to prove she was well-bred. And not frightened. Both untrue.

Parker was adjusting a silver-framed newspaper page of Bill accepting some community service award.

"That's a photo," Alyssa said. "It's not covering a secret safe. Trust me."

"I do. Trust you. Ma'am, again. May I sit?" Before Alyssa could answer, Agent Parker sat on the couch, then leaned forward, hands clasped in front of her. "I apologize. I truly do. I shouldn't say this, but I don't like this any more than you do. It's always difficult for all involved. They told me I should call you into headquarters, and again, being honest, I decided that would give you too much time to get your story straight."

"My story? Straight? With who? About what?" Alyssa shifted in her chair. The manila folder was stabbing her in the thigh. And Bill might be stabbing her in the back.

"I know it's a lot to take in. But we're looking into some of your husband's—"

"Ex-husband's," she said again.

"Not quite yet," Parker said. "Isn't that true? And you have no prenuptial agreement, is that true?"

"How—?"

"So let's talk about his other financial dealings," Parker went on. "He's a fundraiser, I understand, for—"

"Listen," Alyssa interrupted. "He used to go to the office, do whatever he did, then come home—*used* to come home—complain, drink, go to events, drink more, then go to bed. Often I did the same thing. It was a laugh a minute."

Parker nodded. "I understand this is a hard time for you. It's a hard time for me, too. These interviews are always difficult. But how familiar are you with how he handled his clients' accounts?"

"Zero familiar. Nothing." Alyssa's head began to buzz. No food, three glasses of champagne, and a bomb dropped on her life. But she had to keep it together. Why would this agent descend on her like this? Why hadn't she descended on *Bill*?

Agent Parker pulled her briefcase from the floor beside her, unzipped the top. Removed a piece of paper, and handed it across the coffee table. "Mrs. Macallen? Are you aware of this?"

Alyssa looked at it, a black-and-white bank statement from Cataloniana Bank. The account was in her name, Alyssa Westland Macallen. She saw her address across the top, and the last four digits of her social security number were the last four of the account number.

The account balance was $21,862,493.00.

She blinked at it, counting digits. "This is mine? I mean—this is not mine. *Not.* It has my name on it, I see. But I've never seen this. What is it?"

"We hoped you'd tell us," Parker said. "That's one reason I was sent here."

Alyssa examined the back, then the front again. *Customer for two years,* the statement said.

"No idea. None. Maybe Bill's hiding money from my divorce lawyer?"

"Maybe." Parker nodded. "But if he's hiding assets, why put your name on it? Maybe—you're hiding it from him?"

"What?"

"See, your signature was needed to open it," Parker said. "This might be what they call slam-dunk evidence, Alyssa. If I may call you Alyssa. Possibly of intent to defraud."

"I know nothing about this," she said. "And you said you were on 'my side.' So ask Bill."

"Is that your final answer?" Parker sat up straighter, took a deep breath. "What you want me to tell the main office? I mean, this is clearly your money. A lot of money."

Alyssa felt her anger simmering. These waters were too deep to navigate without advice. She put on a bravado she didn't feel.

"Agent? It's time for you to tell me why you're here, if you are indeed on 'my side.' Otherwise it's time for you to leave. And that's my final answer."

"You said you were getting divorced."

Alyssa rolled her eyes, staying strong. "What part of *final answer* didn't you understand?"

"So, yes?"

"Like I said. We're separated. It's in the lawyers' hands now. And Bill's." She looked at the bank statement again. Almost 22 million dollars. In her name. Between her and Bree, they were pretty darn rich. On paper. "May I keep this?"

"I'm afraid not." Parker took back the document. Slid it back into her briefcase. "Let me level with you. I understand, from my own experience, that this is an emotionally difficult subject, so forgive me. But do you know much about divorce?"

Alyssa was surprised by that one. "Enough."

"Have you heard the expression 'ill-gotten gains'?"

"Why?"

"Did your husband buy you all this?" Parker asked. "The art, the antiques, your ultra-fancy kitchen. That guest house in the back."

"It wasn't for me," Alyssa said. "He bought it, sure. It's part of our—marriage."

"Ma'am? And again, I apologize. Are you aware of the term *forfeiture*?"

"For—"

"—feiture," Parker finished. "What that means is, if we can trace any of these purchases, including that car parked out front, and that painting . . ." She pointed to it as she spoke. "Which looks like an authentic Cézanne to me—if we can connect those purchases with money your husband . . ."

She paused, apparently for Alyssa to interrupt again, but Alyssa felt too perplexed to do that.

"Alyssa?" Parker's voice lowered, almost seemed apologetic. "If we can connect those purchases to any untoward activities, purchases using what the law calls 'ill-gotten gains,' they'll be forfeited to the government. To help pay back the victims. Your husband's victims."

"He's not—" Her mind raced, and her bravado collapsed. "Victims? Victims of what?"

"And then you, not-quite ex–Mrs. Macallen," the agent went on, "will be at the mercy of the court."

"I have no idea what you're talking about." Alyssa tried to sound confident, but now all she felt was escalating terror. *Forfeiture? Ill-gotten gains? Victims?* She stood, propelled by fear. "There's nothing I can do for you."

"There actually is. And now I'll let you in on a secret." The agent fiddled with a gold hoop earring, then nodded. "I know, from experience again, that in these cases the wives are often—tragically—collateral damage. I don't want that to happen to you. You seem like a good person. So here's what you need to know. I'll help you. I promise I will. But first, we need your help."

"With what?"

"And if you don't help us," Parker ignored the question, "your future is financially—and legally—precarious. The court is not known for its mercy, ma'am. And neither is the FBI. But at this point, you're only talking to *me*. It's just the two of us. Right here, right now. Deciding your future. And remember, when it comes to a division of assets, half of nothing is nothing."

"My future? *My* future?"

"Sit down, okay?" Agent Parker tilted her head toward the armchair. "Five more minutes. Hear me out."

NINETEEN

Alyssa leaned back against the front door, closing Agent Parker out of her life. She tried clenching her fists, holding her breath, willing her fear away—like a five-year-old, she realized, refusing to face reality. She felt her feet sinking into Bill quicksand again.

What had Bill not told her? What was all that money in her name? She heard the agent's car come to life and drive away, and it was real, all of it, the FBI and the words *forfeiture* and *victims* and she could not pretend it out of existence. The FBI wanted her help. And Agent Parker had promised that tomorrow morning she'd find out how.

Alyssa straightened, tried to shake it off. Nothing more she could do tonight. Parker had instructed her not to call Bill, and wouldn't leave until she promised. Alyssa had his number—one of them, at least—but she'd never leave a message or text. He hated phone messages, never communicated that way. "Why let them track us?" he'd asked one night. They'd been at a hotel in New York, boozy and loose after a glitzy fundraiser, Bill still impeccable in black tie, and Alyssa encased in coppery sequins. "There's too much Big Brother in the world. That's what landlines are for. And in-person meetings. And single-use phones, if there's no choice. We have plenty of those."

"Why let *who* track us?" Alyssa had asked.

But Bill had grabbed her, and pulled down the fragile straps of her gown, kissing her questions away. "Anyone," he'd said, unzipping her dress. "Now hush, beauty." She was an idiot to let him do that. Talk to her like that. Distract her. She could almost hear the sound of that zipper. Look where love—ha!—had left her now.

Alyssa tossed her head, reclaiming herself. Bree and Dez would be wondering about her. She checked her watch, an original Cartier Tank, one of the first gifts Bill had given her. *Would the feds take this, too? In the forfeiture?* The slim black hands on the classic roman numerals showed it had only been twenty-five minutes. Too long for a perfunctory visit, too long for a paperwork transfer, too long for anything except trouble. She couldn't tell those two the truth about Parker. What would she even say? Maybe they'd ignore the interruption. After all, Dez had arrived uninvited, too.

If Bill had harmed someone, she hoped he got what he deserved.

She retrieved her empty champagne flute from the study, and reached for Parker's half-full water glass. She contemplated it, wondering if she should save it for some reason. DNA or fingerprints. Proof of the visit. Angry at her own paranoia, she dumped the water into a black porcelain pot of trailing ivy on a spindly side table. Bree and Dez had seen Parker. Alyssa had the agent's business card in her jeans pocket. She was real enough.

Alyssa touched the rim of her empty champagne glass to her mouth, felt the thin crystal edge against her skin. She envisioned that bank statement showing all that money. In her name. "Cataloniana Bank," she whispered. Twenty-two million dollars.

Seeing Bree's manila envelope again, Alyssa puffed out a breath, alone in the book-filled room. *Money changes everything*. Alyssa had made that pronouncement, not an hour ago. How right that was.

She came through the kitchen, deposited Parker's water glass in the sink. Bree and Dez sat opposite each other on the porch, their legs parallel on the coffee table, the line of battery-powered candles glowing between them. The music was playing out there, too, a piano improvisation, so Bree and Dez must have mastered the sound system. Alyssa drew closer, but her guests, deep in murmured conversation, seemed not to notice her.

"Hey, you two," she said. "Sorry for the—"

"Oh, finally!" Bree interrupted. "All good? You okay?"

"Hey, Alyssa." Dez toasted her with his glass. "I changed to beer. Bree found it in the fridge. Hope you don't mind."

"Did she get the papers?" Bree asked.

"Yup. All good," Alyssa said as cheerfully as she could. "Good you found the beer."

"She couldn't wait until tomorrow?" Bree went on. "That sounds big."

"It does?"

"I suppose not. Too much champagne." Bree shrugged it off. "We need to get you more cheese. Dez devoured most of this batch, though I tried my best to stop him."

Dez got up as Bree did, jabbed a finger at her. "Hey! Not true."

"There's pâté, too, and spinach dip." Seemed like

they believed her story. And why not? They hadn't known each other long enough to lie. "What'd you two talk about while I was so rudely interrupted?"

"Gosh, what *did* we . . ." Bree stopped, pursed her lips.

"Bree told me all her secrets," Dez said.

"Did not!" Bree made a face as she pivoted toward the open french doors to the kitchen, tucking her striped shirt into place in the back of her jeans.

Calling attention to her rear, Alyssa thought, but maybe she'd truly needed to fix her shirt.

Dez followed her, but Alyssa held back, still watching them. Funny, she thought she'd found a potential friend in Bree. Then, quick as a heartbeat, a man had distracted her. Why did women always bail on their friends when the men arrived? A moment of loss saddened her, surprised her.

Men. *Bill.* The FBI. That money. Alyssa barely had brain space to accommodate that, let alone analyze young love. Which, again, was all in her imagination. The two of them had consumed more than a bottle of champagne, and Dez had added beer, so maybe their energy was more about alcohol and less about lust.

"You coming?" Bree's voice from the kitchen.

Alyssa realized she'd been staring, watching the flicker of the battery candles, the twinkling lights that only pretended to be flames. Sometimes it felt as if nothing was real.

But there was no avoiding tomorrow. Tomorrow morning would come all too soon.

She'd have to figure out what to tell Bree about that, she thought, as she wiped a scatter of cracker crumbs from the coffee table. Alyssa had promised to meet Parker at 10:00. She hated the idea of going into that hulk of a gray stone building in downtown Boston, but hated the idea of Parker being in her house even more. Where the hell was Bill? The *FBI*, for god's sake.

Should she call Bill? Warn him? Were they *expecting* her to do that? If they had his phone number, they could be listening. And if they *were* monitoring him, and she *did* call, they'd know. Which meant they'd know she'd lied. And then she'd be in trouble. She gathered the used white paper cocktail napkins from the table, then crumpled them in her fist as hard as she could, imagining they were Bill's head.

No. Bill had left her in the lurch. Now it was her turn to leave him there.

Twenty-two million dollars. She could almost see the words, the numbers glowing like neon as she walked to the kitchen. Bree and Dez stood on opposite sides of the kitchen island, Bree peeling the plastic wrap from a ramekin of pâté, Dez scooping dip from a plastic container. At ease, and chatting, as if the two of them had known each other for years, not days. But the money was her more pressing concern. What did the FBI think that was? She pushed the napkin ball into the wastebasket, watched the triangular aluminum top swing back and forth.

"Oh, hey. Dez is going to drive me to Amherst tomorrow," Bree said. "I still have stuff at my old place, the landlord said he'd keep it for a while, but I'm worried—"

"I feel like crap," Dez said, interrupting. "Freaking Bree out, because of my own ineptitude, and stampeding her to move to the other side of the state with barely the clothes on her back."

Bree pointed a ceramic-handled cheese knife at him.

"It's fine. I told you, I overreacted. I feel dumb about it now. But, whatever, there was nothing holding me in Amherst except my own inertia. Probably you did me a favor."

"Well . . ." Dez flipped his palm, *good news, bad news*. "Just doing my job, Bree."

"Badly."

"Hey. Gimme a break, okay?"

His eyes twinkled at her, Alyssa saw. And for a fragment of a moment, she remembered how she'd felt meeting Bill. Alyssa, struggling to make a career on her own, happened to attend a charity gala, happened to be introduced to an attractive man. She'd known who he was, of course. His name was on the program under *Platinum Sponsors*. And even as she'd understood how impossible it was to unring the money bell, she'd tried, for the sake of her own happiness, to separate the lure of security from her actual emotions. How much did the promise of affluence enhance a person's appeal? Easy one.

Alyssa narrowed her eyes, seeing this kitchen scene through a different filter. Dez's banter and obvious flirting might be about money, too. Maybe it wasn't the new haircut that made Bree attractive. And Bree—who'd scraped for money and tumbled into debt and landed in a grimy suburban hotel—had no personal understanding of how money affected people. She worked in a bank, but that meant she only dealt with other people's money, a matter of paper and numbers. But the reality of money, the power and the control it could buy, and the irresistible allure of it, no way Bree could fathom that.

But Dez could. He might see it happen every day.

Sudden wealth. Then, vulnerability. Then . . . the persuasion.

Sure, Dez worked in a fancy office, with a fancy boss, and seemed to be legitimate. But he'd come to Alyssa's house, that was unusual. And she had to admit he was attractive in a boyish way. Now they were all drinking together at Alyssa's—the soon-to-be divorcée, the newly minted millionaire, and the stranger.

What was he truly after? And Alyssa had gotten Bree into this.

Bree was laughing now. Alyssa, startled back to the present, had missed their whole conversation.

"No, no, no more beer for me." Dez spread spinach dip on a cracker and ate it in one bite. "Got to get up at a reasonable hour if we're going to retrieve your belongings."

"The landlord told me he's leaving at ten," Bree explained. "So we have to leave at what, eight?"

"Brutal." Dez selected a slice of cheese.

"Your penance," Bree said.

"Pick you up at seven forty-five?"

Alyssa wondered if they'd invite her to go along. She'd have to concoct a reasonable excuse not to accompany them. But she had an appointment, that was believable. Alyssa had known Bree for five days. There was no reason for Alyssa to accompany her to Amherst.

Except maybe to protect her.

"You'll be okay here, Lyss?" Bree handed Dez a cracker topped with pâté, which he examined, then sniffed, before eating it.

"Sure, I—" Alyssa began.

"And since my stalker turned out to be a good guy,

I can check back in to that hotel." She grimaced, then looked to Dez. "Or maybe I can afford someplace better? Soon?"

"Well, even if all goes as planned, it'll still take a while for the estate to pay out," Dez said. "There's no obstacle, not that Roshandra or I have found, but it's in probate. The red tape is strangling, and the bureaucracy Orwellian. But we'll make it work. Be patient."

"You can stay here as long as you need." Alyssa made the offer, deciding even as she said it, that it not only made her feel safer, but provided another way to protect Bree from Dez's possible ulterior motives. She saw Bree's expression change. "What?"

Bree downed the rest of her champagne. "I can't—I keep thinking about it," she said.

Alyssa watched tears come to Bree's eyes, saw her shoulders sink. "You're sad? Thinking about what?"

Dez was focused on her, too. "Bree? About what?"

"I guess," Bree whispered, looking at the floor. "That someone had to die."

WEDNESDAY

TWENTY

Every damn place reminded her of Bill. Alyssa clicked her car doors closed, the sound echoing through the full-but-deserted parking garage. All the commuters parked here in the dank and gritty concrete basement of Two Center Plaza were already upstairs in their offices by now, 9:45 was late for regular work hours. She memorized her parking spot number—B-43. Most of the FBI had moved their offices from here in Boston's Government Center to some cheaper building on the edge of town, but Parker had explained they'd retained a few offices here for special meetings.

Alyssa had been in this building before, dozens of times.

Bill had howled with laughter when he'd told her the story, years ago, of where the search for the new offices of the Macallen Group had ended. They'd been side by side that night in their double-sinked bathroom, getting ready for some event; Bill shaving and talking into the ceiling-high mirror.

"The FBI's in the same building we are, can you believe it, sweetheart?" he'd said. He scraped the razor down his cheek, leaving a line of skin between two white puffs of mint-fragranced shaving cream. "It's brilliant. I told the broker, if the bad guys come to get us, I'll just yell for the friendly agents next door to protect me. I'll even put 'em on speed dial. And tax-payers are footing the bill. Talk about a deal."

Alyssa had joked with him about it, checking her eyeliner, offered to bring them muffins. She'd talked to his reflection. "Does the FBI like muffins?"

Bill had laughed again, loving her, pulling at the belt of her thick white terry bathrobe.

She batted his hand away. "We'll be late."

"Late is when we say it is," Bill told her.

He'd ingratiated himself with the feds after that, buddied up to them, Mr. Good Guy.

The parking lot smelled the same as ever, this bleak Wednesday morning: oil, and dust, and the faint murmur of the cooling systems. Exhaust machinery hummed in the background. Someone had painted fresh white lines, not quite parallel, on the grimy asphalt floor. She saw the peeling sign as she approached the nearest elevator: *FBI. Floor 6. Macallen Group. Floor 5.*

She arrived at the elevator door, stared at the scratched aluminum, assessing. Those FBI agents certainly knew where Bill's office was. Certainly knew his premium parking spot was on the lower level, space A-5. And certainly the agents had surveillance cameras installed. She sneaked a look above her. The red warning eye of a lens, housed in an egg-shaped dome, blinked down at her. Daring her.

If she pushed the Down button—and she really wanted to, curious to see if Bill's Mercedes was there—they'd know that, too. And ask about it. Then she'd have to tell the truth, or lie.

How many times had she used this same elevator? Especially in the early days, when she and Bill could not stay away from each other. Once, she'd arrived in a trench coat and little else—right out of a bad movie they'd watched, a now-embarrassing cliché, but he'd adored it, she knew he did. She could hardly picture it now, the extent of their lust. Luckily the door to Bill's corner office could be locked, and the tall windows looked out onto Cambridge Street, where only someone in city hall using binoculars—impossible—could see in. They'd collapsed on his black leather couch, afterward, sticking to the cushions and laughing and drunk on each other and basking in the sunshine pouring through the sparkling glass. A lamp had toppled, rolling across the floor as far as its cord allowed. She'd teased him, asked who he expected to clean up his office after their passionate afternoon. "Everything gets taken care of," he'd murmured. She remembered his voice, his power, his reassurance. How safe she'd felt. Then.

Victims. Forfeiture. Her lawyer had warned her early on, in his sleek, professional, self-protecting legal jargon, that there were no guarantees in divorce. That sometimes the courts divided assets by what each party had brought to the marriage.

"You have no prenup," he'd said as if she needed reminding. "And you brought only yourself."

"And that's nothing?" Her bitter words had come out before she'd had a chance to collect herself, poisoned by the reality of how quickly the balance sheet could change, especially when you were treated as a zero.

She'd lost Bill, somehow. Next, she could lose her home. She could lose absolutely everything.

Alyssa jabbed the elevator button. Up. Up. Up. This Agent Parker had better tell her exactly what she suspected Bill had done. And how she was supposed to "help." *Point us in the right direction,* Parker had asked. Alyssa would point her, all right. She poked the button again. *This* building, of all places.

The elevator clanked into motion, and the doors opened with a swish. Yesterday, an elevator journey had brought Bree a life-changing inheritance. Now, just before ten, Bree and Dez would have arrived in Amherst, and would be talking to Bree's landlord, retrieving her belongings. Changing her life.

Alyssa entered the metal-walled elevator, déjà vu taking away all sense of time and intent. Bree and Dez. In Amherst. Together. "Bree will be fine," she said to the empty elevator. "Least of my worries."

As she traveled up, alone, through time and through fear and through the inexorable knowledge that what was about to happen might change her life forever, too—hell, would *definitely* change her life forever—she smoothed the black light wool jacket she'd chosen for this meeting. Respectful. Not deferential. Her knife-pleated mid-calf skirt would allow her to sit comfortably, and her low heels seemed appropriately reliable.

Twenty-two million dollars. In a bank account with her name on it.

Bill, she thought. *You idiot. What have you done?*

The gray metal door of room 611 was marked *FBI* in peeling gray decals. Alyssa twisted the knob to open it, but it was locked. She pushed a square black button on the doorjamb, heard a buzz from inside. She'd been so surprised by that—a government office should be open, shouldn't it?—that she'd wanted to check her text reminders to make sure she had the correct place. But before she could get her phone unlocked, she'd heard footsteps inside, and then a click, and then Agent Hattie Parker stood in the opened doorway.

"Thank you for being so punctual," Parker said. "Come in."

TWENTY-ONE

It was only Bree's phone call during the drive home that pulled Alyssa out of her spiraling depression. Agent Parker had questioned her. Interrogated her. Threatened her.

"I don't know anything about what Bill does, or did," Alyssa had insisted.

"Really?" She could still hear Hattie Parker's voice, edged with disbelief. "Aren't you married to him? Don't you two discuss things? Like most couples do?"

Even if Parker had secretly taped their session, she couldn't have recorded Alyssa's murderous thoughts, or her imaginings of dark revenge. Bill, the man who had promised her everything, and then—

"Pick a *lane,*" she muttered to the driver weaving in front of her on the Mass Pike. She wanted to go home. She wanted to kill someone. She wanted this to be over.

She'd envisioned that last morning together, a Friday, Bill standing at the kitchen door. He'd been carrying a leather overnight bag, bulging, over his shoulder. He wore his good khakis, a new polo shirt. Their final one-sided conversation was how Bill "needed time" and "space" and how their lives "weren't working." This was no spur-of-the-moment whim, she remembered thinking. This was a plan.

She almost missed the exit off the Pike, now, and had to veer across two lanes, some short-fused driver behind her honking in annoyance. "Shut *up*!" she yelled, and heard her voice quaver on the verge of tears. She slowed for the curve of the exit, but her mind was still going full speed.

"He's good at it," Parker had said. "We need you on our side."

Bill and his damn money, and his ambition, and his supreme self-confidence. If she was in danger of losing everything because of his greed, because of some underhanded, overconfident, self-aggrandizing, illegal cheating . . . she wasn't quite sure how she would deal with that. Or him. If he'd ruined his own life, he should have been smart enough to assess the dangers on the path he was choosing. But "one step at a time," Alyssa knew, could lead to places that defied prediction.

Alyssa had been standing at the stove that Friday as he announced his departure, making his two egg whites over easy and two strips of bacon, her metal spatula in suspended animation and her mind in shock. As the eggs turned brown and then black around the edges, she'd almost not been able to respond to his declaration. The bacon sizzled and snapped as the pan got hotter and hotter. She knew how the bacon felt.

"Time? Space?" She'd waved the dripping spatula at Bill. "What are you, living in some Lifetime movie about a midlife crisis? Might, and just a thought here, *might* your wife be due more explanation than cliché?" Which, she'd instantly realized, made her a cliché, too, and her tone, and her situation, which made her even more devastatingly angry. She'd almost thrown the hot eggs at him, by that time ruined to an inedible charred slab.

But Bill had pivoted, walked away before she could do it.

"*Bill!*" she'd screamed after him, but heard only the slam of the front door.

The kitchen had smelled like burned eggs and blackened bacon for the rest of the day. The warble of the Bluetooth interrupted her now, dissolving her bitter images of the past, of her sorrow and disappointment and confusion.

"It's me," Bree said when Alyssa answered. "You in the car?"

"Just turning the corner to home," Alyssa said, wishing there was another word for a place that used to be home but now was only a transitory shelter, temporary, soon to be only a memory. She was merely a house guest. She grasped for normality, trying to remember what a normal person would say. "How'd it go?"

Bree babbled about her day, prattling and newsy, saying she and Dez would be a little late for dinner, and hoped that was okay, then went on about arranging for her car and packing and apartment leases and final payments on utility bills.

"Moving sucks." Bree's voice sounded more amused than annoyed. "And my landlord is being a jerk. He'll, like, only talk to Dez, like only men can handle business things, you know? Still, we're managing to get my stuff, meager as it is, all into the back of Dez's van, and he's letting me keep it in his garage until I find a new place. Unless your guest house could use a couple of makeshift bookcases and a collection of CDs," Bree said, as Alyssa turned into her driveway. "Music CDs from high school, I mean, Lyss. Not money."

"Ha ha. Understood." Everything seemed to be about money now. Alyssa, running on fumes and still strapped into her seat belt, held up a remote to open her own garage, one-third empty now with her black SUV in place but Bill's Mercedes no longer occupying its spot.

Where was he? This morning, Agent Parker had brushed off Alyssa's insistence that she didn't know.

"Where does Dez live?" Alyssa asked as she drove in. "I've been thinking about that."

"Arlington?" Bree said. "Like a condo. We can talk tonight. Is eight-ish okay? We're bringing pizza. We insist."

We, Alyssa thought. And who was the "we" of her? Alyssa remembered a short story she'd read, something about the human need for belonging. For family, and friends, and support. Now Alyssa had none of the above. And whatever she'd counted on—that word again, *money*—was growing more and more uncertain.

"You're protected if you help us," Agent Parker had laid out the stakes. "If not, you'll be on your own."

On her own. As if she could be any more intensely alone.

But Bree had been equally on her own, too, and her financial future also uncertain, Alyssa reminded herself. Until someone died.

"Pizza." Alyssa tried to keep her voice pleasant, like her world wasn't under siege. She would not tell them about this morning. Not a word of it. "So fun."

"We owe you," Bree said. "Without you—none of this would have happened. I mean it, Lyss. I owe you so much more than pizza."

"Pizza's good," Alyssa said. "But no pineapple."

"Travesty," Bree said. "See you soon."

Bree and Dez. Dez and Bree. Alyssa sat in the silent car, the garage door still open behind her, the afternoon sun shimmering in her rearview.

As if talking to Parker hadn't been unsettling enough. But why had the FBI agent entered her life at this particular time? Parker *and* Bree *and* Dez. More suspicions rose to the top of her mind and floated there, like a thin sheen of oil on water, a veil of doubt that colored everything that touched it. She'd gone to Vermilion on a whim. Someone could have followed her, she supposed. She grasped the steering wheel with both hands, and pressed her back into the yielding leather seat. She'd never have noticed that, especially as wrapped up in herself as she'd been.

She closed her eyes and pictured that Vermilion scene as if she were watching a movie. The cute bartender, solicitous and hovering. The onion ring couple, who'd left soon after Bree arrived. Maraschino cherry man. Had they all been sent by the FBI to watch her?

Scratching her head with both hands, she tried to remember. The bartender had been there when she arrived, but the others—had they been there, too? Or had they come in later?

The only way Bree could have known she was there would be if one of those people in the bar had followed her. Then contacted Bree to make the approach.

She gripped the steering wheel, hard. Then burst out laughing.

"You are a total idiot, Alyssa," she said out loud. She grabbed her handbag, hopped out of the car, and went out into the sunshine. "Let me think," she said to the forsythia, "either some crew of unknown strangers decided to follow you to a bar, for some as-yet-undetermined reason, or—"

She paused, taking a deep breath, smelling the fresh-cut grass and the newly mulched front borders, admiring the tips of the tiny white crocuses, struggling to emerge, and even saw a robin bob across the lawn. "Or, a woman walked into a bar. And sat down next to someone who looked friendly."

She jabbed her key into the front door. Bree had actively not wanted to talk, Alyssa remembered, and it had been Alyssa herself who'd initiated the conversation. So, yeah. One night in a bar. And now a new life. That's how life worked. One day at a time.

The dog barked as she opened the door. Which reminded her, again, of Agent Hattie Parker and what she'd asked Alyssa to do, and she felt her smile vanish as she silenced the alarm.

Now she had to decide.

TWENTY-TWO

"You take the last piece, Dez." Alyssa pointed to the cheesy triangle in the oil-soaked cardboard box. The three of them had taken the Pino's extra-large to the porch, dining al fresco in the May evening.

Alyssa had decided to simply let the night take its course. Alyssa herself had brought Bree to Dez, as they—Alyssa and Bree, another not-really-they—looked for Collin Whishaw. So Bree was a totally random player. And Dez, too.

While Bree showered, Dez stayed in the kitchen, expertly tearing romaine leaves and washing tomatoes and describing their trip to Amherst.

"Her landlord was a jerk," Dez was saying. He'd tied one of Alyssa's aprons over his black T-shirt and jeans. KEEP CALM AND MAKE PI, the apron said. With a picture of three pies and one extra piece. Bill had won it at some event, though only Alyssa thought it was funny. "And we didn't want to tell him about Bree's—you know. Pending financial situation. He'd have probably tried to extort her to pay some penalty for breaking the lease."

"Smart." Alyssa measured balsamic vinegar into a cruet. She wanted to ask more about the "situation," but it was too soon to know anything, and she'd find out eventually.

Dez dumped the romaine leaves into Alyssa's big

wooden salad bowl. "What'd you do today?" he asked.

Alyssa saw her own hand tremble as she poured olive oil into a tablespoon. She focused, adding it to the vinegar. "Not much," she said. "Errands."

"You said you had a meeting, I thought." Dez walked behind her, opened the refrigerator. "Looking for green pepper? Maybe? Oh, I see it. Errands? I know Bree had kind of wondered if you'd want to come with us. But when she brought it up—"

"Oh, right, the meeting. Yeah. Dentist," Alyssa said. "And then errands." She measured more oil, as if distracted. She was terrible at subterfuge. "So. Amherst?"

"Not much," Dez said.

Alyssa couldn't tell if he was being sarcastic, repeating her own "not much." She added salt and pepper to the glass container, choosing her next words.

"She okay? Bree, I mean?" Alyssa snapped the plastic cap onto the cruet, and gave it a shake, mixing the ingredients.

She heard Dez's knife against the wooden cutting board, slicing into the thick green flesh of the pepper. Alyssa turned, still holding the salad dressing, watching him.

"Okay?" He looked up from his peppers, quizzical. "What d'you mean?"

"Collin Whishaw." Alyssa shook the dressing again, saw the brown vinegar coloring the thick olive oil, grains of black pepper floating free, then descending to the bottom. "It's hard for her, I think. Someone—you know—had to die in order for her to—"

"Hey, let's have some music, you two." Bree had yanked open the back door, her shoulders wrapped in one of Alyssa's fluffy white towels. She scrabbled at her soaking hair with the towel, drying it. "Forgive me for being so casual," she said, laughing. "I keep worrying I'll miss something. Yum, the pizza smells awesome. What can I do to help?" She looked at each of them, still drying her hair, expectant. "This is so nice of you, Lyss. Dez and I had a hard day. I could set the table?"

Now, blotting oil from her chin and contemplating a third glass of wine, Alyssa wondered, again, whether Bree had been concerned about what Dez was telling Alyssa. Or what Alyssa was telling Dez. Maybe her newfound wealth was making her wisely wary.

She leaned back against the couch cushions, watching Dez slide a pepperoni-dotted slice onto a white plate. Bree had opened cabinets, looking for dishes, and pulled out the white Rosenthal, almost translucently thin. *Not those,* Alyssa had almost stopped her. The traditional white china had belonged to Bill's grandmother, he'd explained, who'd lived with his family until she died.

His voice had softened as he reminisced, as if he were picturing another time. "She taught me to ask questions," he'd said. "And to always have a savings account. She made me read the paper every morning, even the stock listings, then insisted I discuss the news with her and Papa." Even long after the stock prices went online, Bill had still read the morning papers at their breakfast table, folding the pages into quarters, drinking his black coffee and staring at the newsprint of *The Times* and *Globe* and *The Wall Street Journal*. Until he left. And Alyssa canceled all of Bill's damn papers. She yearned to cancel everything about him. The papers, at least, were easy.

"Perfect plates, Bree." Alyssa gave her a thumbs-up. Maybe someone would break one.

"More?" Bree now lifted the green bottle from a silver-and-cork wine trivet. "I'm about to hog it all. I've never had wine this good. It tastes like plums and rubies."

Alyssa had hit the wine cellar for a big cabernet, figuring, again, she should use it while her access lasted. She sighed, and pictured logo-jacketed FBI agents marching out of the cellar lugging cases of wine.

"Are you into wine?" Dez asked. "Bree? Alyssa?" He toasted them both. "Your wine life is about to change, Bree," he said. "If everything goes as we hope."

"Can we not talk about that?" Bree made a cringing face. "It seems impossible, and a little too sad. Collin Whishaw, you know? I keep imagining him. Still, Alyssa, I'm not sure how to sufficiently thank you. I—"

"All good," Alyssa said, raising a hand to stop Bree. "And you don't need to thank me. Life is full of unexpected connections—what did Kurt Vonnegut call it? A karass?"

Dez smiled. "I haven't thought about that since college," he said. "People who are in a group together, but they don't know it."

"Like us," Bree said. "Or like we were. Before Alyssa."

The sound of the wine pouring into her glass, the underscore of the piano in the background, the rustle of a gentle May wind through the maples in her garden. She hadn't always made the best choices, and had thought helping Bree was, finally, a wise one. A compassionate one, where there was no reward but the joy of doing a good deed.

She watched them tackle their pizza, Dez folding his in half and biting off the end, Bree using a knife and fork, delicately examining each morsel. Alyssa's piece remained untouched. Dez and Bree were on one side of her emotional ledger, the FBI on the other. Her entire body felt clenched, threatened, as if the next phone call or the next text would bring disaster crashing down on her. The vultures loomed. If the doorbell rang again, she would die.

She couldn't ignore what haunted her—the words that agent had used: *kickbacks, illegal, forfeiture.*

You're protected if you help us, Parker had told her, *but you're on your own if you don't.* Alyssa had one day to decide.

She tried to let tonight's small talk distract her; some problem with the transmission in Dez's van, Bree's last-minute goodbye to her bank colleagues. They'd both complained their backs hurt after moving all of Bree's boxes. Just another normal chatty night with friends. Alyssa relished every word, honest conversation where there were no threats or double meanings.

"So how'd *your* day go?" Bree tucked her legs up under her, settling into the green-and-white flowered cushions of the big woven chair. "All good?"

"Ah, sure. Fine," Alyssa began. So much for honest. Here came the shaky ground.

"Dentist," Dez said. "Hate that."

"Yeah, well." Alyssa drank again, drowning her lie.

The room went silent, and it felt to Alyssa that someone was judging her. Which was ridiculous, because no one here but her could know what happened in that Center Plaza office. Parker wheedling, insinuating. Threatening. Bill, revealed as a liar. A con artist.

And she knew he was taunting her. What was she, one little person, supposed to do? She took another sip of the dusky red. The wine began to quiet her mind, comfort it, fuzzing the raw edges of her worry.

She took a deep breath. How was she supposed to do this on her own? The hammer of the United States government was about to—maybe—slam down on Bill Macallen, and on her, too, and sure, she'd talk to a lawyer in the morning, she'd already left a message for the one she wanted, but her emotions were too raw. Growing up, her mother had never provided guidance, or compassion, even on her least cynical days. Bill, finally, had been there for her. Until he hadn't. Could there be more alone than alone?

"You okay, Lyss?" Bree's voice, gently concerned.

She hoped she looked pleasant. "Just soaking up the niceness."

"Aw." Bree nodded, approving. "And yeah, hard to believe all this."

Alyssa watched her take in the lofty white wooden slats of the porch ceiling, the white-framed screened walls, the flickering candles, even the stars peeking through the maple branches.

"Friday, Saturday, Sunday, Monday, Tuesday," Alyssa said. She tried to put her empty wineglass on the coffee table, but misjudged the edge. The glass tottered, hesitated, almost fell. "So much has changed. Since we met."

Her voice had come out a whisper, and she wasn't quite sure who she was telling this to—Bree and Dez, or herself, or the universe.

She felt trapped. Caught in some inexorable whirlpool of impossible inescapable things. Things that pulled and dragged her down into endless oblivion and nothingness. Maybe that was her only way out. Maybe she should . . .

"Lyss?" Bree's voice interrupted, somehow now coming from close to her on the couch. "Alyssa?"

Alyssa felt a gentle touch on her bare arm, startled out of her thoughts. "Huh?"

"I'd asked what's wrong," Bree said.

"Wrong?"

"You're crying, honey."

TWENTY-THREE

So that's the deal." Alyssa paused, seeing the baffled expressions on Bree's and Dez's faces. The two sat side by side on separate cushioned rattan chairs, elbows on knees, chins in their hands, like children riveted by a ghost story. No one had budged as Alyssa related this morning's experience. No one had interrupted.

"The FBI," Bree finally said. She exchanged glances with Dez.

"Yes," Alyssa said. No turning back now.

"Is after Bill. For some tax fraud scheme," Bree went on. "And wants you to help catch him."

"'If you don't help us, you'll go down, too.'" Alyssa air-bracketed the quote with her fingers, used a persuasive tone like Parker had. "Or words to that effect. 'Down' meaning prison. I told her I don't know anything about anything. But she acted like I was lying." She made a dramatic face, lowered her voice again. "*The wife always knows,* she said."

For a moment, the only sounds were the pouring wine and an increasing rustle of leaves. Rain coming again, Alyssa thought.

"The FBI," Dez finally said. He took a deep breath, then flapped down the top of the oily pizza box and stashed it under the coffee table. "That's surprising. Are you okay?"

"What's her name?" Bree asked.

"You know people in the FBI?" Dez looked at Bree.

"Just *asking,*" Bree replied. "So we don't have to keep talking about 'her' and 'she.'"

"Be that as it may. Hattie Parker." Alyssa checked her wineglass, fearing it was empty. It was. And the bottle, too. "We need more wine. If we're going to talk about this. Or maybe . . . I shouldn't have told you." *Too late for that,* she admonished herself again. "Like I said, now I have to trust you."

"Of course." Bree's eyes were wide, her face mottled in the battery-powered candlelight. "You poor thing."

"I'll get the wine?" Dez said it like a question. "The bottle on the kitchen counter? Bree?"

Alyssa nodded.

"Sure," Bree said. "Seems like a three-bottle night. At least. Alyssa, I don't know what to say." She stared at her now-bare feet and their newly pedicured toes. The night air had gone chilly, and crept through the mesh of the open screens. Bree grabbed a yellow-checked gingham throw pillow and clutched it to her chest.

"Listen. While Dez is out of the room? Just tell me. You can tell me. Did you, like, know?" she whispered over the pillow. "That your husband was running some sort of financial—whatever it was?"

"I don't even know what I'm supposed to know."

"Did anyone ever complain to *you*? Like, victims?"

"Victims?" Alyssa winced. "Complain to *me*?"

"They might, if they figured you knew. Were, like, in on it, even."

Alyssa felt the tears begin. "No. *No.* There's nothing to know. There can't be anything to know. And now—now I have to decide what to do, and how do I know, and—"

"Here's Dez," Bree said.

"You've called a lawyer, I hope." Dez set the open bottle of wine onto the trivet. Bree held out Alyssa's glass. "Please tell me you did. A good one. Not your divorce lawyer."

An owl cooed, somewhere in the distance, maybe warning of the impending change in the weather. They'd silenced the music as Alyssa spun her story, and now the quiet seemed unsettling, the room gone hollow.

"Yeah, I did," Alyssa said.

"I know some smart ones. If you want to talk to them."

Bree waved him off. "She told you she has a lawyer."

"Thanks, you two," Alyssa said. They sounded like bickering siblings. "We'll see."

Dez held up one finger, pointed it at Alyssa. "Wait. You said—Center Plaza? You talked to this Parker at the FBI at Center Plaza?" He pursed his lips, as if remembering. "No. That's—no. The offices moved."

"I know. I said that, too." Alyssa shifted on the couch. She'd been sitting for too long, and every cell in her body and brain longed for sleep. To somehow erase the day, and everything that went with it. "Because Bill's office is in that building. He'd always make a big joke about it." She leaned her back against the arm of the couch, stretched out her legs. "The agent said most of the staff moved, but they kept an office or two just in case. And oh, yikes, she told me not to tell anyone the location. So forget I told you.

A private office does make sense, though. If you're a whistleblower. Or an informant."

Alyssa felt the word *informant* hang in the air. That's what the FBI hoped *she* would be.

"And there's a courthouse across the way," she said, looking for some more benign reason for the auxiliary office. "Maybe it's convenient for protecting witnesses."

Another thing she didn't want to be, a protected witness. Especially since she hadn't witnessed anything.

"Sounds like she wants you to entrap him," Bree said. "Isn't that kinda illegal?"

Alyssa dropped her face into one palm, talked through her fingers. "Again. They're the FBI. Whatever."

Dez stood, and paced now, from the kitchen archway to the edge of the porch and back, hands shoved into his pockets.

Alyssa watched him. He faced the backyard, looking out into the night. The garden lights twinkled as if nothing had changed, even though everything had.

"You okay, Dez?" Bree asked.

"The FBI. I'm thinking about that."

"Yeah, Lyss," Bree said. "The FBI is not going away."

"Alyssa? Maybe—maybe you should tell your husband about this." Dez turned, walked back toward them. "Do you still love him?"

"Whoa, Dez." Bree's eyebrows went up.

"It's okay." Alyssa drew in a breath. "I did once."

"And you said, 'Til death do us part,'" Dez said.

"Once," Bree said.

"And, 'For better or for worse,'" Dez went on. "And—"

"This is *worse*, dude," Bree interrupted. "She's got to watch out for herself now. You see her husband protecting *her*? He's only put her in some kind of horrible—ah. Sorry, Alyssa."

"It's okay." Alyssa couldn't help but be touched by their concern. And a sliver of her brain acknowledged that the two of them were disagreeing. An indication that she'd been right. They weren't a "they." She also hadn't noticed any more signs of affection, no teasing or flirting. If anything, Dez had been paying attention to Alyssa herself, not Bree.

"Yeah, so, the divorce," Alyssa went on. "It hardly matters how I feel about him, does it? I mean—right now? I hate him beyond all measure and description. I could go on."

"See?" Bree tipped her glass toward Dez. "You don't understand how women feel. Alyssa made a deal, essentially, to love and honor. Bill agreed, and then just did whatever the hell he wanted. Now he's off wherever he is, and she's here taking the heat."

"They can't blame Alyssa for something she didn't do, or even know about," Dez said. "They can't punish her for that."

"Ha. What planet do *you* live on? And how are they going to prove she didn't? Know?" Bree leaned forward. "That's the thing, right? Proving the negative. And nobody believes the woman. We're just supposed to do what we're told, and say what we're told. Or else wham, down comes the guillotine."

"She *said* she didn't know, and I'm saying I believe her," Dez said.

"Well, of *course,* I do, too, I'm just trying to remind you—"

"But what if her husband *did* do something?" Dez cut her off. "The FBI doesn't fish. They investigate. Alyssa probably knows more than she realizes. She—"

"There's nothing to know!" Alyssa interrupted.

"Oh, Dez, give me a break." Bree ignored her, talked over her. "The feds are—power mad. Devious. You know that."

"You watch too much TV, Bree."

"You have no idea about me," she said. "And this isn't about me, this is about our *Alyssa,* who's worrying she might be sent to prison." She cringed. "Oh, I didn't mean to say that. It's the wine. You won't go to prison."

Alyssa felt as if she were watching a movie about someone else, with these two batting her life back and forth. She was simply too tired, too everything, to make much sense of it.

"Look. You two?" Alyssa stood, dusted off her rear, stretched her arms. "We finished the wine. It's late. Way late. It's almost—"

Dez looked at his chunky silver watch. "Midnight. Wow."

Alyssa paused, considering. He'd had a lot to drink. Was it safe to let him drive? Maybe better to let him leave, if he was somehow a threat to Bree. But nothing could happen overnight. "Listen. I don't want you driving. There's a guest room upstairs," she said, gesturing in that direction. "A new toothbrush in the guest bath. And a bathrobe. Up the front stairs, third door on the right."

"Oh, no," Dez said. "I only had a few—"

"Oh, *yes,*" Bree said at the same time. She jabbed a forefinger at him, as if erasing his refusal from the realm of possibility. "Plus, it means we can talk about this in the morning. Soon as we have enough caffeine." Bree reached under the coffee table, pulled out the pizza box. "I'll toss this. But, Dez? Okay?"

"That's very generous of you, Alyssa." Dez glanced at each of them. "Okay, Bree. You're probably right."

"Imagine that," Bree said.

Alyssa wondered what was up between them. She'd suspected some connection—and now Bree seemed unusually prickly. Maybe they'd had an argument on their drive from Amherst. Maybe about the death of Collin Whishaw? Clearly, Dez knew more than he was saying, and Bree seemed determined to get answers. Though she hadn't brought it up this evening, which was . . . good or bad. Or maybe Alyssa'd concocted the whole thing out of misguided imagination, or, she reluctantly acknowledged, envy of their possibly budding relationship. *Men,* she thought.

"Good," Alyssa said, ignoring the maybe-tension. "We can clean this up tomorrow. Let's—"

A bolt of lightning flashed in the distance, and they all turned to the window, the opaque swimming pool alight for a fraction of a second. Fat raindrops began to splat against the gridded windows of the french doors. Alyssa, out of habit, began to count, *One, two, three, four* . . . And then heard the crashing rumble of thunder. Alyssa caught a glimpse of surprise—fear?—on Bree's face. Then the lights flickered. The kitchen went dark. The garden lights went out, too, plunging the backyard into black. The battery-powered candles on the coffee table glowed stolidly as if they operated in a different universe.

"Yikes," Bree said. "That was intense."

"So annoying, this happens sometimes." Alyssa could smell the rain, the raw fresh dampness seeping through the screened walls. "We're fine. It stays dry in here," she said, "even in the rain, Bill had it designed that way. And the power always comes back on quickly, it's Weston, you know? But hang on, I'll get flashli—"

The kitchen lights powered on again, then just as quickly gave up, leaving them in the dark. "I'm having trouble understanding you," the robot voice of Alyssa's info system complained.

"Okay, then." Alyssa had to laugh. "Never a dull moment. I'll give you both flashlights for tonight, just in case. I could make tea on the stove?"

"I'm fine, thanks, Lyss. But can we just stay here a minute? To see if it maybe stops?" Bree said. "Getting to the guest house is gonna be a challenge. Not to mention being inside it in the pitch dark."

"Good idea." Alyssa held up a plastic candle. "We have these. Might as well stay here a bit. The power might come on any second." She went to the back door, peered out into the night. The rain seemed to be increasing, but they were safe and dry. Bree could stay in the other guest room if it kept storming. May in New England; when storms hit, they hit with unbridled fury. On a typical night, in her other life, she'd have slept through it. Then in the morning, she and Bill would have reset the clocks and coffeepot. *Bill. The FBI. Kickbacks. Illegal.* For a moment, distracted by the surprise darkness, she'd forgotten all that.

Dez plopped back into his chair, crossing his legs on the coffee table, yawned and stretched, his battery-powered candle glowing as he raised it. Alyssa saw

Bree tuck her legs under herself, and nestle in the cushions of the chair beside him.

"Here." Alyssa took one of the fringed cashmere wraps she kept folded across the back of the couch, handed it to Bree. "Cozy up in this," she said. As Bree pulled the herringbone fabric to her chin, Alyssa drew another fleecy blanket from its place, and wrapped herself against the chill. "Dez, you a blanket guy? Want some tea?"

"What did they want you to do, Alyssa? Specifically? The FBI?"

Alyssa stared at him in the unsettling silence, no electricity, no hum of the lights, no music, as if she could feel her support system slipping away. *No power,* she thought. The universe was messing with her, and it wasn't fair. Like everything else.

"Dez? How do you know they wanted her to do something?" Bree had reached from under the blanket and picked up a candle, using it almost as a flashlight.

It reminded Alyssa of her summer camps, in leaky cabins with skittering invisible forest creatures congregating outside, when she and her bunkmates told creepy stories about goat killers and dangerous bad guys with hooks. Now the stories were real, and the dangerous bad guys wore FBI badges.

"Because," Dez said, "Alyssa told us 'Now I have to decide what to do.'"

Alyssa squinted through the candlelight, tried to remember. "I did?"

"Oh. Right. Yeah, you did." Bree nodded. "So what did they propose?"

So there it was, the direct question. Which she didn't have to answer, but she yearned for someone to talk to about it. It would be better, had to be, if she went into her legal consultation at the Fahey Law Firm prepared for what to say. Knowing what her tactics should be. She'd known Mikaela Fahey for years, but under completely different circumstances. Right now, she could barely think rationally, and her mind only recycled the same unknowns, the same fears, the same tortuous doubts about her own best interests. The Fahey Law Firm was well respected, with powerful connections, and Mickey knew her stuff. But still.

"You wanna hear their so-called plan? Fine." Alyssa heard the fatigue in her own voice, the defeat. Kickbacks, victims, tax fraud. FBI, informant, wiretaps. Prison. *Bill.* And now the power was out and she sat in the gloom, as if all the light had been extinguished from her entire life. The sun would rise in a few hours, and the power would come back on, it always did, but she hated the irony right now. She hated everything—her life, and Bill's, and the impossibility of what might happen.

She saw Dez's shadowed face, illuminated, barely, by the fake candlelight.

"What they want?" Alyssa shrugged, drew the blanket closer, swaddling herself for one moment of comfort. "It's the definition of insanity. If I do it, I'm screwed. If I don't, I'm screwed, too."

THURSDAY

TWENTY-FOUR

"Wait. Wait. *She* was the woman who came over that day?" Bree sat at the kitchen island, elbows on the counter, cradling her morning coffee, aiming her questions at Alyssa. "The FBI? The same FBI? That woman who came in here for water? Was FBI."

"Hmm, wonder if the milk survived the night." Alyssa opened the refrigerator, avoiding Bree's questions. She blamed the wine, and the disconcerting power outage, but she'd thought she'd told her and Dez about the visit last night, and this morning she'd alluded to it, and Bree had pounced on the morsel of new information. Alyssa twisted open the top of the milk container, sniffed. Seemed fine. Closed it again. She hated this, probably more than was rational, probably because her mother had always made her do it. *Sniff this milk, Allie,* her mom would say, cajoling. *I might put chocolate in it if you do.*

Once Alyssa—Alice then—had dared to argue. *You do it, Mother,* she'd demanded. *It's gross. Besides, there is no chocolate. There's never chocolate.* She'd been grounded for a week for being "mouthy."

She'd regretted it, though, once she'd realized her mother had probably hated being reminded how sour milk was a metaphor for her own regret and unfortunate choices; for her needy daughter and hardscrabble life and drained bank accounts. To Alyssa, sour milk only meant the power in their comfortable home had gone out, or they'd been at their summer place and left it behind. With a few words, they could get all the milk they wanted.

Turning back to Bree, she twisted the milk container back open. *Sorry, Mom,* she thought. Now Alyssa needed to make a choice about her own life. She poured milk into a white ceramic creamer, put the rest back into the fridge.

She was balancing on the legal thin ice she'd worried about all night. Her lawyer would need to come up with a legal and safe way to extricate her from this, one that didn't require Alyssa to publicly throw Bill under the bus. Which was possibly where he belonged, but with any luck, he'd do it to himself.

"You must have been incredibly upset," Bree was saying. "Why didn't you tell us?"

"Tell you *what,* Bree?" Alyssa answered, putting a smile in her voice. "Can you imagine if I'd prattled on about how the FBI barged into my house looking for evidence that my husband was a criminal? And then say what to you? 'Pass the cheese'?"

Bree winced. "Yeah. I mean, okay." She swiveled her mug back and forth on the sleek countertop. "Thank goodness the power came on. My brain sure didn't. I'd be dead without this caffeine. And don't talk too loudly, okay? My poor head. Apparently, it doesn't matter how good the wine is, if you have too much. You know what I mean. So did you decide anything? About the FBI?"

"I have ibuprofen." She opened the cabinet over the sink. She needed Bree to stop talking about this. She was preoccupied enough already—last night, and the wine, and the power. The confession of her dilemma. And now the relentless morning, with its looming and unavoidable appointment with reality in a high-rise Boston law office three hours from now. "Here. Take as many as you want. And take some to the guest house. Take the whole thing." She slid the pill bottle to Bree, determined to change the subject. "I was wondering. Did Dez ever tell you what happened to Collin Whishaw? I know you were so—rightly—concerned about that. And is Dez still asleep?" She paused. "Upstairs?"

"No idea." Bree shook out three orange pills, slugged them down with her coffee. Went to pour herself more.

Behind them, a little wall-mounted TV monitor flickered the morning news. Alyssa always had it on, for company, with the sound muted, and she'd clicked it on out of habit, when she came downstairs earlier. The weather guy was showing a map of the places still experiencing power outages. Boston, she was disappointed to see, was not among them. Which meant no reprieve from her meeting later this morning with lawyer Mikaela Fahey.

Alyssa's electricity had returned around dawn—the sudden brightness of the overhead lights in her bedroom awakening her. It was naively optimistic that she'd never taken over the middle of the mammoth king-size bed. She'd kept to the left half, as if someday Bill might reclaim his place. Which was ridiculous.

But she'd realized last night, blinking sleeplessly into the gloom and dwarfed by the mattress, that the alarm system might be off. She'd pictured it, staring toward the shadowy ceiling.

Bill stealthily opening the front door. No dog barking. Climbing the front stairs. Opening her door. Would she scream? Gasp? Burst into tears? He'd sent another of his disturbing postcards, this one a bonfire, blazing on a beach, and she'd ripped it up, terrified. Did he mean to threaten her with fire?

Her eyes seemed to adjust, the green glow from her battery-powered bedside clock making that fraction of the room distractingly bright. She'd flapped it down, not only to dim its light, but so she wouldn't be taunted by the reality that time was inexorably moving forward—four in the morning, four thirty, five—and she couldn't get her complicated fantasies to turn off.

Down in the misty limbo of the porch, swaddled in blankets like they were part of some unlikely adult slumber party, she'd told Bree and Dez almost everything Parker had wanted her to do. To catch Bill in the act of pushing his potentially fraudulent tax deduction scheme, the FBI wanted her to help them discover whether Bill would offer an illegal write-off to a new potential charitable donor. A donor she would recruit. A donor who would wear a wire.

Dez had begun asking gentle nuts-and-bolts questions about the procedure and hidden microphones and the investigation—but Alyssa'd had enough.

"No, really. I'm done, you guys," she'd said. "Nothing's going to happen overnight, and my brain is too full to face it. And I'm too woozy to make any decisions. Let's call it a night."

Using one of the ivory battery candles, she'd led Dez—also carrying a candle—upstairs to show him his room. She felt like a heroine in a gothic movie, climbing the darkened stairway with a charming, handsome stranger to the mysterious second-floor chambers. She hoped he was simply a handsome stranger, she thought as they got to the landing. This man had presented her friend with a massive inheritance, and then barely left her side. He didn't seem dangerous. Not physically. And she couldn't throw him out, drunk, to drive on storm-battered streets. So now she'd acquired another house guest, and it was difficult to imagine how he could do any harm tonight. Possibly she was creating a bad movie out of ordinary reality. The power outage had unsettled them all.

She'd shown him the forest-green guest room, but he hadn't gone inside.

"I'll go back down, walk Bree to the guest house," he'd told her. "Thanks again, Alyssa. Me driving in this weather is not the best idea, gotta agree." He'd turned toward the stairs, then back. "Don't worry, okay?" he'd said, the candlelight playing on his face. "We'll figure it out. And you know . . ."

He'd paused, a strange and enigmatic pause, and Alyssa wondered, as the lights from their candles merged to illuminate their shared space on the hallway carpet, what he might be thinking. His cheekbones were sharpened by the flickering light, and she could see the warmth in his eyes. He'd grown on her, she realized. In his not-textbook-attractive way, like a rescue puppy who'd grown into a noble, reliable creature.

She'd heard him blow out a breath.

"Things always look better in the morning. Right?"

"Sure. Good night, then." She'd opened the door to her bedroom. A flash of faraway lightning glowed through the gauzy curtains. "Wait. There are some brand-new T-shirts in one of your dresser drawers, feel free. And Bree knows where everything is downstairs.

Make sure she takes a candle thing to the guest house. And tell her—"

"She'll be fine, Alyssa. We'll be fine." He paused again, that pause. "We'll all be fine."

"See you tomorrow," she said. Alone now, she found the flashlight Bill always kept in his nightstand drawer, and played it around the room. One whole wall was bookshelves, but not even real books, some decorator—Bill's decorator—had shelved them all spines in, so it was only a palette of neutrals. Walls "the color of a mourning dove," the decorator had described them, with accent chairs in chocolate suede. A chocolate-and-white-striped duvet cover with matching pillow shams, and a puffed headboard covered in the accent chocolate suede. Alyssa had pretended to love it, this bedroom of dispassionate, colorless impracticality. Alyssa would have chosen flowers, patterns, vibrant and alive. Loving. But she *adored* it, she told Bill. Because he did. And Bill was always right. Back then, at least.

She heard the last of Dez's footsteps fade away.

Dez and Bree would be alone downstairs, nothing she could do about that. She wondered if they'd both head to the guest house, and then show up in the kitchen one at a time as if they'd slept separately.

Now, with morning sunlight streaming and power restored, Bree's answer about where Dez had slept—"no idea"—made it appear they had not been together overnight. Though that's what any stealthy lover would have done, sneak back upstairs before dawn, muss the bed, and innocently come down for breakfast. Would Alyssa have heard that? Probably not, with her door closed. But maybe. She hadn't heard him come back up, either.

"Alyssa?" Bree's voice snapped her back to the present. "I still can't get over this. The same FBI agent you met with at headquarters was here before. Tuesday. *Pretending* to be from your lawyer's office. You—made that up?"

"What was I supposed to do?" Alyssa poured milk into her own coffee. "Tell you the whole grotesque deal? I feel bad for lying, but you were both essentially strangers, and think of all that had happened that day."

"Yeah, 'it was the FBI' would have been a conversation stopper, for sure. But wait, Alyssa, I'm trying to piece this together. What was she looking for?" Bree leaned forward, focused on her, widened her eyes. "Did she find whatever it was?"

TWENTY-FIVE

Alyssa stirred her coffee for longer than it needed. "There's nothing. To find." She stirred even more, trying to stop herself from sounding peevish. "As I keep saying."

Bree got up and stepped closer to her, cradling an arm across her shoulders. "I'm so sorry, Alyssa. I'm out of line. And I can't possibly understand how this feels. To be taken advantage of—"

"I wasn't!" Alyssa pulled away. "Taken advantage of."

"You were." Bree reached out, sympathetic. "That federal agent came to your house. And accused your husband, and kind of you, when you really face it, of whatever they're talking about. Can I help, at all? What if I could?"

"No." Alyssa took a grateful sip of her coffee. Needed to end the conversation. "There's nothing."

"Nothing what?" Dez's voice entered the kitchen before he did. His hair was wet, Alyssa saw, mussed and finger-combed. He wore his jeans, and one of the black T-shirts they'd kept in the guest room drawers. Maybe she should just give Dez *all* of Bill's clothes, since the T-shirt seemed to fit. Or maybe she should give them to charity. Serve him right, if he expected them to be here when he came back. Expected *her* to be here.

"Hey," Alyssa greeted Dez. "There's coffee. Milk? You sleep okay?"

"Thanks," he said. "When did the power come on? I totally missed it. Black is fine."

"Can I tell him, Lyss?" Bree asked.

"Huh?"

"Alyssa told me that the woman who was here the other day, the one getting water? Was from the FBI. Not from her lawyer's office. And it was the same FBI agent she met with yesterday."

Alyssa, pouring coffee, felt her back stiffen. That was her story to tell, but it would be awkward to be upset, since she'd spilled it to Bree. She understood Bree's fascination with it. Or maybe revulsion. Bree would probably want to leave as soon as she could, and Alyssa couldn't blame her. She'd risk being painted with the same broad brush they'd painted Alyssa herself with. Guilt by association. That kind of paint was permanent.

She handed Dez his mug and a white paper napkin.

He took it, examined the coffee. "Thanks."

"Is it okay?" Alyssa, surprised by his tone, reached out to take it back.

"It's great. I'm just thinking. The FBI? Here?"

"Yeah." Bree nodded.

"While *we* were here. Tuesday. The woman who came into the kitchen."

"Yeah."

The room fell almost silent for a beat, the coffee machine cycling on with a steamy sigh, Bree's spoon stirring, the refrigerator humming again. The picture from the television fluttered distractingly, and Alyssa clicked it off. There could be no good news, nothing that she wanted to hear.

"She was looking for evidence," Bree went on. "Alyssa says."

Dez waved her words away. "Well, none of our business, right? Unless Alyssa wants it to be?"

"Thanks, Dez." Alyssa was grateful for that, at least. Though last night she'd told them more than she should, there were still some lines she hadn't crossed.

Dez blew across the top of his coffee, then set the mug on the napkin. "Speaking of which. Did Bree tell you what we decided last night?"

Alyssa opened her mouth to ask—*Decided?*—then closed it. Looked between the two, perplexed. They didn't have the aura of people who'd slept together, whatever that was, and Alyssa believed she'd be able to tell. These two were behaving like acquaintances, not people with a romantic secret.

"What?" she asked out loud, then paused, surprised at her own demanding tone. "I mean, decided what?"

"Like I was saying a minute ago," Bree said. "How we can help you."

Alyssa felt her chin come up, wary. "Aww. But no. Thank you. I don't need any help."

"Of course you do," Bree said. "And it wasn't my idea, but—"

"Dez," Alyssa interrupted. "I'm serious. No."

"It wasn't my idea, either." Dez tried his coffee, toasted his approval. "It was the FBI's idea. And Bree and I, and you, we can make it work. Bree and I will go to Bill. Wired. The whole deal. Like that agent wanted. See what Bill does."

"No."

"Then you'll be totally off the hook, Alyssa."

"No," Alyssa said. Was she even *on* the hook? What hook? "First of all, it's ludicrous. A terrible plan. Bill would never buy it. He's too smart. Too savvy."

"He left you to take the fall, didn't he?" Dez asked.

"He didn't do anything wrong. There's no fall to take. And it feels completely wicked, luring my husband—"

"*Ex*-husband." Bree jabbed a finger at her.

"Into a trap."

Bree pursed her lips, nodded. "So you'll be nice to him. Thoughtful. Caring and supporting. Like he's being to you? Gotten any postcards recently? I told Dez what you said about those creepy things, Lyss."

"That might be over the top, Bree." Dez put up a palm.

In the silence, Alyssa saw Dez sneak Bree a look. But Alyssa's woman-scorned vibe had to be obvious. Adultery, betrayal, affairs. Because in a divorce that appeared so one-sided, what other explanation would there be?

"Can I ask you, though?" Dez shifted position on his wicker stool. "Why doesn't the FBI use its own people to test your husband? Seriously. It seems preposterous for them to recruit civilians. Risky. Even illegal."

"I wondered about that, too." Alyssa did not want to have this conversation, but these two were not letting it go. "Apparently, this is standard operating procedure. But I suppose there are rules and rules," she finally said. "If you're the federal government."

"And kinda makes sense," Bree said, "in the deeply cynical and arm-twisting way that only the feds can devise. Right, Dez? They want you, Lyss, because you're part of that world, to find someone to pretend they want Bill to handle charitable donations for them. And trap him."

"Yes, but—"

"Can you imagine *that* conversation?" Bree cleared

her throat dramatically. "Hey, Cordelia and Abigail," she said in an affected voice, "guess what about Bill?"

"Exactly," Alyssa said. "And we're done with this topic. No more Bill, no more FBI, no more poor Alyssa. Who wants muffins? Eggs? Bacon? Can't turn down bacon, right?" She paused, wondering why bacon made her sad. Then remembered. "What're your plans for the day?"

"No," Bree interrupted. "Not quite done. Here's the point. I *do* have an inheritance coming. I *do* want to donate some to charity. Right, Dez?"

He nodded. "And I would be there to confirm it. If they wanted to call Roshandra, she would confirm it, too. Bill would believe we were authentic. Because we are."

"*That's* what we figured out last night, Lyss. It's not a risk, because my inheritance is not real money yet. I don't even have it yet. And if I did, the FBI would protect it. It'd be kinda easy. We use the truth to tell lies."

Alyssa jiggled one foot, watching the toe of her black flat swish back and forth across her polished floor. She felt surrounded by betrayal. Bill's, of her. Now the FBI wanted *her* to betray him. Was that justice? Equilibrium? Should she sacrifice her husband to save herself? He'd already sacrificed her, so he deserved it. But it would ruin both of their lives. Though hers felt already ruined.

Bree leaned toward her, moving her coffee out of the way. "We're serious, Alyssa. You've done so much for me. Now it's my turn. Our turn. To help *you*. To change *your* life. You do not deserve to be left alone, and friendless, and—" She hesitated. "Penniless. And it's not a risk."

"It is to Bill," Alyssa said.

"But isn't that the point?" Dez stood, and Alyssa watched him, a silhouette, the sunshine making him a dark outline surrounded by the rain-glistened backyard grass.

"If your husband did something wrong," he said, "do you want to cover it up? If you don't help—" He faced her. "Look. We get intense financial training and legal prep at One Beacon. I understand this world. The transactions. If you don't help, and they get a conviction, that'll look bad for you."

"And what might happen to you then?" Bree asked. "Bill knew, when he did this, that you'd become a target."

"He did not *do* anything."

"That you know of," Bree said. "Or realize you know."

"Exactly," Dez agreed.

"Why do you care about me so much?" Alyssa had to ask.

"Why did you care about *me* so much?" Bree retorted. "I was a stranger in a bar, for god's sake, you could have ignored me. But look. Now I'm sitting with you in your kitchen. And because of you, I'm getting an inheritance. Doesn't it make sense that I'd want to pay you back?"

Dez pulled a stool up next to her. "Look, Alyssa." He moved closer, sitting almost denim knee to denim knee. "Just say no. That you don't want us to do this."

"No."

"But if you say no," he went on, "that doesn't mean the FBI will stop. It means they'll get someone else to—"

"Trap him." Alyssa finished his sentence.

Dez shrugged. "Yup. And if the scheme works, so be it. His bed, he lies in it." He scratched the side of his neck as if trying to organize his thoughts. "But if he *doesn't* fall into the trap, he's free. And you'll be free. And you said they just needed a couple of hours' notice to put it all into action. Right? We can do it quickly. I have to say, saying yes is your only option."

"If Bill is a . . ." Alyssa couldn't get the word *criminal* to come out. "If he took people's money under false pretenses, or pretended to donate it to charity, that's . . . terrible. But I cannot be the one to put him in prison. No matter how much I loathe him."

"Even with how much he hurt you?" Bree whispered. "What about all the families whose finances he might have devastated? People whose lives he might have ruined?"

"But," Dez went on, "if he's not a criminal, this whole thing is over."

"I could tell him," Alyssa said. "Warn him. One phone call."

"Absolutely. Bree and I talked about that last night, too. But once you tell him, boom. You're complicit. You're a conspirator. You're a criminal. There's no coming back."

TWENTY-SIX

"That's quite a story, Alyssa." Mickey sat, leaning back, bracing her arms against her pale wooden desk. A line of frayed yellow leather law books, each title in a red stripe peeling from use, lined the wall-to-wall bookshelf behind her. A chaos of green plants topped a plastic shelf under her window, and the sun glinted on the golden dome of the Massachusetts State House and on the pigeons strutting along the ledge outside the Boston office of the Fahey Law Firm.

"And remind me to be wary of asking you what's new, sister," Mickey went on. "We've had our moments, but I have to say this is—unexpected. Though I'm happy to see you. It's been a while."

"My fault, I know," Alyssa said. It had taken all her courage to call Mikaela Fahey. Eight years ago, they'd been together every day. Mickey and Al, first-year law students. Their whole lives ahead of them.

"It was. But I understand." Mickey shrugged, an indication of affectionate acceptance Alyssa remembered from the old days. "Things change. People's lives grow apart, even if they don't mean them to, especially when their focus changes. We went our separate ways. But again. First. That stinks about Bill. Are you okay, Al? I mean—Alyssa? Hard to get used to that."

Alyssa had confessed everything. Almost everything.

Her baffling but imminent divorce. The postcards. The knife on the kitchen floor, and the disarranged clothing in her closet. Her meeting with Bree in Vermilion, her stray kitten offer of the guest house, the discovery of the ancestry test, Collin Whishaw, and finally, Dez Russo. And then, the FBI. And their request for the trap.

"Yeah, I'm okay." She rattled the ice in her glass of sparkling water, then stabbed the lime wedge with a straw. The Fahey Law Firm was where she'd interned, her one summer in law school, thanks to Mikaela, the newest in the Fahey legal dynasty to become a lawyer. The logo on the firm's website said *Since 1776*. Not true, but no one ever challenged it.

Mickey had been her law school classmate, and while Alyssa dropped out for Bill, Mickey forged ahead to become the successful professional Alyssa once aspired to be. Alyssa had found the latest when she checked Mickey's Facebook page: Lawyer-husband, stepmother to one little girl, puppy, South End town house. Now, seeing her again, Alyssa realized Mickey might be the only friend she had. Not counting Bree and Dez.

Pearls, black suit, manicure, brunette bun. Mickey was hardly the wild-haired karaoke-singing pal she'd hung out with years ago. Alyssa'd changed, too, she had to admit. She'd temp-jobbed through that one law school year, and like other classmates, had been terrified by her soon-to-be crushing student loan debt. But Bill had taken care of that. Was it worth it? She'd asked herself a billion times. Money changes everything—but not necessarily the way one predicts. Was losing it worse than never having it? She was about to find out.

"Maybe I'm not totally okay," she amended her earlier response. "Maybe better to say, 'As well as can be expected.' Which sucks. So I have Burke Slattery, you know him? Slattery and Singh? For the divorce. He's smart, and on my side, and he hates Bill, too. But this insane FBI wrinkle seems like a conflict, and I think I need another lawyer. And I need a friend. I appreciate you fitting me in."

She surveyed the room, the stacks of files teetering on one corner of Mickey's desk, the wheeled leather trial briefcase on the floor. Laptop charging on a side table. "You must be crazy-busy."

"Al, are you kidding me? It's *you*. If we can share first-year law, we can share anything. So, I hear you about Burke. And the potential conflict. And the FBI wants you to get someone to entrap him?"

"Yup." She outlined the fool-Bill offer Bree and Dez had made. How she'd refused.

"Interesting," Mickey said. "Let's think a minute."

She clicked a silver ballpoint pen open, and closed, and open. Just the sound of that—how many nights had Alyssa heard that, studying together in the law library?—made Alyssa feel safer.

A knock on the doorjamb startled them both.

"Mickey?" A young woman, wearing tight braids, a black cardigan buttoned up the back, and a long pleated skirt leaned halfway into the room. "Sorry to interrupt."

"Hey, Odette. You're frowning. Everything okay? This is my intern," she told Alyssa. "Odette."

"The preschool called. Romy tripped on some blocks, and cut her—"

"What?" Mickey stood, her chair rolling backward and hitting the bookshelves behind her.

"Is she okay?" Alyssa said at the same time. Romy must be the daughter. Odette had an accent, Alyssa couldn't place it.

"She's fine," Odette reassured them. "Not truly hurt, but crying. Even after her ballerina Band-Aid, Wusa says. I know you are with a client," she acknowledged Alyssa, "but Romy—"

"Come with me, Al?" Mickey had tucked her pen behind one ear, grabbed her phone and the laptop, and was almost out of the room, gesturing Alyssa to follow. "Or you can wait, maybe ten minutes? It's in this building, top floor. The penthouse preschool. Convenient, at least." And then to Odette, "Tell Wusa two seconds."

Mickey used a key card on the elevator, talking to Alyssa as they waited. "Romy's an awesome kid, she's four, and I know she should learn to regain her own equilibrium, but I can't resist."

The elevator door opened onto a wide, sunlit room, with views across the rooftops of Boston and out to the Charles River. A pod of children stacked blocks in the center, and a scatter of others sprawled on yoga mats with puzzles and books.

"Hold this, okay?" Mickey gave Alyssa her laptop, and stashed her phone in her jacket pocket.

A wiry little girl wearing a pink tutu and one pink ballet slipper raced across the room, and threw her arms around Mickey, burying her face in Mickey's slim skirt. A young woman in jeans and a sleek dark ponytail followed close behind. Mickey stooped to face her daughter.

"How you doing, Romeroo?"

"I fell." The little girl pointed to her knee. "Didn't

I, Wusa? See my ballerina Band-Aid? It's a hurt under there."

"Romy was surprised, I think, when she tripped," Wusa said. "She got a little rug burn."

"Hmmm. You still breathing?" Mickey narrowed her eyes, moved closer. "Let me listen to your heart."

"You're silly! You know I am, MeeKee!" Romy clamped her fists onto her tiny waist. "Of course I'm breathing or I couldn't talk!"

"Okay, then, I pronounce you fully recovered, darling one." Mickey tapped her on the nose with one finger, then touched the Band-Aid. "All ballerina better. I came up so you could meet my friend Al—Alyssa. Alyssa, this is Romy Obeng."

Alyssa held out her hand, and the little girl shook it, her face turning serious. "You're pretty. I'm four."

"Thank you," Alyssa said, and felt tears come to her eyes. "Four is a very nice age. Are you a dancer?"

"Yes!"

"And you're missing a shoe, Romeroo." Mickey pointed to her feet. "Better go find it. And your dad and I will come get you at Romy-time."

"Goodbye!" Romy bounded away on tiptoe, her tutu flouncing.

"That was easy," Alyssa said.

"I hated to bother you, Mickey." Wusa's ponytail swung as she apologized. "She's fine, but—"

"All good. No bother. Life is complicated when you're four. We'll see you later, Wu." Mickey lifted a palm in farewell, then pointed toward the wall of sliding glass doors. "Wait. Okay if we sit on the roof deck? Yes? Okay with you, Al? It's gorgeous out, and the view is amazing."

In a few motions, Mickey had opened her laptop and placed it on top of a latticed wrought iron table, and they sat side by side in the sunshine, looking out over the roofs of the urban aerial landscape; a multicolored patchwork of flat gray asphalt and bulky heat vents, dotted with an occasional sparkle of a sun-kissed skylight or a secret garden with spiky evergreens and manicured shrubs, forbidden barbecue grills in front of voluptuous all-weather couches and rattan chairs.

"Amazing," Alyssa said. She used one hand to shade her eyes, and surveyed from the Charles River to Boston Harbor. She felt small up here, experiencing the world from a different perspective. Maybe her problems were small, too, even solvable. "So peaceful. You should move your office out here."

"Oh, right. In Boston? Even now, the clouds are moving in. But listen, thanks for the Romy detour," Mickey said, tapping at her laptop. She paused. "You and Bill ever think of—?"

"Let's not talk about that, okay?" Seeing Romy, her tear-streaked face and the one ballet slipper, made her aware of another subtraction. Bill had said no to children, and now she was paying for that, and it was all Bill's fault. "Bill is a creature of infinite and toxic destruction. I sometimes wish the FBI *would* nail him."

"Nope. You don't. Okay. Between you and me. Parker? Hattie Parker?" She spelled it. "Is that right?" Mickey tapped on the keyboard after Alyssa nodded. "Told you not to tell Bill."

Alyssa nodded again.

"But you're not saying she told you not to get a

lawyer. That'd be—" She shook her head. "Unacceptable."

"She didn't mention lawyers. Just Bill. Listen, can they ask me to do this? I've never felt this trapped—home alone after Bill, moping around half the time and the other half homicidal; and right when I was getting ready to enter the world again, I pick the one bar where I not only get a martini, I get complications. Lucky for me, you decided to be a defense attorney."

"Huh. That was never in question. Not with *my* father." The lawyer shifted in her metal chair. "Give me a moment." Alyssa saw the light from the screen illuminate Mickey's face.

She'd hated those freckles in law school, Alyssa remembered, and complained no one would ever take her seriously. *Thank the lord for my dad,* she'd said one night, nursing beers at The Local. *No one would dare mess with me.*

You could join me, Mickey had then offered. *If you'd dump that guy—fabulous as he is—we could have our own firm. Dad would send us cases and we'd rock the place. Fight for the little guy. Liberty and justice for all.*

Lovesick Alyssa had dismissed it, unable to imagine anything but a life with Bill. If she'd only said yes to her friend that night, she wouldn't be in this mess now.

If it was a mess.

Mickey was still typing, intent on the screen.

"What're you looking up?"

"Two seconds," she said. "Okay. There is an Embry Lorrance, spelled the way you said, at that bank.

And Desmond Russo at One Beacon. Seems on the up-and-up."

"I know, I checked, too," Alyssa said.

"And that genealogy place seems legit. At least, I looked it up, and there it is. I didn't see a death notice for Collin Whishaw—but no big deal. We can find out why. So, onward. And this proves that sometimes life proceeds via coincidence." She gave a wry smile. "If it didn't, I wouldn't have a job."

"Huh? Oh." Alyssa understood. "Because someone's in the wrong place at the wrong time when a crime happens. Or married to the wrong person." She nodded, acknowledging. "Yeah. But what about Parker? I tried to check her out, but whoever answered the phone at the FBI wasn't about to tell me anything about anything. And I hung up, fast, because I started to worry that she'd know I was checking up." She rolled her eyes. "All I need."

"She's next." Mickey straightened, tapped on her keyboard again. Paused, tilted her head, tapped again. "Okay. There is an Agent Parker," she said. "But—is she *your* agent Parker? I'll get our investigator on it. As for whether the FBI can ask you to get a phony charity donor to entice your husband—well, shit, excuse my language, they're the FBI. They can 'ask' you anything. You know the stuff they've pulled? The bad apples, at least? Pitiful. So I wouldn't put it past them."

"I guess so."

Mickey leaned back, crossed her arms. Behind her, the sky was changing from blue to gray, and the clouds across the sun cast shadows on her face. "But what I'm predicting is that in trying to 'enlist' you, they only want to see what you'll say. Gauge your loyalty. Find out how much you know."

"Nothing!" Alyssa heard the anguish in her own voice. Was there no one, *no one* who'd believe her? This was what they meant about lying down with dogs. Bill was the dog she'd been in bed with. And as a result, there'd never be anyone who'd accept she wasn't part of it. Whatever they thought "it" was. She grabbed her bag and stood, dragging the strap over her shoulder. "Okay, fine, Mickey. I get it. You're a defense attorney. You instantly decide I'm guilty, but you get off on how you can get me out of it."

"No. Al, I—wait—"

"Truly. I'm not one of your criminals who needs to be defended. I'm someone's wife, someone's innocent wife, and if my husband, almost-ex-husband, did something wrong, that's terrifying and hideous. But *I* didn't know about whatever it was. And now . . ." She searched for words. The past however many days of suspicion and walking on emotional eggshells had finally been too much. She felt broken, and utterly lost. "What am I supposed to do?"

Mickey stood then, her metal chair scraping the concrete floor. "Let's go back to my office, okay? We'll get coffee. We'll get water. We won't get bird poop on us."

Inside, Alyssa saw the kids lying on individual purple yoga mats. Nap time.

"I'm a mess." Alyssa collapsed back into her seat. "I apologize."

"No need." Mickey sat. Laced her fingers in her lap. "It's hard. So. Here's a sentence I never imagined saying. I'm your lawyer now, Alyssa. And that means you can say absolutely anything to me. That also means you have to tell me everything. Some lawyers don't want to know the details, plausible deniability. But I do. And it's confidential. The most confidential bond there can be. Every first-year learns that."

Alyssa nodded.

"I know you're upset," Mickey went on. "I know this is disturbing. But we were a good team back then. Friends. We'll handle this just like we handled that psychopath contracts professor. Remember?"

"I wish I had stayed," Alyssa whispered. "What was I, crazy?"

Mickey reached across the little wrought iron table between them and took both of Alyssa's hands. "You were luminous, and ambitious, and brilliant. And absolutely in love. I'd never seen such a thing. That night you brought Bill to The Local—"

"Could you believe he went to that dive?" Alyssa envisioned it, that sweet moment so long ago. "Even ordered those, what were those things? Fried—pickles? And Guinness?"

"He loved you, too. That is my studied legal opinion. But—Al?" Mickey released her hands, and pulled a tissue from her pocket. "Here. It's clean. I'm sorry you have to deal with this. I hope your mascara is waterproof."

"Of course it isn't." Alyssa sniffed, dabbing her cheeks. "This is impossible."

"Nothing is impossible. I promise. One more question—do you have any money of your own? That's just yours?"

"To pay you? Oh. I'll manage, somehow. I promise."

Mickey laughed, the merriment in her green eyes reminding Alyssa of happier times. "You're an idiot," she said. "That's not why I'm asking. I'm thinking that the FBI may suspect Bill has funneled illegal proceeds to you. To try to connect you to whatever scheme they think he's operating. Even make it look like it was your idea. Who knows. I'm just speculating, since we know so little. So—do you? Have a stash of money?"

TWENTY-SEVEN

"Your handbag is buzzing." Mickey pointed to Alyssa's purse. They'd successfully sneaked past the napping preschoolers and returned to Mickey's office.

"What?" Alyssa looked beside her on the pale charcoal carpeting.

"Your phone."

"Yeah. I'm ignoring it." She used to be happy when the phone rang, her heart fluttering that it might be Bill with a new adventure, or an invitation, or someone from the Club with a party idea. Now, except for spam calls, her phone was mostly silent. She paused, reconsidering. She needed a minute to consider what to tell Mickey about the Cataloniana Bank account.

"It might be the FBI," she said. "I shouldn't say where I am, right?"

The buzzing stopped.

"Mickey? How could the FBI make it look like it was *my* idea? I don't even know what they think 'it' is. But you asked about money."

Mickey swiveled in her chair, silent.

"Okay." Alyssa decided. "Money." Mickey would be upset if she found out later, especially after her "tell me everything" speech. And the FBI already knew, so it wasn't as if she was hiding the account from them. "Apparently—" The phone buzzed again.

"Apparently, someone really wants you." Mickey

pointed at the sound. "If it's the FBI, yes, put them on speaker."

Alyssa dug for the phone, and saw the caller ID. For a moment, she didn't comprehend it. Her own phone number. Her landline. At her house. Why would someone be—?

"Hello?" Silence. "Hello?" She tried to picture who might be on the other end. Bree? Dez? He'd gone home to change, and then to his office. *Bill?*

Who? Mickey mouthed the word.

I don't know, Alyssa pantomimed. *No one's answering me.*

"Alyssa?" The voice on the phone came as a whisper. "It's Tammy."

Right. The housekeeper. It was Thursday, so that made sense, but—

"Are you okay, Tammy?" Alyssa's heart raced with worry. Tammy Barker, a fortysomething self-proclaimed cleanaholic, had been there from the beginning of their marriage, and worked for Bill before. Alyssa had often declared she couldn't live without her, but soon she'd have to try. "Is the house okay?"

Silence on the other end.

"Tam? Do I need to call for help? Are you okay? Our housekeeper," Alyssa explained to Mickey. "Calling from the landline at my house."

"What's wrong?" Mickey whispered.

Alyssa tapped the phone to speaker. "Tam. I'm calling 911."

"No, no. Not necessary. I'm fine." Tammy's voice bristled through the speaker. "It's just . . . your husband is here."

The intensity of that surprise brought Alyssa to her feet. Bill. Was in the house. She knew it. She *knew* it. He'd been there before, moving things and changing things and who knew what else, and now he was flat-out flaunting it, and if he had known Tammy was there, or he didn't, it was still the same, still Bill showing off, claiming territory, dismissing her, as if Alyssa was no more than a forgettable interlude. Bill. Always got what he wanted. First it was Alyssa. Then it wasn't. But he couldn't even leave her alone.

"Has Bill seen you?" She tried to keep her voice calm, knew she was failing. But she didn't want to alarm Tammy. "How did he get in?"

"Bill?" Mickey repeated the name, silently, frowning.

Alyssa's mind raced. Bill was in town. Which meant the FBI might know that. Which meant the FBI might be watching him. Were they watching her, too? If they were, they knew she wasn't home. So—that might be good, because it would prove she and Bill were not meeting there. Or it might be bad, because Alyssa had told Parker she didn't know where Bill was.

Mickey picked up a yellow pad.

"Through the front door," Tammy was saying. "I was upstairs, on the landing, and saw him come in. So I ran into the guest room, grabbed the cordless nightstand phone, and hid in the bathroom. And called you. I don't think he saw me, but my cell phone is in the kitchen, so he'd see that. Should I just come out? And act like it's fine?"

Should she? "Hang on, Tam, one second."

Mickey held up the yellow pad. *HE HAVE KEY?* She had written in block letters.

Alyssa nodded. Of course he did. But Tammy had probably turned off the alarm when she arrived. Tammy always came on Thursdays, so if Bill had been watching the house to capitalize on Tammy's arrival, he would have also seen Alyssa leave. Or maybe not.

Mickey was writing again. Held up the pad. *CAMERA?*

No, Alyssa mouthed the word. What the hell was that man doing?

"Tam? Are you there?"

"Of course I'm—"

"I'm trying to decide whether he wants me to know he's there. Or if he's sneaking. Listen, Tam? You're in the guest room bathroom?"

"Yes." A pause. "Has someone been here? The bedspread and towels are all—"

"Oh, right. Yes, yes, I had an overnight guest. There's a friend staying in the guest house, too, she's fine." Oh. No. What if Bree came home? "Red hair, thin, pretty. Let her in, I forgot to tell her you'd be there," Alyssa said, hurriedly. "Her name's Bree, like the cheese, if she shows up."

Mickey rolled her eyes. "Cheese," she muttered.

"Got it," Tammy told her. "So, your husband is downstairs. I hear him in the kitchen, it's right below this room. He's gonna see my—"

"Okay. Right." Alyssa pictured Tammy. She always wore sneakers and jeans and a T-shirt, with a flowered apron tied over her. An apron with big pouchy pockets. "Listen. Can you leave the line open? Put the phone in an apron pocket. I'll be able to hear what you both say. Just go out and act like nothing's wrong. Because nothing really *is* wrong. You're supposed to be there, and he knows you, and you know him. So just be natural. You're cleaning, it's your usual day."

Mickey nodded. Gave a thumbs-up.

"You sure?" Tammy whispered. "I thought I should call you, because . . . I don't know, I was just surprised to see him. Is it even legal if I do that? Let you listen in?"

Mickey waggled a hand back and forth. *Iffy.* Then flipped it, dismissive. *Fine,* she said silently.

"It's okay." Alyssa made her voice sound confident. "It's my house, and it's for my information, nothing else," she lied. Although, depending on how this went, it might be true.

"If you say so. Here I go," Tammy whispered. "Should I maybe flush the toilet? So he knows I'm here?"

Alyssa almost laughed. That might scare the hell out of him. But Bill must know Tammy was there. It was Thursday. Her son always dropped her off at 10:00, picked her up at 4:00. Bill was well aware.

"Sure, flush the toilet," Alyssa said, and Mickey nodded assent. "Good idea."

"I'm putting the phone in my apron pocket. Can you hear me now?"

"I can hear you perfectly," Alyssa said. "And don't worry about it. I'll keep you on speaker, and put myself on mute. So you won't hear anything from this end. Just forget it's there."

"Forget it's there. Sure."

Alyssa heard the water in the toilet swishing, and then a door opening.

Then footsteps. Alyssa could almost see the movie in her mind, Tammy entering the guest room—oh. Had Dez left anything there? Evidence of his stay? It would be obvious that someone had used the bed. If Bill went there to get his damn T-shirts or take something from the closet, he'd be curious. Or judgmental.

But screw him. It was Alyssa's house. For now, at least. She could use it however she wanted. Invite whatever friends she wanted. For now, at least.

Tammy coughed. "I'm at the top of the stairs, going down," she whispered.

"Don't talk to me, remember," Alyssa said out loud, before she remembered she was on mute. Tammy was capable and semi-fearless—Alyssa had seen her pick up a giant beetle and carry it out the door—but she wondered if this would be too much pressure. Eliminating buggy pests was one thing, being trapped between two sides of a warring relationship was another. Alyssa thought about hanging up, to give her an out in case Bill got suspicious. But no. Bill was never going to yank a phone from Tammy's apron. He didn't notice her enough for that.

Alyssa mentally crossed her fingers. And waited.

TWENTY-EIGHT

Alyssa stared at the opaque black rectangle of her cell phone, as if it were about to show the video from inside her house. Mickey had moved closer to her, leaning in to listen to Tammy—and maybe Bill—and they perched side by side against the wide wooden desk. Alyssa recognized Mickey's perfume, grapefruit and lavender, same as she'd worn back in school. The afternoon sun was even more filtered now, gray clouds wisping across it, portending more rain. Three slashes of light sliced through the window and across the law office in front of them, faded, and then disappeared. For a moment, Alyssa worried about what Bill might say to Tammy, and that Mickey would hear it. Too late for that now.

Mickey held up a hand, crossed her fingers. "Here we go," she said, her voice low. "I'm not sure how we could use anything he says, but it will be interesting, nonetheless. And potentially instructive. At least give us some clues."

"Yeah," Alyssa whispered, too, though the phone was still muted.

She heard Tammy walking down the steps; imagined her patting her bulging apron pocket, the unusual heaviness of wearing it, the weighty knowledge that her employer was invisible, on the other end, able to hear every word. The fear that Bill might get suspicious, confront her, catch her. Alyssa regretted that she'd put Tammy at risk.

Or had she? In the silence, Alyssa imagined Tammy and Bill writing notes to each other, as Mickey had with her moments ago. Alyssa would not be able to tell whether Tammy was communicating with Bill in a private way. But she would have to risk it.

Plus, she was being ridiculously paranoid. For the past eight years, Bill had barely glanced at Tammy, not unless he wanted something, had dealt with her the same way he did others he put in her category. Not to their face, of course. Bill was beloved by waitstaff and housekeepers and drivers and gardeners; the ones his family, and then Bill himself, had paid to provide the structural underpinnings of his life. He never noticed the toilet paper roll in the bathroom was always full, or that there were fresh flowers on every table, or that the napkins were always ironed. That's simply how the world worked for him, always had. In private, though, he wasn't such a down-to-earth man of the people.

She'd asked him once, just as an experiment, "How much is a dozen eggs?" Bill had frowned, perplexed. "Why? Do you need some money?" She'd been picking a fight, she had to admit, one of those times, as Bill criticized and complained and the edges of their marriage began to fray, that Alyssa had craved just one moment of power, a single shred of control. But then, as he'd started doing in those perplexing days, he'd waved her off. "Eggs," he'd repeated, as he turned away. "Whatever you need, Alyssa, call someone and tell them."

Alyssa had been brought up differently. Had seen

the world from the other end of affluence. Not that she didn't enjoy comfort, but at least she noticed it.

The silence on the other end of the phone felt charged with energy. Bill was there, in the place they'd shared for their entire married life, and Tammy, who'd been there, too, for much of it, was now on the hunt for him. He'd waited until Alyssa left this morning, she was sure of it. That meant he hadn't wanted to face her.

"Oh, hi, Mr. Macallen." Tammy's voice. Alyssa could tell she was nervous, but no way Bill would notice that.

Bill responded, Alyssa heard the change in the sound, but she couldn't make out what he'd said.

Mickey narrowed her eyes. *Can you understand?*

Alyssa shook her head. *No.* It was unnerving, the way they both felt the need to keep quiet.

"Can I help you?" Tammy's voice was much clearer. Bill must be standing farther away, Alyssa deduced. "Mrs. Macallen is out, and I know she'll be disappointed she missed you. Is there anything you need me to tell her?"

Bold, Alyssa thought. Tammy was initiating a discussion, not waiting to be addressed as she usually did with Bill.

Again, Bill answered, but Alyssa could not decipher it.

"She's got to get closer," Mickey whispered.

Footsteps again. This was beyond frustrating.

"Can I bring you anything?" Tammy was saying. "I'm changing the linens in the guest room," she went on, "you know I don't like it when they sit too long." Another pause. "I'll come upstairs with you, just in case."

Mickey was writing on her pad. *UPSTAIRS?* And drew a frowning face.

Alyssa put up a palm. *Wait.*

A door opened, Alyssa couldn't tell where, and then there was a noise, or a thud.

"I'm fine." Bill's voice came through as distinctly as if he had the phone to his mouth. "You do whatever you need to do."

Alyssa touched her hand to her chest, felt the sleek silk blouse under her fingertips. She recognized that tone in Bill's voice, how he made his demands seem optional.

They must be in Alyssa's bedroom now, *their* bedroom, and she cataloged whether she'd left anything incriminating; a wineglass on her dresser, or the white business card from the FBI. She felt guilty and furious at the same time, guilty because she was secretly eavesdropping on Bill, and furious because he'd invaded her territory. Her territory? Nothing there truly belonged to her, not in reality. She'd been bought and paid for, by Bill, and he had pulled the plug. He clearly felt he didn't need permission to go inside, agreement or not. *It's my damn house,* she imagined Bill saying. She was the house guest, she realized again, if it came to that. Bill could do whatever he wanted. And he did. He always, *always* did.

"Are you looking for anything in particular? We've moved some things."

Tammy was persistent, Alyssa had to admit. Maybe all those years working for her clients had made her into a bit of an investigator. Alyssa had always accepted how much Tammy knew about their lives. Where things were kept—keys, and extra checkbooks, what medications they took, and how many wine bottles were discarded. Where Alyssa had a stash of cash in the second from the left Manolo shoebox on the shelf in her closet. Their emergency phone numbers. Their jewelry. Their passports. How she and Bill blithely left those things in the trust of strangers.

"Damn it," Bill's voice snapped through the phone. It sounded as if a drawer slammed, and then another rolled open. Tammy must have moved closer. Then a door slammed.

"Where the hell," Bill asked, "is my damn suitcase? I need—"

Alyssa strained her ears to hear, but the end of his sentence was obscured by more noises.

"Oh, are you going away?" Tammy was saying. "The big suitcase is in that other closet now. Maybe I can—"

"Tammy, you must have some work you need to be doing?"

Alyssa hadn't predicted how affected she'd be by his voice. How well she knew his inflections, and his agenda. How he'd sugar-coated his instruction that Tammy leave him alone. As if that would go right over Tammy's head.

"Of course, Mr. Macallen," she said, "there's always something to do." Alyssa heard the subservience in her voice. "Just give me a holler if there is anything you need."

"Thank you, Tammy." *Dismissed.*

"Are you going away, though?" Tammy asked. "Maybe to St. Barts?"

Alyssa and Mickey exchanged glances, Mickey nodding her approval.

"Away? St. Barts?"

Another one of Bill's tones she recognized. Annoyance, impatience, surprise.

"Tammy?" Bill's voice had changed again. Got louder. Came closer. "What's going on? You haven't said this many words the entire time you've worked for me."

Shit, Alyssa thought. *Leave, leave, leave.*

"Uh-oh," Mickey whispered.

Alyssa closed her eyes, as fearful as if she were being confronted herself.

"I'm a little surprised to see you," Tammy said. "And since you said *suitcase,* I wondered if maybe you and Mrs. Macallen were—"

A drawer slammed, unmistakably, hard. Alyssa heard Tammy gasp.

"What's this about, Tammy?" Bill asked. "Do you think I'm under the impression that your questions are random? Simply the result of your concern for my well-being? Is this conversation being recorded?"

"Re—?"

"—Corded, Tammy. Recorded." Bill cajoled now, as if talking to a stubborn child. No one could be more persuasive than Bill, Alyssa of all people knew that.

"I'm sorry, Mr. Macallen," Tammy said.

Alyssa crossed her fingers.

"But I'm not sure what you mean," Tammy went on.

"Tell Mrs. Macallen." Bill's voice couldn't have sounded more gracious. "Tell Mrs. Macallen that if she wants to know what I'm doing, or where I am, she can damn well call me. I'm at my office, as usual, every day, as *usual.* You can tell her that my life is as usual, every second of every day, except that she is no longer in it."

Alyssa flinched at the malice in his voice.

Mickey put her hand on Alyssa's arm, comforting her. "It's okay," the lawyer whispered.

"I'm sorry, Mr. Macallen," Tammy said again. "I'll tell her."

"I know you will."

Alyssa heard a sound. And then a thud.

"I'll let you get back to your . . . work," Bill said.

Alyssa heard his voice grow louder, and there were footsteps, as if he were walking closer to Tammy.

"Oh. I don't mean to block the doorway," Tammy said.

"Thank you so much," Bill said, sarcasm in each word. "And one more thing. I'm not sure if Mrs. Macallen has told you?"

"Told me what?"

Alyssa's heart sank. Bill. Bill could be so cruel. She'd heard that tone, so many times. That condescending, privileged, I-have-all-the-power tone. That imbalance that money creates. Tammy had only been doing what Alyssa asked, and now, the woman was a bug on a pin. Had Alyssa herself become as destructive, as manipulative, as Bill? She tried to gauge her own complicity, the indenture of her own sold soul.

"We are grateful for your service, Tammy. But we will not be needing it any longer. You should make arrangements."

"Fun guy," Mickey muttered.

"You have no idea," Alyssa said. "Shhh. Did she answer him?"

But there was no more conversation. Maybe Tammy had nodded, wordlessly indicated her understanding. Typical Bill, picking on someone weaker than he was. Which, if you asked him, was everyone. Alyssa regretted, again, this stupid plan to get information. Still, she hadn't suggested that Tammy push him like she did.

In my office, Bill had said. *As usual.* Which, Alyssa knew, was 8:30 until 3:30.

In the same building as the FBI.

"Tammy?" Bill's voice. "When do you expect to see her next, by the way?"

"I'm not sure," Tammy said. "I'll be in the kitchen if you need me." There was some commotion, some change in the background tension, what must have been Tammy hurrying down the front stairway.

"Tammy?" Bill's voice again.

"Yes?" Tammy called out.

Alyssa pictured him at the top of their curved stairway, light from the double-tall picture window behind him, the voluptuous crystal vases of white peonies Alyssa had arranged on the landing table beside him, the jewel-toned Tabriz-patterned rug under his handmade loafers. She wondered if he'd notice she'd taken their photos down from the gallery wall.

"In fact, why don't you gather your things now." Bill's voice. "And then—let's agree this is your two weeks' notice." He paused, and Alyssa imagined Tammy staring up at him, bewildered and hurt and trapped. Imagined Bill, an entitled tomcat batting around his wounded prey. "Understood?"

"Understood," she said.

A door slammed. Bill was annoyed, Alyssa thought. Having a tantrum.

"Shoot," Tammy whispered, her voice bumping with her motion. "I'm going downstairs, and I'm hanging up. I'm not taking any more chances. He fired me. I hope you could hear. But I—"

Alyssa heard another sound. She looked at the ceiling, imagining. Translating. The doorbell. The front doorbell.

And then the phone disconnected.

TWENTY-NINE

Alyssa stared at the dead phone. "That was the doorbell."

Mickey nodded, then began to pace the law office carpet, jiggling her black pencil between her thumb and forefinger. "You expecting anyone?"

"These days?" She shifted position on the edge of Mickey's desk, watching her lawyer walk back and forth. "Who the heck knows."

"Maybe that Bree you mentioned? Or Dez?" Mickey stopped at the window, rolled her shoulders. "That was pretty tense."

"Tell me about it."

Mickey poked a finger into a ceramic pot of glossy philodendrons. "This needs water. What was all that about St. Barts?"

"Bill will probably see whoever's at the door." Alyssa imagined Bree and Dez. The resulting inquiries. Explanations. Consequences. But she was allowed to have friends. Bill had friends. She could have friends.

"Well, if it was Bree and Dez, so much for their fool-Bill offer." Mickey took a bright red watering can from under a shelf, and tilted the spout into the ivy.

"Right," Alyssa said. "But they're not doing it, anyway."

"I wonder why he was there." Mickey pinched off some browning leaves.

"Good question. He's *supposed* to call in advance,

the lawyers made an agreement. But he wouldn't care." She'd already told Mickey about the disturbing signs of intrusion she'd noticed, *thought* she'd noticed, but if Mickey asked for proof, there wasn't any. "And I'm sure he has a key. Maybe Tammy had turned off the alarm. Maybe he even waited for me to leave and her to arrive."

She pictured him in their bedroom, that not-quite-curly, mostly brown hair, and the crinkles around his eyes. She wondered if he remembered the same things she did. Wondered if he missed her, ever.

Had she partly wanted Bill to come back? At first, of course. Because you get used to things in eight years, even the bad things. The petulant, annoying things. The power things. Some of her life was habit, and comfortable habits were hard to break. But Bill had wrenched them apart, so now she had no choice. *Bill.*

Mickey stashed the watering can, poked the soil again. "Seemed like Bill was trying to send you a message," she said. "All that 'you can tell her' stuff. Again, what about St. Barts? Intriguing, too, that he was paranoid about being recorded. Wow. Tammy must have been petrified."

"I know." Alyssa felt even guiltier. "I hope she's okay. Bill's such a jerk, he can't fire her. And it's so like him, to punch down. Not that Tammy's down," she hurried to add. "But Bill thinks of it that way."

"The patriarchy," Mickey said.

"Tell me about it."

"Not enough time for that, sister. Anyway. Running to the bathroom."

"Sure," Alyssa said. "But should I call Tammy? I want to, but it seems risky. And to answer your question, we have a house in St. Barts. A condo. In Gouverneur." *Even though there's no "we" anymore,* she thought.

"Oh, okay. Huh. You need a passport for that. Be right back."

Alone in the lawyer's office, she stared out the window at the domed statehouse and imagined the Charles River winding in the distance. Maybe Bill was off to Gouverneur. Without her.

She remembered the first time they'd gone to St. Barts, in the drudgy depths of Boston winter, flown first class to Miami and then in a sleek little Embraer jet toward the Caribbean, a twenty-seater, where Bill had purchased every seat. "All for you," he'd said. "Sit anywhere you want. Or everywhere."

Halfway to the St. Maarten's airport, where they'd change for a tinier plane to St. Barts, Bill had instructed the flight attendant to stay in the curtained-off galley, then they'd made love in the emergency exit row. Bill's idea.

"Just leave your coat and Boston stuff on the plane," Bill had told her as the captain announced over the intercom that they'd begun their descent. "Put on your summer things, your St. Barts things."

She'd shimmied into a floaty yellow-lace sundress, slipped her feet into white sandals, and wondered how she'd ever gotten this lucky.

"But our coats?" she asked. "We'll need them when we go back."

"Maybe we'll never go back. Give them to the flight attendant," Bill had said. "I'm sure she can find them a good home."

"Bill!" She remembered being afraid, a gasp of possibility, that maybe Bill was not joking.

"And if we do, we'll get new ones, babe," he'd said. "They're just coats."

At that point, she'd have done anything for him, not just abandon a gorgeous Dolce coat with orange silk lining and a voluptuous hood that made her feel like a movie star. Anything.

The sun had baked her, blasted her, as they finally climbed down the spindly portable stairway to the St. Barts tarmac. A rackety cab ride to Gouverneur, and then the house, stark-white, massive windows, a view of only sand, the turquoise Caribbean, and the shimmering green hills. *Eden,* Bill had named it. And, back then, she'd been so blinded by love, enraptured by luck, that she hadn't registered the irony. Eden, where everything went wrong. And what would happen to Eden now?

Illegal. Victims. Forfeiture.

"What're you seeing?" Mickey was back, joined her at the window.

"Nothing. The world. Just commuters, and happy people, people having lives without the feds breathing down their throats."

"Breathing down their throats?" Mickey looked confused.

"Necks. Whatever the expression is."

She turned her back to the window and leaned against the sill, her feet stretched out in front of her. *Pretty shoes,* she thought, looking at her extravagant suede flats—silly, ridiculous, expensive shoes. Probably would have paid Tammy's salary for a month, if you looked at it that way, and for a moment, tears came to her eyes. She'd forgotten, she really had, what a struggle it had been for her to get where she was. She wondered if a landlord would take her shoes in place of rent.

"Al?" Mickey touched her shoulder. "Where'd you go? I was asking whether you thought Bill was sending you a message. You think he *wants* you to go to his office? He told you exactly when he'd be there." She waved off her own question. "Nah. If he were there every day, the FBI would know."

"That's what I was thinking, too. They have to know. They want me to send someone to see him."

"True." Mickey pulled out her desk chair, tapped at her computer keyboard again. "Their address is still listed as Center Plaza," she said.

"Plus, I need to make sure Tammy gets another job." Alyssa couldn't stop feeling guilty. "I hope she's okay. This is so my fault."

"It is a bit, yeah. You could call her."

"God, no, Bill would freak, if he's still there." Alyssa tossed her phone onto the upholstered chair, as if ridding herself of the option. She had no way of knowing what Bill was doing, or what he was looking for, or taking, or destroying. Or leaving for someone else to find. "I have to wait until she calls me."

When Alyssa's phone rang, they both flinched.

"Answer," Mickey ordered.

"Duh." Alyssa grabbed the phone. Looked at the caller ID. "Unknown," she said out loud. She hit the green button.

"It's me, Bree," the voice said.

"Hi, *Bree.*" She made sure Mickey was listening. "Where are you?"

"In Albemarle Park? I think it's called? On a bench, with Dez, watching the almost-sunset. And smelling the lilacs. I've never seen so many lilacs. Your—cleaning person? She answered the door and told us to leave. You'd told us you had a housekeeper named Tammy, so at least I didn't suspect she was FBI, too."

"You're in the park?" she repeated for Mickey's benefit. "Was Tammy okay?"

"Sure, she seemed fine. Why not?" Bree said. "Where are *you*?"

"Good, glad Tammy's fine," Alyssa repeated. And no reason for Bree to know where she was. "Oh, I'm out. Errands again. Listen, I know that must have been strange. Long story about why Tammy wanted you to leave, but thanks for taking her word for it. Can you stay away a bit longer? I'll call you."

"Oh, sure. Sounds good. Hey. Should we bring back Chinese food? We owe you a dinner, big time. Meanwhile, Dez and I will just sit here. It's peaceful, and smells fabulous. Perfect place to unwind."

Alyssa knew Albemarle Park, a manicured, pristinely green expanse of lawn and lilacs. On a perfect day, the glassy water of Albemarle Pond reflected the lavender blooms, a living watercolor.

Alyssa stared at the floor, remembering. The world was beautiful. But she hadn't noticed beauty, not in a long time. Bill had taken that from her, too. Their marriage, the possibility of their children, their futures, their love. All a . . . a myth. A fraud. A con.

Now she was hemmed in by the trappings of a lawyer's office, the files and books and neutral carpeting, skuzzy seagulls pecking at the mortar in the windowpanes. An old friend, who she'd drifted away from and who she'd now have to hire to save her, faced her in a fancy leather chair, skeptical. No time for lilacs and springtime. *Bill's fault.*

"Lyss? You there?"

"Yes, Chinese food is perfect," Alyssa said. Anything to change the subject. And that meant Bree and Dez were coming for dinner. If there *was* a "Bree and Dez." She still hadn't decoded their relationship. But this was only dinner. "Thanks. I'll call you when I'm home. Your caller ID says *Unknown.* Did you know that?"

"It's a new phone, Dez says I can afford it. But egg rolls it is. We'll go all out. But, Lyss? What long story about Tammy?"

"Too long for the phone," Alyssa said.

"Hang on," Bree said. "Dez wants to talk to you."

"Dez wants to talk?" Alyssa worried her repetitions were becoming obvious. "Look, whatever you want to get for dinner is fine. Use your judgment. Why don't we just—"

"There was a black Mercedes in your driveway," Dez began, without any greeting. "Do you know whose car that is? Is everything okay?"

"It's *fine*!" Alyssa snapped, then she quieted her voice. "It's fine. As I said to Bree, long story."

"But—"

"Got to go," she said.

THIRTY

"Are you sure about those two?" Mickey swiveled in her desk chair, watching Alyssa stash her cell phone into her bag. "Bree and Dez?"

"Sure how?" Alyssa looked longingly toward the law office door. But there was no escape. She and Mickey still needed to decide what to do.

"Yeah, okay." She dropped back into her chair, defeated. "But I've truly deconstructed how this all came about. No one knew I was going to that bar. And no one could've possibly predicted that I would invite Bree home. It's just . . ." She shrugged. Whatever. "I simply don't see how anyone could've planned it. I googled them, like you did. And they were exactly as they said they were."

Mickey stopped swiveling. "I hear you. But then you just *happened* to be right about her ancestry thing?"

"We looked up that site. It showed the brother. We searched addresses like crazy. We found Collin Whishaw, didn't even know if it was the right one. And then Dez was there. I mean, that would be a pretty elaborate web to concoct, and in an impossibly short time. So that's why I have to believe it's true."

"Okay. Say it is. For now. That still leaves us with the separate question of the FBI. My legal advice would be . . ." Mickey clicked her ballpoint again, and again. "If you want to talk to the FBI? Call them, make an appointment, and I'll come with you."

"Should I *tell* them you're coming?"

"You know what? I'm rethinking." Mickey let out a breath. "Let *me* call them. They're manipulative, and devious, and they want what they want. I'm afraid they'll take advantage of how much you don't know about the rules. The law. Sorry, Al." She shrugged. "But that's what I'm here for. To protect you."

"You sure? I mean, you sure you should call?"

"I'm sure. I'll let you know the minute anything happens. So don't worry. Go eat out of paper containers with your new pals. That agent isn't expecting you to make a decision today, is she?"

"No, she didn't say that."

"Okay, then. And I'll call you."

Mickey came out from behind her desk, paused, and then drew Alyssa into a hug. "Not very lawyerly, I know." She pulled back, placing her hands on Alyssa's shoulders. "But you'll be fine. I'll take care of this. You do nothing, Al. Okay?"

"Thanks, MeeKee." Alyssa remembered the little ballerina who'd also needed Mickey's reassurance. "Okay."

But as she closed herself into the elevator and went back to the lobby, she realized that doing nothing might be risky. Because Parker had an agenda, too. And Alyssa had no idea how long the agent would wait before going ahead on her own.

And that could be worse.

• • •

The short walk to the parking lot underneath Boston Common had been reassuringly serene. Alyssa felt the warmth of the milky sun melt away some of her tension, and recalled her Boston history as she walked by the gold-domed statehouse she'd seen through Mickey's window. *Perspective,* she thought again. Everything needed perspective. Simply being outside changed her view, and for a moment, the world did not center around her and her problems. People lived in their own concerns. And had no idea that she existed. Or Bill.

Tourists pointed and clicked, some sporting lobster claw hats and, as always, a few posed under the statehouse's most-Instagrammed spot, a straight-backed soldier on a prancing horse guarding an entrance to the building named after the rider, General Joseph Hooker. The General Hooker entrance, named by someone with no sense of double entendre, had unwittingly created a social media mecca.

Despite her nagging worry, Alyssa had to smile, and that felt good, too.

She passed two coffee shops, but stopped in front of a TV studio, a glass-walled fishbowl showcased to the sidewalk, floor-to-ceiling windows, and a flickering bank of monitors creating a moving mosaic along the back. Inside, a perfectly postured woman on a too-tall stool adjusted the hem of her skirt, and practiced a series of expressions into a chunky camera pointing at her from atop a tall, bulky tripod. If the FBI was right, Bill would be a massive news story. The instant center of attention.

She watched the woman flipping through a spiral notebook. She recognized her, Madeleine Tran. She'd been around awhile, a good reporter, had connections. Madeleine looked up, and caught Alyssa's eye.

Alyssa waved, acting like a fan.

If Bill were charged, Tran would parade him as big-time breaking news, an example of a hotshot financier caught trafficking in greed, trampling on the trusting little guys. Immediately and irretrievably guilty. Alyssa imagined the sneering headlines, and the deliberately ironic photos of Bill in black tie—and her, of course her, no matter what she did or said—both glittering and aspirational and envy-worthy. And, she knew because she'd been there, from envy came suspicion, came doubt, came the certainty that someone so successful must have done something wrong, something unfair, to get where they were.

Which was, sometimes, true. But sometimes the wrong people got hurt.

Like Tammy. Tammy, after two texts and an email, had not called her back. Alyssa needed to get home, whether Bill was still there or not. Had he left a note for her? Or anything?

"Get a life," she muttered.

Her existence was constrained by suburbia and fear now, Alyssa realized. Confined to her house, her car, Dez's company conference room, an FBI cubicle, and her lawyer's office. No wonder she was jumpy. She wasn't even living in the real world.

"No more hiding," Alyssa said out loud. She patted her pockets for the exit ticket, pulled open a heavy metal door to the parking lot, and punched the grimy elevator button labeled Down. The place smelled of exhaust, and dust, and marijuana smoke; out of the sunshine and inside the windowless elevator bay, the air felt gritty and gray.

Twenty-two million dollars, she thought. Mickey hadn't asked the money question again, and Alyssa needed to tell her about the mysterious Cataloniana account. Especially since the FBI already had the documentation.

The atmosphere of the waiting area enveloped her, still and stale and empty. Her life felt like that, too.

Question was: Should she agree to turn her own husband over to the FBI? She could ruin his life—whether he'd already ruined it himself or not. One word from her and he'd be emotionally ravaged, personally damaged, financially ruined. If she truly loathed him, all it would take was her to say yes. And Bill's world would collapse, burying him under the rubble.

Or she could try to protect him. With one phone call, one text, one visit to the office where he'd said he would be, she could tell him everything. He'd even made sure she could know when he'd be there. He could plan, and she could plan, and even—*they* could plan.

Would that be the end of their troubles? If she simply chose his side, and stayed there. Became an ally instead of an adversary. Bottom line, she could save his life. He might be ever so grateful for that. And who knows what he'd do then.

She mentally chewed over that strategy. The FBI had told her their plan to trap him. In exquisite detail, down to her convincing someone to wear a wire. She could pretend to agree, then warn Bill what to watch for. Would they be a team again if she did? She might even be able to clear his name.

All she had to do was give Bree and Dez the okay. As they'd said, it wasn't even their idea, it was the FBI's. And they'd *offered* to approach Bill, she hadn't come close to asking them. The FBI wanted friends, she could give them friends.

She paused, a fraction of a second, drinking in the power. She'd never have felt this way, never, if he hadn't done what he'd done to her. He'd been in her house today. Brazen and officious and audaciously entitled. *Don't poke the bear,* her mother used to say. Bill had poked, and now the bear was awakening.

But Bill, though. Her Bill. Her shoulders sagged with the weight of the question. They had loved each other once, she knew that. Promised things, in the thick of the night and the glow of the morning. Didn't she owe him?

No. He was the one who'd changed everything. And now his future was in her hands. That was a first. An absolute first.

Footsteps behind her. A man. She moved aside, a reflex, though she'd already pushed the elevator button. He was a man, and he'd push the button himself no matter what she said.

But he didn't. He stood, waiting, in jeans and a white polo shirt, navy blazer. Harmless, she quickly assessed, older than she was, graying hair. She nodded, meaninglessly, to prove she was congenial. The man continued to ignore her.

The elevator rattled its arrival. When the doors slid apart, she let the man go first. He entered, but kept the door open for her with his left hand. A slim gold band, an obvious wedding ring, gleamed on his finger. She stepped inside.

The elevator lurched into motion. Alyssa felt the man's eyes on her back.

When the doors opened, she tried not to run. She aimed her key at the car, slid into the front seat, and locked the doors again. Took a breath. Punched on the engine, shifted into reverse, twisted around to look behind her. To the left, nothing.

To the right, half a garage length away, she saw

blinking red-and-white backup lights. But no car pulled out. She quieted her racing heart. A person who had parked in the garage, just as she had, was now leaving the garage, just as she was. Nothing suspicious about that. It would be more suspicious if he *wasn't* leaving.

Her unease was Bill's fault. But his uninvited arrival today, blunt and aggressive and in her face, proved she wasn't paranoid. Bill was teasing her, taunting her, torturing her. Why was he focused on making her fear him? Hate him? His money was one thing, her self-esteem another. It felt as if she couldn't have both, and that wasn't fair. If Bill could have both, she should, too.

She selected the nineties channel on the satellite radio, blasting herself with music as she backed the car out. Tonight was going to be a good night, she sang along, trying to shake her gloom. Bree, and Dez, and Chinese food, and her new life. She'd forget about Mickey, for a bit. She stabbed her exit card into the slot, and the striped arm lifted, allowing her back into the sun. She'd even try to forget about the FBI agent trying to coerce Alyssa onto her side. But what side was that?

Glancing into her rearview mirror, she pulled onto Charles Street. Left onto Beacon. Right onto the curved ramp to Storrow Drive.

The traffic slowed, and Alyssa felt her chest relax as she drove by the pale green branches of the willows on the riverbank, saw solitary joggers puffing along the narrow trails, three poised swans gliding on a cattail-lined lagoon. The outside world was still normal, though Alyssa's was filled with suffocating uncertainty.

The traffic slowed to a standstill. Alyssa saw swirling blue lights ahead, heard the wail of faraway sirens. The music on her radio changed, and the song brought a mist of tears to Alyssa's eyes. The band had played it—some plummy Muzak version—the night she and Bill met. He had come up to her at the charity event, the evening almost over, holding a single white rose. He'd kissed it, and handed it to her.

"Like the song," he'd said. "A kiss from a rose." Then opened his arms to her, and twirled her onto the dance floor, her silver tulle skirt swirling around her ankles. Three nights later, side by side with Bill breathing, spent, beside her, she replayed that moment in her head, as transporting as a classic movie, a moment in time, of surrender, and passion, and a beginning.

And now here she was, stuck on Storrow Drive, and stuck in her life, and forced to choose which way to go at the crossroads.

Someone honked, behind her, and she flinched, wiping her eyes. She carefully accelerated into the space that had opened in front of her, and it was all she could do not to collapse into tears.

This was Bill's fault. Bill's fault.

It was when she steered toward the exit ramp that she saw the car behind her. Saw it copying her fluid motion, easing into the same curve. Saw the face in her rearview. The man in the parking lot.

THIRTY-ONE

No one was following her. They absolutely were not. Alyssa sneaked another glance in the rearview. Was it the same man?

She looked yet again, allowing herself one more time. It was. It was. It was. It might be a coincidence, she tried that for an answer, but instantly dismissed it. And it wasn't that some rando parking lot stranger was following her for nefarious reasons. On TV maybe, but not in real life. There was no one, absolutely no one it could be except someone from the FBI. No one else cared about what she did. Bill? Not Bill.

She felt her face go cold, her mind racing to decide as the cars pinballed around her, changing lanes and jockeying for position at the complicated exit. The steel-gray sedan stayed behind her. She thought about taking the back way home, seeing if he stayed glued to her rear. But why, really, did she care? If someone wanted to find out where she lived, following her was the world's stupidest and most time-consuming way to discover it.

The red light at Mass Avenue forced her to stop. To the left was the guardrail, and a hassled-looking guy wearily toting a hand-lettered cardboard sign saying *NO MONEY FOR FOOD*. She scrambled in the center console for cash, but when she turned to offer it, the man had already walked away.

She could not look behind her again—she knew

Garage Man was there, she could feel it. She remembered his eyes meeting hers in the rearview, and with one more connection, he'd know she'd recognized him.

Parker must have assigned someone to follow her. To see if she led them to Bill? They could have trailed her to Mickey's office, and assumed she'd now have some action plan. *Bill.* All she'd signed up for was to be married to a loving and successful husband, one who'd devoted his life to charity. If Bill was a fraud, that meant her whole marriage was a fraud. And it meant she'd become another of his victims—just like the families who might have been "devastated," or "ruined," as Bree had suggested. Now, because of *him*, she needed to figure out how to survive.

She pressed her lips together, furious. She might be leading them to Bill right now. She'd told Agent Parker she had no idea where Bill was, and at the time, that was completely true. But if Bill was now at the Weston house, Parker would never believe Alyssa hadn't arranged it.

Parker had ordered her not to talk to him. Which she hadn't. But the result? Another stinking pile of quicksand, courtesy of her almost-ex-husband.

"Bill, you complete self-centered jerk," she said out loud.

She felt her expression change, like a cartoon character who gets a brilliant idea. Almost pictured the light bulb illuminate over her head. The best plan—would be simply to go home. If Bill was still there, why not lead this FBI guy right to him? Those people were going to nail him, only a matter of time. Parker had told her they'd gotten "complaints" from "victims." As a result, the feds were taking action. And demanded she choose a side.

When it came to the feds, they considered theirs was the only side. She nodded, agreeing with herself. They wanted cat and mouse? Okay, but she'd be a crafty mouse. A smart mouse. She'd *let* them follow her home. She'd choose a side, all right. Her own.

The song changed on the radio, and she sang along, savoring her good idea. She wanted it her way, too.

If Bill was still at the house, and the FBI nabbed him, she'd be totally off the hook, because she could legitimately say she had no idea they were following her. And Bill couldn't know Tammy had alerted her that he was there. So he couldn't blame her for bringing them.

He could only blame himself, which was pretty perfect. Plus, all of them deserved it. Parker was deviously sneaky for having her tailed. Bill was deviously sneaky for waiting until she wasn't home to have his way with the place.

She pulled into the next intersection. Felt the car behind her do the same thing. She trundled through, inching along. Testing.

He stayed behind her. Which made her laugh, a male driver would never do such a thing unless he were forced to. Most men would honk, impatient and aggravated, as if the world were only about them. She'd seen Bill do it, every time they were in the car. But Garage Man, now certainly FBI Guy, docilely chugged behind her.

She merged onto the Pike, teeming with rush-hour commuters headed west. Unlike every other driver, she kept at the speed limit. FBI Guy did, too.

"You're not very good at this, dude," she said out loud. "If you're trying to be sneaky, you suck."

She'd love to tell him that to his face, but as she

heard her own spoken words, she had to wonder. Were they monitoring her calls, somehow, too? Her car had been in the FBI garage all that time she was upstairs talking to Parker. It would have been FBI 101 to attach some sort of listening device.

"Hope you like nineties music," she said. She turned the radio louder. It made sense that if they were following her, they might be listening to her, too. To find out if she'd report to Bill—or someone—about her meeting with Mickey.

The FBI could do anything. Parker had essentially telegraphed that. That meant using *her* probably wasn't the only strategy.

Parker had told her the FBI was targeting Bill—but Mickey had warned they might be after *her,* too. All the more reason to bug her car. And why should she believe anything Parker said? She wanted Alyssa to do something, so she'd say whatever she thought would be convincing. Even if it wasn't true. Cat and mouse.

The gray highway sped by, a blur of the back sides of buildings, an occasional gas station, and the billboards for marijuana shops and radio stations and furniture. Her escort, as she now thought of him, drove obediently behind her.

If she called the police and gave them his plate number, what would she say? By the time they arrived, he'd be long gone. Plus, she didn't want the police. She wanted to get rid of the police.

But now that she knew about her shadow, and the possible bug in her car, she could make that work for her, too. The feds did what was good for them. She'd do what was good for *her.*

She grabbed her phone from the center console and

popped it into a plastic holder on her dashboard. Eyes on the road, she rummaged for Parker's business card.

Snapping off the radio, she made a dramatic show of dialing, then put the phone on speaker. The trill of the ringing phone echoed through the car.

"Thank you for calling the Boston office of the Federal Bureau of Investigation," a recorded voice said. "If you know your party's extension . . ."

Alyssa poked Parker's three numbers. She was surrounded by rush-hour traffic and determined drivers, the impatient or insane ones darting into different lanes at the slightest opportunity. Her personal escort from Uncle Sam, however, stayed glued to her tail. Three exits until her turnoff. Perfect timing.

She heard Parker's phone ring, miles and intentions away. Two exits to go.

Was FBI Guy cursing her as a typical woman driver? That, for sure, was wrong.

The phone rang again. She noticed her escort's posture change, straighten, focus. Everything she knew about bugging phones or cars she had learned from the movies, but she'd seen somewhere that you could listen via a Bluetooth device if you were close enough. And this guy was resolutely staying close, as close as anyone could be on the highway. She knew he was listening.

The phone kept ringing. Shouldn't the FBI answer the phone? Maybe it was someone ratting out their husband. Ha ha.

Wait. The FBI knew where she lived. They'd sent Parker to visit her. So if this man was following her, either he was FBI and his goal was to listen, or he wasn't FBI. In which case, she had a different problem.

Parker's recorded voice answered. And there was the beep.

"Hello, Agent Parker," she said, keeping it formal. "This is Alyssa Macallen."

She saw the curve of her exit approaching, and knew she had to time this precisely. There was no second-guessing on the turnpike. You turned off, or you didn't. She moved into the exit lane, signaling. Her shadow moved with her.

"I'm on the Mass Pike," she said. "I had an appointment today in town, and—"

She had to stall. The car was still behind her, and her plan relied on split-second judgment.

"Listen," she went on. "I think I'm being followed. I have the license plate. It's a gray car, with a man driving. I can describe him when we talk. I'll call the police if he follows me onto the exit."

The entrance to the ramp was coming close. *Now.* She steered to the right and sped onto the exit.

The gray car kept going west.

He'd heard her. Had to. Didn't want to risk her calling the cops. Which meant he was FBI. Which meant . . . She tilted her head, reconsidering. Her moment of triumph faded as she made the final turn to Weston.

No, it didn't. It only meant *someone* was listening. But who was the someone? And why did they care what she said?

"Thanks," she told the voice mail. "Let me know what to do."

THIRTY-TWO

No black Mercedes was parked in her driveway. Bill was no longer there. No gray sedan, either. She was certain that'd be the last she'd see of that car, at least, though she'd keep an eye out for the driver. The feds investigating Bill was one thing. Following *her* was another. Bugging her car.

Alyssa turned her key in the front door, and no dog barked as it opened. Tammy must have been so upset that she forgot to reset the alarm after Bill left. Although maybe Tammy left first, and Bill had left the place unprotected.

Alyssa realized she'd sniffed as she entered, as if some scent of her husband would remain. But there was only citrusy cleaner, and pungent furniture polish. The nap on the stairway carpeting was vacuumed to smooth perfection. Tammy had not left a note on the entryway table as she sometimes did. Nor had Bill. Alyssa deposited her bag on the bottom stairstep, and out of habit, started for the kitchen. Maybe Tammy had left a note on the counter.

She stopped, halfway down the hall. And ran up the stairs.

In their bedroom—her bedroom—nothing looked different. No notes from Bill taped to the dresser mirror, no card placed on the pillow shams. She'd imagined Bill thumping their large suitcase on the bedspread, but there were no wrinkles on the duvet cover.

Tammy at work, probably, as if she could exorcise Bill's visit. She still hadn't heard from her housekeeper, and she needed to make that right. Tammy shouldn't suffer because Bill was a jerk. Any more than she already had.

The bathroom was untouched, the row of conch shells lined up on the counter, the towels perfectly folded.

She whirled, determined, and yanked open the drawers on Bill's side of the dresser, one by one by one. Empty. Every one of his drawers, empty. Here's where he'd kept his dress shirts, pressed and starched and travel-ready-wrapped with the dry cleaners' thin tissue; this one once had socks, rolled and lined up in color-coordinated rows; this one once full of sleeveless white T-shirts and white underwear. Now there were only the black-and-gold fleur-de-lis drawer liners. Not a speck of Bill remained.

She'd have said it was impossible, she thought as she plopped onto the bed, that Bill could feel more gone than he already did. But now the empty drawers seemed to hold nothing but finality, a fleur-de-lis-lined metaphor that her life would soon be empty as well.

So it was *taking* things, that was his plan. It was a message. Bill could full well buy dozens of replacements for anything. He was saying goodbye to her with every empty drawer. He was erasing himself from her life. As if she needed to be reminded.

She crossed her arms, as if hugging herself. Felt the motion of her breathing. Her life had been a series of decisions, like everyone's was, but she'd tried to improve, be good at what she did, be a better person, be part of something important. Handsome successful

Bill, benevolent generous Bill, had seemed her reward for persevering.

Now she needed to persevere again. And tell Mickey about the bug in the car. Possible bug.

She heard her phone ring and flinched at the sound. Her cell was still in her bag at the bottom of the stairs. Times like this she felt like letting it ring, letting whatever happened simply happen, let other people's decisions carry her along. But she knew, knew completely, that she needed to take action. She needed to empty the drawers of her own life, and move on.

She trotted down the steps, trying to grab the phone before it went to voice mail. She tapped the green circle. Caller ID unknown. "Hello?"

"Is the coast clear?" Bree said. "The moo-shi pork is congealing."

"The coast is nothing but clear," Alyssa told her. "Bring it on."

"Fifteen minutes," Bree said, and hung up.

"Bring it on," Alyssa said again, this time to the blank phone. She narrowed her eyes, deciding. She would not be erased.

• • •

"So what was the long story?" Bree asked. She held a crispy egg roll between two fingers, and dipped it into a pool of orange duck sauce.

They were using Grandmother Macallen's heirloom white china again, which Alyssa thought was only right. Bill could not erase everything, especially not her hold over his future.

Alyssa knew exactly what Bree was asking, but also that answering honestly would be a move she could not undo. The rain had started again, dank and unpleasant, and they had decided to have dinner inside. Even with carry-out, Alyssa decided on full dinner-party mode in the formal dining room, with the antique oval mahogany table, two crystal chandeliers, and waist-high cherrywood paneling topped by upholstered walls; the padded navy paisley fabric woven with gold threads that glinted in the candlelight.

"Impressive, right?" Bill had gone all lord-of-the-manor as the decorator had finished her final touches years ago; leaving three curved white orchid plants, in full bloom, lined on the seventeenth-century walnut sideboard. "Wow," Alyssa had said, not quite sure that "impressive" was what she hoped for in a dining room. Friendly, maybe, cordial, congenial, comfortable. But impressive is what Bill had wanted, and as a result, what they got.

For tonight, Alyssa had placed the white cardboard food containers on silver trays atop a white linen tablecloth, with place mats, and real candles in heavy silver candlesticks. Dez sat across from her, Bree at the head of the table. Places for eleven more guests sat empty, and as she'd struck three matches to light the slim white candles, Alyssa recognized yet again how her past life had been deleted.

"Whew, hot." Alyssa now fanned her mouth with fluttering fingers. "Too much mustard."

Dez was using two chopsticks to guide moo-shi pork from a paper container onto a flat pancake, the brown sauce leaking over the edges and onto his plate. "Crap. I give up. I need a fork. Okay if I grab one from the kitchen, Alyssa? I'll get a beer, too, if you don't mind."

"I'll—" Alyssa stood.

"No, no," Dez said as he stood. "I'll go. Anyone else? No?"

Alyssa pointed a chopstick at Dez's departing back. "So? What's the deal with you two?" she whispered.

"Deal?"

Alyssa couldn't read the look on Bree's face. Embarrassed? She kept her voice low. "You can tell me."

Bree seemed fascinated by the duck sauce on her plate, poking it with one chopstick. "About what?"

"Come on, sister," Alyssa said. "I thought we were friends. You can tell me. Truly, I'll be fine with it."

"With what? And of course you and I are friends. You saved my life. Changed it, too. But about Dez? I'm not sure what you're asking."

"Okay, Miss Cagey. But look. You two are inseparable. And, yes, I know, the world works in mysterious ways. But—since we're friends. Are you okay with him? Trust him?"

"Well . . ." Bree looked toward the kitchen.

"You're about to get a lot of money, Bree. Life-changing money. And I know—"

"How 'money changes everything,'" Bree sang, conducting her words with the chopstick.

"Right. I'm serious. For better and for worse. I know what can happen."

"Anything new on that front? With the FBI?"

"We're talking about Dez now, Bree. I mean—he's cute, and he has that fancy job, but I want you to be careful. You know. Men. You need to make your own decisions. Life can change very quickly. Get out of control." She paused, listening for footsteps. Heard none.

"I'm just saying," she went on, "you're in an extremely vulnerable position. And if you need someone to talk to, I'm here. You're with him all the time, you know. *All* the time. And he knows everything about you. Job, finances, connections. Remember, he and Roshandra Jain had to research you to prove who you were. Now you've allowed Dez into your apartment, and taken him to your job. You even brought him *here.*"

"No, I didn't. He came on his own that night."

"Exactly," Alyssa whispered. "To see *you.*"

Bree's chopstick stopped. The candlelight played across her face. In the silence, Alyssa heard the refrigerator door open.

"I'm okay, Alyssa," Bree said. "I'll be okay. And you will, too. Dez is fine." She paused, swallowed. "If anything, he's interested in *you.* You might want to—"

"What?" Alyssa stifled a laugh. Part of her brain remembered their encounter on the stairway the night the power went out. How the light from the battery candle had changed his face. How he had looked at her. But that was absurd. "He's trolling for soon-to-be divorcées? Doubtful. You're young. And gorgeous. And about to be rich. That's a volatile combination."

"You find everything?" Bree called out. Dez had arrived at the carved archway to the dining room. "I can't believe you were defeated by chopsticks."

Dez held up his fork, triumphant. "No more fighting for my food." He set the beer bottle and glass on his place mat. "I don't know how you two do it. Anyway, we were talking about—"

"The long story about why Alyssa's housekeeper wanted us to leave," Bree finished his sentence.

She was focused on Dez, didn't even look at Alyssa, as if Dez were the only person in the room. As if Alyssa had not just warned her about him.

"Right. She looked—what would you say, Bree? Nervous? Wary? Unhappy?"

"All of the above."

"Exactly." Dez nodded in agreement.

Alyssa took a sip of chilled Chablis. Bill, her darling Bill, had once been her best friend. And he had turned against her, for reasons she could only speculate, each speculation more devastating than the last. Boredom, cheating, lying, stealing, federal crimes, and personal betrayals. And now seemed to be tormenting her for his own sport.

"Is everything okay, Alyssa?" Bree asked. "Why was Tammy so upset?"

So here was the moment. Where she could lie, or tell the truth.

THIRTY-THREE

Bill was here," Alyssa said.

She almost laughed at the silence. The dining room smelled like soy sauce and wine, and one of the waxy white candles on the table had started to flicker and smoke. She pulled it toward her, puffed it out. The wick glowed for an instant, then sent up a final dying wisp.

"Here? In this house? When we were at the door?" Dez propped his fork against the side of this plate. He leaned toward her across the table, looking concerned. "When *we* were at the *door*?"

"You mean today," Bree said. "When your housekeeper told us to go away. He was here. Inside. That's whose car it was."

"Yup."

"Are you okay, Lyss?" Bree asked. "Is everything okay?"

"As okay as things are these days," Alyssa said. "I mean, he didn't steal the silver or slash the sheets, far as I can see. Gone without a trace."

"Did you know he was coming?" Dez asked.

"Of course not."

Silence again. Alyssa saw Bree and Dez exchange glances, as if they thought she'd been lying to them about her situation with Bill. After all, she'd made it clear that he had gone, *was* gone, *stayed* gone, and their relationship was over. So of course they'd be perplexed. But she hadn't lied. She *did* hate him, or some damaged emotion like that, and she'd been baffled and disturbed at his arrival. She obviously hadn't invited him. But again, trying to prove she wasn't "involved" was impossible. She was learning that, over and over, every day. From Agent Parker. From Mickey. And now from Dez and Bree.

"How did you know he was here?" Bree asked.

"*When* did you know, she means," Dez interrupted.

Alyssa needed a plausible explanation, and it couldn't include eavesdropping on a hidden telephone with her lawyer. Though Bree and Dez might think it was funny, she still felt hesitant.

"I was on the phone with Tammy." That seemed reasonable, a woman talking to her housekeeper. "And Bill showed up, and she said so, of course, and then, you know, we hung up."

"Did you talk to him?"

"Oh god," Alyssa said. "I want nothing more to do with him, not ever."

"Does he have a key? Isn't he supposed to call before he comes over?"

"Bill doesn't care about 'supposed to,'" she said. "And a key? Bill has anything he wants." Still, she thought, if Bill could sneak in, why make such a display of it, arriving when Tammy was there? Alyssa had gone through the drawers in the guest room, and the secret compartment in the closet. Nothing was added or missing or disarranged. The study looked untouched, nothing out of place. He'd come to get shirts and underwear? That made no sense, but nothing else did, either.

"I suppose Tammy let him in," she went on. "Anyway,

he's gone. He's out of my life and I hope he'll never be in yours."

"You sure he didn't take anything?" Dez twisted his beer glass. "Or—leave anything? Did you check?"

"Did *Tammy* know why he came?" Bree persisted. "Did she ask?"

"Hey. You guys." Alyssa reached for the nearest white carton, didn't care what was inside. "I agree it's strange, and I appreciate your concern, but I can tell you the answer to all your questions at the same time. I have no idea."

"Where is he now?"

"Men, right?" Bree pointed a chopstick at Dez. "She said she didn't know, Dez."

"Did you tell that FBI agent?" Dez went on. "That he was here?"

"Why would I do that?" Alyssa thought about the bug in her car. Possible bug. "Do you think I should have?"

"Dez, chill. Let the woman have some peace."

"Look," Dez said. "I'm concerned about you, Alyssa. Because Bree and I are still thinking that—"

Alyssa saw Bree look at him, inquiring. Dez put up a palm, took a pull from his beer.

"How about you two?" Alyssa poked at her now-tepid dry-fried green beans as if she hadn't noticed their mimed duet. They'd spent hours alone together today. She wondered what they'd discussed when she wasn't there. "How about we talk about *you* for a while? Any news? Anything about Collin Whishaw?"

As always, she felt a little guilty, watching their uncomfortable reactions to her go-to subject changer. They never wanted to talk about him, and she understood that. Bree especially seemed upset when his name came into the conversation, and she regretted her own heavy-handed use of it to detour the discussion, but she did not want to talk any more about Bill or the FBI.

"Bree, go ahead," Dez was saying. "You—"

"No, it's fine," Bree interrupted. "You're the one with the inside track. It's upsetting to me, and you know that."

"There's nothing more about Collin Whishaw." Dez looked at Bree as he talked. "The office has been assured it's nothing sinister. Natural causes. Arrangements in the works, and we'll handle it. You know I'm sorry, Bree."

"Thanks," she said.

She looked so pitiful, Alyssa thought, and felt even worse about her subject-matter strong-arming. "I'm sorry, too," she said. "Truly."

"It's okay," Bree said. "But Lyss?"

"Yeah?"

"Um. We really want to help you. That's why Dez and I were together today, Alyssa. Talking about your situation. Right, Dez? And we kind of—"

"Insist." Dez finished her sentence.

"Exactly." Bree nodded.

Alyssa blinked, confused. "Insist what? Help me what?"

"Look. The feds are after your husband," Dez said. "No question about that. And they'll get him, no question about that, either. They have all the force and power of the U.S. government. The only question is whether you'll go down with him."

Alyssa bit her bottom lip, imagining.

"You keep saying you have no idea where he is these days," Dez went on. "Did your housekeeper Tammy get any idea about that, though? You said *you* didn't talk to him, but did she? Did he say anything to *her*?"

"Well," Alyssa began.

"Ah," Bree said. "And?"

Alyssa propped her chin on her hands, talked through her fingers. "She said he mentioned being at his office. That he was working at his office. As usual."

"Good." Dez nodded. "Does that make sense to you? Is there any reason he wouldn't be there?"

Alyssa shrugged. "It's where he works." She picked up two food containers, held them up, offering. "Anyone?"

Bree waved her off with a chopstick. "Like I said. We insist."

Alyssa knew it. Bree *had* been keeping a secret. "Insist what?"

"We do what your FBI agent wants," she said. "We have to do it. We *have* to. We know you told us no, but it's the only way. It's not dangerous. We'll use our real names. We'll say I came into some money. I want to donate a bunch to charity. All true. Dez will be my financial adviser. Also true. Sort of. And maybe he'd heard of Bill, right?"

"Everyone has heard of Bill," Alyssa had to admit. "But listen, no. Still no. You two are amateurs, forgive me, and you can push this big plan after a couple of beers and a bottle of wine and some good intentions, but can you imagine this as a movie? The entire audience would be screaming at you. And at me." Alyssa contorted her voice into a strangled cry. "*It's a trap!*" She shrugged, became herself again. "So thanks, you two are generous and crazy, but not a chance."

"See?" Bree said. "I told you she still wouldn't buy it."

"You think it's a trap?" Dez narrowed his eyes at her, leaned toward her. "You know what? I think you're right."

"You do?" Alyssa drew out the word. "So why—"

"The FBI is setting a trap for *you,* Alyssa." Dez sat up straighter, pointed at her. "Listen. They want to see if you'll *agree.* If you agree, then they'll see if you call Bill and warn him. If you don't call, that puts you in the clear."

"What?"

"Like Dez says, think about it, Lyss. For one second. I thought he was wacked at first, too, but now I get it. Because the *only* reason you'd agree is if you really have no idea if Bill's doing anything illegal." Bree nodded as if replaying a conversation. "Got to admit he has a point. Saying yes is the only way to protect yourself. Do you trust anyone else but us to do it?"

Alyssa pressed her lips together, watching the two of them watch her.

Dez drained his beer. Put the glass back on the table, the last foamy remnant sliding down the inside. "The minute you tell them yes, this will all go away."

"You mean—they'll call it off?" *This will all go away* was a concept Alyssa could barely imagine.

"Oh, they'll still go the whole nine yards. They won't want you suspecting it's a trap. And who knows, maybe your husband will fall into it."

"Bonus," Bree said.

"But. If you don't agree to it, they'll simply try some other way to get him. Here's my final point. You're either a target in this, Alyssa, or an innocent means to an end. Trust me, I know this stuff. The FBI has you in their sights. They are experts. This is their life. There's no way out."

Alyssa stared at the brown sauce streaking her white plate. She'd be putting her own husband—her lying, deceiving, sneaky, user of a husband—into the hands of the FBI. But if she didn't, she be putting herself in jeopardy. Maybe Dez was right. Maybe this was the only way to prove to the feds that she was not involved in whatever Bill was—might be—doing.

She covered her face with both palms, wishing she could disappear. Someone clattered their silverware against a china plate. Bree put a comforting hand on Alyssa's shoulder, then took it off as Alyssa turned to her, a question in her eyes.

"So here's what we need now." Dez's words came slowly, carefully. "You call Hadley Parker, and—"

"Hattie," Alyssa corrected him, almost a whisper. "Hattie Parker."

"Right. You call her tonight—"

"Tomorrow is fine," Bree gently interrupted. "It's almost ten now."

"Tomorrow, then. And tell her you have the people she asked for. And tomorrow we'll see what your Bill has to say about Bree's pile of newfound money."

"He's not my Bill," Alyssa said.

THIRTY-FOUR

They'd ended dinner by cracking open their fortune cookies, crispy remnants scattering on the tablecloth as the three removed their tiny strips of printed paper. Alyssa's had promised "All obstacles are illusions," and Bree's read "All the world is a stage."

Dez had frowned, shaking his head. "Mine says 'Never give up.' These aren't fortunes," he complained.

"Sure they are," Alyssa had insisted. To her, at least, they foretold the future.

Tomorrow, they'd decided, they'd offer themselves to the FBI. Tomorrow, Bree and Dez would pay a visit to Bill Macallen. It felt as if maybe, finally Alyssa had some power. *All obstacles are illusions.* She hoped that was true.

This was Bill's mess. And his carelessness had brought her to the brink of personal and financial disaster. Until that FBI agent arrived, she'd tried, dredging her imagination and her memory, but failed to come up with a reason for Bill to have so abruptly dumped her. Now she could only think he'd been hiding something. Something so devastating that he couldn't even discuss it with her. Something so criminal that he'd decided he was better off without her. How many trusting clients had he ripped off? *If* he had. She could either sit back and passively wait for her own similar destruction, or try to take control.

After hugging each of them, awkwardly, Dez had gone home. Alyssa couldn't see the look on his face as he'd hugged Bree, but their bodies had stayed far apart, like brother and sister.

"Wonder if his company offers such personal services to all their clients," Alyssa teased as the door closed behind him.

"Ha ha." Bree brushed a sprinkle of fortune cookie crumbs from the front of her black sweater, and pointed one foot in front of her. "I left my shoes under the table. I thought I felt short. But let's clear the dishes, and then I'm fried. I'll need some sleep if tomorrow happens. I'm kind of excited, tell you the truth. I always wanted to be the good guy."

Alyssa stopped, stood under the foyer chandelier. "Bree?"

Bree paused, mid-stride to the dining room, and pivoted to face her.

"What?" She scratched her forehead. "Come on. It's late. Let's do this, then crash. 'Kay?" She started toward the kitchen.

Alyssa didn't follow her. "Is he pressuring you?"

"Who?"

"Dez."

"Dez? To what?"

"To do this thing with the FBI."

Bree put up two palms. "Where's this coming from?"

"Because it's ridiculous."

"It's reality," Bree said. "I know it must be hard, Lyss. And that's why it's so lucky we met."

"Lucky," Alyssa repeated. Luck? She'd been told by Parker that the FBI suspected her husband was a criminal. Now, at least, she had someone to talk to about it. Which was lucky, she supposed; otherwise, she'd be going out of her mind instead of eating egg rolls and drinking Chablis. So, fine. Lucky. "Okay. But let me ask. What does Dez get out of this?"

"Dez?" Bree narrowed her eyes. "Is this you talking, or is it the wine? You want to discuss it in the morning instead?"

"I just—" Alyssa needed to set the alarm system, started to key in the numbers.

"Look, Alyssa." Bree came closer. "It must be difficult, I can't even imagine, having your husband deceive you. Having the FBI show up at your door. Accusing him. And it's awful that you have to deal with this. But did you two *never* talk about . . . anything like this? I mean, you were married, and—it seems surprising. How could you not discuss things?"

Alyssa turned to face Bree. "I told you." She sighed. "We talked, sure. But he was pretty—private. I never pushed him, he pulled away when I tried, so I stopped trying. But *I'm* asking about Dez. What's he telling you, to convince you to do this?"

Bree's expression hardened. "If you, for one moment, think I'm the kind of person who would be, I don't know, manipulated by some *guy*—"

"You ran from that stalker person, 'boyfriend,' if I remember correctly." Alyssa heard the bitterness in her voice, and maybe Bree was right, maybe it was the wine. "And you never told him to stop."

"Oh, but I did." Bree raised a forefinger, making a point. "Yesterday, while Dez and I were in the park, I called Frankie, and confronted him. I told him to leave me the hell alone. He hasn't called me since. And I have you to thank for it. You gave me courage."

"Good." Alyssa hit the last button, triggering the alarm. It began its final cycle, pinpoint pings counting down before it fully activated. If she had helped Bree once, maybe she could help again.

"But now you have to tell me about Dez," Alyssa said. "Because he was *also* calling you. And because you two *do* talk."

"What about Dez?" The warning pings of the alarm punctuated Bree's words. "We'll have to turn that off for me to go out back."

"He's—" Alyssa yearned to say *I'm worried for you. He's manipulating you. He's conning you. He's after your money.* But how could she? Alyssa's world was completely upside down, so she might be unfairly suspecting menace and duplicity in every relationship.

The pings ended. No one could come in now without the shriek of the alarm. And the dog barking.

"Look. Alyssa." Bree put her palms together as if in prayer. "No one tells me what to do. You taught me that. Not Frankie, not Dez. Not anyone. Give me some credit."

"Credit?"

"I make my own decisions. Just like you do. And I can help you. Please. *Please.* Please let me do this. Let us do this. Please let this be. I owe you. Let's just clear the table, okay? The place is going to smell like soy sauce if we don't."

"You can still call it off," Alyssa said.

"I'm well aware," Bree told her, walking toward the dining room.

With the last of the leftovers wrapped, Alyssa had tapped the code to silence the alarm and flipped on the backyard lights so Bree could see her way to the guest house.

"Sorry for freaking out a little," Alyssa said.

"Who wouldn't?"

"Well," Alyssa began, "I suppose—"

"And I'll leave tomorrow. I mean, I know it's past midnight. But after everything," Bree said, the open door behind her letting in the peaceful May night.

It was too early in the season for a full symphony of crickets, but somewhere a bird hooted, and another responded.

"You don't have to leave. Stay as long as you like."

"I can't." Bree took a step toward the threshold. "You've already done too much. And, Alyssa?"

"Hmm?"

"We're trying to help you. Dez is—okay. I'd let you know if he wasn't. Deal?"

"I hope you *would* know, is all I'm saying."

"Deal?"

"Deal."

Alyssa watched her walk away, down the bluestone path, in and out of the bright white spotlights illuminating her. Once under the glow of the lantern light at the door of the guest house, Bree turned, and waved good night.

THIRTY-FIVE

Once Bree was safely inside the guest house, Alyssa had re-set the alarm, taken a glass of Chablis up to her room, snuggled under the comforter, and plugged in her cell phone. She needed to call Mickey. Tell her about the plan.

Whether it was a good idea, Alyssa still wasn't sure. But she needed to protect herself, that *was* sure. And it did seem, as Bree and Dez had emphasized at dinner, it might be a pathway for Alyssa's new life. And, as they also kept saying, it had been the FBI's idea. Parker had told her they only needed a few hours' notice. So how could *she* get in trouble about it?

Famous last words, she knew. And she worried there was some pitfall, some trap. For *her.* But whatever she told Mickey was confidential, and even if her lawyer objected, they could work it out.

And definitely Mickey should talk to the FBI first. Alyssa and Bree and Dez could not simply bop into the FBI's office on their own, like characters in *Scooby-Doo.* She knew, from their many late nights in law school, that Mickey was a night owl.

She picked up her phone, deciding what to say.

She put down the phone. Took a sip of wine. Examined her deepest true beliefs. If Bill had cheated people somehow, cheated *charities,* he deserved to be caught and punished. Even if she was harmed by it, too. Bill might lose every cent of his money—and hers—to penalties and fines and forfeiture. No matter what, she'd be guilty by association, by proximity, by speculation and gossip. Guilt by outrage.

Guilt by marriage.

But as Parker had explained, she could still choose the good-guy side. She might be pitied, or reviled, or ignored, but she'd be free, at least, and able to move on.

Her cell phone glowed on the comforter beside her. The minute she called Mickey, her life would be set on an unchangeable path. The stillness of the bedroom surrounded her—the opulence, the sophistication, the luxury. The closed white doors of the expansive closet, her mirrored dressing room, the glittering bottles of perfume lining her makeup table. The scented white towels and ribbon-tied stacks of Egyptian cotton sheets. If she lost all this, at least she would have herself.

Mickey answered before the end of the first ring.

"I was about to call you," Mickey said. "But then I worried it was too late."

"Never. If you have news, I need to hear it. No matter when. So you go first. What's up?"

"I called Agent Parker. Hattie Parker."

"You did? And what—"

"She hasn't called back yet. But I'm wondering. Did she ever talk to you about compensation? Did she say that word? Or anything like that?"

"Hmm. Let me think a minute." Alyssa leaned back into her pillows, looked at the swirls in the eggshell-white ceiling, trying to mentally replay that conversation. Hattie Parker had been almost sympathetic in her bare-bones office, an institutional room with weary-looking plants and a battered wooden desk.

"I know this is difficult." Parker had pulled her

chair up next to Alyssa as if they were friends, confiding in each other. "I know you're upset. But forget who I am for a minute, okay? Listen. I know men can be . . . difficult. And women, don't say I told you this, are always the victims."

"Victims?" Alyssa had said.

"Your husband took people's savings, their pensions. Money they thought they were investing in real charities. He also showed them how to take tax deductions. Illegal deductions. You don't need all the details, Mrs. Macallen. But it's devastating. Those people lost everything. Regular, real, hardworking people who trusted him. Are ruined."

"Bill? Did that?"

"I could get in trouble for telling you. But he conned you, too, didn't he?" Parker had sounded almost reluctant. "We know there's no prenup. We know he's ordered his divorce lawyers to be relentless." She'd sighed. "Let me just ask you, Mrs. Macallen. What is a con artist but a person who lies to get what he wants?"

Alyssa had stared at her, that stranger, the straitlaced federal agent who had made her understand a new reality. Alyssa had bought into it, the comfortable life that emotional con artist Bill had sold her. Bought into it because it provided exactly what she needed and longed for—someone who loved her, and made her feel safe. But it was all to get what *he* needed. Until he didn't. And then he erased her.

"Mrs. Macallen?" Parker had whispered. "Please don't cry. The agency cannot protect your feelings. But it *can* protect the law. And that's why you're the only person who can help us. It's your turn to have the power. And we can make it worth your while."

"Mickey? Maybe." Alyssa now repeated what Parker had told her.

"'Worth your while,'" Mickey said. "Yup. She's offering to pay you."

Alyssa pulled her knees up to her chest. "For what?"

"Long story short, the feds can pay cooperating witnesses, or whistleblowers, or simply people with knowledge of a potential crime who agree to assist them in the conviction of a suspect. Like a reward."

"So—"

"So if as a result of your help, and it's a big if, *if* Bill were convicted of fraud, and ordered to forfeit his ill-gotten gains and pay restitution to his victims, then you might be eligible for a payment."

"No." Alyssa shook her head, even though Mickey couldn't see her. "Impossible. If Bill cheated people, I couldn't—I mean, those victims should get every penny back. Paying me from that money? Forget it."

"Listen, no," Mickey said. "It's money from the feds. They have a budget for it. It's as if they're hiring you, as an investigator. It's separate."

"It still feels wrong." Alyssa drained the last of her wine.

"I'm just telling you. Compensation."

"Well, *I'm* telling *you*. No."

Silence on the other end.

"Just so you know, it appears to be on the table," Mickey finally said. "I'll check with Parker. I'm your lawyer, that's my job. But you called me. About what?"

"Three things." In quick bullet points, she told her about the Cataloniana Bank account, and the possibility that the FBI had bugged her car. And then the new offer from Dez and Bree to approach Bill.

Mickey had listened, silent. "I'll ask Parker about

the bug. Could be, and they may have turned it off now. But that money—the money's not yours? You know nothing about it?"

"Nothing," Alyssa said. "But Agent Parker has paperwork."

She heard Mickey draw in a breath. "Okay. Let me think about that. As for your friends . . . Let me know if you want me to make the call. But tomorrow, first confirm Bree and Dez are serious. If they think better of it in the light of day, that's fine. You tried. All good. You'd get the good-guy points. And the . . . compensation."

"No," Alyssa said. "No money. That's what's poisoned this whole thing."

FRIDAY

THIRTY-SIX

Ready in one minute!" Bree called from the dressing room.

Alyssa sat, waiting, on the edge of her bed. By shopping in her own closet, Alyssa had selected what she knew was the perfect fool-Bill outfit for Bree. Soon the plan would be in motion. *For better or for worse,* she thought.

"Alyssa?" Bree now stood in the doorway of Alyssa's dressing room, the mirrors behind her duplicating the image over and over. "So? Do I look rich and charitable?"

She twirled, slowly, giving Alyssa the full picture. Simple black Prada sheath, two strands of South Sea pearls, the ultraconservative Ferragamo pumps Alyssa had found in the back of the top shelf of her closet. Clip-on gold earrings, and a touch of coral lipstick. Bree's new haircut was still in place, but off-handedly casual.

"You think your husband will recognize the pearls?" Bree touched her fingertips to the princess-length necklace, luminous against her black dress. "Or the dress? That's what worries me."

"He'll have no idea," Alyssa said. "I bought those pearls myself, in Hong Kong. I'm not sure I ever wore them. And to Bill, a black dress is a black dress. He'll only see your money."

Alyssa felt sad, suddenly, but tried to hide that.

"You look just right," she said. *Right for what?* went through her mind. Seeing dressed-up Bree proved this was not a game, not a moment of vengeful make-believe, or woman-scorned, divorce-induced anger. This was action. This was battle. This was Alyssa deciding to allow the FBI to trap her husband. And confirm he was a criminal.

Ever since Parker outlined what Bill might be doing, her entire sense of herself, of him, of their marriage, of their lives, had collapsed. She had relied on the marriage, grounded herself in it, given herself to it, trusted it. If she had to let it go, release every single thing she'd believed over the last eight years—was she capable of that? She'd have to be. She'd find a way to be.

"Why are you doing this, Bree?" Alyssa asked.

She surprised herself with her own question, but there it was. Her own actions, those she could understand. A mix of being hurt, and damaged, and used, and abandoned, combined with her honest revulsion at the idea that her revered husband might be pretending to be generous and benevolent, when in reality he was only helping himself. That he had cheated people, and accepted credit and adulation for doing it. And all without her knowledge. He had lied to her, too, that meant, throughout their marriage. Or for however long he'd been doing whatever he'd been doing. She could imagine his excuse, *I was only trying to protect you.*

Which was a lie. His arrogance had led to disaster, and he had left her to face the consequences.

But Bree. Why would *she* get involved?

Bree stopped posing, her smile vanished. "Why am I—what's wrong, Lyss?"

"I'm still thinking there's no need for you to do this."

Bree put her hands on her hips, narrowed her eyes. "Look. I'm thirty-two years old. Have I ever done *anything* brave or good? Have I ever done anything but max out my credit card, slog through a menial job fighting off a hideous boss, and go home at night to ramen and bad TV? My one boyfriend, *one,* turned out to be an asshole who thinks threats are the same as conversation. Then, tail between my legs, at my lowest point of all the lows, I meet you, and my life completely changes."

"It would have changed, no matter what. Dez would have found you, sooner or later."

"Maybe, but that's not what happened. You helped me, I help you. That's the world, Alyssa. Like I told you, I quit my stupid job at the bank. Because of you. I jettisoned Frankie. Because of you. I'm free. Because of you. Don't you think that's enough reason to—I don't know. 'Pay you back' doesn't seem like the right phrase, but I *will* pay you back, and now, it's my turn to be a good guy. Don't you think Dez and I discussed it? That's why we've been together so much, don't you see? And hey, what could go wrong?"

Alyssa raised her eyebrows. "You're really asking that? This is all verging on—" *Crazy? Ridiculous?* She couldn't even decide on a word. And everyone, even Mickey, seemed to be dealing with the trap as if it were an everyday occurrence. Who knew, Alyssa thought, maybe it was.

"The FBI will keep us safe," Bree went on. "I have a chance to do a good thing, Lyss, finally. For once in my life. And it's all because of you."

The doorbell rang. The dog started barking.

"Dez must be here," Alyssa said.

"Game on," Bree said.

"No." Alyssa stood, smoothed down her black pants. "It's not a game. And that's exactly what I'm afraid of."

THIRTY-SEVEN

I had to get away from there," Alyssa said, digging into her bag for the keys to the Osterville cottage. The gray shingles and white trim of their sprawling Cape Cod home seemed impeccable, One Ocean Place untouched by the winter's battering storms and the relentless spring rains. "I keep thinking about it. How can they just cancel? After all that?"

Alyssa had tried to decide whether it was a good thing that Hattie Parker had shut down the undercover operation—because, since she hadn't yet mentioned Dez and Bree's offer, it meant she hadn't conspired to betray her husband. Or a bad thing, because she'd lost her leverage with the FBI. Frustratingly, it didn't matter what she thought. She was vulnerable, no matter what happened. "I still can't believe it. Can you?"

"Kinda." Bree followed her up the weathered wood front steps, Dez close behind her. "I have to say, I'm a little bummed, because it would have been—" She paused. "Are you meeting her again? And whoa, no more FBI sting. That means you're off the hook."

"And your Bill is, too," Dez added.

"You think? And he's not my Bill." Alyssa fumbled deep into her tote bag. "And no, she didn't talk about meeting again. Maybe it *is* over. Where the hell is the key?"

The federal-blue front door in front of them was

flanked by white ceramic pots overflowing with white pansies, and a wreath of antiqued hydrangea encircled the brass lion's-head doorknocker. Alyssa had navigated the two hours of surprisingly light Friday afternoon traffic to the Cape—she'd left the Volvo behind, in case there was a bug, and taken her black SUV—and they'd arrived just before sunset. Now the pinking sky to their south promised a beautiful Saturday morning to come.

Dez had arrived at the Weston house soon after the mortified Parker had almost run for the exit, pleading "top brass" and "meetings" and "strategy sessions."

Alyssa, too, had wanted to escape, and the Cape was her peaceful place. But it seemed rude not to invite Bree, and if she invited Bree, she was obligated to invite Dez. Who somehow had become part of their lives. But Bree had latched onto him, and he was relentlessly attentive to her. For better or worse. The power balance felt off, although maybe Alyssa was making too much of it. She'd expected them to decline, maybe go off somewhere alone. But neither had been to the Cape, they'd told her, and they had seemed sweetly excited about the prospect. At least if they were all here, Alyssa could watch out for Bree. Vulnerable, almost-rich Bree.

Alyssa texted Tammy that she'd be out of town, but Tammy had not responded. And why should she? Bill had fired her. Leaving Alyssa even more vulnerable. She'd been extra diligent about the alarm.

"I was thinking, too," Dez was saying now, "this also means you don't need a lawyer anymore. Another good thing."

Was it? She'd already called Mickey to get her take on Parker's surprise announcement, but Odette had said she was out, and would call back. She'd focus on the present now. Sit on the beach. Watch the waves.

"Oscar and Eddie keep the place stocked and ready for us," she said, ignoring the lawyer topic, "like they do for everyone, so the guest rooms will be—hang on, the keys are in here somewhere."

"Like they do for everyone," Bree said to Dez, as if she were explaining to a child. "Do Oscar and Eddie come to *your* house, too, Dez?"

Alyssa held up the key, pretending to be annoyed. "Hush, you two. Oscar and Eddie cornered the market in house-sitting around here, and it's a service, like everything else."

Watching Bree and Dez exchange more amused looks made Alyssa realize how out of touch she'd been. How happily she'd slid into luxury. Teenage Alice would have been awed by One Ocean Place, and house sitters, and abundance. Her mother would have been envious, even bitter, and asked about the market value. But grown-up Alyssa thought she'd won the lottery of love and life—and now, if the feds believed that Bill's income was actually legitimate, then Bill was safe, his income was safe, and his inheritance was safe. Her fair settlement in the divorce might even be safe.

No matter what Dez said, though, she needed to consult with Mickey. She'd authentically devoted her married life to Bill, and that had value. *She* had value. If he wasn't on his way to prison, terrific. If he hadn't left victims in his wake, terrific. But Bill was still the jerk who had dumped her. For reasons unknown.

The key slid into the lock, and the door opened to a white-wood entryway with a great room on one side and Bill's library on the other. A long skylighted hallway led to an open plan kitchen, and beyond that, the gray wood slats of the back deck and the rope-banistered steps to the beach, the way lined with waving seagrass and scrubby beach roses.

"Come in, if you can convince yourself to stop making fun of me." Alyssa stepped aside and let Bree and Dez into the grasscloth-papered foyer. Eddie and Oscar had filled a huge mason jar with fresh green seagrass on a sleek white-wood side table, and deposited a pile of unimportant-looking mail beside it. Someone had scrawled a note on top of the stack. She picked it up.

"From Eddie and Oscar," she read it out loud. "Welcome. Wine and beer and OJ and limes in the fridge, as always, among other treats. Lobsters and corn will arrive for dinner as soon as you let us know how many and when, vodka in the freezer. The Little Market will deliver whatever else you need. Have fun. Text." She put the note back on the pile. "So yeah, you two. If you don't like it, I can call you an Uber to take you back wherever."

"You had me at wine. I'm totally in." Bree stood under the arch of the great room, her overnight bag—one of Alyssa's—still hanging over one shoulder. "This is gorgeous. All that light, all those windows." She pointed at the far wall. "The fireplace is as big as my room at Vermilion. Seems like such a long time ago."

Dez placed his travel bag on the lowest of the stairs to the second floor, and strolled into the library.

"This is amazing," he said, looking up at the beamed ceiling. He took a deep breath. "Beach houses always smell like the ocean to me. This is not where I thought I'd be today, gotta say. Now I'm far from your husband's clutches, and out of my financial adviser disguise." He patted two hands from the neck of his well-worn navy-blue crewneck sweater down to its ribbed waist, hanging loose over his khaki pants. "See? I'm not even wired with a hidden camera. So you two have nothing to fear."

"Right," Bree said. "If I were you, Alyssa, I'd still be careful. The FBI can be pretty sneaky."

"Nice office, though," Dez went on. "All the bookshelves. This where Bill worked? I mean, your husband?" He stepped closer to the framed artwork hanging on the hunter-green wall. "This looks like an original Audubon."

"Nope, it's a repro. Pretty sure." Alyssa thumbed a quick text to Eddie and Oscar. *Three, before 8pm, thanks!* "It'd be silly to keep anything valuable down here, the weather's too unreliable. Hurricanes and nor'easters. If it's not ruined by salt water, it'd be ruined by ice. This place is super casual."

"Huh." Dez continued to look at the print, one of Alyssa's favorites; the great egret, beautifully awkward, with its long bill and graceful neck and intricately painted feathers.

"Dez, come see this view." Bree tucked her arm through the crook of Alyssa's elbow, drawing her along. "Look at that deck. Can we sit out here and watch the ocean?"

"It's Nantucket Sound," Alyssa said. "And sure. But first, you two take your stuff upstairs, your choice of guest rooms; the yellow one, the wallpaper one, the pale blue one. They each have a bathroom. They each have a view. I'll meet you in the kitchen."

Alyssa watched the two tramp upstairs, bags over their shoulders, heard them discussing the sunset, graying now as the evening edged into night. Alyssa walked through the familiar hallway to the kitchen, a place she'd come to love, white and light and accessible, which always smelled like summer to her. She remembered the bite of a salty margarita and the laughter and conversation. She must have gone so bafflingly wrong with this. With Bill.

She pulled open one door of the stainless steel refrigerator, which, as promised, held cheese and clam dip, and limes, a carton of eggs, and a container of cream.

The divorce lawyers had told her—in preliminary discussions, at least—that she could ask for Ocean Place as part of her settlement. And she could imagine living here; reading, and swimming, and forgetting. Forgetting the Club, and those women, with their haughty and transitory power. She could watch the birds, learn about flowers. She closed the refrigerator door, and felt tears welling. She'd thought she could escape if she left that ghost-filled house in Weston.

But the memories here were equally indelible, and every one of them contained Bill. She had never been here without him.

She should have known from the beginning that he had no intention of obeying the "call in advance" agreement, an agreement he'd made with the cavalier attitude he flaunted at everything and everyone. She predicted her divorce lawyer's future explanations. That Bill was ignoring the divorce settlement, stalling, changing, conniving. She should have known there was never "settlement" with Bill. Never agreement. There was only what Bill wanted, and only when he wanted it. And now even the FBI was giving up. Bill would win again.

She would never be safe from him. Sinister postcards, secret visits, his "you can tell her" message to Tammy—it was only the beginning. She recognized his tactics. He was setting the stage. To be even more destructive. But why? She couldn't survive if she didn't know the rules.

Her phone buzzed in her jeans pocket. She reached under her bulky fisherman-knit sweater and fished it out. Connected.

"Hey, Mick," she said, seeing the caller ID. "You will not believe what happened. You got my message, right?" She paused. "Sounds like you're driving."

"Yeah, I'm on 128. But I haven't checked my messages. What happened? You okay?"

"I'm mad as hell," Alyssa said. "Or maybe not." She stared out the kitchen window, across the close-cut lawn and down to the beach. Things were so pretty here, on the outside. "The FBI—"

"How'd it go?"

"It didn't. She told me to forget about it. The sting." Silence on the other end. "Did you hear me?"

"Yes. And now I'm trying to understand. What happened? Did Bill catch on? Maybe she left a message for me, too. Are they rescheduling?"

"Nope. It's off. Off-off. It's a long story about some higher-ups interfering. Parker was pretty vague about it, almost seemed embarrassed," Alyssa explained, quickly as she could. "I never even told her about the offer from Bree and Dez."

"Huh," Mickey said. "That doesn't sound kosher to me. *Damn* it."

"You okay?"

"There's a train. I'm stopped while the commuter

rail goes by. But I'll try to check with her. She should have called me. Those *people.* You can't trust them, I should know that by now. They'll say anything. You okay, though? Where are you? Hold on, I'm getting a call. Don't hang up."

Alyssa opened the back door, and stepped onto the deck. The briny smell of the Sound, and the freshly cut back lawn were nostalgic, too, triggering all her Cape Cod memories. The invisible strings of tiny white fairy lights had come into full bloom. They'd installed them for their first anniversary party, an old-fashioned clambake, with steamed lobsters and corn on the cob, and oysters and champagne for everyone. *Let's keep these lights forever,* Alyssa remembered saying as they watched their guests laughing and mingling on the lawn, the solar-powered tiki torches flickering in the moonlight, a sense of peace and joy and celebration. *Our own personal fantasyland,* Bill had said, and she'd believed him.

Now she wondered just how much of her life was fantasy.

"Al, you there?" Mickey's voice came back in her ear.

"Yup. I'm at the Osterville house, by the way; Dez and Bree are here. But do you think it means Bill is off the hook? If there was even a hook."

"Well . . ."

"And does it mean *I'm* off the hook? What do I do now?"

"Let me think about that," Mickey said. "But I'm wondering about that bank account. The twenty-two million dollars in your name you finally told me about. Did Parker mention that again?"

"Huh. No. I asked, but she didn't answer." Alyssa

sat down on the back steps, the faint outline of the wood underneath her still warm from today's sunshine. She heard a train whistle on Mickey's end, long and far away. "Then I got upset, and kind of yelled at her, and then she left."

"You didn't get a copy of it, if I remember."

"Right. I asked, that day, but she took it back." Both women were silent for a beat. "Mickey? You think that was fake? You told me, not even a minute ago—you said: they'll say anything."

"Well . . ."

Alyssa could almost hear Mickey analyzing. It *was* fake. That's what made the most sense. She hadn't opened a bank account like that, and it seemed unlikely that Bill had. It was all part of their scheme to unsettle her, to make her feel as if Bill was doing things she didn't know about. Hiding things from her. Like Dez thought, using her. To make her angry, and unsure, and to goad her into betraying him.

But it was Bill who was betraying *her*. That's why she'd drawn those precise eyeliner dots on her marble table, and sacrificed flowers on her front steps, and monitored the hiding place in the closet. To catch him at it. Now he wasn't even trying to cover up his home invasions.

"Okay. Law enforcement officials are allowed to lie," Mickey said. "It might be that's what they were doing. To try to trick you into incriminating yourself. At least they didn't go through with the sting. That was too much, apparently, even for them."

Alyssa put one hand on the smooth wooden handrail, and slowly drew herself to her feet, gazing over the endless water. "But, Mickey? What if they lied today, too? What if this is not really over?"

THIRTY-EIGHT

They'd taken webbed beach chairs down to the edge of the waves, Dez lugging all three of them while Bree carried the blankets and Alyssa balanced a thermos of hot lemonade laced with vodka, three red Solo cups, and a big stainless steel bowl of popcorn and pretzels. Now they sat in a row, Alyssa on one end, Dez on the other, all in bulky sweaters and draped in beach blankets, their backs to the lighted house behind them, gazing at the water.

Alyssa was always mesmerized by the waves lapping at the edge of the sand, as if teasing them in some secret constant rhythm, inching closer to the aluminum legs of their chairs as the tide came in. Now she was consumed with secret recordings and mysterious money and constant lies.

"Weird that Bill is out there . . ." She waved a hand in the general direction of everywhere. "And has no idea about any of this. Oblivious to a scheming FBI agent, an ongoing federal investigation, and to you guys, and me. Even Mickey. Then today happens, and Bill simply goes on with what he was doing."

"With what, though?" Bree asked. She waggled her fingers at Dez, asking for the popcorn.

"Ask the FBI." Alyssa tried her spiked lemonade. Bill always complained it tasted like cough syrup, but on a spring night like this, not quite summer, with the stars above and the sound of the waves, and the blanket cozy from the wind off the water, the warmth brought her a kind of peace. The lobsters were in the fridge, waiting, but cocktail hour on the beach was a treasured time. A ritual she would be sad to give up. If she had to give it up.

"And now Bill gets away with it," Alyssa said to the waves.

"With what?" Dez asked.

"Ha ha," Alyssa said. "You two are a laugh a minute."

For a moment, the only sound was the slosh of the water, pulling and fizzing across the flat spackled sand. Tiny shorebirds skittered through the foam, barely visible in the dim moonlight.

"This is our anniversary, you know, Bree," Alyssa said.

"Hmm?"

"We met a week ago. A week ago, I was having a pretty good martini in a pretty dreary bar, the rest of my life taunting me like a tightrope I had to walk. Over Niagara Falls. Honestly, I was not eager to find out what happened next. I was so—ah—seethingly angry at Bill, I still couldn't believe there was any path for me out of it."

"I know the feeling," Bree said. "I'll always be grateful that you talked to me."

"No, you spoke first, remember?"

"Did I? We're like an old married couple. Remembering things differently."

"We're not old. And we are definitely not married."

"Except you are."

"Technically."

"Well, actually, legally," Dez put in.

"Can we not talk about that, you two? Not talk

about Bill? I can't get over that he just—barged in. With Tammy there. Like he owned the place. Which he does, I know, but still. It's—"

"I heard about people like him all the time at the bank," Bree said. "Rich people who think they're different. That the rules don't exist for them. They also think I'm not listening. Men never listen to women. Or notice them. Especially ones who work for them."

"So true," Dez said.

"Shut up," Bree said. "Or I'm keeping the popcorn."

"Are you talking, Bree?"

"You guys," Alyssa said. "I know what you mean, though. Bill and his crowd taught me about 'rich people.' They always . . ."

"'They' would be you, I feel I should remind you." Bree handed her the bowl. "So it's not *every* rich person."

"And 'they' would be you, too, right, Bree? Soon, at least," Alyssa reminded her. "Now that Dez is in your life."

"Ha. Got me." Bree took a sip from her Solo cup. "But back to *real* rich people. If the feds are calling off the investigation, wouldn't that be a good thing for you? I mean, not to be crass, Lyss, but if Bill's legit, you could get big bucks in the divorce. Dez, you think?"

"Sure," Dez said. "If Bill did nothing wrong and Alyssa did nothing wrong, then all's right with the world."

"In a way." Alyssa took a deep breath, smelled the sand and the lemonade and the salt from the popcorn. A lone gull soared overhead, maybe assigned to handle nature's beach surveillance. "But—as you said, not to be crass—that divorce settlement is now in the hands of the lawyers. Bill's lawyers. And judges. Probably Bill's judges. I can't rely on anyone, really."

"You should get what you deserve." Dez was resting his head on the back of his chair, and his words went skyward.

"Thank you, Dez." Alyssa was surprised at the vehemence in his tone. Bree had probably told him how upset she was, how she felt belittled and dismissed. Her contribution to their married lives—tangible, but not financial—did not carry much weight in a ledger book.

"At least you're not going to prison," Bree said. "Here's to staying out of prison. Toast to that, right?"

The three touched cups together, and Alyssa almost felt comforted. The edges of the waves curled closer to their chairs, but it was so peaceful, and so serene, it seemed a shame to move. And Bree was right. Though she'd tried to avoid having the specter of prison creep into her consciousness, whatever legal judgment hammered Bill might have slammed her as well. Maybe she was safe now. She was still angry, and sad, but safe would be good.

But then it hit, like the wash of a rogue wave. She wasn't safe. Bill was still a danger. Bill's plans. Bill's power. Bill's access.

The stars had begun to emerge, and she watched them twinkle into life—Orion, and the Big Dipper, and a scatter of constellations she couldn't name, all a reminder of how small she was. How small the three of them were.

"May I just say," Alyssa began, searching for words even as she spoke them, "I don't know, I . . . Thank you." These two had selflessly helped her, had generously offered to put themselves in a potentially precarious situation. For her. To protect her. "And not only for the FBI thing."

"It's—" Dez began.

"I'll never understand the world," Alyssa went on. "Or Bill. But thank you for—being here for me." She felt the vodka blanketing her mind, the rhythm of the waves, the rustle of the seagrass. "I feel so much safer, Bree, with you in the guest house. You're way better than a fake dog. I'm grateful."

"Woof," Bree said. "I'm grateful, too, Lyss. Without you? Zero money, zero prospects, trapped in that damn bank with idiot Frankie hounding me, and—"

"I would've found you," Dez interrupted. "Eventually."

THIRTY-NINE

Alyssa pulled back the white-slatted shutters and opened the bedroom windows wide, letting in the night. The gauzy white curtains caught the intermittent Cape wind, and it gave them a life of their own, luffing and fluttering like indoor sails.

The three of them had polished off the popcorn, pretzels, and hot lemonade, and as the darkness descended, dense as only a beach night can be, they had packed up their beach chairs and trooped inside to do battle with the lobsters.

Taking the stapled paper bag out of the refrigerator, Alyssa had been hit with unexpected emotions, another reminder of her upended life. Bill had always cooked their lobsters, or the caterers handled it. Tonight, hearing the live creatures rustling inside the bag, and faced with doing it on her own, she'd decided she'd have to bluff it through. After all, people did this every day. But, maybe noticing her hesitation, Dez had offered to "do the honors."

"You have to hypnotize them first," he'd said.

Alyssa had already filled a blue enamel pot with water, and brought it to a rolling boil on the stovetop. "Hypnotize?"

"Watch." Dez plucked one from the bag, rubbed a forefinger against the lobster's neck. The scrabbling claws soon relaxed, then fell motionless.

"Wow." Bree's eyes went wide. "That guy's *out*."

"See?" Dez had held up the limp creature. "The massage makes them comfortable and clueless. They'll never know what hit them."

Dez plunged it, head first, into the huge pot, droplets of hot water splashing on his bare arms. Then picked up the next one, began his hypnosis trick again.

"Hey, Lyss, you can imagine them as Bill," Bree said, laughing. "He's in hot water, too, right? *Die,* you monster."

Alyssa winced, embarrassed at being entertained by the comparison. She'd enjoyed it more than she should, she knew, and the imaginary torture of her duplicitous husband was somehow satisfying. *Take* that, *Bill,* she'd silently decreed at the second doomed lobster. *And* this, *too,* she told the third. The vision of harming Bill, even by crustacean proxy, was, unsettlingly, more triumphant than disturbing. *You should get what you deserve,* Dez had said out on the beach. She couldn't agree more.

But now, a few hours later, Alyssa had to admit *she* was the one who was more like the lobsters. Bill had hypnotized her, too, with comfort and luxury, for so long that the eventually clueless and complaisant Alyssa had not realized what was happening to her. And then, like the poor lobsters, he'd plunged her into disaster.

She yanked her hair back into a ponytail, and soaped her face over the tiled bathroom sink. Conch shells, with their prickly white outsides and voluptuous pink insides, were lined up by size across the drainboard, shells pointing the same direction, just as they were in their Weston bathroom. Bill had once compared her to the inside of one of them. *You're just like this,* he'd whispered, *mysterious and sleek and pink.*

She blushed now, even remembering. You don't say that to someone you don't care about. He had cared about her. He had. She must have done something, something she could not even imagine, to make him go.

Or he *did something,* the same inner voice reminded her.

She patted her face dry with a fluffy white towel, monogrammed, and wondered if she could somehow cut all the monograms off. She reached out to pull down the blue-and-white-striped duvet, then paused, bare arm in midair. She had never been in this bed alone.

Now she stared at it, a thing suddenly from another life. The elaborate headboard had been crafted from local driftwood, buffed and painted a bleached blue, like a stone tumbled by the waves and left in the sand. Blue-striped linens, thin white matelassé blankets, and an oversize, almost-threadbare antique quilt of pale blue and white diamonds draped across the foot of the bed, so lavish that both ends pooled on the floor. Bill's favorite ship model, the *Cutty Sark,* he'd explained, still sailed to nowhere atop three steamer trunks, stacked like unpacked Russian dolls in the corner. She had half a mind to throw the thing over the balcony and onto the grass below, and it gave her chills, thinking about destroying Bill's possessions. Destroying what he loved, just the way he'd destroyed her.

But if she demolished Bill's precious ship, she thought as she slid under the covers, he'd complain to his posse of lawyers, not to mention his snarky Club friends, whose minds he'd clearly already poisoned, and that would cement her reputation as the psycho wife. Even more than it already was. She pictured that self-important Lylah, all supercilious, commenting on Alyssa's "troubles" and alluding to some connection with Bill. And Camden Hollis, the hostess, passive-aggressively deciding to make her wait.

She pictured them all as doomed lobsters, and pulled the tiny chain to click off the bedside light. The green of her charging phone and the brightness of the May moon gave the room a pale glow, and scudding clouds splayed shadows across the bedroom walls.

And now she was here in this bed, alone. She refused to reach out her hand and touch the emptiness beside her. Where was Bill, this very moment?

She pulled the covers up, walling herself from the rest of the bed. She still had some ammunition in her back pocket, though. Still had the knowledge that the FBI was after Bill. Had suspected him. Had more than suspected him. Had planned to nail him in an undercover sting.

"And let's say," she said out loud, nestling into a pillow. "Let's say Bree and Dez went, anyway." She imagined the scene unfolding, Bill opening the door to his own office, congenial and engaged, ushering in Bree and Dez. Bree, in the black dress and pearls Bill had paid for himself. Dez would do the talking, since Bill only listened to men, and Bree would sit there, prim and silent and rich, in those expensive Ferragamos. Alyssa had envisioned it before, happening under the imprimatur of the FBI, but who needed them? She stared into nothingness, the movie unspooling in her mind. Bree and Dez could still play their roles. They didn't need fancy wiretap equipment or listening devices or tiny hidden microphones. They could just—go. And then get Bill to, maybe, sign something.

And then she, Alyssa, bombshell evidence in hand, could offer it to the FBI. She edited her mental image. Probably not Parker, since she apparently was no longer in the picture, but someone in the FBI. Mickey could find out who was working the case. She could call them and reveal what she'd discovered.

There had to be a flaw in that plan, somewhere, but her one year in law school was not providing answers. Still, she couldn't let the idea go. She turned over again, trying to get comfortable. Her phone showed 2:10 a.m.

They could still offer Bree's money, money Dez was confident she was about to get, and . . . maybe that was the flaw. Bree's money might be at risk if they no longer had Uncle Sam's protection and guarantees. And even though she could imagine Bree saying she didn't care, Alyssa did. And Dez sure would. She was still suspicious of him.

She sighed, thinking about Bree down the hall in the wallpaper room, and Dez next door in the green room. It had been a fun night, and Alyssa had almost forgotten what had brought them together today. They'd had no hesitation eating the lobster once it was cooked, and they'd devoured them all, drenched in butter and lemon.

"Where can I take these shells and stuff?" Dez had asked as they cleaned up afterward. "They'll stink up the place if we leave them inside." They'd dumped them all into a white plastic garbage bag, along with the thick white paper plates they'd used and the silly disposable bibs Oscar and Eddie had left them.

"Very chic," Bree had said, tying one around her neck and smoothing it over her chest.

"It's the Osterville look," Alyssa reassured her. "Your sweater will thank you."

"*Your* sweater, Alyssa," Dez corrected her.

She'd pointed Dez to the recycling, outside and beside the little shed. "The outside lights are by the door."

"You okay?" Bree had asked her after the screen door closed behind him.

"Me?" Alyssa had been stashing wineglasses and green dessert plates into the dishwasher. "Other than too much vodka and wine and a year's worth of lemon butter, I'm fine."

"Don't make a joke of it. You had a narrow escape today."

Alyssa had closed the dishwasher and leaned back against it, her feet—in flip-flops, pushing the season—stretched out in front of her on the tiled floor. "You think?"

"Yeah, Alyssa, I do." She'd glanced at the doorway. "And I still think you should be careful."

Alyssa had stopped, perplexed at the look on Bree's face. "Careful of what?"

"Nothing. Everything."

"That's helpful."

"Look." Bree seemed to reconsider. "I saw the joy on your face when Dez killed those lobsters."

"No, really, I . . ." Alyssa was still uncomfortable about her vengeful imagination. But that's what imagination was for, to dull the edge of desire.

"Lyss? You don't want to tell me, at all, what Bill did? Why he left?"

Alyssa had clapped a hand to her forehead, pretending annoyance. "I don't know! I don't know! How many times have I told you . . ."

"That's the thing. No times. None. You've never told me. How much have we talked about everything else? And how little have we talked about Bill specifically? Does that make any sense? And it's upsetting to see you so unhappy. I know it's—let me pose one tiny observation. The balance of power in your marriage. It was all Bill, wasn't it? You did what he said, accepted what he did, followed his lead. You didn't initiate anything."

"Well . . ." Alyssa had batted her eyelashes. She hadn't been sure what Bree was getting at, but fine, girl talk.

"I'm not talking about sex, Alyssa, you dope. I'm being serious. It was all Bill, all the time. You didn't ask questions."

"I suppose. Sure. But that worked for us. I thought it did, at least."

Bree had looked at the back door again. "And what did you do when the FBI confronted you?" She lowered her voice. "You didn't call your husband and ask, *What the hell are you doing?* Or tell him the feds were on his tail. You—"

"Of course I didn't. He'd erased himself from my life."

"He didn't, though. That's what I mean. He may have left, physically, even emotionally. But he also left you in danger. He broke into your house! He ignored the agreement. Did what he wanted. Are you hearing me?" She hefted herself onto the kitchen island, perched on the edge, her sneakers dangling above the floor. "You'll be trampled in this divorce settlement. He still has all the power. And you just sit here in this fancy house, killing lobsters."

"Oh, come *on* about the lobsters."

"There's more to you, Alyssa, than you let on. You're not a . . ." She looked at the back door again. "A doormat. You're smart, and funny, and generous. Different than I thought at first."

"There's more to you, too, Bree. More than that pitiful creature in the hotel bar. And that's why I keep worrying about Dez. And you are, too, the way you're watching him now. You've checked the back door at least three times."

"Well, yeah. You're right. I am. But this is about you, Alyssa. You spent however many years in that man's clutches. And now, even when he leaves you, he takes control."

"He doesn't." Alyssa had put her back to Bree, yanked on the water in the sink, and fussed with a yellow sponge, pretending to wipe the stainless steel clean.

"For once, you should protect your power," Bree had said. "Be careful of who might have ulterior motives."

Alyssa almost felt the words hitting her in the back. "You don't have to tell me that." She turned, dripping sponge in hand. "Oh. I don't mean to sound so critical."

"Not the point. Right now, you should be careful as hell, because—"

"You don't think I am? Careful?"

"I know you are. But—"

"I think I saw a fox," Dez had said as he opened the back door. He winced as it slammed shut behind him. "I'm telling myself it was a fox and not like a . . ."

"A rat?" Bree said. She'd looked at Alyssa, as if to emphasize *rat*.

"It might have been a fox," Alyssa had said, ignoring the rat remark. "We have a lot of those around here this time of year."

And now Bree was probably asleep, and Dez, too. Full of wine and lobster and butter, and only bright futures ahead of them. She snaked her arm out from inside the duvet, and smoothed the empty place beside her.

SATURDAY

FORTY

When her cell phone rang, Alyssa tried to convince herself it was a dream. But the phone kept ringing. She flipped over and felt for it on the nightstand, managed not to knock it to the floor, answered it with her eyes still closed.

"Hello?" Her voice came out a croak. She took the phone from her ear. Looked at the screen. 5:27 a.m. Tried to focus on the caller ID. A voice was already talking.

"Is this Alyssa Macallen?" the man's voice said.

"Who is this?" She cleared her throat. *Not Bill,* went through her mind. As it always did.

"Weston police. We got an alarm call at your house. Is everything okay?"

"Is everything okay? You tell *me*!" Alyssa's instincts kicked into fear mode, the back of her neck icy and her heart clenching. "I'm not there, I'm on my cell." She blinked, trying to regroup. Got an alarm call, he'd said. "Someone called from there? Someone's in there? Inside?"

"No, ma'am, the alarm went off."

She'd had two hours of sleep, maybe, and willed her brain to cooperate as he went on. The sunrise, a yellow-orange haze, diffused across the water below, and the light of a new morning inched through her open shutters.

"No one answered when we called your landline, ma'am, this was the backup number. Are you okay?"

"I said I'm not home." She was awake enough now to be angry. She scooted herself to sitting, leaned against the driftwood headboard. "I'm on the Cape," she added, unnecessarily. "What's going on? Is there—are you—wait. It's not a fire, is it?" She swung her legs over the side, and stood barefoot on the carpet, getting her balance, trying to acclimate to the whole thing. A fire. *That last postcard from Bill, a bonfire.* A million horrors raced through her imagination, unnameable.

"We have someone on the way now, ma'am," the voice said. "But your smoke detectors were not going off, and they aren't now, either, so I'd say no."

Okay, then, no fire. She tried to calculate. It would take her two hours, at least, to get there. By that time, whatever happened would be over. She had to call someone. Tammy. Mickey. Even—should she call Bill? She couldn't, but—or what if it *was* Bill?

Her entire being went heavy with certainty, and she sank onto the bed again. Of course. It was Bill. How did he know she was not home? The answer came instantly. Oscar and Eddie. They would have called him. Innocently, without intent, simply out of habit. Protocol. She hadn't texted them not to. Her fault.

Now he knew where she was, and knew where she wasn't. Knew she was two helpless hours away. He could have defeated the alarm system, as she knew, just knew, he always did. He was upping his game. And when the police arrived, he could simply tell them, *Yeah, it's my house.* And it would all be true.

He was taunting her. Showing her she had no power whatsoever. Exactly as Bree had warned. Her first time alone on the Cape, and Bill had to prove she would never be free of him.

"I'm staying on the line," she told the officer. "I'm two hours away. In Osterville. I'll wait here until you tell me what they find. And I'm pulling up the alarm video on my phone."

"I'm just dispatch, ma'am, but I'll contact the officers on duty."

"I'm putting you on hold. Checking the video. Don't hang up. Okay?"

Alyssa tapped the password for the alarm. Checked the video. Nothing. Nothing recorded.

But Bill could erase it as easily as she could. Damn it. *Damn* Bill. If the camera showed nothing, did that mean it *was* Bill?

She changed to the live view. An empty porch.

But the front door was open. Wide open. Was he hiding inside? Doing what?

She clicked back to dispatch. "Hello? My front door is—" But there was only white noise.

Alyssa tapped it onto speaker. She had to go back there. She took the phone into the bathroom, got ready to leave as fast as she could. Bree and Dez were probably still in their beds, sleeping off the wine and butter, unaware. She'd put a note on the kitchen island, explaining, and then she'd call them later. She yanked on her jeans, zipped them. No. She couldn't leave them here alone together. Could she? She pulled on a sweater, tied her sneakers.

Still only static from her cell phone.

Both the other bedroom doors were closed, she saw, as she ran down the stairs, phone in hand. "Hello?" she said into it, checking. "Hello?"

She'd make coffee. Put it into a travel mug, leave

a note. She could be back by noon, if all went as planned. And maybe the two of them would still be asleep. She put the cell phone on the counter beside her, and picked up the landline and dialed, tucking the receiver between her cheek and chin as she started the coffee. "Hello?" She aimed her voice at the cell on the counter. "Hello?" But nothing.

Her landline call connected. "Mickey," she said, "it's me. Alyssa. I just got a call from the—hello?" Voice mail. "Mickey, it's me, Alyssa," she said after the beep. "I'm on the Cape, the police called and said they got an alarm from the Weston house, and I was wondering if . . . Oh, I'm sorry, ah, it's too early. Sorry. Call me."

She hung up. Her cell phone sat in staticky silence. But outside—there was a noise.

A definite noise.

She paused, listening. Nothing. Picking up her cell phone, she crept, as quietly as she could, toward the sliding glass doors. She had locked them, she was certain of it, the night before. But they were not locked now. She slid one open, and there, standing on the deck, was Dez. She saw his cell phone on the table beside him, and one of the bottles of water from the fridge.

"Oh, hey," she said, "I didn't know you were out here."

"Are you okay? Did I frighten you?" He stood, his hair mussed, a gray long-sleeved T-shirt over jeans and loafers. "I know it's early, but I wanted to see the sunrise. I tried to sneak downstairs without waking anyone up."

She waved the cell phone at him. "The police called. They said the alarm went off at my house."

"Oh, no—a fire? Okay," he said, acknowledging her reaction. "Good, at least. But what happened?"

"No idea. No idea." She held up her infuriatingly silent phone again. "I'm on speaker with them, waiting." She tried again. "Hello? See? Nothing. The alarm system video shows nothing. But the front door is open. I tried to call Mickey, see if she could go check on the place, but it's too early. And I can't call Tammy, not under the circumstances. I have to rely on the police. Which means I need to get there as fast as I can."

"I could go," Dez said. A golden sun bloomed in full behind him, making him almost a silhouette, winged with the bright rays of the morning. "I'd have to drive your car, but—"

Alyssa weighed that for a second. "No," she said, "thanks, but that won't work. You wouldn't know what to look for."

"What d'you mean, 'what to look for'?"

"It's too complicated," she said. "I'll go. You and Bree stay here." She'd made the decision before she'd even thought it through. "Hello?" she said to the phone again, heard the exasperation in her own voice. "How long can it take the police to get somewhere?"

"Do you have any friends you can call?"

Which is precisely what Alyssa had asked herself, and, mentally scrolling her contacts list, had realized the answer with sorrow, then anger. As soon as she was nothing to Bill, she'd been nothing to any of them as well.

"It's early," she said, avoiding reality. She went back into the kitchen, and he followed her, sliding the door closed. "The police will get there more quickly than anyone else can."

The coffee hissed through the machine. Her cell phone was still white noise. "So frustrating. If I hang up, I might lose the connection, and if I call back 911, I'll get some operator, and not Weston. I just have to leave the line open, and go. I'm imagining every terrible thing. Will you tell—"

"Hey, you guys." Bree padded into the kitchen, blinking. She wore a gray T-shirt, too, and jeans, and the two of them looked like siblings. She yawned, then shook her head as if to clear it. "Isn't it way early? Why are you up?"

"I was looking at the sunrise," Dez began, "but—"

"The Weston police called and—"

"What?"

"They said the alarm was going off at my house." Alyssa poured coffee into a travel mug. "I'm trying not to be freaked out. They're going to let me know." She held up her phone. "Allegedly. It's been fifteen minutes."

"Fire?"

"No," Dez began, "they—"

"No, they don't think so." She filled Bree in. "So I've got to race back, and you two can—"

"No, no." Bree waved her off with both hands, erasing that idea. "I can be ready in five. In three. I'm coming with. Dez can stay. Definitely. If you'll make a coffee for me, and give me two minutes, I'll come with you."

"I'll be glad for the company," Alyssa admitted. "And you can handle the phone while I drive. You'll hold down the fort, Dez? The Little Market is a short walk away, turn right at the end of the driveway, and they have everything you might need. And I'll call you. Your number's in my cell."

"I have it, too," Bree said.

"Know what? I should go with you," Dez said. "Bree should stay here. It's better if I'm there to talk to the police."

"Why, because you're the man?" Bree fluttered her eyelashes, apparently to show she was teasing. "Seriously. I'll go."

"You guys?" Alyssa tapped the coffee maker to start Bree's cup. "In about two minutes, I'm going with you or without you, whatever."

"I'm coming with you," Bree said over her shoulder, and she was gone, her footsteps trotting up the stairs.

"Looks like you're the security now," Alyssa said. "We'll be back by noon, if nothing's really wrong. Hello?" she said into the phone again, then shook the device as if it were tormenting her on purpose. "This is *so* frustrating!"

"It'll all be fine," Dez said. "The police know where to find you."

FORTY-ONE

I just realized what I don't know," Alyssa said as she edged the SUV out onto Route 6. She hated negotiating the rotary, a sadistic and anarchistic traffic interchange where every driver decided that they deserved to go first, no matter what the rules.

Bree twisted toward her on the front seat. "Wait," she said, "you're gonna make me choke on my coffee. Which of the things are you talking about?"

"Listen, first, can you use your cell to look up the business number of the Weston police? And call them for me? Tell them the deal. That I'm still waiting for a report on what happened at my house. It's been a ridiculously long time."

"Sure." Bree put her coffee back into the console cup holder and pulled out her phone. "What's the name of the police officer who called you? Or the dispatcher, you said it was?"

Alyssa squinted, trying to remember, her eyes on the two-lane road ahead. "I'm not sure he told me. But there's a record of it. The alarm at my address."

Route 6 was already its start-of-the-weekend self, all the Boston vacationers who had decided to get an early start on Saturday morning had apparently chosen the same version of "early" and were now mired in the traffic heading east. Alyssa had a clear shot west, and even here on the Cape's notorious speed trap, she pushed the accelerator faster than the signs allowed.

"Yes, Macallen," Bree was saying into her phone.

"Anything?" Alyssa asked.

"Hang on, they must be checking. I can hear them talking in the—yes, I'm here." Bree held up one finger. "Okay, so, no one inside? Okay. And—no sign of anything disturbed." She looked at Alyssa, gave her a thumbs-up. Then her expression crumpled. "The door was open?"

"Just the front?" Alyssa tried to keep her eyes on the road and on Bree at the same time.

"Just the front?" Bree asked. "Just the front," she repeated, confirming.

Alyssa pointed at the phone. "Put it on speaker, okay?" She paused while Bree pushed a button, then talked across the console. "This is Mrs. Macallen. I'm on my way there."

"As I said, the alarm went off, ma'am, and the front door is open. But nothing seems disturbed." The officer's voice made him another passenger.

"Did you look in—" Alyssa began.

"We checked the premises thoroughly, ma'am. Your house is empty. Basement, first floor, second floor."

"Guest house?" Bree whispered.

Alyssa's eyes widened. She tried to concentrate on the traffic and the possibilities. "There's a guest house in back, and—"

"All secure, ma'am."

Bree clapped a palm to her chest, relieved.

"Are you sure you didn't leave the door open, ma'am?"

Alyssa narrowed her eyes. *They never trust the woman,* she thought. Easier to handle an incompetent female than solve a potential home invasion.

"The alarm went off, Officer, is that not correct?"

Alyssa added some honey to her voice, as if talking to a child. "So it's unlikely that I left my own front door open."

She made a face at Bree, who mirrored her exasperation.

"I'm actually terrified to go inside, though," Alyssa admitted, imagining. "What if—"

"We'll stay here until you arrive, ma'am," the officer said. "We need you to confirm nothing is disturbed. And you'll need to relock the door."

Alyssa bit back a hostile reply. It didn't matter. She needed to get home.

"Thank you," she said. "I'm so grateful. We'll be there as fast as we can. And you have my cell."

"Drive safely, ma'am."

"Right," she said. "Thank you." She pantomimed to Bree, *Hang up*.

"You think it was Bill?" Bree asked.

Alyssa took a deep breath, considering, and trying to calm her roiling thoughts. "Yeah. I do. He . . ." She quickly outlined her suspicions. The altered cushion on the office chair. How he'd moved the carefully placed tulips, seeming to prove he was onto her tactics. The knife on the kitchen floor. How he'd intensified his game even more, brazenly arriving while Tammy was there.

"Didn't even try to hide it, even with the agreement," she finished her recitation. The traffic slowed, for some inexplicable reason, and she felt her shoulders sag. "I just don't get it."

"It seems so—calculatedly destructive," Bree said.

"It's impossible, it's truly impossible." Alyssa touched the accelerator as the traffic started again. "I don't know anything, the FBI is insane, the whole thing is insane, I'm about to be expelled from a life I thought I knew, and I didn't do anything to deserve it."

"That's not how the world works, Lyss, and you know that. It's not about 'deserve.'" Bree sighed, and sank lower into the passenger seat. "It's about the combinations of things that happen, and how we're caught up in them all. It's about decisions we don't even realize we're making. And then what we have to do as a result." She paused. "Whether we like it or not."

They rode in silence then, past stands of newly budding maples and tender green elms, the ones that had survived the brutal winter; others, savaged and destroyed by the storms, with leafless trunks split and splayed and grotesque.

She and Bill had driven this trip together, countless times, in every season. The SUV was always filled with wine and provisions, and when the weather cooperated, they'd have party plans underway and a raft of visitors eager to dive into the waves and play drunk badminton and share champagne under the stars. She'd embraced it, felt part of it, and now she was pretty sick of thinking about it. Annoyed with herself for the depth of her sorrow, and her masochistic—was it?—need to replay those eight years over and over.

Deception was the worst emotional evil there could be, she decided as the mile markers went by, because truth is a comfort, a reliable comfort. And destruction of truth is more than the act itself, it's proof that the victim is weak. Someone who can be deceived cannot see reality. They're vulnerable. Stupid. Insignificant.

If there were stages of marital sorrow, like the stages of grief, she had been through them now; disbelief, and bargaining, and heartache, and on into anger. She was past that now, too, way past anger. And into . . . what would be next? Acceptance? Or action?

Bill seemed to have his own agenda. He'd worked, actively worked, to make her hurt go deeper than sorrow. One of the other postcards he'd sent had been a fresh pineapple, sliced into a row of glistening half-circle slices, and a still-wet carving knife. Another knife. How could that be anything but a threat? This was his personal and strategic dismissal of her. Of their marriage. Of what she'd thought was their love. As if only *his* voice counted. Only *his* feelings.

"Lyss? When we got on the highway, you said there was something you didn't know. What?"

"Phone," Alyssa said at the sound. "Grab it. Might be the police."

"It's connected to Bluetooth, right? Just put it on speaker."

"Oh, right." So frazzled. She clicked the button on the steering wheel. The dashboard readout said *Call from CLB*. The Club? Maybe Bill was calling from the Club?

"Hello?" She heard the trepidation in her own voice.

"Mrs. Macallen?"

Not Bill. "Yes?"

"This is Camden Hollis. I regret having to call you so early."

Bree made a simpery face. *My, my.*

"Hello, Cam." Alyssa used the diminutive, keeping the woman at arm's length. "What can I do for you?"

"It's a bit delicate, I fear," the hostess said. "Are you in a place you can talk?"

A car passed them on the left, swerving in front of

them. Alyssa had to tap the brakes, her grip on the steering wheel tightened.

"What can I do for you?" she repeated.

"When you came for luncheon on Sunday, with your friend?"

"Did we leave something?" Alyssa asked. Although what could be delicate about that?

Bree was listening, concerned. There was no way she could avoid hearing, Alyssa realized, so she might as well not pretend.

Cam Hollis cleared her throat. "It's a matter of the lunch bill."

"Oh, did I not sign it?" Alyssa thought she remembered signing it, but maybe not. She'd been upset by Lylah, she had to admit, and then had that afternoon wine.

"You signed it, yes," Cam's voice came over the speaker. "But the Club's monthly invoices went out yesterday? And we received a call from Mr. Macallen's administrative assistant indicating—and as I said, this is delicate—that he was no longer responsible for charges you incur at the Club. I'm sure it's an oversight, but shall we forward this to you?"

Alyssa felt the blood drain from her face. She could not feel her fingers. The highway in front of her threatened to blur.

"Of course." There was no need to say any more, and she wasn't sure her composure would last if she tried to form actual words.

The woman didn't respond. Was Bill there, listening? Wanting to hear whether she got upset, fought back, burst into tears? She wouldn't give him the satisfaction.

"If there's nothing more?" Alyssa heightened the disdain in her voice.

"There is, I'm afraid." Cam Hollis matched her tone. "Since you're no longer listed on his membership, you'll need to discuss your future access here with him. As for the luncheon bill, are you still at the Weston address?"

As if telegraphing the inevitable brevity of her stay.

"Of course," Alyssa said.

The other woman stayed silent. "Lovely," she finally said. "I'll tell Mr. Macallen it's all settled."

"You do that," Alyssa said. And hung up.

FORTY-TWO

Alyssa felt the echoes of her rancor as the phone call connection vanished. The emptiness. Almost the undercurrent of a chess game being played, one where she was a pawn. As if her sorrow weren't enough, or confusion, or grief, or social exile, or loneliness. Now Bill had to layer on humiliation. The roadside trees and billboards had changed into the outskirts of Boston, first construction and scaffolding, then a skyline staggered with glass buildings and towers approaching in the distance.

Alyssa was completely over this. Chess game? No. She'd sweep all the pieces onto the floor, and smash the chess board into a million pieces. She'd play *her* game now, and simply had to decide on the rules. Even making the decision, emotionally signing it, empowered her.

"Stupid lunch bill." Bree almost whispered. "That's horrible."

"It's fine," Alyssa said. "He has access to all my credit cards. He knows everything I do. Every place I go, probably."

"Maybe you should tell someone."

"Tell who what? That Bill's decided he won't pay for my lunch?"

"You know what I mean. He's aggressive. He sneaks into your *house*."

"It's *his* house, right? And there's no proof of any

dark intent. No proof of anything about anything, except Bill's gossip and bullying. You heard Lylah at the Club, alluding to my 'troubles.' Insinuating that my iced tea was alcohol. That's Bill, all Bill, sowing the seeds of my instability, couching them in sympathy and phony concern. And now he stiffs our lunch bill. This is Bill, and perfect Bill, because he never leaves a trace. Infinite deniability. He's the master at it."

"Huh."

"And he's never satisfied with winning." Alyssa was building up angry steam now, her animosity simmering. "He's got to make the other person fail. Publicly. Shame them. I've known that, but it seemed like business. Bill's power, and confidence, and success. Admirable, unless you're on the losing end of it. Like I am now. Trampled. And helpless."

"Hmm. I wouldn't say you're helpless." Bree shifted in her seat. "How far are we now?"

"An hour, if we don't hit traffic. Which, you know, Boston."

"Could we stop, then? I am incredibly sorry, but the coffee wants to go right through me. I know it's a pain, and you probably wish I'd stayed back with Dez."

All she wanted to do was get home, but thankfully, the police were there guarding the place, and she was glad for Bree's company. Even if she'd been an earwitness to her humiliation. "Next exit okay?"

"Thanks. I'm such a wuss about this. I know it's terrible timing."

Bree's bathroom trip reminded her. "So what's-his-name, Frankie, has he called you lately?"

"Nope." Bree sat up straighter, pride in her voice. "Got to tell you, Alyssa. Once I stood my ground, he caved. Once he knew I wasn't scared. Maybe making me miserable wasn't fun for him anymore. And, Lyss? What if it's the same for Bill? What if you confront him? I don't like seeing you unhappy."

"Oh, he doesn't care what I say. He's got some insane emotional agenda, and I'm his target. He's midlife, he's rich, he's probably in bed with—well, she's in for a surprise, is all I can say."

"You really think it's the 'other woman' thing? Seems so predictable. Dez thinks—"

"What's the deal with you two these days, by the way?"

"Deal?"

"You're about to be rich, and he's—well, money means power. And I know what that can do."

"Dez has no designs on me, I'm sure," Bree said.

"Then why's he hanging around?" Alyssa smiled at Bree's naiveté. "He's hardly interested in *me,* sister."

"Don't be too sure," Bree said. "Is that the exit?"

"Oh, yeah, yikes. And I need to get gas, so good thing we're stopping. We never would have made it."

"Good, then. Now I don't feel so guilty."

"You're avoiding me about Dez," Alyssa said as she took the exit curve, then steered into the gas station. "Why is that?"

Bree unlocked her door as they pulled up to the tanks. Opened it. The sounds of the highway, the whoosh of traffic and honking, wafted into the car, along with the layered pungency of fuel and oil and grease. "You're very intuitive. I'm honestly not sure how I feel about him. But I know he's not after my . . ." She paused. "I'll be careful, I promise. But now we need to make sure your home is safe. And that you are, too. There's a lot going on, Lyss."

"Yeah. Okay." Alyssa poked off the ignition, and swung her feet onto the grimy asphalt. "I'll get the gas, and—you want food? Twizzlers, coffee, Fritos?"

"Sure, anything." Bree waved as she headed for a metal door marked *L*.

Alyssa, inhaling gas fumes, watched the numbers tick up on the gas pump, somehow measuring more than gallons. They were measuring *time*.

What the hell did Bill want?

• • •

When they pulled into the driveway, two uniformed police officers stood sentry at her open front door.

"I'm Alyssa Macallen," she said as soon as she got within earshot.

"Officer Chu," the woman said, pointing to a black plastic nameplate pinned above her shirt pocket. Slim, almost elegant, her impossibly unfashionable uniform of chunky navy pants, thick belt, and starched navy shirt seemed tailored to fit. "And this is my partner, Officer Ramsey. The alarm company shut off the bells remotely. And the dog."

"A fake dog?" Ramsey looked confused.

"Seems to work just as well." Alyssa arrived at the front door, Bree behind her, but the officers, like mismatched bookends, one sleek and one stubby, did not move apart to let them inside. She saw one edge of the security dogwood blossom she'd placed on the top step, the rest of it was hidden under one of Ramsey's boots. "I have to go in," she said.

"Of course. And I'll have to come with you," Chu said. "It looks untouched to us. Like someone opened the door and left. As they told you on the phone, it's an all clear."

"Nothing is disturbed, ma'am." Ramsey's basset hound face and his gravelly voice made it clear he was weary of the whole thing. *Just another ditzy woman,* Alyssa figured he was thinking.

"The alarm went off, dog and all, and they left," he went on. "Without closing the door. Is there anyone other than you who has the key? Husband? Maid service? House sitter? Friend?"

"Sure," Alyssa told them, "but they wouldn't set off the alarm. And no reason for them to run out and leave the door open, right?"

"Unless they were scared of what was inside," Bree said. "I'm her friend," she explained.

"There's no camera?" Officer Chu looked up, scanning the eaves over the front step.

"Yes, there's a camera," Alyssa said. "But I pulled up the video, and nothing was recorded."

"Does the camera always work?" Chu asked.

"I—I don't know," Alyssa admitted. "I mean, how would I know?"

"Her husband may still have access," Bree began, and looked to Alyssa for permission. "And they're newly separated. Ms. Macallen is worrying it may be some sort of petty harassment."

"Have you reported that?" Chu took a spiral notebook from a cargo pocket in her pants, flipped it open. "Would you like to do that now?"

Should she? What would she even report, out-of-place tulips? An unpuffed cushion? "See, he's not supposed to be here without calling in advance," Alyssa said.

"Have you contacted him?" Ramsey asked. For the first time, he looked interested. "Or asked him to leave you alone?"

"It's fine." Alyssa tried to decide if it was. "There's an agreement that he'll make an appointment before he comes over. I was upset when you called, because it's never good when alarms go off, but you got here, fast as you could, and knew there was nothing wrong from the beginning, right? I'll call my husband, see if it was him." *But what if it wasn't?* Alyssa thought. "But maybe—the alarm did its job? Someone tried to break in, heard it, and ran?"

"Oh," Bree said.

"The dog worked," Officer Ramsey said. "The guy booked. Could be."

But Chu was focused on Alyssa. "We've given your home the all clear," the officer said, "but we'd like you to see if anything was taken. Or disturbed. I'll come with you."

"I'll check the guest house?" Bree offered. "I know you've already looked."

Chu nodded. "Sure. Ramsey, go with her, please."

Chu hovered in the study archway as Alyssa scanned the room, opened the desk drawers, traced a finger along a row of first editions. The Cézanne was untouched. She'd positioned a pencil on the desk blotter—it was still there. Chu followed her upstairs and into the master bedroom. Her one diamond earring was still in place on her dresser. A real burglar might have taken that bait. Bill might have ignored it.

She knelt and searched under the bed. Slid her hand between the mattress and box spring. Opened all the drawers, fleur-de-lis liners on Bill's side, her possessions on the other.

"My jewelry is all here," she said. "Undisturbed."

Bree had arrived. "Guest house is fine," she said,

and came up close behind Alyssa. “Anything here, Lyss?” she whispered.

“Nope.” Alyssa opened the doors to the closet, but everything was the same as she’d left it. Her shoebox stash of cash was still there. She pushed back the clothing, counted two slats, pushed on the second one. Tap, tap, and the door popped open. The closet cubby was empty. She understood it then, knew Bill’s weapon was simply invasion. His looming constant threat, and his unfathomable intent. What she could not understand was why he needed to invade at all.

She shook her head at the officer. “Nothing.”

“Nothing missing. Nothing moved. Nothing changed?”

“Not that I can see.” Alyssa took a deep breath, and part of her wanted to cry. “I’ll call him, though,” she lied. There was nothing these people could do. Bill would lie and deny and make her look hysterical and vengeful and out of control. There was absolutely no evidence that he’d been there. And he’d simply say, “It’s my house,” and that would be case closed.

“I’ll go back downstairs,” Bree said. “Ramsey’s at the front door.”

“Good.” Chu didn’t move as Bree went by.

“Mrs. Macallen?” Chu now leaned against the doorjamb, did not seem eager to leave. “Between us. Are you worried he’ll come back? Your husband?”

Was she worried? Yes, she was worried every second of every day.

“Ma’am?” the officer prompted.

“No,” Alyssa said. She was vulnerable if she pushed it. Crazy abandoned wife, she’d be labeled. Accusatory. Manic. Unable to cope with reality. “Look. I’m—

he's used to other people cleaning up after him. So he wouldn't care if others were disturbed by his carelessness. That's how he is."

"Your husband ignored the fact he was setting off an alarm." Chu nodded, skeptical. "You okay with that?"

"Maybe it wasn't him," Alyssa said. "A would-be burglar set off the burglar alarm. How it's supposed to work."

"Right," Chu said. "If that's how you want it."

They'd gone back downstairs, found Bree and Ramsey in the entryway, Ramsey examining the alarm pad.

"All clear," Ramsey reported. "Alarm's back in service. Just needs the code."

"Kitchen's fine, too," Bree said.

"Are you staying here now, Mrs. Macallen?" Chu had stashed her notebook into her jacket.

"We planned to go back down to the Cape," Alyssa said. "Is that okay?"

Ramsey cocked his head at the alarm. "We'll watch while you set it."

"And you know where to find us," Chu said. "If you ever want to tell us the truth."

The moment the cruiser pulled away, Bree grabbed her arm.

"You know it was Bill."

"He's tormenting me," Alyssa said. "As if he's trying to make me as angry as he possibly can. Does he *want* me to lash out? But why? I have nothing to trade. Nothing to offer. There's no way I can hurt him."

"Really?" Bree said.

FORTY-THREE

"What did you mean, 'really'?" Alyssa mulled over Bree's one-word question as they headed back for the Cape. Bree had taken a final look upstairs, while Alyssa checked the basement. The doors were closed, locked, and alarmed. The alarm company on alert. Alyssa wanted to be on the Cape, and Bill was not going to intimidate her to stay away. "Do you have some big idea?"

"No, but . . . ," Bree said. "You'd said there's no way you can hurt him. And I said—really? Because everyone has a way of hurting someone else. Don't they? Especially someone they've known for a long time. Some fear, or secret, or thing in their past they don't want anyone to know. Secrets are power, don't you think?"

"Sure," Alyssa agreed. Midafternoon Saturday was the best time to drive from Boston to the Cape, the early birds had already arrived, the procrastinators had made it to the bridge over the canal by now. Only the last-minute deciders—or those with other concerns, like Bree and her—were left on the road. They'd make good time. "I suppose I could tell everyone at the Club that Bill cheats at golf. Which he does. But they must already know that." She glanced at the rear-view, changed lanes. "He's the kind of guy they let cheat, you know? He's the—okay, I know there's no such thing as a king bee. But if there were. It's better to have Bill on your side. Keep him happy."

Bree ripped open the second bag of Fritos. "Why?"

• • •

"Nothing at all in Weston?" Dez met them at the kitchen door, holding an IPA.

"Nothing at all." Alyssa deposited her handbag on a wicker stool. The leather handles flopped over the sides, showing a half-eaten bag of Fritos and a crumpled Twizzlers wrapper.

"We looked everywhere," Bree said. "But like the cop told us, remember, Lyss? It had that atmosphere of emptiness, and it looked the same as we left it. I even checked to make sure the pilot light on the gas stove was working. And no one got into the guest house, either."

Dez swallowed. Put down his beer. "You sure?"

"The gas stove? So you agree," Alyssa said. "You agree he's . . ."

"Dangerous?" Bree's laugh sounded bitter. "There's physical danger, and there's emotional danger. And one way to create emotional danger is to instill the fear of physical danger. Every step you take, you wonder—will Bill be around the corner? Every time you go to lunch now, you'll wonder if Bill is watching you. You know that Hollis woman called him when we were at the Club." Bree perched on one of the kitchen stools, hooked her running shoes through the slats. "I saw her smirk at you when she came back."

"I'm changing the subject," Alyssa said, giving Bree a look. No need to go into the lunch bill with Dez. Might as well avoid another opportunity for embarrassment and pity. "What did you do today, Dez?"

"I met Eddie and Oscar, for one," he said. "They came over. Nice guys. Very Cape. They brought the beer." He held his up, illustrating. "And you were right, they *did* tell Bill you were here. Apparently, that's the procedure?"

"Yes, I'm . . . I should've told them not to. I forgot, and now—the whole thing is too complicated. Never mind. Any info from them? Bluefish running, celebrity sightings?"

Dez blinked, twisted his beer bottle on the counter.

"What?" Bree asked.

"What?" Alyssa said at the same time.

"They wondered if I was here—as a potential purchaser of the house. That maybe you were showing it to me."

"What?" Alyssa said. She heard her voice come out as a high-pitched yelp of surprise and wounded discovery.

"I know. I, ah, said no."

"You have got to be kidding me." Bree leaned forward, elbows on the island, chin in hands. "Can he even do that?"

"He's Bill Macallen." Alyssa yanked open the refrigerator. Considered the chilled rosé, but it was too early. She took out a bottle of sparkling water and some limes. Cheese. And the wine.

"I'll have some of that, please. If you are." Bree pointed at the rosé. "What a complete jerk."

"Got to give him credit, the bastard." Alyssa peeled the heavy foil from the neck of the wine bottle. "Selling this house? We're not divorced. There aren't any divorce papers even drawn up yet. Bas—"

"Is your name on the deed here?" Dez interrupted.

"Good question." Alyssa paused. "Bill does the

financial planning and bookkeeping, or someone does, our accountant. I just sign things. And if you're not worrying about your future, whose name is on what document sort of recedes into unimportance. We'll deal with that when the time comes, that sort of mindset."

She opened a cabinet, pulled out a box of water wafers, and bit the edge of the sealed cellophane packaging to open it. "Who'd have thought the time was now, right?"

Bree raised an eyebrow, traced a pattern on the kitchen island counter with one finger.

"I know this is pushing it," Dez said, "and feel free not to answer. But because of my job, I'm fascinated, professionally, by how different couples handle their finances. So—you have no idea if you're on the deed."

"Let me open this first," she said, pulling the stopper from the wine. "I'm so fried from today."

• • •

The three of them sat in yellow web-backed director's chairs on the deck, wineglasses balanced on the wooden railing, watching the distant sunset over the empty beach, a streak of ruby slashing across the gray water. *Red sky at night,* Alyssa thought.

"I bet Bill doesn't really even want to sell." Bree inched her chair closer to the railing, then propped her sandaled feet up on the fence.

"Ha." Dez lifted his second IPA bottle. "But you're in the process of divorce, Alyssa. We did a few case studies on this very situation in our training. It's a tactical manipulative maneuver, an asset-amassing power grab, that some retaliatory spouses do. He apparently thinks he can get away with it."

"Bill always gets away with it."

"It's so special out here," Bree said. "Smells like salt, and sand. But Lyss, even I, an almost-stranger, can see Bill's trying to mess with you. Make you worry. And get you so destabilized that you agree to anything his lawyers propose. Make you *grateful* for the crumbs he leaves you." She poked Alyssa's arm with one finger. "You gonna stand for that?"

Was she? What would she have done without Bree and Dez to talk to? She'd been at Bill's mercy, that's how it felt, at least, but these two had helped her realize she had some skin in the game, too. She hadn't been the loving and patient wife for eight whole years to be discarded, abandoned with a scatter of what Bree called *crumbs*.

Alyssa leaned back in her webbed chair, stared into the changing-to-violet sky, wondered how her life had become so tumultuous. Or maybe—it was Bill's life that had gone wrong. "I keep thinking about that FBI investigation," she said. "Dealings with me aside, they must have had *something* on him, mustn't they? I mean, Parker was pretty specific. Fake charities, and pension money. Devastated victims. Where there's smoke, you know?"

"The FBI? Who knows with those people." Bree shrugged. "Maybe they had the wrong guy."

"Anyone want a beer? Or anything?" Dez held up his empty. "No? Be right back."

Alyssa heard the sliding glass doors open, then close and click shut. Heard the hiss of the waves, intensifying as high tide crept in. Soon the water would be halfway up the beach, leaving perfect fractal curves that bubbled, then vanished. The cycles of nature, Alyssa always thought, so inevitable and reliable. Unlike everything else in her world.

"Alyssa." Bree's voice was a whisper, almost lost in the waves. "Dez and I have been talking."

"What about?" She frowned. "And when?"

"When what?"

"When did you two—"

"Shh," Bree interrupted. "We only have a second. I just found out he looked up Hattie Parker."

"What? Looked her up?"

"Ask him about it."

"Huh?"

"But not right now. He'll know I told you. And we can't let him know that. Tomorrow."

"But—"

"It's fine. It's all good. Just ask him. But leave me out of it. Maybe—get your lawyer to mention—" She stopped. Widened her eyes. Alyssa had heard the doors slide open, too. "Don't you love this color?" Bree held up her foot, showing her pale-blue polished toenails. "It's 'so Cape,' as Dez says."

Clearly trying to change the subject as Dez returned, Alyssa knew, and she barely had time to register this perplexing new information—what had Dez discovered? *It's all good,* Bree had insisted.

"I have an idea," Bree said. "I was thinking about your Bill—"

"He's not—"

Bree waved her off as Dez settled back into his chair. "I know. Here's my thought. If Bill told Eddie and Oscar that he's selling the house, maybe, let's just say, they told me, too? Me with my nice new inheritance? And what if I offer to buy it, and see if he agrees to sell. Then we tell your lawyer, and he gets into trouble for undercutting you. Since that's what he appears to be doing."

"That's good. And doable," Dez said, twisting off his bottle cap. "I'm hearing that your probate procedure is progressing as planned. You'll be a rich woman soon, Bree."

"That makes one of us." Alyssa put an apologetic hand to her chest. "Yikes, sorry, Bree. It's hard not to be bitter."

"You're apologizing?" Bree swung her legs down, turned to face Alyssa. "You have to stop doing that, Alyssa. Let me list what I know after one week: your husband left you, with no explanation, high and dry."

"Not so dry," Alyssa said, holding up her wineglass.

"This isn't a joke," Bree said. "He walked out, but he's apparently broken into your house several times, once quite brazenly. He knew you were here on the Cape—and made you drive home, panicked, in fear, to be met by the police. He's probably laughing at you now. He's poisoned your reputation among people who used to be your friends."

"They apparently weren't—"

"Let me go on. From the smallest, nastiest lunch bill thing, to the biggest, most antagonistic threat to sell this very house, he's made your life miserable. Look how we even met! You were alone in a bar. Drinking. Alyssa, that's not you. It's not!"

"She's right." Dez had gentled his voice.

The fading light had hollowed his cheekbones, and his eyes, Alyssa saw, seemed to register concern.

"You two trying to make me cry?" Alyssa poured more wine into her glass, set the bottle back on the uneven weathered deck floor between them. She probably should have some food. Or maybe she would never eat again. What would be the point? As empowered as she could make herself feel, that swelling of personal determination was as fragile as a helium balloon, inevitably deflating. She felt like that now, limp and useless. For better or for worse, she'd vowed, and Bill had, too. As it happened, he got the better and she got the worse. "Trying to make me even sadder?"

"The opposite," Bree said. "I'm trying to help you. *We're* trying to help you, like you helped us."

"Bree and I were talking," Dez began.

Okay, Alyssa thought, *this must be what Bree meant.* She pretended this was new territory.

"And at this point, if you get divorced—" he went on.

"Not if." That was one thing Alyssa knew for sure.

Dez nodded, took another swallow of beer.

"When you get divorced," he said, "the money you'll receive, and the assets, can likely never be more than half. And you have no prenup. In my view, judging by Bill's current behavior, it will only become increasingly contentious. He's trying to prove the extent of his power over you. That's a tactic. To pressure you. To make you give up."

The sky had darkened to ink and charcoal, the last of the light edging the shallow waves. A single night bird, on the day's final mission, swooped over the water.

"He's deliberately trying to diminish you, Lyss." Bree narrowed her eyes at Alyssa, leaning closer. "Personally. To let you know he thinks your eight years of devotion to him—and don't make that face, I know you were devoted, I've seen all those photos online. Bill the center of attention, you in those expensive outfits, gazing at him adoringly. He never looked at you, did you ever realize that?"

She had, in fact, thought the very same thing. But

she didn't follow their logic. "You'd think—wouldn't you—that he'd try to be *nicer.* Conciliatory. So I don't fight him."

"He doesn't want you to even consider a fight. He wants you to feel defeated. That it's a done deal," Bree explained. "He *used* you—you're gorgeous, after all—and you did whatever he said to do. Why wouldn't he think he controls you? He always gets what he wants, how many times have you told us that?"

"And I'm the loser, you're saying."

"You don't have to be," Bree said.

FORTY-FOUR

Me? Not the loser? What world are you living in, Bree?" Alyssa felt as dark as the gathering night, and nothing the two of them were saying was making her feel any better. They'd foraged a dinner of cheese and crackers, and stayed out on the deck with the last of the pretzels as the stars came out.

"Rich people can get away with things," Bree said.

"Like Bill." Alyssa heard the bitterness in her voice. Her brain was embracing the wine, and the oblivion. For tonight, at least. Why did men always get to make the rules? Even Dez, who she still felt uneasy about. Bree seemed to defer to him, and Alyssa couldn't figure out why.

"I've seen it at the bank," Bree went on.

"I'm sure you have," Dez interrupted.

"All the time." Bree ignored him. "That's why I was so happy to leave. There's so much financial brinksmanship. Game-playing."

"Like what?" Alyssa asked. At least they'd stopped talking about Bill.

"Oh, duplicate bookkeeping. Multiple bank accounts in the same bank, or using different banks. Or making cash transactions just under the federal reportable amount. If the customer is a high-flyer, a big shot, there's a lot of looking the other way. And making sure the auditors never catch it."

"Huh," Alyssa said.

"And of course if a bank employee were to discover that and not report it in a timely manner . . ." Dez pointed a finger at Alyssa. "That's a crime. Just saying. It's called misprision of a felony."

"But my *point,*" Bree said, "is that if Bill's not in trouble with the FBI, there'll be no forfeiture. And that's good for Alyssa in the divorce."

"There's legally, and then there's realistically," Dez said.

"Thanks a lot." Alyssa toasted them with her glass. "It's so much fun to have my future be in someone else's hands. Especially when those hands seem to be trying to harm me at every turn."

Bree flapped the cracker crumbs from her navy-blue Osterville sweatshirt. She pulled the hood over her head, and yanked the drawstrings tight. Made an exaggeratedly sinister face. "You'll get it all if he dies," she whispered.

"Brilliant." Alyssa applauded, laughing. "I'll just make the divorce drag on for forty more years. Good plan."

Alyssa heard Bree puff out a breath as she pushed back the hood. Dez had propped his feet on the highest rail of the deck fence, and leaned back, precariously, in his chair. He'd taken all his empty beer bottles back into the kitchen, and now his eyes were closed, his breathing steady.

"Look at him," Bree whispered. "Out."

"A hard day doing nothing on the Cape," Alyssa said, remembering. "You and I were the ones who raced all the way to Weston, dealt with skeptical police, scoured an empty house. Hey—you checked the gas stove. You don't think Bill was trying to kill me, do you? Ha ha?"

"It's not funny." Bree examined the moon through her wineglass as she talked, sloshing the pale liquid back and forth. "You know Bill did something bad, don't you, Lyss?"

Alyssa looked over at Dez, his chest rising and falling. Asleep? She lowered her voice. "He's asleep. Tell me about Parker. What Dez found."

"What?" Dez seemed to sputter awake.

Bree widened her eyes at Alyssa, disapproving.

"We were talking about whether I thought Bill was trying to kill Alyssa," Bree said. "Just girl talk."

"You think he is?" Dez blinked, raked his hair away from his forehead, sat up straight again.

"Are you two joking?" Alyssa felt a chill cross the back of her neck. Animosity was one thing, even petty harassment, but homicide was another. "I've had too much wine, maybe, but . . ." She watched the two of them exchange looks. "Regular people don't just kill people. It's not a thing. Regular people are unhappy, and furious, even, and hurt. But killing someone is for crazy people. Over the edge, or drunk, or on drugs, or deeply disturbed. No matter how controlling Bill is, killing me would not make his life any better. Especially from prison."

"Unless it looked like an accident," Dez said. "Like you were so distraught and unhappy and—as he's apparently been gossiping—drinking so much that you, whatever. Left the gas on. Fell down the basement stairs. Drove off the road into a tree. Ever had any strange people following you on the highway?"

Alyssa tried to clear her head. Maybe she should make coffee. "You guys are fun," she said.

"Well," Bree said. "It's just a thought."

A few tiny bugs skittered across the lantern sconces

on each end of the porch, and the strings of fairy lights had bloomed on across the back lawn, as if some invisible hand had flipped a switch and pronounced it nighttime. It was transporting, almost, her fuzzy brain and the brilliance of the lights, and the depth of the darkness over the water. The pale glow of her friends' faces.

"What thought?" Alyssa persisted. "You think Bill wants to kill me?"

"Nothing," Dez said. "Forget it."

"Really?" Bree sounded confused, Alyssa thought. "We're not gonna talk about it?"

"Alyssa's not into it," Dez said. "So let's not go there. It's late. You two had a difficult and complicated day. Maybe we should hit the hay, get some sleep. Maybe tomorrow we'll do whatever you do on the Cape. Get cotton candy. Fry clams."

"I'm not into what?" Alyssa felt her emotional alarm systems begin to ping. Maybe heard the barking of an imaginary dog.

"Okay, so this is nothing," Bree said. "This is—theoretical. Imaginary. Not a real discussion."

"Okay," Alyssa said, but the dog did not stop barking.

"But Dez and I were talking, you know. And like I said before, if Bill were dead, all this would be over."

"Bill. You're talking about Bill dead. Not me dead."

"It would be sort of self-defense, you could say." Bree licked a finger, and swiped up the remnants of salt from the bottom of the pretzel bowl. "Emotional self-defense."

Alyssa shook her head. "I don't think so." *End of discussion,* she thought, and the dog went quiet.

"So, Alyssa?" Dez said. "We called Parker."

"Who's we? You and Bree? You called the FBI?" Alyssa tried to understand that. It seemed meddlesome, invasive, over the line. Dangerous, even. "I'm not sure . . ."

"No, no, not Bree. And not me, personally. Roshandra Jain. I was worried about you, frankly. Roshandra is very connected, very back channel, and I told her what had happened." He put up two palms as Alyssa continued to protest. "All totally confidential, because I knew she had experience in these things. So she did some digging, and says the FBI has given up on Bill. That's why I said that in the car. He's—they've decided, internally, to consider him small potatoes. But she told me she gets the feeling they're actually embarrassed. That Bill might just be too good at it."

"At what, do you think?" Maybe this was what Bree had been alluding to, about Parker.

"You know," Dez said.

Alyssa stood. "No. I don't."

"Okay. Okay," Bree reassured her, a patient parent. "Sit, okay?"

Alyssa lowered herself back into her chair. Maybe they'd been out here too long, in the too-warm-for-May evening, lulled by the spring breeze and the squawk of a gull or two, the relentless constancy of the waves. And the wine. What did they all have in common, really? Money, Alyssa realized again. Alyssa and Bree had each needed a friend, and Dez had joined them professionally, and they'd bonded over pizza and a power outage.

"So I told Dez," Bree spoke as if that moment of friction had never occurred. "What you and I had talked about that day on the way to find Collin Whishaw. *Strangers on a Train.*"

"What? That was nonsense," Alyssa said, remembering the Hitchcockian crisscross. That Alyssa would kill Collin Whishaw, and Bree would kill Bill Macallen. But Collin Whishaw was already dead. And clearly Alyssa had no part in that. "We were exaggerating. Joking. Because it seemed like such a goose chase. And we'd been watching movies."

"But it might be . . ." Bree paused as if deciding what to say. "When it comes to Bill . . ."

The night breeze picked up, rustled through the beach grass and the scrubby beach roses.

Alyssa burst out laughing. "Oh, right," she said, almost choking on her wine. "All our troubles would be over. If you killed my husband. Brilliant. Genius."

She took a beat, trying to gauge their responses. The fairy lights danced and twinkled. "I'm kidding, let me just assure you. For the record. In case you're wired with some hidden microphone." She cupped her hands around her mouth to make a megaphone, and spoke each word precisely. "I do *not* want to kill my husband. I do not want *you* to, either."

"Okay," Bree said.

"It's not even funny," Alyssa said.

"I'm not laughing," Bree said. "But the FBI says he's cheating charities, stealing money from people, and not only is he doing it, but he's so good at it they can't even catch him. So he just gets to win? Again? As always?"

"I hate him, you know I do. I didn't want to, but that seems to be his goal, and he's definitely succeeded. Have I wished he were dead? I cannot tell you how many times I've wished it. But a wish is simply a fantasy, a defense mechanism, the way we cope. Maybe even an effective way to cope with our failures, or our disappointments. But this is the real world."

"My very point." Dez tilted the mouth of his beer bottle toward her, emphasizing. "And in the real world, things happen. Falls. Car accidents. Food poisonings. Look at all the movies and TV shows about it."

"Precisely," Alyssa said. "And on all the movies and TV shows, the bad guys always get caught. People always get caught."

Dez raised one eyebrow.

"Of course they don't," Bree said. "You just hear about the ones who do."

"This is just alcohol-fueled babble, right? About movies? Just making sure." Alyssa heard the dog growling again, quietly, insistently. What did she know about Dez, really? Only what he'd told her.

"Don't you think Bill has enemies?" Bree asked. "Don't *you,* Dez?"

"Absolutely. People who are angry with him. People who know they've been cheated, or defrauded. People who've lost money because of him."

Bree nodded. "How furious might they be? Mightn't they be more logical suspects than, say, two people who are not connected with him in any way?"

"The FBI can't come up with anything," Alyssa said. "Parker never mentioned specific victims. And no one is going to kill Bill Macallen for cheating at golf, or for being arrogant and controlling. Half the men in the country would be dead."

"She's got a point," Bree said.

"Ha," Dez said. "But so, you think your only option is to sit back passively and wait for him to take action? That's what you're saying?"

"Well, I—"

"You know whatever Bill's doing to you is not

going to stop." Dez was leaning toward her, insistent. "Look, we've only known each other—"

"A few days. Six, maybe," Alyssa interrupted. And they'd been together for part of every one of them.

"And you are so generous, first to Bree, and now to me. But this is my training, Alyssa. I've dealt with people like him. The ones who let greed poison their very souls until nothing seems too outrageous. If you're dead, Alyssa, he doesn't have to share anything with you. Not a cent. No one has to make any decisions about the Cape house or the Weston house or the St. Barts villa or that little Cézanne. He thinks of his money as His Money. With capital letters. His. He's escalated and escalated, and it's only a matter of time before his gaslighting of you—yes, Bree told me—turns into true and physical danger."

"I . . . no. That can't be true," Alyssa said.

"If you're happily and blissfully married, you're not going to kill yourself, are you?" Bree asked. "But if you're despondent and drinking and off your rocker, then, huh. You're poor Alyssa. Poor, dead Alyssa. And Bill is rich and free."

She stood, trying to get her bearings. "You think that's what this is about?"

"Look. I know it's the oldest, boringest story in the book. But if Bill is—oh god, I hate to say this, because it's conjecture, but say he's in lust with someone else. He knows—and *she* knows—that as long as you're alive, you're nothing but a drain on the Macallen bank account."

"And since you don't financially contribute to the household . . ." Dez half shrugged.

Alyssa's eyes widened as she realized what might be coming next.

"He'll likely be forced to support you for as long as you live. And he doesn't want to do that."

"Or *she* doesn't." Bree paused. "Lylah Rhodes, with the mystery man who fathered her daughter. Did you ever find out who that was? Hmmm? Even Camden Hollis. Who seemed to take great glee in humiliating you. I wonder why. Don't you?"

Not a bird cooed, not an insect buzzed. Even the fairy lights had stilled.

"I know it's hard, Alyssa." Bree's voice had dropped to a whisper. "But we're—outsiders. We can see reality better than you can."

"You have to stop him, Lyss." Dez leaned toward her, a fraction of an inch. "Can you think of any way you can stop him?"

"Like what?" She sat down again, half to prevent herself from running.

"Like helping the FBI, maybe," Dez suggested.

"Or—making a move on your own," Bree said. "Somehow."

"How can I?" Tears came to Alyssa's eyes. "I don't know anything about anything."

"You sure?" Dez said. "Or maybe, if you think about it, you do?"

Alyssa crossed her arms over her chest, taking control. She was finished with this. A slithering non-conversation with two people who were acting like friends, but who were actually strangers.

"Look," she said. "All I have is my own integrity, in the end, whatever the end is; and don't we need to do the right thing, the good thing, no matter what forces are threatening us? We only have ourselves, that's the lesson I've learned. I counted on Bill, I counted on the world working the way I thought it should. But that's—not life."

"It can be," Dez said. With Bree's chair between them, he faced her head-on. "Life is not about being a victim. If you could wave a magic wand, with no ramifications, how happy would you be if he were out of your life?"

"Very," Alyssa had to admit.

"And you'd get all the money, Alyssa."

"Which would be pretty useless in prison. Where we all would be, forever, in one split second."

"No, we wouldn't," Dez said.

"You're scaring me, you two." All the things she didn't know about Dez and Bree—which was, basically, everything—stacked up in her mind, a tower of uncertainty. She'd been frantic about *Bill* possibly being in her house—but these two actually *were*. And sounding like characters in one of those old movies.

"Seriously. I'm not sure what you mean by 'out of my life,'" she went on, "but if for some crazy reason you're not joking, please, please, *please* erase this whole conversation from your brains. Erase, delete, and double delete. We've had a lot to drink and you're supportive and caring friends, and I am so touched that you're being honest and trying to take care of me. It's been a long time since I've had a wine-fueled late-night theoretical existential discussion with anyone but my pillow. But if you ever allowed one shred of possibility to enter your minds about putting Bill 'out of my life,' please annihilate it. No one is killing anyone. No one is even thinking about it."

"It was just talk," Dez said.

"Just talk," Bree repeated.

"Okay." Alyssa pursed her lips, nodded. "The end."

The night sounds filled the silence that surrounded the three. Alyssa had lost all track of time, in that limbo of too much wine and unsettling conversation and the unpleasant feeling that what Dez and Bree were pretend-proposing was more tantalizing than Alyssa dared to admit to herself. But plotting ugly revenge was one thing—that could be satisfyingly restorative. Plotting an actual murder was another thing entirely.

"Deal," Dez said. "This conversation never happened."

SUNDAY

FORTY-FIVE

Mickey hadn't texted her back, and Alyssa supposed that wasn't surprising. Most people didn't check their messages after midnight on Saturday. Sunday morning. Now, at way past four, Alyssa was sitting in bed, still wide awake. And still using the laptop she kept hidden in the bottom drawer of her side of the dresser. And what she'd discovered—in addition to tonight's disquieting and unsettling conversation—made her close and lock her bedroom door. And text her lawyer.

Not her divorce lawyer, not a chance. Professional as he was, he was a man. She didn't trust men right now. Especially after tonight. She almost didn't trust anyone.

Alyssa leaned against the driftwood headboard, and stared at her computer screen. So Bill was trying to sell this house. Fine. She'd known exactly how to find out if he alone legally owned it. The Registry of Deeds, she remembered from her secretarial job at her mother's real estate office, showed the ownership and mortgage records for each house in the county. Online, and in black and white, and for the entire history of the property. But it wasn't only *this* house, One Ocean Place in Osterville, that Alyssa had just searched. And not only the Weston house. She'd also looked up 2357 Partridge Street in Marbury. *All prime numbers,* Alyssa could almost hear Bree saying it. The place where Collin Whishaw had lived.

Where Dez had *said* Whishaw lived.

But there was no Whishaw listed, Collin or otherwise. Not from the beginning of the record-keeping, 1956. Which would have been arguably inconclusive, just like Alyssa's name not being on the Weston house deed didn't mean she didn't live there. But the deed for "Collin Whishaw's house" was in the name of Roshandra Jain. Roshandra Jain had purchased the home in 2011. And when Alyssa searched the directory of town residents, Roshandra Jain was listed as residing there.

She and Bree had been directed to Roshandra Jain's house.

Alyssa tried to trace the thread to the beginning. *Collin Whishaw,* she typed the name into Google again. And gaped at an unfamiliar screen. Where before they'd found that one address on Partridge Street, now there was nothing. No listings for a Collin Whishaw. No listings at all.

As if the man had never existed. And maybe that was true.

Her chest tightened as she tried to understand the words she read, again and again, on the registry deed. The words that taunted her. The words that meant the man now sleeping in the guest room down the hall was not who he'd told her he was. Or who he'd told Bree he was. Alyssa's brain collapsed into lockdown, not from the wine, or the lack of food, or the fact that she was still awake—she'd watched the sun set over Nantucket Sound the evening before, and now she was about to watch it rise. But Alyssa was now living in a completely different world.

She had to get to Bree without waking up Dez. She had to tell her what she'd discovered, and they had to figure out what to do. There was one pale-green wall between her room and the one next door, the one where Dez was sleeping. One pale-green wall between her and someone she had trusted, someone she had invited to be a house guest. She was holding her breath, she realized, as if he might be able to hear her breathe. As if he was listening right now, maybe hearing the faint tapping on her laptop keyboard, wondering what she was doing on the computer.

Or maybe he was listening to Bree. Dez had chosen the room between them, such a seemingly casual choice at the time. But maybe not, because it meant Alyssa would have to walk by Dez's room to get to Bree. Or Bree to get to her. And if he was on alert, he'd hear. He'd get up, too, and join them, all jovial and convivial and pretending, maybe, to have a hangover, and not let her and Bree have any time alone together.

He'd tried his best to keep Bree from going with her back to Weston. He'd wanted Bree to stay behind. And, thinking about it, he'd insinuated himself into this visit to the Cape. Alyssa had once thought his attention to Bree was romantic, that he'd wanted her affection. And then she'd suspected it was predatory, that he'd wanted her money. Her second idea was more likely. Poor Bree.

Alyssa closed her eyes briefly, willing herself not to panic. Her two guests—one innocent, one a liar—had no idea she was suspicious. She still had a little bit of time, though. She was awake. And they were both asleep. Dez, in particular, had a lot to drink, and was so woozy he'd fallen asleep on the deck.

Or pretended to. But all those empty beer bottles did not lie.

If they had really contained beer.

She closed the laptop, almost hugging it to her chest.

Alyssa had been the one who'd led Bree to Dez—but no, not really. She'd only suggested that Bree follow up on the gift from her mother, the access to the ancestry search. And together they'd found that online. So that was real.

And it had sent them to Partridge Street. So at least *something* about *that* was real, too.

And Dez had been there. And he knew about Collin Whishaw.

That meant Bree must have been his target. For some reason. He'd been ready to pounce as soon as she clicked "Yes, I'm sure" on the ancestry search. Alyssa was collateral, simply Bree's friend. If Alyssa had not gone to Vermilion that night, none of this would have happened. Or if it had, she simply wouldn't know about it. And now she was involved, and now she had to help Bree. Somehow.

She shifted position, adjusted the pillows behind her.

Her phone sat on the nightstand, stubbornly silent. The minute it hit 6:00 a.m., she would call Mickey, even if it woke her up, because now she was locked in her own bedroom in a house with a person who wasn't who he said he was, and who had—with his now-sinister colleague Roshandra Jain—offered her friend Bree an inheritance of millions of dollars.

And what made it worse, significantly and gruesomely and terrifyingly worse, they'd spent the last evening talking about—joking about, yes, joking about but still saying the words—killing and murder and death. About Bill killing her. About her killing Bill.

Or Dez killing Bill. Or Dez and Bree doing it. What if they were serious?

Her brain could not make those puzzle pieces fit, not into anything instructive, at least, but only into a dark picture of lies and manipulations. For reasons she could not fathom.

She put a hand to her chest, trying to quiet her heart, and realized she was wearing the T-shirt she'd put on the day before. She'd gotten the idea to look up the Whishaw house as she'd climbed up to bed the night before, around two, she calculated, and had become so curious she hadn't even washed her face before she got out her laptop. And if she did it now, turned on the water in the bathroom, she might not hear if Dez—or Bree—went down the stairs. And he'd know she was up, too.

And now if Dez Russo—or whatever his name really was—had lied about everything from moment one, what did that leave to be true?

Five minutes until 6:00.

To hell with it.

She grabbed her phone, tapped in Mickey's number. And then, hand trembling, instantly hung up. If she had to speak out loud, and if Dez was listening, he'd hear. It didn't matter what she was saying or to whom—he'd understand that Alyssa on the phone at the crack of dawn was probably not a good sign. She flipped to the text screen. *Yes, I called you,* her thumbs flew across the keyboard. *Don't call me back. Text.*

She waited, hearing her own breathing, as she watched for the three dots indicating Mickey was typing. As if watching would make them appear. As if Mickey, a married woman with a young child, a woman who had a life of her own, would be looking at her cell at this time of the morning. She imagined the three of them—Mickey, and her husband, Ross, and little Romy—cuddling together, blissfully and peacefully asleep. Like a family should be. Like *she* would never be.

But this was not about Bill anymore, not now. This was about the man in the room next door.

And about Bree.

Clutching her phone, Alyssa carefully got out of bed, easing down one foot at a time, then tiptoeing across the room and putting one ear to the wall, feeling like an idiot. She waited.

What?

The word bloomed onto the cell phone screen. Message from Mickey. Still standing by the wall, she typed, quickly as she could, explaining. The registry, the deed, Jain. The crisscross discussion about Bill. Their enticement to kill him. Her refusal. Their insistence it was a joke.

Get out, Mickey typed back. *Leave.*

Leave them here?

Yes.

What if

Go downstairs. Get in your car. Drive away. Then call me.

More words appeared before Alyssa could respond.

I have more. Confirmed. Parker not FBI. Bug? Get out.

FORTY-SIX

Alyssa put one hand on the bedroom doorknob, kept the phone in her other, and took a deep breath. She'd thrown on a sweater and jeans, jammed her feet into sneakers, stashed her laptop into her tote bag. She paused, stealing one second to survey the bedroom: her beloved quilt, the gauzy curtains, the view of the lawn and sand and sky, the vast rippling water that had given her so much peace. She'd never see it again, she somehow felt—not from here, at least. So many things were infinitely uncertain, as infinite as the waves to the shore.

Get out, Mickey had ordered. *Parker not FBI.*

Goodbye, she thought.

Holding her breath, she turned the doorknob, wincing as she heard the first click, and then the second. She paused, listening for an answering click from the room next door. She imagined Dez, or whoever he was, with his hand on the knob a wall's width away from her.

But it was okay, she reassured herself. If she saw him, she'd just flutter a wave, and head down the stairs as if she were in search of coffee or a look at the sunrise. And then run out the front door. *My car keys!* she thought, and then realized she had them. She'd been awake a solid twenty-four hours, and her brain was fraying around the edges.

Go.

She pushed open the door, hearing the edge brush against the hallway carpeting. She paused, couldn't help it. Turned to the left.

The door to the green bedroom was open. Wide open.

Bree's door was open, too.

Were they downstairs, laughing and chatting over a cup of her coffee, lounging on her deck? *Pretending* to lounge? Waiting for her? What had Dez told Bree? What did she think was going on?

She took the four steps to the room next door. It was empty. Bed perfectly made. No sign of a travel bag. No sign that anyone had ever been there. A few more steps to the open door of Bree's room. She was gone, too. Bed made, no travel bag, not an item moved from where it always was—dried flowers on the night-stand, shells on the bathroom counter, even the shower mat lined precisely along a row of tiny white tiles.

She flew down the stairs, one hand on the banister to keep her balance. Swung herself around the corner and down the hall, knowing, with terrifying certainty, that the two of them were gone.

Which meant that either Dez had taken Bree against her will, or they were somehow in it together.

She stopped by the entryway table, regrouping, clutching her tote bag to her chest, her heart racing out of control now, even more than before. There was not a sound from the kitchen. Not conversation, not the burble of the coffee maker, not the rush of the waves through an open screen door. If they were in it together, what was "it"? The last thing they'd discussed was killing her husband. And, she now fully understood, trying to get her to agree.

Parker not FBI. Bug?

If she ran to the car as Mickey had instructed, she'd never know if Dez and Bree were still here. And if Bree was in trouble, there'd be no way to warn her. She'd pushed Bree into this, into the genealogy search. She'd only meant to be benevolent and helpful, but all her good intentions had led Bree into some kind of danger. Or trap.

Parker not FBI.

On day one, Bree had told her she was running. Running so hard that she'd packed up what she could and left her entire life behind to hide out in a no-frills hotel.

It was Alyssa herself who had offered the "abusive boyfriend" excuse, which Bree had instantly accepted, and embellished. She'd even commiserated with Alyssa about the tyranny of "men." But after a few texts and phone calls—which always seemed to happen when Bree was in the bathroom—the mysterious "Frankie" had conveniently disappeared.

Maybe Dez—and his offer of "seven million dollars"—was the trap. Clearly, Roshandra Jain was in on it. And Alyssa had no idea why. But it had to be connected to whatever Bree was trying to escape.

Her cell phone vibrated in her hand. A text. From Mickey.

You gone?

She looked at the front door. And turned the other way. In a few steps, she was at the entryway to the kitchen.

It was empty.

• • •

"Where do you want me to go? Home? Your office?" Alyssa talked into the speaker as she once again navigated her SUV through the rotary and onto the highway. Yesterday, she and Bree had driven this same road in panic, fearing what they'd find at the Weston home. Now Alyssa feared what had happened at the *Osterville* home. She now, ridiculously, felt as if she had no safe place in her life. So heartbreaking that Mickey—a friend from another time—was the only person she could rely on.

"And Parker?" Alyssa said into the speaker before Mickey could answer. "Not FBI? What the hell? Who is she? What does that mean about the bug? Why would she—"

"Just head toward Boston, Al," Mickey said. "Then we'll decide where you should go. I'm still home. We don't know what'll happen in the two hours it'll take you to get to town—well, yes, come to my office. I'll get there as fast as I can. Are you okay to drive?"

"I'm not okay for anything," Alyssa said. "And now? Dez and Bree are gone. Totally. As if they were never here. Mickey? Should we call the police?"

Alyssa heard a sigh on Mickey's end. "I'm not sure what we'd tell them. But listen. Remember when we first talked, I told you there *was* a Parker on the FBI roster?"

"Yes." Alyssa nodded. Checked her rearview. Moved to the fast lane. "And you said you'd have your investigator confirm."

"Exactly. And investigating FBI agents ain't the easiest task, let me tell you. But listen. There *are* agents named Parker. Several of them. Hattie's real first name is Stetson, which is why it took a minute. But turns out she quit, several years ago, and now lives in Marrakesh. I talked with her, via Zoom, and she's just as surprised as we are."

"So who was—?" Alyssa frowned. "The office in Center Plaza?"

"Vacant."

Alyssa's head buzzed, she could almost hear the sound as she tried to focus on the Sunday traffic filling the highway ahead, cars with surfboards bungee-corded to their roofs and bicycles of all sizes attached to their rear doors. She needed sleep. She needed explanations. She needed her life back.

"Vacant," she repeated. She envisioned the room where Parker had questioned her; the folding chairs and the ugly metal desk. Parker's starched white shirt. Her insistence that Alyssa must know the inner workings of Bill's business. Her plan to have her recruit "friends" to entice Bill to do something illegal. Her cajoling, her sympathy, her persuasion. Her threats about the dire consequences for Alyssa if she refused.

Kickbacks. Illegal. Forfeiture.

Twenty-two million dollars in a secret bank account in her name. Now certainly a fabrication.

She sighed. But better for the money to be imaginary than to have to explain her way out of some financial land mine Bill had planted. Plus, the account wasn't secret if the FBI—*wait*.

"If she wasn't FBI, who was she?" Alyssa asked. "You can't just impersonate an FBI agent."

"Look, Alyssa," Mickey said. "Right now, you've got a more imminent problem. And possibly so does your husband. This Dez person, who you say—"

"Wait, Mickey?" Alyssa did her best to focus on the road, yearning for coffee and wondering if her brain was working properly. "Can you get your investigator to go to One Beacon Place?" She narrowed her eyes, replaying her mental video. "Go to room 2102.

Find out what that is. See if there's a Roshandra Jain there. That's where Jain and whoever Dez is gave Bree the documents saying she had seven million dollars. I saw them. Those documents were at my house, in fact. They're still in the guest house, I bet. I tried to look at them in Jain's office, but I never read them."

"It's impossible to prove what happened there." Alyssa heard the defeat in her lawyer's voice. "If this is some scam, they'll flat-out deny it all. Documents, millions, inheritance. Pretend it never happened. You're deranged. Vindictive about Bill. You made it up. And that's even if we could find those people."

Alyssa frowned, then steered into the middle lane, playing it safe. And then remembered.

"Mickey. Hey. Yes, we can. Prove it. I recorded that conversation. On my phone."

"You recorded it?" Mickey's peal of laughter came through the speakers. "Forgive me, Al, I realize nothing is funny. But you recorded it? Why the hell would you do that?"

"Oh, you know, I just—thought what they were saying, Dez and Jain, might be confusing to Bree, or complicated, and maybe it would be helpful to listen to it all later."

"Do you still have that?"

"Pretty sure." Had she deleted it? A mile marker went by, and a tantalizing billboard for Starbucks. "Yeah, I have it. But Mickey, what's going on? That whole meeting was about the dead Collin Riley Whishaw, the long-lost brother of Bree Lorrance, who'd left her seven million dollars."

Silence on the other end.

"Mickey? What if—"

"Yeah, sweetheart." Mickey took a long breath.

"I've got to tell you—it seems like none of that is true. There's no Collin Whishaw. Never was."

"You really think—"

"And one more thing," Mickey said. "You may want to warn Bill that someone is on their way to kill him."

FORTY-SEVEN

Alyssa hit the gas, swerved into the fast lane, and set her sights on Boston.

"Warn *Bill*?" she said. "Me? Call him? And tell him—Mickey, that's—how am I supposed to do that? He'll never believe me, first of all, and probably think I'm trying to frighten him. Or, can you imagine? Even threatening him." She rolled her eyes, at the world and at her life. "Just like he's been doing to me. He'll think I'm pitiful."

"Well, if he does, he may wind up dead. He may be playing games, but you aren't."

"He'd probably call the police. No, he'd call his lawyers. And, yes, tell them I'm threatening him. That like—" The landscape swept by, billboards and power lines and wind farms, and it was as if her life was going by at eighty miles an hour, too, maybe faster. "That like I'd hired those people to kill him. And was trying to make an alibi for myself."

"So we'll call the police."

"And tell them what?" Alyssa heard the pitch of her voice rise, heard the fear and the uncertainty and the tension. "That two people whose real names we don't know and whose whereabouts we don't know and whose addresses we also don't know are plotting to kill him for reasons we don't know? They'll throw me right in the loony bin."

"Well—"

"And two people, essentially strangers, who I invited to my actual house, are involved? Maybe I *should* be in the loony bin. I hate Bill for this, I really do."

"A sentiment that, speaking as your lawyer, you might not want to be saying, Alyssa."

Alyssa clamped her mouth closed.

"Hang on," Mickey was saying. "I'm sending my investigator to One Beacon. But it might be too early. The building might not be open to the public yet. But she's good, she'll get in, hang on. Stay with me. I'll leave the line open."

Something pinged in Alyssa's brain. "I'm putting you on hold," she said. "I have an idea." And she tapped the Hold button before Mickey could respond. Flipped to her contacts, trying to keep her eyes on the road at the same time. Hit Call. It was probably too early, still before seven, but they were early risers.

"Hey, Alyssa, you're up at the crack," Eddie said. "Is everything okay? You need more lobsters? Oscar's going to The Yard at eight, so perfect timing."

"Nope, yup, all good." Alyssa tried to keep her voice breezy and casual. "My friend Dez told me you'd come over yesterday with beer, and I wanted to thank you."

Silence from Eddie. "Oh, right, no," he said. "He was at the Little Market, and he was already buying beer."

"Right," Alyssa said, narrowing her eyes. The traffic had slowed for a road construction project, and the merging lanes inched along, jockeying for position between rows of bright orange cones. That's not what Dez had described. "And he was telling me about—well, what's the latest on the sale of One Ocean Place?"

"What? You're selling it?" Alyssa could hear the surprise in Eddie's voice. "That's—a shock. Are you looking for a new place? Want Os and me to help? You're not leaving us, are you?"

Alyssa took a deep breath. Tried for indulgent good-wife cheer. "You know Bill. Always thinking about deals. I'd thought Bill might have mentioned it to you, and you told my friend. But my friend must have heard it somewhere else." She paused. "He does love his beer, as you could see. Probably got confused. But no, we're not selling."

"That's good to hear. Whew. And your husband's never talked to us about that."

"Got it," Alyssa said, and the traffic started again, picking up speed. She needed to get moving. The construction delay had eaten up valuable time. She hit the gas a little harder, risking it. So Dez had lied. Again. "Between us? I thought it was a terrible idea. So let's . . ." She lowered her voice, and whispered dramatically. "Never speak of it again."

"Never," Eddie played along. "Anything else?"

Was there? "Yeah," Alyssa said slowly. "I'm in town today, and my friends will be in and out. Could you stop by at some point? Just see if they're there? And let me know? Don't tell them I sent you, we had a big talk about how they'd be fine on their own."

"Gotcha," Eddie said. "I'm the vault. Ciao."

"Ciao," Alyssa said.

When she clicked back to Mickey's line, there was only white noise. "Mickey?" she asked, just in case, but there was no response. The Dorchester Yacht Club appeared to her right, the venerable but rickety structure a haven for family boats since as long as anyone could remember, with Boston Harbor stretching into the horizon beyond. It was early enough that the frantic commuter traffic hadn't started, and Alyssa had an odd feeling of separation, as if she were alone in the world, and speeding toward the unknown.

Dez had, for some reason, tried to make her hate Bill even more. And had pretended to be distressed and concerned about the sale of One Ocean Place, when actually he'd concocted the entire story. They'd headed upstairs about two in the morning. She'd found their open doors around six. If Dez had *forced* Bree to go with him, wouldn't Alyssa have heard that? Maybe. Maybe not. She'd been focused on the computer, and early on, footsteps and murmured voices would have seemed normal. It might have been as long as four hours before she'd realized they were no longer there.

Were those sirens? She eased to the right, gently steering into the slow lane, realizing how fast she was going, making room as the sirens grew louder. Two sets of them. Must be something big going on in Boston.

She noticed the other cars slowing, too, guilted into obeying the speed limit.

The sirens grew louder, closing in on her, and she braced herself for the velocity of them going by. But the cruisers stayed in her rearview. She slowed even more, perplexed, since she was down to about fifty now, molasses here on the Southeast Expressway.

A siren chirped behind her. Then again. And then a blue-and-gray state police car pulled up alongside her, matching her speed, keeping perfectly parallel. She glanced out her window. A trooper in one of those big hats was in the passenger seat of the cruiser, and with the wave of one hand and a pointed finger, signaled her to pull over. Her brain flared, her heart raced, and her conscience kicked in. Yes, she was guilty of going too fast. But all she needed, *all,* was to be stopped for speeding. And why *her*? The excuses scrambled to the top of her mind. She was only going the same speed as everyone else. Why not stop *them*? Why, today of all days, did they choose her? Because she was a woman, she decided, in a fancy SUV, and the staties were out to get her. As was, clearly, the universe.

"Fine. Fine. *Fine,*" she whispered. Probably the only time a driver had been pulled over by the cops when their lawyer was already on the phone.

She eased to the breakdown lane, and then onto the shoulder of the road. One trooper car pulled in behind her, and then another. Lots of firepower for one speeding driver, she thought. She buzzed down her window, reached into her tote bag for her wallet and license.

"Mickey?" she said into the phone. "You're not gonna believe this."

"Ma'am?" The trooper, as square-faced and hard-edged as if he'd been carved from the trunk of an oak tree, stood angled outside her window. His sunglasses were tucked into his navy-blue uniform shirt pocket.

"What's wrong?" she asked. Still only white noise from her phone, but the timer was still counting, so she knew the connection had not been broken. Mickey was still investigating Roshandra Jain's office.

The trooper consulted a slim spiral notebook, then looked at her, then looked at the notebook again.

"Sir?" she prompted, trying to be respectful and

submissive. Anything that would get her back on the road. She had to get to Mickey's office. Dez and Bree had vanished—and either they'd simply gone out for coffee without her, or they were about to kill her husband. And then implicate her in the conspiracy for some reason she could not even imagine. Getting nailed for speeding was exactly what she didn't need.

"Are you Alyssa Macallen?"

"What?" Nothing could have surprised her more. Although maybe they'd run her license plate. And who knew what fancy technology the cops had. She thought of Hattie Parker. At least this guy was authentic.

"Yes," she said. And had to ask, "How did you know that?"

"Did you have a woman named Embry Lorrance living with you?"

All the blood went out of her face, the cop must have noticed her distress, and she struggled to find her voice. It wasn't working.

"We don't have time for this, ma'am, we know she was staying with you," the trooper said. "You might be in danger, ma'am."

"Danger? Me?"

Another trooper had stayed in the front seat of their cruiser, and two more, she saw in her rearview, sat sentry in the matching car behind her. Traffic zoomed by behind them. The sun sparkled on the harbor, and a few gulls swooped and sailed, scouting for their Sunday breakfast.

"We need you to come with us, ma'am."

"Why?"

"Right now."

"But why? You said I was in danger. How did you even know where to find me? You can't just—you have to tell me."

"Look, ma'am, it's difficult."

"Difficult? Mickey!" she yelled. The officer looked perplexed. "I'm on the phone." She pointed at it. "With my lawyer, in fact. So anything you need to tell *me*, you can tell *her*. Mickey!" she yelled as if raising her voice would make a difference.

"Alyssa? I'm back now." Mickey's voice crackled over the speaker. "Our investigator is on the—"

"Mickey, hang on," Alyssa interrupted. "I'm here with Trooper—" She paused, read the trooper's metal name tag. "James Rose. He pulled me over on the Southeast Expressway. And there's another trooper car behind me, with two officers inside."

"Are you okay? What happened? Why?"

"I'm okay, but I don't know," Alyssa said. A radio clipped to the trooper's epaulet blurted a squawk of static. "They knew who I was. They told me I was in danger."

"Officer?" Mickey's voice came through the speaker more loudly now. "What can I help you with? I'm Mrs. Macallen's lawyer."

"We need her to come in," the officer said.

"Listen," Mickey said. "You pulled my client off the road. You frightened her. Now is the time to tell me what's going on. And by now I mean now."

Alyssa saw the trooper's shoulders deflate. Watched his face change. He consulted his notebook again.

"What's your name?" he said toward the phone.

"Mikaela Fahey. With the Fahey Law Firm. Now it's your turn."

"We've arrested Embry Lawrence and her brother, a Desmond Russo, on suspicion of attempted murder."

"Her *brother*?" Alyssa's brain shattered into infinite pieces. "Murder of who?"

"Murder of who?" Mickey said at the same time.

"Your husband," the officer said.

Two cars, then three more, powered by as Alyssa let that sink in.

"Is he—dead?" Alyssa asked. *Attempted* murder, her brain reminded her. "Is he okay?"

"He's fine," the trooper said. "The suspects were intercepted before the crime occurred."

"But why—" Alyssa began. Then stopped. Visualized what might be happening this very minute. Or had already happened. She'd realized, with growing dread, that right now, Dez and Bree might be sitting in separate rooms in some miserable police interrogation office, spinning a story. Telling them that the murder of Bill Macallen was all Alyssa's idea. Angry, bitter, devastated, soon-to-be-penniless Alyssa. Why else would she have been involved with them? Why else would she have invited them into her life?

This traffic stop was a thinly disguised arrest in process. Her only defense was to insist that the tale Dez and Bree were relating was a lie. But what evidence did she have of her innocence? Absolutely none.

The trooper's radio squawked again, then, "Six-oh-two, requesting status," a scratchy voice said. The trooper keyed a mic with his thumb. "In process." A massive big rig rumbled by, mud flaps fluttering, kicking up a cloud of road dust and leaving a plume of pungent exhaust.

"Officer?" Mickey's voice came over the speaker. "So why do you need my client any further?"

"It's Lieutenant. And for obvious reasons. One, she knew these people. And we'll need to ask her some serious questions. And two? It's possible that she might be next."

FORTY-EIGHT

Don't say anything, Mickey had ordered her. Mickey had negotiated with Lieutenant Rose that Alyssa could drive herself to Mickey's downtown office, and they would all meet there. The troopers made no attempt to hide that they were escorting her, but Alyssa had no intention of going anywhere else. This was all Bill's fault, she couldn't help but think. Her hands clenched onto the steering wheel. *Bill's fault.*

She took the final exit, staying under the speed limit. The two cruisers followed, predatory and watchful, and their caravan navigated the twisty, narrow streets of downtown Boston.

Bill's fault. She wouldn't have been at Vermilion in the first place, sitting in that middle stool and mooning over her vodka, if Bill hadn't walked out and left her miserable. She'd never have met Bree, their paths would never have crossed. Which left her sad, surprisingly, since she'd truly felt a bond with her. *Shows you about my judgment,* Alyssa thought. *Even when I try to do a good thing, it backfires.*

She clicked on her blinker, so law-abiding, and steered into the underground parking lot of Mickey's steel-and-glass office building. Lurched over the traffic bump, and down the ramp. No sign now of the troopers behind her. Maybe they'd parked on the street for a faster getaway. *She* was the one who needed to get away, but that was hardly in the cards.

She wasn't as surprised by Dez—she hadn't trusted him from moment one, and it was only Bree's reassurance that quieted her doubts. *Brother and sister,* Alyssa thought. And remembered how often she'd described them to herself as behaving like siblings.

And if they were siblings, why didn't they have the same last name? Millions of possibilities. But they were equally complicit, and equally liars, and equally guilty, and she was a complete hopeless idiot.

She found a parking space, pulled in, switched off the ignition. Sat, behind the wheel, in the gray stillness. In a few minutes, she would get some answers. Wherever that would lead.

Answers about the duplicitous and manipulative Bree and Dez.

About the not-dead and nonexistent Collin Whishaw. About the equally squirrely Roshandra Jain.

About Hattie Parker. If she wasn't an FBI agent, what the hell was she doing?

And, if it was even connected, answers about Bill Macallen's erratic and inexplicable behavior.

"Come in, sweetheart." Mickey had embraced her as she buzzed open the glass entryway doors to her law firm. "No one else is here yet, and I've made coffee. You've never said no to coffee. You okay?"

"I'm terrific," Alyssa said. "As you can imagine."

"Right."

They walked to Mickey's office, Mickey's comforting arm draped around her shoulders. "Listen. First of all, it was the FBI—the real FBI—who alerted those troopers to stop you," Mickey told her. "And the feds are in charge. They'd been watching Bree Lorrance and Desmond Russo, and turns out those are their real names by the way, because they'd both made statements about Bill in the past." She indicated the visitor's chair. "Have a seat."

"I can't sit still, can't possibly," Alyssa said. "Statements about Bill?"

Mickey put her hands over her face for a second, then took them away. "They said he'd bilked their parents. Defrauded them out of their pension money, life savings, something like that, who knows what's true. We'll eventually get the facts. Bree and Dez had decided that the way to take Bill down was to ingratiate themselves with you. Maybe find out Bill's secrets. From you."

"They planned it? *Together?*" Alyssa sank into a chair, her body leaden but weightless. She'd been so afraid for Bree. So proud of her. So protective of her. Her *friend.* She would never trust anyone again. Not ever. That was the only solution. "*Brother and sister?*"

"They didn't hurt you, did they?"

"Not physically," Alyssa said.

"Okay," Mickey said. "They were looking for evidence that Bill had some kind of ongoing scheme."

"But wait." All the coffee in the world would not make this any clearer. "Parker. If she isn't really the FBI, who is she? What about the bug? And there *is* an FBI investigation?"

"There are lots of questions. I know. I'm only telling you what the troopers told me."

"But Bree and Dez—so when I wouldn't help them get Bill, they decided to *murder* him? And incriminate *me*?" She tried to imagine it, any of it. Couldn't. "Really?"

"Their parents died, apparently. Penniless. As a

result." Mickey clasped her hands under her chin. "Maybe they—couldn't face the loss. So they decided to avenge it."

Alyssa nodded, reluctantly. Exhaustion would kick in soon, and she welcomed it. Oblivion would be nice. But again, not in the cards. She took another sip of coffee. Realized.

There *was* a scheme. Bill *was* a criminal. "Where's Bill now?"

"Yeah. I don't know. One step at a time."

A buzzer sounded, two short bursts of insistent static.

"The cops," Mickey said. "I'll let them in. Don't you say *anything*. If they ask you a question, don't answer. Wait until I tell you it's okay."

"I'm not involved with this, you know that, right?"

"You think I suspect that you conspired with those people to kill your husband?"

"I'm just asking," Alyssa said.

"Don't even talk about that." Mickey's voice had hardened. "Don't bring that up. Don't even think that. Let's hear what they have to say."

"You think that's what they think." Alyssa made it a statement.

"I don't know what they think," Mickey said. "That's why I don't want you to say anything. One step at a time."

"Mickey . . ."

"Alyssa. I'm your lawyer. Stop talking. I don't mean to be harsh, but sit there, and stay quiet. Drink your coffee. Let me take the lead."

"I told them, Bree and Dez, not to—"

Mickey whirled, one hand still on the doorknob. Narrowed her eyes. "Do not say a word."

FORTY-NINE

Mickey was gone longer than Alyssa might have predicted. Alyssa used the time to contemplate the last of her coffee, and to wonder where Bill was. Whether he'd left her because law enforcement was on his tail. To protect her, maybe? And what about Hattie Parker?

Her coffee cup contained only a scattering of soggy grounds. Reading the tea leaves, she thought. *Hattie Parker.*

Had Bree and Dez sent "Hattie Parker"? To come after her from two sides? That had to be it. They were all working together to get back at Bill. By using her. Staying in her house. Gaining her trust.

And that's why Bree and Dez had seemed eager to take part in Parker's "sting." It was *their* sting, too. Why had they called it off? Because they'd decided to murder Bill instead.

She pressed her lips together, imagining. Ashamed. Of her neediness, her dependence on money, her rage at Bill's behavior. Her self-centeredness. Her hubris about how she'd "changed Bree's life," pushing her to do the genealogy tests, buying her friendship with manicures and macarons. Had she almost caused the death of her husband?

Bill was a miserable person, sure. But she wouldn't have wanted *that,* no matter how miserable he was.

Now that her house guests had actually tried to kill

him, the depths of her sorrow increased. Two people—one of whom, at least, she had trusted—had duped her.

Even tapping into her angriest moments of grief and rage, Alyssa could not understand the suffocating depth of Dez and Bree's cynical manipulation.

But rage and sorrow and even love must have poisoned their better judgment, turning it into an obsessive desire for revenge. Bree didn't seem like the type, but what was the type?

Alyssa heard footsteps in the carpeted hallway, and steeled herself for the accusatory interrogation to come. She had not done anything wrong, she reminded herself. She had not agreed to anything. Exactly the opposite, she had told them no, and in no uncertain terms. Delete, she had said. Erase, forget. She almost hoped they'd been recording her. The possibility brought tears to her eyes. Dez was a mystery. But she had connected with Bree.

Mickey arrived alone. No cops.

Alyssa stood. Even more confused. Her heart was running on empty, but her brain was full. "Listen. I figured it out. Bree and Dez," she began. "*Hired* Hattie Parker—"

"Al? I'm going to tell you something." Mickey put up a palm. Stopping her. "But it's absolutely confidential."

Alyssa could not read her lawyer's face, could not take instruction or guidance from the lack of expression. She trusted Mickey. Although she'd trusted Bree, too. And Bill, for that matter. But now she'd risk it. She had no choice. "I understand."

• • •

The dog barked as Alyssa opened her front door. After her sleepless night, her devastating betrayal by Bree and Dez, and the gut-punch of the revelations from Mickey, it was all she could do to put one foot after the other. Her body only wanted to think about washing her face in the sweet creamy almond soap on her bathroom counter, peeling off every stitch of her clothing, yanking on an old T-shirt, pulling up the puffy comforter and sleeping forever. But her brain would not turn off.

"Bill's off the hook," Mickey had said.

"Off the . . . what?" Alyssa had tried to translate.

"The FBI was investigating him. All true. And they knew he was aware of it. But they're dropping the investigation for now."

As Alyssa, brain in flames, had lowered herself into the visitor's chair again, Mickey bullet-pointed what she'd just been told. Someone at some financial institution had been suspicious of several of Bill's transactions, including the Russo/Lorrance dealings. Had reported those to the FBI. Because of that, the feds had looked into Bill's finances. And found nothing untoward.

"Edgy, yes," Mickey had explained. "Pushing the envelope, yes. Out of the box, yes. Any of those clichés that you choose. But arguably—and that's the key—not illegal. And the return on investment of their time and energy to prove any potential transgressions was, in their words: not worth it."

"Not worth it," Alyssa repeated, her exhausted brain now a charred ember.

"The FBI told that to Bree and Dez," Mickey went on. "They were—disappointed. So apparently, those two offered to investigate Bill on their own. Using you as a source."

"They let them do that?" Which was exactly, Alyssa

realized, what "Parker" had suggested Alyssa do to Bill.

"As I've said, Al. They can do anything they want. As long as it works."

"But Bree and Dez—they tried to convince me to let them *kill* him! They pressured me. Pushed me." Alyssa remembered *Thelma and Louise. Strangers on a Train.* "Bree had it in her head from almost day one."

"Yeah, the feds were upset about that. They called in the staties, and voilà, today. They 'apologize profusely.'" She bracketed the quote with her fingers. "Well. Fast-forward. I threatened to sue the FBI for invasion of privacy, unauthorized surveillance, unethical behavior, and an additional mind-blowing list of transgressions. And also to make it blazingly public."

"Hell yes. Go for it. Government intrusion. Manipulation. Entrapment. That bug. We should—" She'd stopped, seeing the expression on Mickey's face. "What?"

"Well." Mickey seemed to search for words. "They threatened—mentioned—that they could charge you with conspiracy to murder."

"What? I never—"

"I know. You play chess?"

"Huh?"

"It's stalemate. The endgame. Long story. We won't sue, they won't charge you."

Time had stopped, Alyssa was sure it had. She could almost see Lady Justice holding those scales, the two sides rising and falling and trying to balance.

"Can they *ever* charge *him*? Bill?"

Mickey shrugged.

"So Bill gets away with it again." Alyssa dragged

her hands down her face. For all her relief, she still saw who was coming out on top. Always, always, *always* Bill. And it might make *her* the one under public scrutiny. "What about Dez and Bree? Will I have to testify?"

"No. I told them under no circumstances."

"I need to go away," Alyssa whispered, almost a plea.

"I think that's a good idea, sweetheart."

Yes. She'd leave Boston, leave her ridiculous life behind, let Bill sell whatever the hell he wanted and screw whoever the hell he wanted and never think of him again. She'd learn to be someone else. Or even better, be herself. She felt her eyes well, felt the exhaustion and defeat through to her bones.

"Bill wins again." She stood, fists on hips. "Bill always wins."

Mickey stood behind her desk for a beat, then in a few steps had gathered Alyssa into a hug. "You win, too," she whispered. "Count your blessings it wasn't worse."

It was all Alyssa could do not to cry. "Thank you, Mickey." She spoke the words into her lawyer's shoulder. "I'll let you know where I am."

"You'll be fine," Mickey said. "I promise."

"I guess so," was all Alyssa could manage.

And now here she was again, at a little after five on a waning Sunday afternoon, alone in this echoing home, an expanse of wood and bricks and possessions and somehow full and empty at the same time. Full of shadows and lies and the residue of betrayals, empty of all she'd believed in. She looked at herself in the mirror over her bathroom sink, saw her eyes sad with fear and confusion, realized she hadn't looked at her hair for the last ten hours, wondered how her very soul, defeated and disappointed and in despair of the future, could be so visible in the wide pane of silvered glass. The scatter of pink-centered conch shells multiplied in the mirror, too; shells she and Bill had carried back from St. Barts, meant to be memories, but now only—she stopped, mid-thought.

The shells had been moved.

Alyssa stared at them. When she'd left for the Cape, they'd all been lined up on the left of the mirror, the biggest in the back, the smaller ones in the front. Tammy always arranged them that way. Now all the spiky white shells were on the right side of the mirror, nearer the door. And the tip of every shell was pointed the same way. Toward the closet.

THE NEXT WEDNESDAY

FIFTY

It was almost magic, Alyssa thought, how certain fragrances could elicit such deep memories. The sweetness of the frangipani blossoms that encircled the railed balcony where now she stood, alone, at the St. Barts condo Bill had named Eden. The coconut sunscreen she'd applied to her bare arms and legs. The pungent fresh pineapple she'd cut and cored and sliced by herself, now arranged in a chunky ceramic bowl, her favorite one, painted in the same intense turquoise as the Caribbean that stretched out to the almost-matching blue horizon before her, past the serene waters of the still-breathtaking infinity pool three marble steps down, past the treetops of the palms beneath the water's edge, and the vast vacant expanse of pearlescent sand.

It had taken less than a day for her to make all the arrangements. She'd used her credit card to buy her tickets. She'd quickly packed the little she needed; they both had Eden clothes so they'd never need luggage. Ubered to the airport, arrived on the island. A different world now. A beginning.

She'd make new memories, she decided, tasting the sweetness of the fruit and the possibilities of what was to come. Licking the juice from her fingers, she selected another piece of pineapple, and let the almost-equatorial wind play with the hem of her gauzy white sundress. Her bathing suit was underneath, the tiniest she could find, and she'd taken a moment, looking in the coconut-shell bordered mirror in the entryway, to recognize that the weight she'd lost in grief left her looking pretty darn great in a bikini. She'd left her hair wild, untouched, and it had curled and waved with the humidity and salt air.

When the doorbell rang, she expected the groceries she'd ordered from Étienne's or the fresh towels their majordomo had promised to provide. She adjusted her filmy dress, making sure it was presentable—though St. Barts had its own particularly lax rules about "presentable"—tossed her hair and opened the door.

Bill.

She took two steps back, feeling nervous and somehow uncovered, put her fingers to her lips.

"Bill." His name was all she could think of to say. What she did now, what she decided, would change her life, and his, maybe, and she knew it.

"Lissie," he said. "You look amazing."

She hadn't seen him in—more than a month? So no reason to be surprised that he looked the same, but he looked even better than the same; a white linen jacket, a Caribbean turquoise linen shirt over white jeans. Woven sandals. Sunglasses. His hair seemed somehow already sun-kissed, and Bill, too, had his own fragrance.

"How did you know I was here?" She almost didn't recognize her own voice.

"Oh, Lissie." He hadn't moved from the doorway, and stood, with the succulent-bordered walkway behind him, palm fronds from graceful cylindrical tree trunks almost touching the top of his head. "I *always* know where you are."

"But—" Her mouth and brain were not connecting,

and her knees were not quite right. "How?" was all she could think of to say. "Why?"

"Don't you know that by now? Every time you use a credit card, I see it. It's my connection to you. And my airline person called me the instant you booked St. Barts, babe. Sometimes I come visit you when you're not home. I know the damn rules, but I can't resist. I touch your clothes, check your mail, sit in my chair."

She could only stare at him. "You left a *knife* on the kitchen floor."

"Knife falls, gentleman calls? Right? Did you get that? And how about Tammy? She must have told you I was there." Bill kept talking, his words encircling her. "She's an idiot if she didn't. I *told* her to tell you! I rehired her, by the way. Just to make you happy." He pointed at her with one forefinger, amused. "*You.* She told me you sent her the emerald necklace I gave you. The house necklace. You're too much, babe. And we'll get you another one."

"What about last weekend?" She'd make him admit that, too. And she'd never tell him about her traps. "The alarm? Why would you terrify me like that?"

"Terrify? You'd gone to Osterville with . . . those people. That was *our* place, Lissie. Only for us." He made his pleading-puppy face. "I screwed up about the door, okay? And I erased myself right after, I was so embarrassed. I was just . . . missing you."

She saw longing in his eyes. He *missed* her?

"May I come in?"

She caught herself, took another step back. Tried to remember the last time Bill had asked for permission for anything, remembered all the things she'd promised herself she'd say if she ever saw him again. She'd expected, for a long time, that it would be in the contentious iciness of a lawyer's office, not standing on the warm terra-cotta tiles of their stucco island villa.

"What are you doing here?" she finally said. "Are you trying to take this, too? My peace? My privacy? Everything I have left?"

"Babe." Bill's voice was the old Bill's voice. Beguiling. Persuasive. She'd heard it so many times. Been enticed by it, swayed by it, seduced by it. "You got my postcards, I hope? To remind you how much I was missing you? Our time together? Hon? Will you let me talk?"

Alyssa shivered, even in the heat. "I'm freezing," she said. "I'm getting a wrap. Don't move. If you stay there, I'll know I can trust you."

"You have one minute," he said. A rangy black bird fluttered to the railing behind him, and perched there, blinking its yellow eyes at her.

Alyssa whirled, felt the gauze floating behind her, and felt Bill peering through the translucent fabric. She came back wrapped in a black terrycloth robe, belted hard and tight, its shawl collar up to her neck. He was still at the door. Still smiling. Still watching her.

"I'd seen you in far less than that," he said.

Alyssa smelled the tequila on his breath. He always drank on the plane to Eden. "You said you wanted to talk." Alyssa adjusted her bulky robe. "Talk."

"It would be easier if I came in." He took a step across the threshold. Sniffed. Drew in another long breath. "Smells like Eden," he said. "I've missed this. Missed you."

FIFTY-ONE

"You said you wanted to talk," Alyssa said again. She chose the fan-backed wicker chair, leaving Bill to sit alone on the flowered couch across from her. She'd created several oversize arrangements of deep red frangipani encircled with glossy green leaves, and one sat on the end table beside him.

Bill had taken a folded piece of paper from his pocket. Held it up. "I got this awesome letter from the FBI," he said.

She blinked, waiting.

"There'd been an investigation into my finances. Those assholes. And I knew it, knew it from moment one. Some moron at some bank decided I was a—" He paused. "Whatever, it's not important, that's why I had to leave. I couldn't risk you being drawn into it."

"Into what?" she asked.

"Oh, Lissie, it doesn't matter. As soon as I got this, though, I couldn't wait to find you. The letter says it's over. It was bullshit, but now it's in writing."

"Really?"

"The letter doesn't protect us going forward, but—"

"Us?"

Bill shrugged, amused. "Well, me. But I'm out, you're out, we're in the clear."

"I'm out of what?" Alyssa's eyes narrowed. "I didn't do anything."

"Of course not." Bill put the paper back into his jacket pocket. "I didn't, either. Ha ha." He leaned toward the frangipani, drew in the fragrance, closed his eyes. "Eden," he said.

"Out of what?" Alyssa said. "In the clear of what? Ha ha what?"

"You don't need to pretend anymore." He leaned back on the couch, crossed one bare ankle over a white denim knee.

She opened her mouth to answer, but Bill kept talking.

"Remember Parker? The FBI agent you talked to?"

Alyssa blinked, silent. "The FBI agent?" she finally said.

"Oh, come on, babe, it's over now. You have no secrets from me, never have. I know you know her, because I sent her. I hired her. Sorry, not sorry, not FBI. She's an actor, a damn expensive improv actor, and gotta say, she played her part to the hilt. That office in Two Center? A floor away from mine? I knew those feds, even the real Parker, who'd retired to some weird place. And that day you talked to *my* Parker? Come on. I heard everything you said, and even if her wire hadn't worked, she told me you didn't divulge one word. That you defended me, even when she threatened. You refused to let her search my study. Even when she tempted you with twenty-two mill in a secret bank account. Even when she offered to compensate you. You're the best, Alyssa, my girl. That's when I knew I could trust you. That's not a real account, FYI."

"She wanted me to send people to—" Alyssa began. She remembered what he thought she knew. "Wait, she wasn't really—you *hired* an actor to pretend to be an FBI agent? Is that even legal?"

"Legal. Like that's the problem. I had to see if you'd agree, babe," Bill said. "But you held out. I had you followed home that day, wondering if you'd head for the cops. Even had a bug put in your car, which, sadly, malfunctioned soon after."

"A bug. In my car."

"I heard about your two new friends, too—and I had to wonder what *that* sweet little arrangement was. But you're allowed to have your fun, however you want to change partners or entertain yourself. You thought we were separated. And we're all adults. I forgive you."

Even with the robe, Alyssa felt a chill, and made sure the fleecy black folds were in place.

"So water under the bridge, or over the dam, we're home free. I had to test you. I had to see how loyal you would be. I figured if I made you hate me, truly hate me, and if even then you passed the loyalty test—"

"Loyalty test," Alyssa whispered.

"Big-time. And if even *then* you passed," Bill went on, sounding pleased with himself, with his own ingenuity. "After that, I knew you were truly on my side, and no matter what, if I managed to get through this, we could be together again. We had something, Lissie. I knew if I could trust you, we'd always be together. And safe. And rich." He patted the jacket pocket, almost caressing his letter. "Can you forgive me?"

"You . . ." Alyssa tried to decide. "Made me miserable. *Miserable.* On purpose."

"Babe. I knew you'd get over it. You'd understand it was for the greater good."

The greater good, she thought.

"So . . ." She could hear her own heart beating. "You don't want a divorce?"

"Hell no. You're my wife, and we're gonna stay that way. Isn't that awesome?"

"Awesome." Alyssa nodded.

"Is there champagne?" Bill leaned forward, twinkling at her, closing the space between them. "We should celebrate, right? You up for a swim? No suits allowed."

"Just wondering," Alyssa interrupted. "Before we get champagne. So that means even if they asked me to testify in court, I wouldn't have to."

"Hundred percent. You're a smartie. Always were. I couldn't be forced to testify against you, either. But—I knew I *could.* Right? If it came to that? If worse came to worst, I'd simply say you knew all along, and helped." Bill leaned back again, his arms open across the back of the couch. "And which of us would they believe? You saying you didn't? Or me saying you did? If that bullshit investigation led to an indictment, it would be a massive crapshoot. But now it's over."

"Sounds perfect," she said. "So what was the bullshit investigation about?"

"Come on, Alyssa. You passed the test. But you don't have to pretend with me."

"But maybe I'm wrong," she said. "You'd never really explained anything, and if I said something incorrect, then you would be in trouble. So since it's over, and since you're so—" She thought of their times together. Of silver chiffon, and a kiss from a rose, and that first plane ride to St. Barts. Of loyalty tests. "Since you're so safe. But maybe *I* should be prepared? About what not to say?"

Bill looked up as if asking providence to be patient with his dense, benighted wife.

He cleared his throat. "Did you ever wonder how I did so well raising money for charities?"

"Not really," Alyssa said. "I assumed they paid you?"

"So, hon, it's complicated."

"We have time." Alyssa let her robe fall open a bit, sliding down one bare thigh. She nestled the collar even closer, as if keeping part of her secret. A promise.

"Hmm." He eyed her, the old Bill. "I have missed . . . everything. So, babe, if you insist. See if you can understand this. People give me money, I give it to charity, the charity pays me a portion. The donor gets a tax deduction. Then, all good and everyone is happy. But sometimes, the charities weren't completely . . . charitable. To anyone but me. Us. Me. And then, to make it win-win-win, they got some of their money back. From me."

"You accepted money for fake charities. Sometimes kept it for yourself. Then kicked back a chunk to the donors. All under the table. And got paid for doing it."

"Bingo. Look. The trust fund was headed underwater—yeah, for a while the market was killing me and I was bleeding money—and I needed the cash influx to keep things afloat."

"Oh, okay. But when those people took deductions for fake charities, why didn't someone find out? Like, the IRS?"

"Well, yeah, obviously, they did. Eventually. After I heard they were onto it, I went a little crazy for a while. I felt like crap, and probably took it out on you.

But two big things. Rule number one of finance, deny everything. And rule number two, deny everything. The stupid feds finally gave up."

"Rule number one and rule number two, deny everything," Alyssa repeated, nodding, an obedient student. "I hear you. But weren't you worried? At all? At how mad someone might be? Even a victim of some kind?"

"Nah." Bill leaned back, laced his fingers behind his head. "The real charities got the real money, so there weren't any actual victims. I mean—who would be a victim? Uncle Sam? As if."

"That's all? 'Only' the federal government?"

"Okay, fine. Sure. Some other people came to me for advice about their pensions and savings. Worker-bee types. Heard about me in the news, I guess."

"They did? And you told them—"

"My advice was to give me the money. Right? Though I never put it that way. Their fault for not checking it out, am I right? As if I'm supposed to babysit for them. The IRS may audit them, but hell, they signed. If they got greedy? It's on them. The losers. Let 'em sue me. Life doesn't come with guarantees." He made a dismissive snort. "Instead of champagne, do we have any of that gold Patrón?"

"I'll look." Alyssa stood. She paused, thinking. "Actually, no. We're out. And I know how you love it. I'll change, quickly, and run to Étienne's. You rest."

"Perfect." Bill shifted on the couch, tucked a pillow under his head and stretched out his legs, planted his shoes on the farthest cushion. "I've missed you, Lissie. And maybe we'll never go back to Boston—like I told you on the plane that time. Remember? We'll stay here for the rest of our lives, eating pineapple and drinking mai tais. We're together. And free."

"And rich?" Alyssa said.

"And rich," Bill repeated. "Nothing sweeter than living on someone else's money."

THE NEXT DAY

FIFTY-TWO

"I think we should get a dog when we get home," Alyssa said. The seductive scent from the white-flowered tropical vine that twisted across the trellis above them on the lanai combined with the pungency of the lush foliage and the sharp perfection of their coffee. Their al fresco breakfast, surrounded by voluptuous nature, stayed perfectly private. She sat across from Bill at their rattan breakfast table, sipping her sweetened coffee, keeping one of her jewel-toned frangipani bouquets between them.

They'd discussed sleeping arrangements—Bill had assumed they'd sleep in the same bed, even teasing her to take off her terrycloth robe. But she couldn't, not after all that had happened. The Patrón and Bill's jet lag and a few promises had helped her negotiate, and she'd eventually led him, docile and staggering, to the guest room, where she'd deposited him on the flowered bedspread. Out cold.

"It felt sad," she went on now, "having an imaginary dog. Even sadder when I had to be there all by myself. I was really frightened."

"You know I'm allergic," Bill said. "And how I feel about dogs." He selected a cinnamon scone from the wicker basket, broke off an end. Tasted it, and put the rest back. Took a blueberry muffin. "And now you won't be alone. Now you'll have me. And Lissie?"

He slowly peeled away the muffin's pleated paper wrapper. "I can't wait to do this to you." He held up the sugary-sparkled muffin and eased away the last of the paper, leaving the pastry's bare sides exposed. He took a bite. "Delicious."

"Allergic," she said. "Right. There's more food coming today, by the way. I ordered from Étienne when I got the tequila and the breakfast. I couldn't carry the rest."

"Again." Bill licked his fingers. "Now you'll have *me*."

"I know that," Alyssa said. "More coffee?"

Eden's doorbell was three quick fairy twinkles, high and soft, like the waving of a magic wand. She and Bill both looked toward the door.

Alyssa drew her flowered cover-up closer, put a hand to her chest. "I'm not really dressed for—"

The bells chimed again.

"This is Eden, babe. Nobody cares what you wear. Or what you don't wear. It's only the food, or the pool people, or the cleaning people."

Alyssa made a pouting face. "I thought I had you," she teased. "What's a husband good for, except to protect the little wife from whoever's at the door?"

The bells chimed a third time. Bill stirred his coffee, leaned back in his turquoise canvas chair.

"For heaven's sake," Alyssa said, and smiled sweetly so he'd know she was teasing. "You are impossible."

She gave him one backward glance as she went to the door. Opened it.

"Who is it?" Bill called from the lanai.

He couldn't see the doorway from where he sat, Alyssa knew. "I'll handle it," she called back.

"Hey," Dez said.

The man who—just a few days before—had offered to kill her husband.

Now, his khaki suit looked rumpled, as if he'd just come off a long flight. Alyssa knew that was precisely the case. His white shirt and yellow tie, however, were impeccable. He had a look in his eyes Alyssa had never seen before. Determined. He even seemed taller.

"What's taking so long?" Bill's voice came from outside. "Alyssa, you need cash?"

"No, thanks," she called back.

She widened her eyes at Dez, inquiring. Whispered, "What do I do now?"

"As we discussed. You stand there. Let me do the talking. And Bill, of course. Can't wait to hear what he has to say." He raised an eyebrow, exaggeratedly polite. "So? May I come in?"

Alyssa moved aside. Felt her heart race with a gathering knowledge. An irrevocable decision. She gestured toward the open sliding doors to the lanai.

And then she watched as Bill, maybe hearing their footsteps on the yellow-and-white tiled floor, or maybe sensing a change in the oxygen, glanced their way. Seemed to register surprise. Then disbelief. Then maybe, fear. He stood, almost toppling his chair, his flowered linen napkin falling onto the tiles.

"William Macallen?"

"Who is this, Alyssa? And why'd you let him in?"

Alyssa took a step back. Away from him. Too late to stop anything now.

"I'm Special Agent Desmond Russo of the Federal Bureau of Investigation." Dez took a folded piece of paper out of his jacket pocket. "And I have here a warrant for your arrest for—"

"Bullshit," Bill said. "I'm calling—"

"Mr. Macallen?" Dez interrupted, handed him the warrant.

Black type on white paper, Alyssa saw, signed and dated.

Bill brushed it aside with a string of muttered and indecipherable expletives. "I have a letter, you moron, probably from your damn boss, which says—"

"That letter is from me, actually, Mr. Macallen. And it's not worth the paper it's written on. You, of all people, should know not to believe everything you read." Dez placed the warrant on the tablecloth next to the crumpled muffin wrapper. "Except for this warrant. Which says you are under arrest for tax evasion, conspiracy to evade federal taxes, subornation of tax evasion, interstate financial fraud, misprision of felony tax evasion, creating a fraudulent charitable institution . . ."

As Dez's voice continued, Bill's face twisted into a mask of raw, unbridled anger. Alyssa watched him, fascinated and horrified. Bill hated to lose, how many times had she said that? And now, witnessing the end of Bill's career and reputation and most likely his freedom, she felt nothing for him but pity. He'd always gotten whatever he wanted. She'd lain awake the night before, knowing what would happen the next morning, preparing for it, the slatted wooden louvers of her windows cranked open, letting in the Caribbean night and making slashes of moon shadow across the king-size bed.

A loyalty test. The ugly phrase, three words that Bill used to camouflage what was, in truth, his power and manipulation and influence. Three words he'd used to make her miserable and terrified and doubting her very worth. She'd passed his insane loyalty test, that was indisputable. She'd proved she was loyal to *herself*.

"Why don't you arrest *her*, too?" Bill's voice was as grotesque as his face. He pointed at Alyssa with one forefinger, and she thought she saw it tremble.

She stood tall, silently daring him. It was all she could do to stay quiet as another chess game played out to endgame in front of her.

"She was in on all of it," Bill went on. "Every single bit of it."

"I agree. She was." Dez nodded. "Mrs. Macallen was 'in,' as you put it, on every single bit of this."

"So cut the crap," Bill said. "I'll tell you everything you need to know. This was all her idea."

"What was all her idea?"

"Screw you," Bill said.

"Do you deny the allegations, Mr. Macallen?"

"I fully and totally deny them. I deny everything."

Alyssa tried not to smile.

"Indeed. The first rule of finance." Dez nodded as if Bill were a good student. "Want to go on with your second rule?"

"Screw you."

"That's not what you said last night," Dez replied. As Bill glared at him, Dez pulled a cell phone from his jacket pocket. Tapped it, scrolled through, and held it up. "Allow me to read from a transcript. I'll pick it up mid-sentence." He cleared his throat. Recited from the screen. "Two big things. Rule number one of finance, deny everything. And rule number two, deny everything." He paused.

Bill had taken a step toward him. Alyssa saw his fist was clenched. He stopped, then scowled at Alyssa. "You incredible bitch."

"And here's one of my favorite parts," Dez wen on as if no drama were underway on the sunlit pati "The part where you say . . ." He read from the phon again. "'The stupid feds finally gave up.'" He touche his phone, replaced it in his pocket. "I'm afraid, M Macallen, we didn't give up. In fact, you might sa that's our rule number one."

"I want my lawyer." Bill's demand came out in on long growl.

"Of course you do," Dez said. "And you can tell hi or her to meet us at Logan, at the general aviation te minal. And don't start throwing around words lik *extradition* and *local authorities*. We have that all i hand. Your choice, Mr. Macallen, is to accompany m back to Boston. Or spend some quality time in the S Barts lockup. I assure you, there will not be muffins.

Bill had pulled his cell from his robe pocket, an tapped the screen so hard, dialing, it looked like h was trying to stab it.

"And I suggest you enjoy the flight, Mr. Macallen, Dez went on. He'd sneaked a wink at Alyssa. "We'r figuring it'll be the last one you'll take for a long time.

"You'll pay for this, Alyssa." Bill sneered at he "You'll get nothing. Absolutely nothing."

"I'm not so sure about that," Dez said. "The pro bate judge might have a different idea. There's n prenup, so you're at the mercy of the court, Mr. Ma callen. Good luck with that."

"At least I can get a dog now, right?" Alyssa fel the gentle breeze in her hair, heard the faraway call o a laughing gull, a derisive soundtrack to this closin scene. *Eden.* Where, some say, the very first betraya took place. "Someone who truly loves me. And some one who is truly loyal."

FIFTY-THREE

"You can see why they call them infinity pools." Alyssa, floating on an orange plastic raft, looked past her toes and out to the glistening turquoise Caribbean. "I'm still not quite sure how they work. Do you understand it?"

"I don't even try," Bree said. Like Alyssa, she was wet, her skin shiny from water droplets beading on her sunscreen. And like Alyssa, wore a black tank suit, a black floppy hat, and Jackie O sunglasses. "I'm soaking up the niceness, as you always say, and being grateful my raft has a holder for this delicious orange juice. It's been a long time since I could float and look at the sky—or do anything, in fact—without worrying that your husband would find out I was the one at the bank who'd ratted him out."

Bree had arrived by private jet that afternoon. Alyssa picked her up at the airport after waving a complicated goodbye to a fuming—and handcuffed—Bill, who'd be returning to Boston on the same plane that brought Bree to the island. In return for her help, the feds had not only underwritten this final part of Bree's journey, but also let her off the legal hook.

"But what leverage did Dez have over you?" Alyssa hadn't gotten the whole story yet. "You'd reported Bill. Weren't you a good guy? A whistleblower?"

"Ha. You'd think. But I waited too long, they told me. And it was like—going through the looking glass.

Remember when Dez talked about 'misprision of a felony' that Chinese food night? That was aimed at reminding me. Putting me in my place. I was a bank official, they'd told me, and I'd taken months to report the irregularities, which allowed the scheme to go on. That's a crime. So, they said, to stay out of prison, I had to help trap him."

"Did you ever talk to him, personally?" Alyssa tried to picture it; accountant Bree, analyzing Bill's financial transactions, discovering the illegalities. Questioning him.

"Nope. It was all about you. Dez had people follow you, watched you go into Vermilion. Then it was my turn. I had to pretend to befriend you. To see what you knew."

"I saw the profile in your yearbook. Math Club, you love numbers. Mensa, you're smart. Drama Club. You can play a role."

Bree made a dismissive sound, and two white butterflies fluttered near her. "Oh, I had my FBI-approved script, all right. Pitiful me, big bad boyfriend, big bills, bad boss. Not true, none of it, and I'm so sorry, but we had to make it believable. But then—you were instantly sympathetic. Humble. And so generous. The whole pretend-to-like-Alyssa thing got harder when I realized I wasn't pretending."

"I believed you," Alyssa said. "Stories about mistreated women are all too easy to believe."

"I know." Bree trailed one hand through the turquoise water.

Alyssa felt sad for a moment, then realized why. "But now, I guess, I don't really know anything about you. It's almost as if I just met you. The real you."

"Maybe we can start over?" Bree said.

"Hmmm." Alyssa didn't know how to answer that. Could people start over?

"My orange juice—fresh orange juice!—is almost gone." Bree's pronouncement broke the silence. "I'll be right back. I'll bring some for you, too."

Watching Bree clamber out of the pool and walk, dripping, across the patio, Alyssa thought about friendship, and about how they'd wound up where they were today.

Alyssa and Dez had FaceTimed this morning, she on the sunlit patio, Dez in Boston's real FBI headquarters. Bill in lockup.

"So listen to this, Alyssa," Dez had told her, his face almost in focus. "The recording was totally clear. We heard every word."

"I was worried." Alyssa had wrapped her terry robe closer, the same one she had worn to conceal her microphone. "I had to email the files while I was at the grocery store."

"Well, we had to crash a transcript from the listening devices we gave you to put in the flowers and from the body mic, and from that we got a warrant, and then we had to get to the island as fast as we could. So good job, Alyssa." Even blurry, Alyssa could recognize Dez's thumbs-up. "Your Bill is a huge fish. And we got him. In his own words. Thanks to you."

"He's not my Bill," Alyssa had said. "Is Bree okay?"

"You'll have to ask *her,*" he said.

"You don't make a very good dumb guy, you know?" Alyssa teased. A bright stripey butterfly had landed on her knee, and it perched there, folding and unfolding its wings. "I was always suspicious of you, Dez with a Z."

Dez laughed, more than a thousand miles away. "But not suspicious of Bree?"

The butterfly's wings were black and white on the outside but luminous orange inside, a secret that only showed when the wings were opened.

"We had our moments," she said.

"See you soon, Alyssa. Again, thank you."

And the screen went dark.

Now, Bree was handing her a clear plastic glass of orange juice with a mint leaf floating on top, the tropical sun was lowering in the pristine blue sky, and the two of them floated in a world that was utterly reconfigured. Exploring their new reality.

"Um, Lyss. To clear the air." Bree shifted on her raft, facing Alyssa. "Like you or not, at first I was convinced you must have been in on it."

"Yeah, well. As I kept telling you, I didn't even know what 'it' was."

"I felt awful," Bree went on. "Like I had to trade away your freedom to get my own."

"You had to play 'Let's Make a Deal.'" Alyssa couldn't read Bree's eyes through her sunglasses. Unsettling, to have this transactional discussion in such a tranquil setting.

"It was my career. My passion. I was trying to—get ahead. I was low on the ladder, working my way up to the bank's executive offices, and then I saw it, in the Macallen transactions. Bill's. The numbers didn't add up, or I should say, they did. I stared at them, a clear pattern of avoiding currency transaction regulations. And I thought, no. Leave it alone. Let the big guys handle it. But no one did. And the violations kept happening."

"And if you mentioned it," Alyssa said, "you'd be a

troublemaker. Or a bitch, or pushy or nosy or whatever they call women who are smarter than they are."

"Exactly." Bree look a long sip of her drink. "And it'd sound almost like bragging—*I found a potential crime in progress and you didn't.* Not to mention a potential crime by one of their biggest customers. But, finally I guess my conscience outweighed my ambition. Plus, I knew it was a violation for me not to report it."

"Doing the right thing can be complicated." *Understatement of the day,* Alyssa thought.

"Well, look where it left me." Bree shrugged, rueful. "Screwed. And being forced to sacrifice *you* to save myself. Still, I was so angry that someone would break the law like that, part of me was relieved when they proposed it. It seemed like a way out for me. Even a way to get justice. Until I got to know you, Lyss. Alyssa, I am so sor—"

"It's okay." Alyssa put up a hand, stopped her. "I know about choices. They seem smart at first, then, not so much."

"Yeah. Like the Collin Whishaw story. My idea, I have to admit. After you told me about Lylah Rhodes's DNA thing, I called Dez from the bathroom at the Club, and his people set up the fake ancestry site. It's down now."

"Pretty elaborate."

"Not really. Mine was the only listing. I'd told Dez that if you thought I was rich, like, a seven-million-dollar equal, you'd trust me. You'd know I wasn't gold-digging, or a con artist after your money. I said it would help us 'bond.' It also made it logical that Dez would hang around. It was completely impromptu, and we had no idea how you'd react, but yet again, you were genuinely helpful. I felt awful. I almost backed out, that rainy day on the porch."

"Maybe I was *too* helpful. I discovered 'Collin's' house was Roshandra Jain's. And decided you were in danger."

"Yeah, well, best-laid plans." Bree sat up on her float, straddling it, feet dangling in the water, the cobalt-blue plastic raft bending in half. "I know your lawyer told you Jain is FBI, too. One Beacon is one of the fronts they use."

"All to get Bill."

"He stole a lot, Lyss. Millions. The charities all got what he promised, that was authentic, and that was his cover. But the rest of it, all those people he ripped off, that was smoke and mirrors and intricate triple bookkeeping. People, moms and pops and salts of the earth—they trusted him, and lost everything they had. Pensions. Savings. In other news, Lylah Rhodes is soon going to be even more unhappy with her husband. Camden Hollis, too, Dez says. They're about to be arrested."

"Poor things." Alyssa sat up, too, water from the front edge of her float dripping into the pool below. "So much greed."

They let the whispery breeze and coconut fragrance surround them for a beat. Bill had ruined so many lives. Almost including hers.

"*I* feel bad, too, about one thing," Alyssa began.

"What, that I don't really get seven million dollars? Got to agree."

"Seriously. Listen." Alyssa touched Bree's raft, connecting. "I was more than willing for you to trap Bill. Let you risk potential danger. Who knows how he might have reacted if he'd gotten suspicious."

"No, no, Lyss. Forget it. We were never in real jeopardy. Because, like, Dez *was* FBI. The moment you told us the FBI contacted you? He knew—and soon I knew—that was absolutely not true. That something else was going on. So when we offered to nail Bill, it was 'Parker' we were really after. She's in custody now for impersonating a federal agent. It took about four seconds for her to talk."

"Bill must have done quite the sales job. I almost . . . feel bad for her."

"Well, listen to this. Bill apparently told her some specifics about his operation. Details that were true. The stuff she told you about. Plus, he paid her to do it. So now she can stay out of prison—*if* she agrees to testify against him. His own scheme comes back to bite him."

Alyssa shifted, balancing, adjusting the brim of her hat. "Schemes. What if I'd agreed to murder Bill? What would you have done?"

"Dez is . . ." Bree grimaced. "An FBI guy. They're relentless. And I have to say, he would've probably tried to lure you further in, and then arrested you. As you yourself said, that day on the way to Collin Whishaw's, all hired killers are really undercover FBI agents. I even told him you'd said that! But he just laughed. Plus, you said no. You passed another test."

Tests. Alyssa was sick of tests. "So why did the feds tell Mickey you were brother and sister and that your parents were victims? That you'd actually tried to murder Bill?"

"To give Dez and me cover. And to give the feds leverage. They figured if you complained about their methods, they'd threaten to arrest you for conspiracy unless you kept quiet. But, Lyss? As I got to know you, as a *person,* not a target, I had to believe you knew nothing about Bill's crimes. And I decided—I had to warn you. I almost did, a couple of times. But in the end, there was no way to do it in person. So I had to leave that note. Telling you everything."

"I can't believe you found Bill's secret compartment in the closet."

"I didn't 'find' it, Alyssa. You showed it to me, kinda, that day that Bill broke in. I saw you count; then tap, tap. Right? When I ran upstairs to check after Officer Chu left, when you were in the basement? That's when I left the note. I'd written it before, but couldn't figure out when to give it to you. When we were in the car on the way to Weston? You were already so upset, it seemed wrong to say, 'Oh, by the way, Dez and I were both lying to you.' So that's when I moved the shells. Stashed the note. And crossed my fingers you'd understand my signal with the shells."

"But that was—"

"I know, risky. But riskier to leave something where Bill might find it. But since they'd nabbed the fake Parker, I knew Dez and I were . . . about to vanish from your life. Our job with you was done. I was torn, I really was."

Alyssa played out Bree's decision.

"Wasn't it dangerous for you to write down the truth? That Dez was FBI, and you were an undercover informant, and both of you were after Bill? That they were using me?"

Bree shrugged. "Yeah. I knew it might ruin my deal. Which would not be optimal, prison-wise. But I couldn't let you think I was a killer. Or that you'd been unwittingly conspiring to kill your husband. The FBI are a different breed. That's why I also wrote that you should call me. And I'm glad you did."

She'd paddled her raft to face Alyssa. "It felt like you and I were both being—"

"Being what?"

The women sat opposite each other, bobbing on the glassy water. Alyssa peered over her sunglasses, saw the sky turn to stripes of impossible pink and lavender and purple, the white clouds lining the horizon beginning to glow a shimmering gold.

"We were both being used," Bree said. "Pressured. Manipulated. I—respected you too much to let it go on."

"You could have gone to prison," Alyssa said.

"So could you," Bree said.

A moment went by, the sun glinting on the water, the past fading with the afternoon.

Alyssa picked up her glass, held it up to toast. "To freedom," she said.

"To freedom." Bree held up hers to clink. "Go back to being Alice, maybe?"

"You knew about that?"

"Yeah. I really am Embry, though. At least that part was true."

Alyssa wondered how it had come to this, but maybe, it would turn out for the best. She'd find a life. Maybe go back to law school. Maybe work with Mickey. Someday, maybe, have a husband, a child, a real dog. Or not. But either way, be happy. And she hoped Bree would, too.

They should define themselves, not wait for others to make them who they were. No more expectations from others. Only expectations from herself.

"Alyssa?" Bree put her glass back into the cup holder. "There's one more thing."

EPILOGUE

At their request, Emmett had turned the television over the bar to the noon news, and the trumpeting theme music of Channel 12 had just begun, an insistent underscore. At this time of day, Vermilion was nearly empty. Except for Alyssa and Bree, sitting on the barstools they'd occupied when they first met. Though they'd been back for a few days, Bree's nose was still peeling from the St. Barts sun.

"Vermilion is the perfect place to watch this," Alyssa said, pointing at the screen. "Sort of the end and the beginning. End of Bill, beginning of me. And of your new life, of course."

They'd still been floating in the pool when Bree had paddled to the side and clambered out. She'd stood, dripping, on the tiled floor of the lanai. Behind her on the rattan table, a pile of folded beach towels, and that vivid frangipani arrangement, now simply flowers, and no longer hiding a tiny microphone. Dez had removed it with a flourish, which Alyssa had to admit was secretly entertaining. Bill had not been amused. She wasn't sure she wanted to remember the destructive and bitter words Bill had spoken to her as Dez led him away, although maybe they'd eventually make her life easier. He was gone, and as her mother would have said, good riddance.

"You okay?" Alyssa had followed Bree, concerned,

water pooling at her feet. *One more thing,* Bree had said. "One more thing what?"

"My skin is pruning," Bree had said, wrapping herself in a turquoise-striped beach towel. "And I think it's time for alcohol."

"I hope we're celebrating." Alyssa took her own striped towel from the pile, and tucked the ends in place across her chest. "One more thing what?"

"I hope so, too." Bree had turned, facing the ocean. "It's so pretty here."

"You're stalling." Alyssa slid her feet into flip-flops, hooked her sunglasses onto her bathing suit. "But okay, I'll get some wine. And glasses. And food. But when I get back, you'll tell me whatever it is."

Bree nodded, and Alyssa had tried to figure out what she was thinking. Bree had made a deal with the devil, if you looked at it that way, to be an FBI informant in return for her own immunity from prosecution. But pretending to be a potential heiress must have been difficult when she was constantly watched by the law enforcement officer who controlled her future.

When Alyssa returned, Bree was still standing on the edge of the terrace, watching the sunset.

"Did you see the green flash?" Alyssa had asked, setting her tray on the table.

"Green flash?" Bree had turned to her, looking puzzled.

"Yup. Some people insist that on certain perfect evenings, the sun disappears below the horizon with a green flash." She pulled the stopper from the pink bottle of rosé. "I've never seen it, though."

For a moment, there were only the sounds of the wine pouring, the rush of the faraway waves, the squawk of a seabird.

"This is yours," Alyssa had said, holding a glass out of reach. "But if you want it, you have to tell me the 'one more thing.'"

Bree adjusted her towel, and brushed her hair from her face. "Okay. Like I said, Dez and I aren't brother and sister. They had to tell you that to make you believe the murder conspiracy story."

"Yeah. Go on." She lifted the wine again, keeping it out of Bree's reach.

"But we got to know each other over the investigation. Especially that last week. We developed—a way of communication. He's a pretty fascinating guy. Smart. Wise. Authentic. And he was doing his job, right? Plus, he could have sent me to jail, or at least threatened to. But he didn't."

Alyssa narrowed her eyes. "What are you telling me, girl?"

"So, um, I won't be going back to your guest house, lavish as it is. Dez and I are going to see how we are together. As our real selves. I'm getting an apartment in his building. Separate, definitely separate, but nearby. And we'll see."

Alyssa burst out laughing. Couldn't help it. "Oh, I'm so—but—that's so beyond. What a meet-cute story. Boy arrests girl, boy makes girl informant, boy falls in love. Girl falls in love. Boy and girl live happily ever after."

"Well," Bree began. "I—we—we're not sure. I need some time for just me, too. You taught me that. Like you said, you can't really love someone else until you can love yourself."

"Good luck, honey," Alyssa had said. "I mean it."

Their empty rafts drifted across the pool, colored by the changing sunset. The day ebbed and flowed, and somehow felt infinite, like the pool and like the universe. People could only try to do the best they could, hoping for peace and fulfilment.

"I have to admit you were a good team," Alyssa went on. "For better and for worse." She lifted her goblet. "Maybe there'll be happiness for both of us, Bree. Maybe it could happen."

"I know it will, Lyss." She toasted back. "You're an amazing person. Strong and brave. With your whole life ahead of you. And, if Dez is right about the divorce settlement, the Weston house is also ahead of you, and the Osterville house, and even the Cézanne." She paused. "Whoa. Even after Bill pays whatever fines and penalties and legal fees. You might get millions."

Alyssa watched a row of brown pelicans skimming across the shore, sleek and determined and far away. And silently wished.

"Nope. That life is over," she'd said. "Some people will never believe I didn't know what Bill did. People will hate me, some of them. But we both know I'm used to that. And listen, if you need a lawyer someday, call me. Wait a few years, though, until I graduate. Mickey's already invited me. And I'm envisioning an apartment, by myself. With a dog, of course. Maybe the Cézanne over the fireplace. I can keep that because I love it. The other stuff, hey. Whatever's left, it'll be my turn to donate to charities. When that life starts, I could become Alice Westland, good guy."

"Really?" Bree sat in a turquoise chair, wrapped her towel closer.

"Like I told you early on, it's not the money that's bad, it's how people use it." Alyssa blew out a breath. "Everything I thought would make my life wonderful and happy . . . well, it didn't. And I can also help make sure Bill's victims—the ones who lost their pensions and their savings—get full restitution. I know *your* parents weren't actually harmed, but *someone's* parents were."

The two sat in silence, just a beat.

"Alyssa? A long time ago you told me—well, a week or two ago." Bree sighed. "Weird, that seems like a lifetime. Anyway, you told me you weren't gorgeous, or brilliant, or brave. Or special. But you are, Alyssa. You're all of those things."

A puff of wind rattled the palm fronds above them, and a flutter of jasmine petals landed on the pool's shimmering surface.

"You are, too, Bree." Alyssa had scanned the luminous sunset. "Oh!" she said, pointing. "The green flash. I saw it!"

"It's an omen," Bree had said. "I told you. You're special. It's all going to work."

Now the green-and-white light of the newscast attracted their attention. Alyssa sat, elbows on Vermilion's bar, chin in hands. Bree mirrored her position, and the two of them watched as the news anchor introduced Madeleine Tran, the same reporter Alyssa had watched in that TV studio the evening after she first talked to Mickey. The graphic on the screen said *Fraudulent Fundraising*. And then, with a swirl, changed to *Local Man Charged as Scam Artist*.

"They sure don't pull their punches," Emmett muttered. He stood at the end of the bar, wiping out a wineglass, just as he had done the first time Alyssa and Bree had been there. Today they'd ordered coffees. "On me," Emmett had told them. "That guy's toast."

"Can you turn it up?" Alyssa asked.

Emmett aimed a remote at the screen.

"I'm live here at Boston's federal courthouse." Tran's voice sounded almost confiding as she stood in front of the modern redbrick edifice, holding a logoed microphone, her posture taut with anticipation of the big reveal. "We are awaiting the arrival of William Macallen, the once-lauded and now notorious fundraiser. He is about to be arraigned on a series of serious and shocking charges of federal financial fraud that threaten to topple many of the inner-circle power elite of—"

Alyssa swiveled her stool, turning her back on the television. "Can you turn it off, Emmett? Do you mind?"

She heard the click, and then the silence. Emmett disappeared into the back of the restaurant, leaving her and Bree alone, while Bill's future played out in a courthouse miles and worlds away. In the arithmetic of her life, she was subtracting him. Deleting him. Counting only on herself.

"You okay?" Bree asked. "Don't you want to—?"

"I don't need to see it. We'll hear soon enough. It's not over, I know that." Alyssa slid off her stool, brushed off the back of her jeans. "But I've got my own life to live, best I can. And so do you. Let's get out of here."

Vermilion's red exit sign seemed to glow a special message to her—offering the route away from one life and into another. New beginnings, and infinite possibilities.

She thought about addition. Adding friends. And love. And hope.

"So, Bree?" she asked. "You ready?"

As they walked toward the exit, the afternoon sun streamed through the stained glass panels of

Vermilion's front door, spilling rays of jeweled light across Bree's face.

"Life, take two?" Bree asked.

"Or as many takes as we need," Alyssa said.

"As friends?"

"As friends." They were a few steps from the exit, and as they drew closer, somehow Alyssa felt her heart breaking. No, not breaking. Her heart was changing. Filling, even overflowing, with the awareness that life was fragile and surprising. That she had made a good decision. That the path ahead might be rocky, but she could handle it.

"Should we meet here some Fridays?" Bree was asking. "For old times' sake?"

Alyssa pushed open the door, and the warm sun felt full of promise. "Not a chance."

"What?" Bree had stopped at the threshold. "No?"

"Not for *old* times' sake, Bree, not for one minute." Alyssa smiled, inviting Bree to join her in the luminous afternoon. "But for *new* times' sake? Absolutely."

ACKNOWLEDGMENTS

Writing the acknowledgments is the very last thing I do with a new book. I remember when I wrote my first ones, fourteen books ago, and what joy it brought me to be doing this *thing*, this rite of passage thing, this acknowledgment of an accomplishment that I had dreamed of for so many years. I have to say, all these years and books later, and all these adventures later, and all these triumphs and tragedies later, I still feel the same way. I am honored to get to write this, thrilled, and it brings tears to my eyes. There were days when I thought this book would never work, and yet, loving it and embracing my life, I just kept typing.

Because it proves, doesn't it, exactly what you are holding in your hands. It's the creation of all of us. The team at Forge Books is unceasingly stellar, devoted, motivated, savvy, and wonderful. My total genius editor, Kristin Sevick—I have often reminded her my book is not truly complete until it is Kristin-ized. The wise and patient editorial assistant Troix Jackson. The indefatigable Alexis Saarela, who'll make sure everyone knows about *The House Guest*. It's probably Ploy Siripant and Katie Klimowicz who caused you to pick this up—the incredibly talented Ploy designed the cover, art directed by the amazing Katie. Inside the book, you cannot believe how much work copy editors Sara and Chris at ScriptAcuity Studio did—thank you for protecting me from career-ending errors. Thank you as well to Melissa Frain and NaNá V. Stoelzle. And so many thanks to managing editor Rafal Gibek, production editor Sam Dauer, and production manager Jacqueline Huber-Rodriguez. And whoo-hoo for marketing—thank you Julia Bergen and Jennifer McClelland-Smith. Sales, yay, every fabulous brilliant one of you is a rock star. The leadership of Linda Quinton, you never cease to amaze me, and the powerhouse combination of Lucille Rettino, Eileen Lawrence, Laura Etzkorn, and Laura Pennock is unstoppable. Devi Pillai, who continues to make dreams come true.

Agent Lisa Gallagher, you are a treasured friend and wise shepherd, thank you. I love everything you do and every decision we make. Long may we decide things.

The artistry and savvy of Madeira James, Charlie Anctil, Mary Zanor, Andrea Peskind Katz, Pamela Klinger-Horn. Ann-Marie Nieves, Suzanna Leopold, Keri-Rae Barnum, Christie Conlee, Nina Zagorscak, and Jon Stone. You are all so fabulous. Karen Bellovich and Margaret Pinard and Bosie Rand at A Mighty Blaze, you are perfection. Maxwell Gregory and Mary Webber O'Malley, I am in awe.

Sue Grafton, always. Mary Higgins Clark, ditto. You are both still with me. Heather Gudenkauf, Lynne Constantine, Samantha Bailey. Lisa Scottoline. Lisa Unger. Erin Mitchell. Barbara Peters, Kym Havens, and Robin Agnew. Jenna Blum, what a rock star. James Patterson, you are a treasure.

My incredible blog sisters at Jungle Red Writers: Julia Spencer-Fleming, Hallie Ephron, Roberta Isleib/

Lucy Burdette, Jenn McKinlay, Deborah Crombie, and Rhys Bowen. And my Career Authors posse: Paula Munier, Dana Isaacson, Jessica Strawser, and Brian Andrews. What would I do without you? And Ann Garvin and the Tall Poppies, standing ovation. Thank you.

My dear friend Mary Schwager—we have been through it, right? And my darling sister Nancy Landman.

And speaking of life-changing: Bookstagrammers! If I list you, I will forget someone, but you know who you are. I am grateful every single day.

And also life-changing: my partner in fictional crime, the brilliant bestseller and treasured friend Hannah Mary McKinnon. There would be no First Chapter Fun without you, and my life would be significantly different. You are incredible in every way. And the amazing Karen Dionne—our collaboration on The Back Room has been a constant joy! And you are a dear and brilliant pal. And to all of you, Funsters and Blazers and Back Room attendees, it is always a joy to see you. Thank you.

Jonathan is my darling husband, of course. Thank you for all the carry-out dinners, your infinite patience, and your unending wisdom. (And for being my in-house counsel.) Love you so much.

Do you see your name in this book? Some very generous souls allowed their names to be used in return for an auction donation to charity. To retain the magic, I will let you find yourselves.

My true inspirations are you, darling readers, and those who helped this book become a reality. It's not fully realized until you read it, and I am so grateful to you for keeping it alive.

Sharp-eyed readers will notice I have tweaked Massachusetts geography a bit. It's only to protect the innocent. And I adore it when people read the acknowledgments. Keep in touch, okay?

Read on for a preview of

ONE WRONG WORD

Hank Phillippi Ryan

Available in Winter 2024
from Tom Doherty Associates

A FORGE BOOK

Regret has consumed him, and fear too, and Cordelia wishes she could let her husband know how well she understands his spiraling terror. She's never seen him cry, not like he is now, anguished, head on his knees, taking up all the space on the folding chair in the waiting area off the courtroom. A metal-tipped cord attached to the grimy woven curtains keeps tapping against the window, tap tap *tap,* aggravated by the rattle of the ancient heater. How much sorrow this room has seen, this limbo between guilty and not guilty. Some who sit here, waiting, will go home. Some will not. But no one will ever be the same.

Because regret itself can be lethal. Remorse, too, and the toxic second-guessing that gnaws away the edges of reality. All those "if only" moments. Cordelia knows Ned must be—yet again—replaying that night, over and over, as if somehow he could make it end a different way. But that is impossible. "If only" is now his nightmare.

His coffee, two sugars one cream, sits untouched on the pitted metal table. Nyomi Chang, who'd dramatically defended him, stays silent, staring out a meshed window. The door to the courtroom stays closed. The jury has been out two days and four hours. *Commonwealth v. Bannister.* Three counts. Operating under the influence, reckless driving, and vehicular homicide.

Ned is the defendant, but *her* future is on the line, too. Pip's, too, and Emma's.

"I didn't see him, Dee," Ned says. "I didn't."

"I know, honey." She touches her hand to the back of his navy blazer, feels his shoulders trembling, feels the soft worsted of the too-expensive suit, has a flash of prison orange canvas. Ned is tough, and capable, but he'll never survive. He'd navigated his way up the corporate ladder, now he faces fifteen years in state prison. Where the power structure is terrifyingly different.

"He wasn't supposed to be there. He was trespassing."

"I know, honey."

"And I *wasn't* drunk. I had, maybe, two glasses of champagne. It was a party. But I know drunk. I know myself. I was tired, sure, after all that. But . . ."

She isn't sure who he's explaining it to. Himself, maybe. He'd explained it on the stand, allowed himself to be cross-examined by a gorgon of a DA, admitting he was tired, denying he was drunk. Admitting he was driving fast, *maybe,* but he was the only car in the place, and then repeating those four words, over and over, a refrain of anguish. *I never saw him. I never saw him.* One reporter had actually laughed. The headlines had not been kind. REAL ESTATE EXEC SEZ: WHAT GUY?

Cordelia knows, from the nights he's writhed and tossed in their bed, and as she fails to find any way to comfort him, that he repeats that New Year's Eve moment in his mind as if it were something he could edit, or alter, or hit some cosmic undo button. The curved pavement of the parking garage, Ned's big Mercedes barreling up toward the exit as skateboarder Randall Tennant careens down; the younger man trespassing, certainly, in the private building. Ned had been exactly where he belonged, and Randall Tennant hadn't. But only one had survived. The punishment for trespassing is not—usually—death. Except this time.

She'd been home with Pip and Emma, as she'd told everyone, over and over, and a little angry, she'd admitted that, too, after everyone *kept* asking, to have been left alone with two sniffy whining kids while Ned had lorded it over the bacchanalian fireworks party at his lofty harbor-view office.

Apparently the champagne had been unending, no matter what Ned said, and now their lives hang in the balance, and that damn jury, ten men and two women who would leave and go back to lives of whatever, have no idea how much power they wield over her future. She tries to imagine that: Ned gone, his pillow empty, his place at the dinner table vacant, Cordelia herself either doomed or free, their children constantly having to explain what happened to their once-revered father. One mistake, one missed turn, one wrong word.

Sometimes we lose the ones we love. And what will she do?

A knock at the door. It opens. A blue-uniformed court officer is framed in the doorway. Cordelia tries to read his expression, but cannot. She stands, almost in tribute, a reflection of the pivotal moment. Nyomi Chang stands, too, the burden of past verdicts, Cordelia imagines, weighing her shoulders. Ned does not budge.

"Mr. Bannister?" the officer says.

PART ONE

ONE

ARDEN WARD

Hey Warren, how's *your* Friday going?" Arden stood as her boss entered her harbor-front office. She smoothed the sleek wool of her cashmere pants, adjusted the double strand of her trademark vintage pearls, then gestured to the video of the courthouse shown on the wide-screen TV mounted in her bookshelves. "Better than Ned Bannister's, I bet. Time's running out for him. Verdicts always come on Friday. Jurors want to go home."

Warren, tie loosened and bespoke cuffs rolled, carried a crystal rocks glass filled with some dark liquid. Likely bourbon, Arden knew. Fridays at the Vision Group, the drinking started early. *Solving other people's problems was thirsty work,* Warren always said. Whatever tired cliché he chose, he always spoke as if he had originated it.

"They should have called us before the trial, you know?" Now he toasted the television screen, watching the muted video of an earnest reporter stationed outside the gray marble exterior of Boston's Suffolk County Courthouse, the building blending into the November sky.

He took a sip, contemptuous. "Coverage of this debacle's been a total shit show. The Parking Garage Killer." He shook his head. "Pitiful. We'd have nipped that phrase in the bud."

"Agreed." Arden nodded. Of course she agreed with her boss, she understood the balance of power. She'd even stopped what she'd been doing to watch with him. The banner crawling across the bottom of the screen spelled it out: *Jury still deliberating in Bannister drunk drive trial.* "You'd think a guy as connected as Ned Bannister would realize he needed crisis management help."

She paused at Warren's silence. He hadn't arrived in her office to chat about this latest gossip fodder—Boston's elite and powerful partying high above Boston Harbor, the deadly crash, then business exec Bannister publicly branded a careless boozy criminal. It wasn't entirely surprising, she had to admit, Warren often made end-of-the-week visits, the benevolent dictator, to check on Arden's clients, her progress. Her billings.

And sometimes to celebrate. The last time Warren showed up unannounced, he'd bestowed her with a bouquet of white English roses, a wildly extravagant bunch studded with shiny green foliage. The Vision Group had Patterson's Florist as a client, Arden knew, so the pricey flowers had not come from Warren's pocket. Still, she'd buried her face in them, deeply inhaling.

"These are spectacular," she'd said. "And you know I love flowers. But what's the occasion?"

"The occasion is your—our—big score. Arthur Swanson is a done deal. And *you* get the Miss Congeniality bouquet."

Arden had rolled her eyes, hidden her derision behind the fragrant roses. *She'd* done all the hard work, getting the pretentious and privileged Arthur Swanson onto the board of Caldecott Hospital. But

Vision Group CEO Warren Carmichael was the boss, and he was her lifeline, and he'd taken a chance on hiring her after she'd fled her old life in Allentown.

Not that there was anything left of it; back home the taint of being Governor Porter Ward's daughter wrapped her with a permanent shroud of embarrassment. But in Boston, the name "Ward" was just a name, not a label, and she'd done well here. Maybe bad things sometimes happened for a reason. To allow the good things.

"Arthur Swanson's perfect for the role." Arden had been authentically enthusiastic. "All that money. All that influence. The hospital ate it up. And his wife totally believes it was the result of his merit and her social standing. Patience Swanson seems to live in her own glittery world." Arden, daring, could not resist the possibly inappropriate dig. She shook her head. "People."

Now Warren took a sip of his probably-bourbon. Arden could smell it, sweet and smoky.

He'd focused on the television again. "No verdict yet, huh?"

"There's still time," Arden said. "Though Fridays they recess early."

Warren took another sip.

"You okay?" she asked. Might be a little personal, but she thought the Arthur Swanson deal had brought them closer. Warren had been the face of it, and she the supposed "associate." But Warren had no idea that throughout the negotiations Arden had endured—and ignored, or pretended to—Arthur Swanson's advances; the unnecessary touch on her shoulder, the gratuitous hand on her back ostensibly guiding her through a door, the too-personal jokes about her "single-girl" apartment or her weekend plans. The sideways looks, as if they shared some secret, which, indeed, they did not. The dinner à deux invitations she always refused.

In this day and age, she thought. But for men like him, there was only *his* day and age, meaning *now* and *today.* For Warren, too, she had to admit. Who always did whatever was in his own best interest.

"So Arden," Warren began. "About Patience."

"Sit," Arden said. She had a flash of dismay. "Is everything still on? With the deal? Do not tell me she's—"

Warren settled into the butterscotch tweed club chair. "We should talk."

"Sure." Arden calculated the possibilities, speed of light. She hated surprises, *hated* them. *We don't like surprises,* she taught her assistants. *Our job is to stay ahead of the surprises.* Now, surprise, Warren wanted to talk.

"So Patience herself barges in last week, like, loaded for bear."

"And?" Arden heard the bourbon in Warren's voice. Saw his posture wilt. Alcohol always hit him hard, and he'd powered this drink down.

"And she was—pissed."

"What? About what?"

Warren looked at the ice in his glass, the bourbon gone. "So you remember Capital Grille?"

"Sure. . . ." Arden couldn't help but frown.

The week before, the Swansons had invited the two of them, along with Warren's hoity-toity jet-setting peripatetic wife and a group of their friends, to a closed-door celebration of Swanson's not-yet-public new position. Dinner at Capital Grille, in a mahogany-paneled private room with flowing wine and hovering waitstaff. Asparagus, hollandaise, filet, caviar. Food and setting as rich and overstuffed as some of the guests themselves.

Arden had noticed Patience seated her as far away from Arthur as possible, but she'd been grateful for that. She had tolerated enough uncomfortable and insulting moments of removing his hand from her leg. She would never tell Warren, of course. The deal needed to go through, and some things, by necessity, women handled on their own.

"And then she says the weirdest thing," Warren went on.

Warren rarely gossiped with her. She was curious about his new tone, but embraced it. It felt like progress. "What'd she say?"

"'She smells of joy.'" Warren was actually imitating Patience Swanson, that imperious but impossible-to-identify accent that some of her ilk adopted. "I had no idea what she was talking about, you know?"

Arden remembered, in the weird snippets of moments we remember, having sensed a kinship with Warren that night at the Swanson dinner. Feeling she had finally made it as his equal. She'd perceived, with a glimmer of hope and even confidence, that they were a team.

"Joy the perfume?" Arden guessed now. "What 'she'? And why did that matter?"

Warren's face changed. Hardened. He carefully placed his crystal glass, contents diminished to ice, on her side table. Centered it on a copy of *Boston* magazine.

"Yes. Perfume." Warren nodded, once. "And the 'she' is you."

TWO

Arden took a moment to unpack Warren's words. She stood, uncomfortable in her own office. Then sat in her swivel chair, kept the desk between them.

"I? Me? I smelled of *Joy*? That's kinda random. Well, I guess so. I wear it, sometimes. My mother did, too. It's . . ." She shrugged. "O-G, maybe, but classic. Ask *your* wife."

"Well, seems that's something you and Mrs. Swanson share. Joy. She uses it, too. And she says she recognized it on you at the Capital Grille. That night."

Arden tried to decipher Warren's expression, his growing discomposure. One polished loafer tapped against the steely pile of her office carpeting.

"Okay." Arden took a plastic bottle of water from her bottom desk drawer, twisted off the top. The TV flickered above them. The lower-third crawl repeated the lack of news: *No verdict yet in Bannister case.* "Joy. And?"

"And she is not happy about it."

"About what?"

"More than not happy. Extremely unhappy. Because her husband has a habit of . . . Shit, Arden, she thinks he gave you the perfume. Apparently, this is what he does. Hits on women. Gives them Joy. The perfume I mean. It's like, a pattern."

"What? And—so what?" She stopped. "Oh. Is there

some *woman* thing? That we didn't know of? Is the board appointment in jeopardy?" Arden's mind raced with the possibility that their hard work would blow up because of some idiot man's inability to appreciate what he had and stop greedily wanting more. *Perfume?*

Arden stood, came to the front of her desk, team player. "We *warned* him. Told him he needed to tell us everything. That we can't fix what we don't know. We told him we hate surprises. Right?"

Warren actually gulped. She'd never seen his face so ashen.

"Listen, Arden. I don't like this any more than you will. But understand. The Swansons are major clients. Lucrative clients. Company-supporting clients."

"Well, I know. I *brought* them to you. When we met at my Saving Calico childhood leukemia fundraiser. Remember?"

"Oh. Right." Warren picked up his glass, rattled the ice. "I didn't think anything could make this more difficult."

"Make what?"

"So Patience Swanson thinks you and her husband have a . . . thing. That he gave you the Joy."

Arden clapped a palm to her chest. "She's insane."

"Possibly. Probably. But that doesn't change anything. She demands that we let you go."

"She? Demands? You let me go?" Every nerve cell in Arden's brain burst into flames.

"I have no choice."

"Choice? Of course you do." Arden took a step toward him, arms spread in exasperation and disbelief. "Who does she think put her husband where he is today?"

"I'm sorry, Arden. It's a situation. I don't know what to say."

"You don't? Well, I do." She jabbed toward him with a forefinger. "You can say 'she's lost her freaking mind.' You can tell that woman I'm a valuable employee who brings in big bucks, and new clients, and will continue to do so. And who, it goes without saying, is not having some sort of sordid affair with her vile entitled husband who clearly she has problems with. But the 'problems' are not me. A *situation*? It's my *life*!"

"I'm sorry, Arden. Unless you can prove he didn't give you perfume. Unless you can prove he didn't—"

She rolled her eyes to the heavens, then harnessed her outrage. "*I'm* not going to prove one thing on this planet. Ask *him*, right? First of all, I can't prove something that didn't happen, that's through the looking glass, and I cannot believe you're even asking me that. Is that what you think of me? Let me ask *you* that. That this is *true*?"

"No, of course not, no." Warren lurched to his feet, turned away, not looking at her, looking at every place else but her. "He'll deny it. So I can't force him to—"

"Ah. I see. Warren. Look at me. So you believe *her*, not me? Is that what you're saying? Because if that *is* what you're saying, Warren, I could file so many lawsuits it'd make your head spin. Hey. You're a pro. Imagine the headlines. Blame the victim? Or wait, would you paint me the vixen, the temptress? Oh, yeah, do it. *Please* do that. I'd love that. Bring it."

Warren had to know this was bull. "Are you hearing me?" she persisted. "Are you ignoring me? *Look* at me. I know the rules. I know the deal. You cannot do this. I'll go to HR so fast it'll—"

"Be careful, Arden." Warren interrupted her. "Take a beat. If you sue me, well, that's not gonna help you, is it? Suddenly you're . . . a problem employee. A liability. On the defensive. It's not a good look. You know that."

"What I know—and what *you* know—is that it's not true."

"What I *know* is that if the Swansons leave us, if they take their billings, I'd have to fire three other people to make up for it. Do you want to be responsible for that?"

"Oh, no. No. That's not fair." Arden wiped away the space in front of her, erasing Warren's words. "Do not make me feel guilty about people losing their jobs over a lie."

"We won't let this get out," Warren said. "It'll stay between us."

"Right. Between us." She choked down a bitter laugh, focusing her anger. "*And* Patience Swanson. And Arthur Swanson. And whatever gossip mongers and sycophant confidantes and social media jackals—I cannot believe I'm saying this. A *secret*. As if anyone could keep a secret." She drew in a breath, her judgment obliterated by expanding rage. Narrowed her eyes. "Unless they're dead."

"You can say whatever you want about why you're leaving," Warren kept talking, trampling over her words. "That you're on to new opportunities, or . . . and we'll support you. Whatever you want. We'll back you—"

"I don't want anything. What I want—at least until about a minute ago—is to do this work. Where I have changed people's lives for the better." Arden struggled to find the right words. Her vocabulary had vanished, along with her balance and place in the world. "You can't do this, Warren. You can't."

"You'll find another job." He backed toward the door. Watched her, as if she'd change her mind. "You have two weeks. Maybe I can even find you one last client. Go out big. Prove that you left on your own."

"*Bull*," she said. "You want me to lie to protect your lie?"

But he was gone.

Her universe had crashed. Everything she believed in, everything she relied on, everything she cared about. She stood, staring into the empty hallway, set adrift by power. And money. And the power of money.